JUST AROUND THE CORNER

Gilda O'Neill was born  ast End, where her grand   r grand-father was a tu   ked as a minder for a Ch   t school at fifteen but re   tudent, studying with th   hnic of East London, and   the University of Kent while lecturing part time. She is now a full-time writer, and has had seven novels and three non-fiction books published. She lives in Essex with her husband and family.

Praise for Gilda O'Neill

'Tarts with hearts, dastardly villains and a happy ending.
A thumping good read'
Lesley Pearse

'This novel has everything ... a cracking read'
Martina Cole

'Peopled with an irresistibly vivid cast of characters and
told with warm-hearted sympathy ... a great read'
Oxford Mail

'The characters are brightly and freshly drawn ... the
dialogue is spot on, and she writes with a real feeling for
the time and the place'
Western Evening Herald

Also by Gilda O'Neill

FICTION

The Cockney Girl
Whitechapel Girl
The Bells of Bow
Cissie Flowers
Dream On
The Lights of London
Playing Around

NON-FICTION

Pull No More Bines:
An Oral History of East London Women Hop Pickers
A Night Out with the Girls: Women Having Fun
My East End: A History of Cockney London

Just Around The Corner

Gilda O'Neill

ARROW

Published by Arrow Books in 2001

1 3 5 7 9 10 8 6 4 2

First published in the United Kingdom in 1995 by
Headline Book Publishing

Arrow Books Limited
The Random House Group Limited
20 Vauxhall Bridge Road, London SW1V 2SA

Random House Australia (Pty) Limited
20 Alfred Street, Milsons Point, Sydney,
New South Wales 2061, Australia

Random House New Zealand Limited
18 Poland Road, Glenfield,
Auckland 10, New Zealand

Random House (Pty) Limited
Endulini, 5a Jubilee Road, Parktown 2193, South Africa

The Random House Group Limited Reg. No. 954009

www.randomhouse.co.uk

A CIP catalogue record for this book
is available from the British Library

Papers used by Random House are natural, recyclable
products made from wood grown in sustainable forests.
The manufacturing processes conform to the
environmental regulations of the country of origin.

ISBN 0 09 928048 5

Printed and bound in Great Britain by
Bookmarque Ltd, Croydon, Surrey

For Auntie May and Uncle Alf
with my love

My acknowledgements and thanks to Michael Odell from Essex PACT, Jackie Grant from the Colchester Physiotherapy Clinic, and Neil Winton from Voice Recognition Computers. They know why.

1

'Thank Gawd yer got me this gas stove while there was still a few bob about.' Katie Mehan wiped the back of her arm across her sweat-soaked forehead, then, using both hands, lifted the big pan of neck of lamb stew from the hob. 'Honest, Pat, I couldn't have stood this heat if I'd had to have that old Kitchener going in here.' She looked over her shoulder at the big, black-leaded range that took up the whole of the kitchen fireplace.

'We bought that stove in time all right.' Pat leant back so that Katie could put down the pan. 'No matter how hot the weather would've turned, there'd have been no affording one now.'

Pat Mehan sat at the head of the scrubbed kitchen table, holding up his bowl in his big, rough hands, while his wife ladled thick, glistening gravy, pearl barley, chopped vegetables and dumplings into his bowl, then topped it up with the choicest pieces of lamb. During the past eighteen months Katie Mehan had learnt all kinds of tricks to stretch the bony bits of meat she bought in the market into tasty, filling suppers for her ever-hungry tribe of a family.

Pat put down his bowl in front of him with a nod of thanks, and ran his finger round the neck of his collarless

1

shirt. 'Yer know, I reckon it's bloody hotter this evening than it's been all day.'

Katie flashed her eyes at her husband. 'Language, Pat,' she said primly and jerked her head along the table to where their five children and Nora Brady, her mother, sat waiting for their food.

Pat winked conspiratorially at eighteen-year-old Danny, the oldest of the Mehan children, before turning to his wife. 'Sorry, love. I forgot meself for the minute.'

Danny made sure that his mother couldn't see what he was doing before grinning back at his dad: a man's gesture of unity against women's unfathomable ways.

'I should think you are sorry,' Katie said, and dropped an extra dumpling into her husband's already brimming bowl as a reward for his apology. 'You just remember to keep that language for down the docks, if yer don't mind. We don't need it here indoors, thank you very much.'

As she made her way round the cramped table, filling up her family's bowls and correcting their manners, Katie hummed happily to herself. She was a woman who had what she had always wanted: a fine, healthy, happy family. And even though her kitchen was, like the rest of the little house, crammed full of second-hand odds and ends that even in easier times were all she and Pat could afford, she still considered herself a fortunate woman – a lot better off than many. Crowded and a bit threadbare the terraced two-up, two-down might have been, but Katie Mehan was thankful for what she had, and lavished as much care on her home as she would have done on any grandly furnished West End mansion.

She saw the upkeep of number twelve Plumley Street, Poplar as her duty, but she also took pleasure in knowing that she kept her place immaculately clean and would never be ashamed no matter who came knocking at her door. It all took a lot of effort, but so long as she had breath in her body there would not be any mouse droppings in *her* food cupboard. The fact that the cooking basins and pots stood on a simple, painted dresser rather than on shelves made of fine oak couldn't be helped, but there was never a trace of grease left on any of them when Katie had finished with the washing soda and wire wool.

And, as she always liked to tell her kids, although she might not have much in her purse now, there was always the hope that there'd be better times just around the corner, but, until those better times arrived, she could still keep up her standards. A bar of laundry soap didn't cost much, she told them, which was a good job, considering the amount of the stuff she bought from the corner shop. The evidence of her labours with the soap and scrubbing board could be seen in the pure white lace runner pinned round the mantelshelf over the fireplace, and the spotless vests and underpants airing on the cord stretched across the chimney breast.

Above the hearth, a wooden overmantel took pride of place, its gleaming looking-glass a testament to regular polishing. Katie never allowed junk to accumulate on the overmantel, nor to be poked under the mantelshelf below it, as happened in some houses in Plumley Street, including number ten next door, her mother's house; not that she thought it any business of hers what her mother did in her own home. Even though Katie's four sons slept in their grandmother's two upstairs bedrooms, what happened in number ten was her mother's concern. It wasn't that Katie didn't care about other people – she would always do anyone a good turn – it was just that she wasn't the sort to go sticking her nose into other people's affairs. She was content with making sure things were just so in her own place – that was her life, and she had no reason to complain or for it to be otherwise.

'Here you are, Michael, love,' she said, ladle brimming and ready to pour.

Michael looked up at his mother as she filled his bowl. At ten years old, he was the youngest but one of the Mehans; the advantages and the burden of being the baby of the family going to eight-year-old Timmy.

'I'm glad we don't have to have the range alight and all, Mum,' he said, busily spooning through the gravy in a search of bits of meat, "cos I really hate going down Levans Road to fetch the coke for yer. It'd be all right if I had a proper barrow, but all the kids laugh at me when I have to push that old pram down there.'

Banging the saucepan back down on the table, Katie straightened up and wagged her finger at her son. 'But I'll bet they don't laugh at yer when yer tell 'em I treat yer for going, now do they?'

Michael wasn't sure how to answer that one, so he gulped down a spoonful of stew instead, burning his lips and tongue in the process, making him cough and splutter all over the table. His grandmother, Nora, slapping him hard across the back only made matters worse. His eyes ran and his shoulders stung.

'Good boy, Michael,' she encouraged him. 'Cough it up. Who knows, it might just be a gold watch.' Despite living in the East End for over thirty years, Nora still spoke in the lilting Irish brogue that marked her out as not being Poplar born and bred as her daughter and son-in-law had been. 'And even if yer did start gobbling down yer grub before yer should,' Nora added, 'yer a good boy for reminding me.'

Michael smiled, his smarting mouth forgotten; he was being praised.

4

'I was having a look under those stairs of mine next door and I noticed me coke's got a bit on the low side. So yer can go and fetch some for me later. How'd you like to do that for your old nanna, eh, Michael, love?'

'But Nanna!' he wailed. 'It's summer. Yer don't need no coke in this weather.'

'And how about me cooking?' Nora demanded, looking around at the family for support.

Michael's freckled forehead creased into an anxious, thoughtful frown. 'What cooking? You have all yer dinners and that in here with us.'

'And how about the heating up of the water for me bit of washing?'

His voice took on an even more desperate, whining tone; if he didn't do something fast he'd wind up spending the whole of Saturday night running errands instead of playing out in the street with his mates. 'But Nanna, you and Mum do all the washing in here.'

Nora thought for a moment, then leant back in her chair, her arms folded across her apron-covered bosom. 'Well, I suppose that's all right then. Yer'll not have to bother fetching me none, will yer?'

Michael's mouth dropped open. He appealed to Katie: 'Mum! Nanna's tormenting me again.'

'You're such an easy one to string along,' grinned Nora, chucking him under the chin. 'Like putty in me hands, sure you are.' Her smug expression softened to a wistful smile. 'Just like I was with yer grandfather. He could kid me into doing or believing anything. Talk about the gift of the Blarney.'

'Here we go, let's hear about the good old days,' Michael said, his voice laden with sarcasm in an attempt to get his own back on his grandmother.

Katie glared at her son. 'Button that lip now, Michael,'

she hissed into his ear. She lifted the pan and carried it round to the other side of the table and set about serving up a portion of stew for young Timmy.

Michael knew better than to argue with his mother but he allowed himself a sulky pout as he sat there, a picture of injured innocence, watching her through his gingery lashes as she finished seeing to Timmy and then sat herself down at the opposite end of the table from his father.

'Bow yer heads,' Katie said and pointed to sixteen-year-old Molly, her and Pat's only daughter. 'You can say it tonight.'

Molly sat up straight, dropped her chin demurely and put her hands together.

Danny curled his top lip into a sneer and whispered so that only his sister could hear him: 'Goody-goody.'

'For what we are about to receive,' she began in a sweet voice that covered the fact she had one eye open, was sneering back at Danny, and was about to kick him hard in the shin, 'may the Lord make us truly thankful.'

'Amen,' the eight of them said in ragged unison, as spoons and forks were lifted, ready for the attack.

But Katie didn't seem interested in her food. She put her spoon down again and folded her hands in her lap. 'Yer know what I saw this afternoon, Pat?'

'No. What was that, love?' Pat looked at her across the table, as he reached for the salt.

'That welfare woman. She was over the road at number three again.'

'What, over at the Miltons'?' asked Michael, his mouth full of potato. 'On a Saturday afternoon?'

'Yes, over at the Miltons' on a Saturday afternoon, but I don't think I was talking to you, was I, Michael? Thank you very much.'

'Sorry, Mum.'

Pat shook his head and let his spoon dangle from his hand. 'He looks haunted, that poor feller. Can't be more than, what, thirty years old? And he's bent over like an old man with the aggravation of it all.'

'As far as I can tell, they ain't had a carrot coming in from nowhere except the RO, not since he got laid off.' Katie fiddled absent-mindedly with the edge of the oilcloth table covering. 'See, what's worrying me, Pat is . . . well . . .' She lowered her voice. 'I know it's none of my business, but yer know what them welfare people are like.'

He nodded. 'What's happening in this world, eh? Tell me that.'

Nora sighed loudly. 'They'll take them children away from her, first chance they get, and they won't be satisfied till they do neither. And you know what they'll do then? They'll put them in one of them homes. Terrible places. Terrible. And it'll kill that poor girl, losing her kids, you see if it don't.'

Michael and Timmy looked at their grandmother, appalled that such a thing might happen to their friends.

'All right, Mum,' Katie said under her breath. 'Not in front of this lot.'

Nora shrugged. 'It's only the truth I'm speaking.'

Young Timmy looked wide-eyed at his grandmother, then turned to his mum, his little face tense and solemn beneath his heavy auburn fringe. 'When we was playing footer this afternoon, I give Robbo Milton the bread and dripping what Nanna made me. Right starving he was, Mum. Growling, his belly was.' Timmy clutched his stomach by way of demonstration. 'But that filled him up. The welfare lady could have seen for herself he weren't hungry no more. They can't take him away if he

7

ain't hungry, can they? And our Michael's got them spare shoes what don't fit Sean no more. He could have them. They'd make him look right smart, they would.'

Katie narrowed her eyes and looked purposefully at her mother. 'You was eating in the street, was yer, Timmy? Bread and dripping what yer nanna give yer?' She slowly turned her head to look at her son. 'And yer can wipe that gravy off yer chin and all.'

Timmy rubbed his shirt sleeve across his mouth. He looked offended. 'I thought yer'd be pleased I give it to him. Yer always saying how we should share things. And he was really starving hungry.'

'I suppose,' Katie said warily. 'But don't you let me catch yer showing me up eating out in the street again, all right? Now be quiet and get on with yer tea.'

Nora didn't seem in the least concerned that she had got her youngest grandson into trouble. 'I see that Relieving Officer was round at the Miltons' again and all yesterday afternoon.' She snorted contemptuously. 'Going in for his Friday nose around, I suppose. It makes me laugh. What does he think – that they've suddenly come into a fortune since last week and are trying to fiddle the flaming means test for a few bob?'

Timmy hadn't learnt his lesson. 'Robbo Milton says the Relieving Officer's a rotten bastard. He taught me a song about it and all. Shall I sing it for yer?'

Katie reached out and rapped her son sharply across the back of his hand with her spoon. 'No you will not.'

'Ouch!' he said, nursing his tingling knuckles and his injured pride.

'See?' Nora hissed at him. 'Yer should have done what yer mother told yer and kept quiet.'

Pat, used to such goings-on around the table, had been eating as though nothing had happened, but now he put

8

his spoon down. He had a faraway look in his eyes as though he were watching a scene playing in his head. 'He was down the docks the other day – Milton – to see if there was any casual about. There was nothing, of course. It's bad enough for the regular crews.' Pat rested his elbows on the table and rubbed his hand over his chin. 'I tried to have a word with him, to cheer him up, like, make him realise it was nothing personal, but he was so down, poor bloke. Couldn't get through to him at all. Joe Palmer reckons he's scared out of his sodding life they're gonna make him go down to Essex to one of them labour camps. Poor bleeder.'

'Padraic!'

The sound of their mother using their father's full name alerted the children; all eyes were on Katie.

She was outraged. 'Whatever's got into everybody round this table? All this language. And just look at you with yer elbows on the table and all. What example's that to set to the kids?'

'Yer worried about language and elbows?' Pat said the words ominously quietly. He picked up his spoon and jabbed it at Katie as he spoke. 'Yer've told us what *you* see, well, d'yer wanna know what *I* see on me way to the docks yesterday morning?'

The children sat in fascinated silence as they waited to see if their parents were actually building up to a row. Their mother flying off the handle and almost immediately calming down again was a familiar sight to all of them. But even though their big, dark-haired father looked tough, and dwarfed his slim, red-haired wife, he was usually such a mild-mannered, gentle person that, no matter how she flared and blustered at him, he very rarely lost his temper with her, or anyone else for that matter – except when he thought that

9

another man might even be thinking about looking at Katie – and it was this that made the exchange of rare interest to them.

'I'll tell yer what I see,' Pat went on. 'I wasn't going to 'cos I thought it might upset yer, but yer need to get yer priorities right by the sound of it.'

Katie's face was scarlet at being spoken to like that, especially at her own kitchen table.

'Four miners, I see, with all their gear on – their lamps and helmets and everything. And what was they doing? They was singing, that's what.'

Timmy wanted to ask what was suddenly so wrong with a bit of singing – they'd only just told him off for offering to sing them all a song – but the look on his father's face made him change his mind.

'They'd come down here all the way from Wales, they had. And they was standing by the dock gates singing for sodding pennies. Pennies!' He spat the words out. 'I ask yer. Skilled men who've risked their lives and their health for this country. And for what? For bleed'n charity, that's what. Hoping that the few men round here what have still got a bit of work would feel bloody sorry for 'em and give 'em a handout.'

The sound of their father using so much 'language' had the children – all except Sean – spluttering into their hands. Their mother would skin him.

It was Sean, interrupting his father, who rescued him from Katie's rising fury. Calmly, he put down his spoon and fork and said to no one in particular, 'I'd rather go out nicking than have to beg.'

Katie's focus was immediately on her son. 'Would yer like to say that again, Sean?'

Sean looked at her, his blue eyes vivid in his pale, redhead's face.

10

Katie bobbed her head towards him. 'Go on. That, what yer just said. Say it again. Nice and loud, so's we can all hear it.'

Sean, with the recklessness of his fourteen years, actually started to repeat himself but Pat stepped in, returning his son's earlier favour of deflecting Katie's wrath.

'Least the boy's got pride in himself. And he's showing a bit of interest in things,' said Pat. He gestured towards Danny with his chin. 'Wouldn't hurt for you to show a bit more interest in what's going on in the world.' He warmed to his subject. 'All you seem to bother about is getting out and meeting them mates o' your'n. Kids nowadays, no interest in nothing 'cept enjoying themselves. Terrible state of affairs. Terrible.'

Danny looked bemused. What had he done? His dad had never complained about him seeing his friends before. In fact he'd always encouraged Danny to have a good time – within reason – before he had to start taking on the responsibilities of keeping a home and a family of his own. 'You enjoy yerself, son,' he'd say.

Danny looked at Molly to see if she had a clue what it was all about.

Molly shrugged. 'Don't ask me,' she whispered behind the cover of her hand.

'You might be lucky enough to be working, Danny,' Pat continued, 'but yer wanna remember that's only 'cos Joe Palmer's good enough to keep you on. Most boys get the elbow when they're coming up to eighteen. Soon as they start expecting a man's wage they're out, right out on their ear'oles. You should think yerself lucky – more than lucky.'

'Dad . . .' Molly said, smiling, using the voice that usually made him smile back in return.

'And *you*, madam,' he said. His tone was harsh, not what his daughter had expected at all.

'Me?' asked Molly. 'What have I done?'

'You? The world just passes you by, don't it? Yer think yer so safe in that tea factory,' Pat said, 'but you take my word for it, no job's safe nowadays. Not even tuppenny-ha'penny girls' jobs like your'n. I mean it, no one's safe, no one. Not even stevedores like me.' Pat jerked his thumb over his shoulder in the direction of the street. 'There's skilled men out there, on the scrapheap. Well, I've come to me senses lately. I've realised just how much we've all taken for granted in this house, and things're gonna change.'

'Have you finished?' Katie asked serenely.

Pat's face was rigid. 'What d'yer mean, have I finished?'

'Yer stew.' She pointed to her husband's bowl.

Pat nodded. 'Nearly.'

'A bit more?'

He nodded again and shoved his dish towards her. 'It's just that they ought to know the truth about things, that's all,' he said defensively, looking across at his wife as she began to scoop more stew from the big enamel pan. 'They can't go through life like it's all one big lark. They've gotta learn.'

As Katie was about to pour the stew into the dish she saw Molly lean towards Danny with her hand to her mouth. Katie banged down Pat's bowl on the table and glared at her daughter. 'Before you two even *think* about making plans to go out tonight, I want both them dishes o' your'n licked clean, right down to the pattern. D'you hear me? And you, Molly, I expect you to set a decent example to the young 'uns and clear the table *without* being asked. Not even once.' Katie pointed dramatically

12

at the saucepan as though it was evidence in a court case. 'Yer father worked his fingers to the bone to put that food on this table and I expect you two to show some gratitude. And a bit of respect.'

Relieved that whatever their father had thought they had done wrong now appeared to be either forgiven or, more likely, forgotten in all the commotion, and that their mother was back in her usual position of supporting him, whatever he said or did, Molly and Danny nodded and got stuck into the remains of their supper, eating as quickly as they dared.

Satisfied that order had been restored, Katie handed Pat's bowl to Sean to pass to his father. 'I was thinking me and Mum might go hopping this year, earn a few extra shillings. Maybe put a bit by for Christmas, 'cos that'll be here before we know it.' She turned to her mother. 'You'd like to go, wouldn't yer, Mum?'

Nora swallowed a mouthful of dumpling. 'I would, girl. Do me good to get down to Kent for a bit. Fill me lungs with some decent country air.' She looked at her granddaughter. 'And how about you, sweetheart? Would you like to come with me and yer mam? Get some of them roses back in yer cheeks?'

'I ain't sure really, Nanna. Me and Lizzie Watts was talking about it the other day, and she was saying, now she's settled in her job with me and everything, how she don't wanna risk losing it or nothing.' Molly glanced across at her father. 'And it ain't just that I don't wanna go without me mate, 'cos I ain't a baby,' she added, ignoring Danny's sarcastic gasp of disbelief. 'It's just that I feel the same as her. Dad's right, yer've gotta look after yer job nowadays. Me and Liz're lucky to be in work.'

Nora grinned. 'You sure it's just that tea warehouse that's got such a grip on the pair of yer, and that yer haven't gone and got yourself a couple of young feller-me-lads? I mean, yer both young ladies now, so you are.'

Molly dropped her chin; she didn't need the country air to put colour in her cheeks, not with her grandmother around. The last thing she wanted was for her little brothers, particularly Michael, to see her blushes. They teased her rotten as it was, whenever she even spoke to a boy. Molly loved her nanna fiercely but the trouble with Nora Brady was that she had no shame and worst of all, no inhibitions either.

Katie, having been the object of her mother's embarrassing behaviour on many occasions herself, helped her daughter out by changing the subject. She pointed at Michael with her fork. 'If you dare feed another one of them bones to that dog while we're still sitting at this table, Michael Mehan, yer do know what yer'll get, don't yer? The back of my hand round yer legs.'

Michael looked stunned by the accusation. 'But it ain't my fault, Mum,' he complained. 'Rags nicked 'em off me.'

'And don't you lie to me neither, yer little monkey. God's watching yer, yer know.'

Defeated, Michael slumped down in his chair and ran his greasy fingers through Rags's tangled brown fur, muttering sulkily to himself about how it was always him that everyone picked on.

Molly glanced around the table, then said, 'Right, everyone finished?'

They all nodded.

And so, with another rowdy family meal over, Molly stood up and began collecting the dishes and cutlery.

'I'll put the kettle on for the washing up,' said Katie, 'and then we can all have a nice cuppa tea.'

'Not for me, girl,' said Pat, stretching his arms high above his head. 'I'm off down the Queen's for a pint.'

14

'Well, don't bother making one for me neither then,' said Nora. 'I'll have a nice stout brought over from the Jug and Bottle instead – if someone fancies fetching it for me, that is.'

Katie stood up, untied her apron and looped it over the nail behind the kitchen door. 'I'll go over for yer in a minute, Mum.' She took a clean tea towel from the dresser drawer and draped it across the top of the saucepan. 'I'm just gonna see to something first.' She leant closer so that only her mother could hear her. 'I'm gonna pop the rest of this grub over to Mrs Milton. Yer know how it is when yer short. If I was a gambling woman, I'd lay money she's been going without so's she could feed her old man and her kids. Like a bag of bones, she is.'

Nora touched her daughter's cheek. 'Yer a good girl, Katie. But will she take it off yer?'

'Yeah. I'll make up a story like I did before. I'll say we got a load of lamb from down the docks or something.' Katie paused and crossed herself. 'God forgive me for lying,' she said to the ceiling. She looked over to where Pat was standing in front of the mirror tying a paisley stock round his neck, and smiled. 'Yer know how everyone reckons dockers are always on the thieve.'

Nora sighed. 'And so they all are, except your sainted husband, more's the pity.'

Ignoring her mother's remark, Katie straightened up and turned to Molly and Danny. 'Off yer go, you two,' she said, jerking her head towards the door. 'I'll see to the washing up later on.' She looked at Sean who, unlike the others, had made no attempt to move away from the table. 'You going with your brother and sister?'

'Might as well,' he said sullenly, scraping back his chair.

15

Katie shook her head. He was so moody lately, but then, she supposed, weren't all boys of his age? And he probably still hadn't got over the disappointment of being let down by the cabinet-maker Bill Watts had introduced him to. Bill's mate had promised Sean an apprenticeship, but had had to change his mind because his business had got so bad. 'Well, mind yer all back in here at a decent hour. Mass in the morning.'

'We will be. See yer later then, Mum,' said Molly, pecking her on the cheek. 'Come on, Dan,' she urged her older brother. 'Get a move on.'

He was peering round his father's bulky frame trying to get a look in the mirror so that he could check his thick dark curly hair that made him look like a younger version of Pat.

Molly rolled her eyes. 'You ain't gonna stand there all night titivating, are yer? Yer just like a big girl.'

His hair forgotten, Danny slung his jacket over his shoulder and chased Molly as she ran jeering and sniggering out of the kitchen. They were followed in quick succession by Michael, Timmy and Rags, and finally Sean, who slouched over towards the door.

But the two youngest ones and the dog didn't get very far. Katie stepped nimbly round Sean and blocked their exit to the passageway. She grabbed hold of Michael and Timmy by their shirts, tipped her head sideways, indicating that Sean could go round them, and then dragged the two little ones back into the kitchen with Rags trotting along after them, his pink tongue lolling from his grinning snout.

'And where, would yer mind telling me, d'yer think you pair are off to?'

'Out with the Milton kids,' said Michael, trying to wriggle his way out of his mother's formidable grip.

16

'Well,' said Katie, letting them go and, much to Michael's shame, straightening his collar for him. 'So long as yer keep yerselves out of trouble. And so long as yer keep away from . . .' She paused, going through a mental list of forbidden activities. 'Well, all the things yer meant to keep away from. And you, Michael, I expect you to keep an eye on Timmy. Do you hear me? I don't like the way he's been acting this evening.' She raised her eyebrows first at Nora and then at Pat. 'Eating in the street,' she said pointedly. 'And using language like that. Whatever would Father Hopkins have to say if he found out?'

'All right, Mum,' said Michael.

'And no fighting.'

'No fighting.' With that, Michael and Timmy dashed from the kitchen, raced along the passageway and burst out of the ever-open street door, with Rags yelping and yapping close behind them.

'Bundle!' Katie heard her two youngest children yell as they launched themselves across the street towards the swarm of variously sized young Miltons who had been waiting for them.

Satisfied that he looked respectable, Pat checked the battered silver pocket watch that his father had given him just before he died, and pulled his cap over his thick dark hair. 'That's me ready,' he said.

'I'll walk out with yer,' said Katie, picking up the saucepan.

He motioned to Katie's bare throat. 'Yer top's all undone.'

'Leave off, Pat.'

He didn't move or say anything, he just looked her steadily in the eye.

With a weary sigh, Katie put the pan down and did

up the two topmost buttons of her dress that she had opened while she was cooking. She then dragged her cardigan from the back of her chair and pulled it roughly over the thin cotton. 'That suit yer? Or shall I put me overcoat on and all?'

Pat still didn't respond. He just stood there.

'You just wait and see,' Katie said, picking up the pan again. 'Wrapping meself up like a suet pudden in this heat, I'll wind up having a turn. Then you'll be satisfied, will yer?'

Nora didn't even have to look at Pat to know that by now he would be swallowing hard and scowling disapprovingly at his wife through unblinking, narrowed eyes.

'I mean, I don't wanna go showing meself off to all the neighbours now, do I?' Katie said sarcastically. ''Cos let's face it, Phoebe Tucker'd never let me hear the end of it if her old Albert got a look at me neck.'

'Nor would your old man,' Nora mumbled to herself, as she took hold of one of the kitchen chairs, ready to carry it out into the street for her evening vigil.

'Here, gimme that,' said Pat, lifting the chair as though it were made of matchwood.

'Yer a good boy,' said Nora pathetically. 'Kind to yer poor old mam-in-law.'

Pat snorted. 'Get away with yer, Nora. Yer still a young woman, and tougher than the rest of us lot put together.'

Nora waited for Pat to disappear along the passage. 'I've said it before,' she said to her daughter, 'and I'll say it again. He's a good man, your Pat – been like a son to me, he has – but yer wanna watch yerself with him, think before yer let yer tongue run away with yer all the time. Jealousy's a terrible thing, Katie. It can turn a

18

man.' She reknotted the strings of her crossover apron and patted her wavy auburn hair, an unconscious act of straightening herself up before she went outside to the street. 'I'm telling yer, girl, you push that man too far with yer carrying on, especially when he's got all these other worries driving him mad.'

'Have yer quite finished?'

'It'd do you no harm, Katie my girl, to listen to yer mother for once. I know you and your temper. You go on and off the boil like a kettle. But I'm telling yer, yer might think you can wrap Pat around yer little finger if he ever looked like really getting nasty, but there's some things that are too much to take for a jealous man like him.'

Katie put down the pot yet again. She stuck her hands on her hips and cocked her head to one side. 'Mum, what are you talking about? I'm not far off being forty. I'm hardly gonna have men chasing around after me, now am I? Even if I was stupid enough to be interested in that sort of thing. I know what Pat's like, but if there's anything worrying him, it's all in here.' She tapped her finger on her temple. 'All in his own mind. His imagination. It ain't my fault.'

'I'll say no more. But you just remember what I've said, and how well I knew his mother and father, God rest their souls. There's plenty of stories I could tell you about what went on in this very house when they lived here. Murderous rows they had, murderous. Yet his father was a good man deep down, just like your Pat.' She rolled her eyes heavenwards. 'But jealousy turned him. That woman had more black eyes and split lips than a prize fighter.'

'Aw, just leave off, can't yer, Mum?' Katie stuck out her bottom lip, making her look like a grown-up version of Michael when he was sulking. 'You know very well, Pat's dad had good reason to be jealous, the way his mum carried on. But I ain't nothing like her – nothing at all.'

'I never said you were, Katie, and I'd batter anyone who even suggested it, but when a kid's been brought up seeing and listening to them sorts of carryings-on, well, it can make a deep impression on him. Make him nervous, like; make him think that maybe it could happen to him one day. That his wife might start taking a fancy to some other feller.'

'Yer talking rubbish, Mum,' Katie snapped.

'Am I? I just think yer should realise what's at stake, my girl.' Nora waved her arm around her, taking in the whole of the kitchen, the whole of Katie's domain. 'All this could all go down the shoot tomorrow if yer not careful. You've gotta make that man feel secure.'

Katie glowered at her mother. 'Yer talking to me like I'm stupid.'

'If you two are gonna stay in there gabbing, I'll be off down the Queen's,' they heard Pat holler along the passage. 'Won't be long, love.'

Katie smirked triumphantly at her mother. 'See? Nothing's wrong. He ain't even upset.'

Nora shook her head. 'For such a clever girl, Katie Mehan, you really *can* be stupid at times.'

2

Pat set the chair he had carried outside for Nora on the pavement by the front door. He glanced along the street and saw his two youngest children in the middle of the road, engaged in a rowdy, knockabout game of football with a crowd of assorted Miltons and a whole throng of other kids he didn't recognise. He laughed out loud as Michael threw himself to the ground, grabbing the ankles of a much taller boy, dragging him down on top of him, whilst protesting loudly that it was he who was being fouled.

'That Michael!' he said to Danny before straightening his cap and striding off along the road to the Queen's.

Danny just nodded. He wasn't in the frame of mind to be amused by his little brother, or by any of his brothers for that matter. He and Molly should have been off long ago, but there they were, still standing by the street door, trying to prise out of the gloomy-looking Sean exactly what his plans were for the rest of the evening. And they weren't getting very far.

'Look, yer welcome to come with us, yer know that,' Molly said with more patience than she was feeling. 'But I mean it, Sean. We ain't gonna stand here all night begging yer to come with us.'

'What makes yer think I'd wanna go anywhere with you pair?' Sean leant back against the grimy brick wall, his hands sunk deep in his trouser pockets. He glared down at his feet and kicked hard at a stone, sending it spinning into the gutter. 'Walking up and down the flaming street with a bunch of idiots. What's the point of that?'

'So what *are* yer gonna do then?' As much as Danny wanted to be off, he, like Molly, felt obliged at least to try to find out what Sean was up to; their mother would expect it of them and it was always wise to attempt to keep her happy. 'Are yer meeting yer mates or something? Is that what yer doing?'

Sean lifted his chin and stared arrogantly at his brother. 'What's it gotta do with you?'

'Bloody hell, Sean, I only asked.'

'Keep it down, boys,' said Molly through her teeth. She looked anxiously at the open street door for any signs of their mother appearing from the passage.

'But it ain't none of your sodding business where I'm going, is it?' Sean sneered contemptuously at them. 'I'm fed up with having to tell everyone what I'm up to all the time. Can't yer get that into yer thick heads?'

That was too much for Molly. She stuck her fists into her waist, just like her mother did when she was angry, and pushed her face close to Sean's. 'Now look here, you. Me and Dan couldn't give a tinker's cuss what yer up to, if yer really wanna know. It's just that Mum worries about yer. Just like she worries about all of us. And we should think ourselves lucky that she does, and all. There's plenty of kids round here who'd give anything for a mum like our'n.'

Sean turned his head away. 'Piss off, can't yer? That's all I get from you lot. Treating me like a kid.' He twisted back round to face her. 'Well, I ain't a kid no more, am I? I've left school now and, even if that geezer has let me down, I'm gonna be earning soon, you just see if I ain't. Independent I'll be, and I'm gonna make meself a packet. And you all wanna remember that.'

'Sean,' pleaded Molly, 'don't start. We only wanna know where yer going so's we can all meet up after and come home together. Then Mum won't know we ain't all been out like a nice happy family. And she won't have nothing to lead off about, will she?'

Sean repaid her concern with a look of total disdain.

Molly threw up her hands in exasperation. 'I can't stand this lark, Dan. You'll have to do something with him.'

'What can I do?'

Whether Molly could have told Danny what to do or not didn't matter; it was too late. Sean wasn't going to listen to anything either of them had to say. He pushed himself away from the wall and disappeared at a fast trot round the corner of the house and was off along Grundy Street before either of them could stop him.

'Aw wonderful, now yer've done it, ain't yer?'

Danny's mouth fell open. 'Me? What did I do?'

'Nothing. That's the trouble. Yer know what he's been like lately. He's had the right devil in him. Gawd alone knows what he'll get up to. We'll never find him now. Yer could have tried to stop him, Dan.'

Danny didn't bother to disagree with his sister. Molly could be as stubborn as their mother, and also like her, she could out talk him any day. Since they had been tiny Molly had been able to tie him in knots with her arguments. So, instead of wasting his breath, Danny decided that action was called for. He tipped his head towards the other end of the road, the end that was blocked off with a six-foot-high brick wall, and began walking slowly backwards in that direction. 'Shall we

23

get going then? Before Mum and Nanna come out and
wanna know where that little sod's taken himself off
to?'

Molly didn't move.

Despite his mounting frustration, Danny tried an
encouraging smile, but still she didn't budge. She just
stood there by the street doorstep, her eyes fixed on the
wall at the end of the turning – the wall that made
Plumley Street different from every other street in the
neighbourhood.

In all other ways, Plumley Street was exactly like the
rest of the little turnings in that part of Poplar, that
either ran parallel to, or led off the market in the road
known to everyone locally not by its proper name of
Chrisp Street, but as Chris Street. Just like its
neighbours, Plumley Street was home to a tight-knit
community that saw its fair share of births and deaths,
rows and feuds, friendships and marriages, tragedies
and laughter. But when the two-up, two-down terraces
of Plumley Street were being built over forty years ago
– not long before Katie's and Pat's parents had arrived
from Ireland and had moved in next door to each other
in numbers ten and twelve – the builder had intended
that the far end of the street should open out on to the
busy East India Dock Road. It was with the potential
passing trade on that bustling, major thoroughfare that
linked Barking in the east to the Commercial Road, and
beyond to the City of London in the west, that the builder
had in mind when he built the little general shop and
the pub, the Queen's Arms, at that end of the street.
But, before the project was completed, the builder had
disappeared.

It was a complete mystery as to where he had gone.
Some said that his money had run out, others that he

24

had been put into prison, some even claimed that they knew he had been murdered in Stepney in a drunken fight with the landlord who employed him, and had been buried in the foundations of one of his very own building sites. But, whatever the reason for his disappearance, Plumley Street was left as it was: blocked at one end by the solid brick wall that had been erected during building to stop through traffic from interfering with the work. So, instead of being on the busy corner of East India Dock Road, the shop and the pub stood at the far end of a cul-de-sac with a blank, six feet of wall between them, and the only way in and out of the turning was at the other end, where Plumley Street butted on to Grundy Street. It was at that open end that number twelve Plumley Street, the Mehans' home, stood on one corner, facing number eleven where a widower, Frank Barber, and his little daughter, Theresa, lived downstairs, and upstairs was 'Nutty' Lil Evans.

Having the wall at the other end of the street had never been seen by the residents as a hindrance. Instead they thought that it made their turning special, different, because it was back to front, what with the shop and the pub being at the 'wrong' end. And the wall had its practical uses too. It had served generations of local children as a football goal, a wicket, a blackboard to scribble on, a target to pelt stones and tin cans at, and something just to clamber over for the sake of it. It also kept the street free of carts and lorries cutting through from the market, making it a safe playground.

Strangely, the back-to-front nature of the street hadn't harmed trade for the general shop or the Queen's; both were as busy as any similar establishments in the East End, even though there was plenty of competition in that area, particularly from Chrisp Street and Upper

North Street. The neighbourhood looked affectionately on Plumley Street as a cherished oddity, and the cheerful, friendly personalities of Mags and Harold Donovan, who ran the pub, and Edie and Bert Johnson, who owned the shop, hadn't done any harm to that reputation either. Plumley Street had the added advantage for people using the pub and the shop that they knew their kids would be safe playing in the street outside. It didn't occur to them that a mere six foot of wall was no barrier to a child determined to find its way on to the East India Dock Road; and it was that very route that Danny, despite his comparatively mature eighteen years, was impatient to take.

He walked back to his sister and leant close to her, trying to figure out what she was staring at. 'Oi, Molly, wake up, will yer? You coming or what?'

She flicked her thick auburn hair away from her eyes. 'I was thinking.'

'Blimey, mind yer don't give yerself a headache.'

Molly either didn't notice, or, more likely, she chose to ignore her brother's sarcasm. 'I was thinking,' she said slowly, 'that I might walk round, go through Chris Street, so's I can have a nose at the stalls.'

'But, Moll, we're late enough as . . .' Danny began, then a look of realisation gradually dawned on his face. 'Stalls, my eye,' he jeered. 'Nanna's right, you have, haven't yer? Yer've turned into a *right young lady*.'

This time Molly took the bait. Her cheeks reddened. 'No,' she snapped, 'I have not.'

'Well, what's up with yer then? Yer always go shinning up and over that wall like a good 'un. You gone soft, have yer?'

Molly pursed her lips indignantly. 'I'm too hot to go clambering about, all right?'

'Yeah, course you are.'

'You go whichever way you like, big mouth. I'm walking round through the market.'

'Well, I'd better come with yer then, hadn't I?' Danny couldn't resist taking another dig at his sister. 'I mean, I don't want a delicate little flower like you to go tripping over no match sticks or nothing, now do I?'

Danny took one look at his sister's face and took off as fast as his legs could carry him. Molly immediately took up the chase, yelling for revenge. Despite the skirt of her cotton dress flapping round her legs, she pursued him round the corner and along Grundy Street, and managed to catch hold of him just as they skidded into the crowds who, even at that time of the evening, were milling around the stalls in Chrisp Street.

'Yer can still run then, sis?' he grinned, pulling away from her.

She punched him hard in the shoulder. 'Yeah, and I can still fight and all, so yer'd better watch it.'

'Mind how yer go,' Danny complained. He circled his arm and rubbed at his stinging shoulder. 'That ain't very ladylike behaviour, now is it?'

'No, but it's very Mehan-like,' she said, grabbing hold of his shirt sleeve again. 'Now let's walk nice and slow, all right? I wanna have a look.'

'Don't you girls ever get fed up, gawping at flaming stalls?'

'No,' she said with a challenging stare. 'Why? You got something to say about it?'

Danny shrugged. 'Well, don't be too long,' he said importantly. 'I've got someone to see about a bit of business.'

Molly didn't give her brother the scornful answer he more or less expected, she was far more interested in one of the stalls. It was piled high with toppling towers of vividly coloured bales of dress material. There was one pattern in particular, an intense cornflower blue with sprigs of tiny yellow flowers, that she knew would be just right for flattering her blue eyes and her auburn hair.

She ran her fingertips over the smooth, crisp cotton; with her slim build, she would only need a couple of yards for a frock, even for the new longer length, and she was sure she could persuade her nan to make it for her, or better still, Liz Watts's mum, Peggy, who was a dab hand with a needle. But material cost money and even if skirts whizzed right up to her thighs – which they might well do the way the fashions they showed on the newsreels kept changing – Molly still couldn't afford to buy half a yard, even at market prices, let alone enough for a dress. Much as she would have loved to spend something on herself, she knew that with the way things were, it was only fair to hand over most of her miserable wages to the family kitty each week; but that didn't stop her looking. She hadn't had anything new for ages, and it was such a lovely colour. Still, it was no good dreaming. Things would have to get a lot easier in the docks for her dad before she could start spending money on bits of material again, whether it was cornflower blue with yellow flowers, or sky-blue pink with purple spots.

Reluctantly, Molly moved away from the stall, but she wasn't miserable for long. There were, as always, enough things in Chrisp Street market to distract anyone. It was a noisy, exciting, kaleidoscope of a place, full of tantalising smells and seductively presented goods. There were toys and cups and plates and shoes; huge, engineered items of salmon-pink satin ladies' underwear; make-up and hair brushes; dresses and little boxes full of tonic powders that guaranteed to improve everything that could possibly need improving; food stuffs and stockings, pot scourers and great slabs of dark green soap. Each stall had its own enticements and never-to-be-beaten prices. And the crowds loved it, as they strolled along, stopping to barter and buy, or just to look while enjoying the warm evening air.

Even though it was almost seven o'clock, the sky was still clear and bright with summer sunlight, and while the stall holders might not have had their naphtha lamps burning yet, the summer fruits and vegetables, piled in drifts and pyramids of colour, on carpets of luridly green straw grass mats, glowed as brightly as any lantern. It being a Saturday night, the market would be busy until at least ten and even then there would still be customers eager to get any last-minute bargains before the stalls were packed away.

Back from where the stalls were jammed together along the roadside, Chrisp Street had another line of activity, centred around the shops which were all as busy as the barrows. Woolworth's in particular was chock-full of people looking for anything from household goods to cheap trinkets, or just hanging around listening and swaying in time to the latest sixpenny records. Then, when the browsers had had their fill of the sights and sounds of the shops, they could go back to the market and refresh themselves at the coffee and food stalls. Wherever one of these stood, there were as many dogs hanging around as people; each mutt sniffing under the canvas side flaps, whining in the wistful hope that someone just might drop a bacon sandwich or a slice of dripping toast – or even better, one of the greasy saveloys or savoury faggots – right there on the ground before them.

But for anyone Molly or Danny's age, Chrisp Street market, with all its attractions, couldn't begin to compete on a Saturday night with the appeal of what awaited them just around the corner. For Saturday night on the East India Dock Road meant the Monkey Parade, the weekly promenade attended by what seemed to be all the young people from Poplar and the surrounding neighbourhoods. They strolled along in groups, gossiping and laughing, cheye-eyeking and yelling at one another, checking to see who was walking with whom, giving what they were wearing and how they had their hair done the once-over, and generally commenting on everything and anything about them. But what was most important of all about the Monkey Parade was the sorting out of who you did or didn't take a fancy to, and, with everyone knowing everyone else, there was never much of a secret about it. The Monkey Parade was the reason that Danny and Molly had been so keen to get out of the house, even though Molly had insisted on taking the roundabout route.

As soon as they turned into the East India Dock Road someone was calling out to them.

'Danny!' They stopped on the corner and waited while the stockily built, brown-haired boy, who looked to be about Danny's age, came trotting over to them. He smiled at Molly. 'Hello,' he said, looking her directly in the eyes.

Molly tilted her head to one side. 'Hello,' she answered, looking up at him through her lashes.

Danny punched him matily on the shoulder. 'Bob Jarvis, you old sod. What you doing here? I thought we was gonna meet up later, after yer'd seen them blokes yer was going on about.'

Bob held out his packet of Woodbines. Molly shook her head but Danny took one. 'I was on me way when I saw you two. So I thought, here's me chance. I'll see if Danny fancies coming with me to meet the chaps, and I can get him to introduce me to that beautiful sister of his at the same time.' Bob stuck a cigarette in the corner of his mouth and put the packet back in his coat pocket. 'Two birds with one stone, see. Here, you are his sister, ain't yer?'

Molly lifted her chin. 'I might be.'

Danny squinted as he lit his cigarette and then held out the match for Bob. 'Yer know she's me sister. Yer've had yer eye on her since I've known yer.'

Molly's expression hardened. 'Well, I ain't never seen, *you* before. You been talking about me behind me back, Dan?' She turned on Bob. 'If there's anything yer wanna know about me, you ask me yerself, all right?'

Bob gave an amused nod, but Danny sounded rattled. 'Blimey, Moll, give us a chance. I've only known the bloke a couple o' weeks. I ain't had time to say nothing about yer.'

Molly stared at Bob, daring him to lie. 'That true?'

'Yeah.' He leant towards her and held his hands melodramatically to his heart. 'I have had to be content with admiring you from afar, but with knowing nothing about yer.'

'That's all right then,' she said haughtily. 'And, anyway, if I'm being truthful, I have seen yer around. Once or twice maybe.' She stuck out her hand, as Danny always did when he met someone new. 'Molly Katherine Mehan. How d'yer do?'

Bob took her hand, but instead of shaking it as she had expected, he raised it gently to his lips. He looked along her arm to her shocked face. 'Bob Jarvis. Pleased to meet yer, Molly Katherine Mehan. Yer a very lovely young lady. Very lovely indeed.'

Molly snatched her hand away and wiped it on her skirt. 'You fancy yerself, don't yer?'

'Yeah, and I fancy you and all.' Bob winked at her, then turned to Dan who, to Molly's intense annoyance was now grinning like a fool. 'So, what d'yer think, old son? Yer wanna come with me to meet these blokes I was telling yer about? Yer'll like 'em.'

'I would, Bob, but . . .' He hesitated before adding wistfully, ' . . . there's Molly here to think about.'

'They wasn't expecting me to bring no one else, Dan.' Bob blew his breath out noisily between pursed lips and slowly shook his head. 'I'm gonna have to explain how I bumped into you as it is. I dunno how they'd react if I had the two of yers tagging along.'

'Well I can't just dump her, can I?'

Molly folded her arms and tapped her foot impatiently. 'Yer don't have to worry about me, Dan.' She was doubly annoyed – her brother was not only making a very good job of showing her up by talking about her as though she were a bag of dirty laundry he was having to cart about, but worse still, his friend already seemed to have lost any interest he had in her. She could have kicked herself for the way she'd acted all stupid and flattered; it had obviously put him off. The trouble was, she told herself, this was all so new to her, all this caring about what a feller thought about her. And there was something about Bob, something about the way he looked at her and the way he had kissed her hand. She couldn't explain it, but he made her feel as though she were ready to do whatever he wanted. It scared her. Now she'd made enough of a fool of herself, and she was blowed if she'd let him know what effect he'd had on her.

She shrugged carelessly. 'It's all right with me if I ain't invited. There's plenty of people round here to keep me busy.' With a pointed smile Molly waved cheerfully at a noisy group of boys who were strutting past on the other side of the street. 'And anyway,' she added, looking slyly at her brother, 'I'm meeting Lizzie Watts, ain't I?'

Molly could barely disguise her pleasure at seeing that it was now Danny's turn to look disappointed with the arrangements.

All thoughts of teasing his sister in front of Bob were gone from his mind. 'Yer meeting Liz? Yer never said. When?'

'Soon as she gets here.'

Bob smiled at Molly. 'I reckon he likes this girl, whoever she is.'

Molly smiled sweetly. 'Reckon he does.'

'Tell yer what, how about if me and Danny nip off for a while to see these fellers. It won't take long. Then, when we get back, us three and this Lizzie can all go off to the pictures together. How'd that suit yer?'

Determined not to sound too eager, Molly looked casually around her. 'I don't mind,' she said lightly. 'I'm easy. But here's Liz now.' She pointed. 'You can ask her yerselves.'

The two boys turned and looked back along the East India Dock Road. Liz Watts, Molly's best friend, was walking towards them. She was brushing the dust off her dress, a sure sign that she had just shinned up over the wall at the end of Plumley Street.

Whereas Molly was vivacious and good-looking in a striking, red-haired way, Liz Watts was softly pretty with fair hair gently curling around her pale pink cheeks. Like Molly she was sixteen years old and worked in Terson's, a warehouse near the docks, packing tea. She and Molly had grown up together and, everyone in the street said it, they were so close that they were more like sisters than friends.

Molly, emboldened by the sight of her ever-faithful ally, called out loudly, 'Wotcher, Liz.'

'Hello, Moll, Dan,' she answered, as she looked their brown-haired companion up and down. 'So who's this then?'

'His name's Bob Jarvis,' said Molly, standing next to her friend and joining her in her appraisal of Bob's looks. 'Mate of Dan's. What d'yer reckon?'

Liz cocked her head to one side and considered. 'All right if yer like that sort of thing, I suppose.'

'Does your mother know yer out?' Bob asked with a cheeky wink.

'Yeah,' Liz snapped back, with a wink of her own, 'and she give me a farthing to buy a monkey – you for sale, are yer?'

Bob shook his head. 'Here, Dan, these two off their heads or what?'

'Just a bit,' said Danny, smiling soppily at Liz.

Molly noted the expression on her brother's face; he looked like Rags dribbling at the marrow bones in the butcher's shop window. Molly narrowed her eyes thoughtfully, nudged her friend and said something to her quietly behind her hand. Then, continuing in a mock whisper so that Danny and Bob could hear every word, she said, 'He mentioned us all going to the pictures together, Liz. What d'yer think? D'yer think yer could stand it?'

Liz wrinkled her nose flirtatiously at Danny. 'Wouldn't mind. But only if Danny'd sit next to me. Would you like that, eh, Dan, sitting with me? 'Cos I'd really like yer to. Especially as it's so dark in the flicks. I get really scared when the lights go out, but I'd feel all safe if I

34

knew yer was sitting there next to me.'

Danny eyes widened. What should he say? He coughed exaggeratedly into his hands, hoping his seizure looked convincing, while he desperately tried to think of something clever.

Molly didn't seem very concerned about her brother having a turn. She took her purse out of her dress pocket and began raking through the farthings and ha'pennies. 'How much yer got?' she asked Liz.

'Enough. Mum let me keep a bit extra this week.'

'Lucky cow,' said Molly, clearly unimpressed by her own total wealth. She shoved her purse back into her pocket. 'You wanna have five kids and a nan in the family like us, that'd teach yer.'

Liz put her finger on her chin and flapped her eyelashes. 'Yer should have been the baby of the family like me.'

'Don't I wish.' Molly pulled a face at her brother. 'In fact, I wish I was an only child sometimes. One of them little spoilt brats with ribbons and shiny shoes and all the frocks I could ever want. And just laying in bed until I felt like getting up.'

Danny, his composure miraculously recovered, raised his eyebrows. 'Girls, eh, Bob? She's getting mixed up with the films, ain't she? I ain't never seen no one like that round here.'

Molly pouted. It wasn't an expression she usually favoured but, what with Bob being there, she didn't want to start a slanging match with Danny; she felt she should try and hide her usually loud and mouthy self and act how her mum would call 'nicely' instead. 'Shut up, Dan,' she said quietly, but she still couldn't resist adding, with a meaningful curl of her lip, 'or yer'll start that cough of your'n off again, won't yer?'

In complete contrast to his sister's sudden venture

into demureness, Danny had overcome his earlier reticence and was now more than happy to be loud. He flicked his jacket back over his shoulder and then jabbed his finger at his sister. 'You reckon yer've got it hard, do yer? Yer don't know yer born, Moll, yer've got life so easy. You girls don't have no trouble getting work, not like us blokes. Yer cheap labour.' He looked shrewdly at Bob. 'And yer don't cause no trouble for yer governors neither. *And* yer don't have to go breaking yer back doing poxy labouring jobs 'cos there's nothing else.'

Molly's girly pout disappeared. She stuck her fists into her waist. 'Didn't you listen to a word Dad said, Danny Mehan? Everyone's having it hard now. Everyone.'

Liz rolled her eyes. 'Here we go. Saturday night and the battling Mehans are still at it. Don't you lot ever take a day off?' She shook her head knowingly at Bob. 'I'll guarantee that neither of 'em's got a clue what they're on about. Just any old excuse for a ruck'll do.'

Bob smiled at Liz as he pulled a wallet from his inside pocket. 'Typical brother and sister, eh?'

Molly's rage with Danny was instantly forgotten. Like Danny and Liz, she was far too busy staring at Bob's hands. No one from round their way even owned a wallet, as far as they knew, let alone a flash-looking leather one like Bob was waving about.

He cracked it open and took out a ten-shilling note. 'Tonight'll be my treat, if that's all right with everyone.'

Liz and Molly gawped at each other.

'Fine by me,' giggled Molly.

Danny stuck out his chest, proud to be friends with such a man of the world.

Bob slapped him chummily on the back. 'Well, Danny old son, if we're going, we'd better get a move on. You on?'

'I'm on,' Danny agreed with a nod. 'Now, how about if we meet you two in, say, half an hour?' He looked at Bob for approval. Bob dipped his chin to give him the go-ahead. 'In Commercial Road?'

Molly linked arms with Liz. 'That'll do us fine. We'll see yer near the Eastern.'

Bob frowned. 'No, yer don't wanna hang around near no pubs by yerselves. Couple of pretty girls like you – yer'd get bothered by all sorts of creeps and no-goods. No, you walk along a bit and we'll see yer on the corner of Three Colt Street.'

Molly raised her eyebrows at Liz. 'Ain't he the bossy one?'

Bob chucked Molly under the chin. 'Yer'd better remember it and all. And if yer a good girl, I'll get yer a nice marzipan fish in the interval.'

Molly wrinkled her nose. 'Yeeurrr, no thanks. I hate the taste of almonds. But I tell yer what, yer can get us a big block of honeycomb to nosh. Something nice and sweet.' She shoved Liz so hard that she stumbled sideways. 'We like that, don't we, Liz, something nice and sweet?'

'Don't get me involved,' said Liz testily, rubbing her side.

'You can have whatever you fancy, darling,' said Bob with an exaggerated wink, "cos I'm the man to get it for yer.' He reached out and ran his finger slowly up and down her cheek. 'You just remember that.'

Open-mouthed at such familiarity, the girls were still speechless as they watched Bob lead Danny dodging across East India Dock Road and down one of the turnings that led onto Poplar High Street. They waited until they had disappeared from view, and then strolled along arm in arm in unspoken but agreed progress towards the place they had arranged to meet them in half an hour's time.

They were intrigued by what the exchange with the boys had revealed. Both girls had been fancied, and both girls knew it – that was more than clear – but what was keeping them silent was the possibility that they'd make fools of themselves, if they had over-estimated the boys' interest in them. For all their bravado and cheek, they knew they were dangerously close to being out of their depths; Molly and Liz had never actually had boyfriends before, and weren't really sure what they should expect to happen next.

But by the time they had walked just a few yards further along the crowded pavement, Liz could keep quiet no longer. 'So, what d'yer know about this Bob Jarvis then?' she asked, trying to sound as though it was of less interest to her than what Rags had had for his tea.

Equally casually, Molly ran her fingers through her hair. 'I've seen him around,' she said, 'but it's the first time I've met him proper, like. Seems all right, I suppose. Bit flash though.' She waved hello to a giggling girl who was dashing across the road between the traffic to join a crowd of her friends. 'Look, there's old Phoebe Tucker's granddaughter. She's got herself done up a bit lairy, ain't she?'

'Don't change the subject, Moll,' said Liz, waving too. 'I reckon he's nice. Bob, I mean. Well, not nice exactly, more sort of, I dunno, exciting, like. How about the way he touched yer?' Despite her resolve to remain cool, she chuckled suggestively. 'It was obvious what he had on his mind. Made me go all funny, it did.'

'Made *you* go funny?' Molly put her hand to her cheek where Bob had touched her 'How about what it did to me? All goose pimply I was. Anyway, you're one to talk. How about you and our Dan? First time you two ain't just talked about football.'

'He was a bit of a giveaway, wasn't he? Did yer see his face when I asked him if he'd sit next to me in the pictures?'

Molly joined in with her laughter. 'No wonder. You was a bit forward, yer know. Right quick off the mark.'

'*You* told me to say it! Anyway, you can talk. You was as bad, way you dived in with that Bob. No wonder he got going. Mind you, he ain't bad-looking, is he? Quite handsome really. And lovely big shoulders. Bit like Clark Gable.'

'Yeah, if yer squint yer eyes and stand on one leg, he's a dead ringer.'

'Silly mare,' she said, squeezing Molly's arm affectionately.

'You thought any more about going hopping this year, Liz?' Molly asked, stepping off the kerb, ready to cross Upper North Street. 'Mum's thinking about going with Nanna and the little 'uns, and I think she expects me to go and all. I ain't that keen though, to tell yer the truth.'

Hauling Molly back on to the pavement to let a van pass by without running her down, Liz said nonchalantly, 'Only the little 'uns going, yer say? So Danny ain't going for the pole-pulling this year, then?'

'No. He was gonna go, but now Joe Palmer's promised to keep him on regular like, he's staying home with Dad.'

'I think I'll be staying home and all this year.'

'Here, I thought I was having yer lead our Danny on for a laugh, but you fancy him, don't yer? That's why you don't wanna go, 'cos Danny ain't going.'

'*No*,' said Liz indignantly. 'You was right what yer

said before. Jobs *are* getting harder to come by. Even for girls our age.'

Molly sighed and nodded, suddenly serious. 'That's what Dad reckons.' But, as usual, her sober mood was as short-lived as a soap bubble. 'Here, Liz,' she said, prodding her friend, 'look at them blokes over there. They're only doing that hand thing.'

'What hand thing?'

'Over there, look.'

Liz looked across the road towards Saltwell Street where Molly was pointing. There she saw a group of four boys, all about fourteen years old, slapping anyone who passed them on the back as though they were old friends. 'What?' she said. 'What am I looking at?'

'Look at the state of their shirts and dresses when they've gone past 'em,' Molly explained.

Liz looked again. Everyone who received the friendly greeting was left with a black sooty impression of a hand marked clearly on their back.

'Little sods,' laughed Molly.

'You can say that again,' said Liz, biting her lip to stop herself from laughing. 'Look a bit closer, Moll. One of 'em's got red hair.'

'Red hair?' Molly took another look, then, with an angry tutting, she put her hands either side of her mouth to make her voice carry. 'Sean Mehan!' she screeched. 'You just wait till I get my hands on you.'

The four boys scarpered before Molly could cross the busy road, leaving her fuming helplessly on the pavement.

'I'll swing for that flaming Sean one day, you just see if I don't. I'll have to stop the little bugger before he gets himself in trouble, or Mum'll do her pieces. And yer know who'll be to blame.'

Liz's shoulders slumped. She was used to the Mehan temper and the family's talent for flying off the handle, and knew what to expect. The prospect of an evening spent trailing along behind Molly while she shouted the odds as they searched for the wayward Sean, presented itself in all its miserable likelihood. And Liz had really got used to the idea of going to the pictures with Danny, as well.

Molly was about to drag her across the street in a gap in the traffic, when an opportunity for Liz to distract her friend presented itself right on cue. Coming towards them, in one of the big huddles of young men and women who were milling about on the pavement, was a girl they both knew. She was a very obviously bottle-made blonde, who, whenever Molly and Liz saw her, always seemed to have the latest length skirt, too much red lipstick, and a new boy on her arm. And she was a girl, they also both knew, who had her eye on Danny.

'Get a load of her,' hissed Liz, as they neared the group she was with.

'Yeah,' Molly sneered supportively. 'All cased up as usual. Thinks she's flipping Joan Blondell, that one. She wants to get herself a mirror, ugly mare.'

'She's a flashy-looking cow, all right,' Liz agreed. 'But I reckon she could be in the films, if she wanted, yer know.'

Molly was shocked into silence. Stopping dead in her tracks she eventually managed to blurt out. 'What? Her? In the films? You been on the turps, Liz?'

Now she had her attention, Liz started walking again, dragging Molly along beside her. 'No. I mean it. Just think. Once them Indians have finished with 'em, I reckon them cowboys could always do with a few more horses. And with a face like her'n, she'd be perfect with a saddle on her back.'

When Molly burst out into loud, coarse laughter, Liz grinned happily with relief, all her friend's thoughts of hunting for Sean seemingly forgotten – for the meantime, at least. It looked as though they would be going to the pictures after all.

They were now nearing the big intersection where West India Dock Road peeled off towards China Town, Burdett Road led away to Mile End, and Commercial Road followed the route into the City – not far from where they had arranged to meet Danny and Bob – but Molly again came to a sudden halt, jerking Liz to a standstill beside her. 'Cor, I could take a fancy to him, Liz,' she breathed, her voice full of undisguised admiration.

'I don't know what's got into you,' Liz said primly, looking around for the object of her friend's attentions, 'but don't let that Bob hear yer.'

'Ne'mind Bob Jarvis,' Molly whispered. 'Just have a look at him, will yer?' She nodded over the road to where a handsome, black-haired young man of about twenty was coming out of a side street. He had clear, olive skin and, even from that distance, Molly could see that his eyes were so deep brown they were almost black.

'I know him,' said Liz.

'You what? Call him over then.'

'Well, not exactly *know* him.'

'That don't matter. You just call him.'

Liz sighed in resignation. Like Danny, she knew she would never win in an argument with Molly, so she put four of her fingers between her lips and let out a piercing whistle. Several people looked round, some even smiled hopefully at the pretty blonde girl, wondering if it was their attention she was trying to attract. But the dark-haired young man was one of the few who ignored the shrill signal and he carried on walking away along Commercial Road.

'Too late,' said Liz.

Molly nudged her hard in the ribs. 'Lizzie Watts,' she said threateningly.

Liz knew when she was beaten. 'Oi!' she hollered. 'Simon. Simon Blomstein. Over here.'

As several disappointed young men turned away, Simon Blomstein stopped and looked round. He seemed puzzled. Tapping himself on the chest, he mouthed, 'Me?'

'Yeah, you.' Liz nodded and beckoned him over.

Molly kept her eye on Simon Blomstein as he did his best to get safely across the busy junction. 'Quick, tell me what yer know about him.'

As he drew closer to them, Liz automatically patted her fair curls. 'Not much really. I took in some printing what he delivered to the warehouse the other day and we got chatting. He ain't got no mum or dad. He lives with his Uncle David's family but used to live with his auntie somewhere – North London, I think it was – can't remember now. And he works for him, his uncle, I mean, at his printing works off Cable Street. Aw yeah, they're Jewish and they live up Whitechapel way and all. Him and his uncle's family.'

'What, don't tell me you don't know his collar size,' Molly said, tearing her eyes away from Simon – who by now had almost made it to the pavement – and turning to stare at her friend. 'How d'yer know all this?'

Liz winked broadly and tapped the side of her nose with her finger. 'Psychic, ain't I, just like Nutty Lil.'

'Liz!'

'I told yer, he come into the warehouse the other day to deliver some printing, and we had a little chat.'

43

Molly grinned and shoved Liz sideways. 'Some little chat.'

Liz signalled with her eyes for Molly to shut up as Simon Blomstein finally arrived beside them. His face lit up with a smile of recognition. 'Terson's Quality Teas,' he said, snapping his fingers.

Liz returned his smile. 'That's right. Lizzie Watts, remember?'

'Of course.' Simon held out his hand.

Molly grabbed it before Liz had a chance. 'Molly Katherine Mehan,' she said, noticing the softness of his long pale fingers, so different from the big rough hands of the men in her family.

'Hello, Molly,' he said with a nod.

There was a moment's pause and then Molly opened her mouth and out it came. 'We was thinking of going to the pictures. Fancy coming with us?'

At first, Simon looked a bit taken aback and Molly was convinced that this time she and her big mouth really had gone too far, and that she had scared Simon off before she had even had a chance to get to know him. Despite her protests about what her nanna and Danny had said earlier, now she could have kicked herself for not being a bit more ladylike.

But Molly was wrong. Simon hadn't had very much to do with girls outside of his family, and the enthusiastic, fox-haired Molly Katherine Mehan seemed so exotic compared to his quiet dark-haired cousins that he couldn't help but be charmed by her.

'I'd like that very much,' he said.

Molly turned to Liz and raised her eyebrows with a surprisingly nervous grin. 'He's all right, ain't he, this Simon Blomstein?'

For want of something better to do, Liz grinned

dumbly back. She didn't like even to think what Bob Jarvis might have to say about this unexpected addition to their party.

'But,' Simon added with a shrug, 'I'm really sorry, I can't. Not tonight.'

Molly echoed his shrug, swallowing down her disappointment before she spoke. 'It's all right. I just thought yer might like to, that's all.'

'I would, truly, but I'm meant to be somewhere else. I really have got to rush.' He began walking quickly away, but then stopped and turned round. 'Look, I'm sorry about tonight. Really. But it's family. You know.'

Molly did her best to sound uninterested. 'Family, yeah, I know.'

'But, how about,' he continued, 'if we meet up tomorrow?'

Molly's mask of unconcern slipped and she beamed like an electric light bulb. 'Yeah, I'd like that. When?'

'During the day sometime? Would that be all right? I have to get up early for work, you see.'

'Me too.' Molly was bubbling. 'Tell yer what, I've got to go to church, then have me dinner, but after . . .'

'Church?' Simon asked.

'Yeah,' laughed Molly. 'Same problem as you: family. Me mum'd kill me stone dead if I missed Mass, and then I wouldn't be able to give you the pleasure of me company, now would I?'

Liz stood beside her friend, watching in awe, as though she were witnessing the theatrical skills of a great actress. It really was quite a performance. Molly wasn't beautiful in any conventional way but she had a vivacity, combined with the cheek of the devil, that boys, a lot of them anyway, seemed to fall for, and she never ever seemed to notice what effect she was having on them.

45

Well, up until now, she hadn't, Liz checked herself. Now Molly looked all too aware of the effect she was having on Simon Blomstein.

'I know what'd be a good idea,' she said, flicking her thick auburn waves away from her eyes. 'I can meet you at the top of Preston's Road. Know it?' She jerked her thumb back over her shoulder in the direction of the Isle of Dogs.

'I know it.'

'Good. Then we can go on to the Island and through the foot tunnel to Greenwich. It'll be smashing in this hot weather.'

Simon hesitated for just a moment, then smiled and nodded. 'That sounds nice. Half past two?'

'Half past two,' she agreed.

Then, without another word or so much as a wave, Simon trotted off in the direction of Aldgate.

He was still in view, dodging in and out of the increasingly boisterous Saturday evening crowds, when Molly felt someone grab her arms from behind, pinning them to her side. Furious, she twisted her head round to see who would dare take such a liberty. It was Bob Jarvis, his face pale with anger.

'Good job we finished our business a bit earlier than I thought,' he said through barely open teeth.

Molly dragged herself away from him. 'What the hell do you think yer doing?' She stabbed a finger at Danny who was standing there beside Bob, looking as though he wished he wasn't. 'And what's up with you, letting him grab at me like that?'

Danny stared at the ground, nervously drawing designs in the dust with the toe of his boot.

'Danny?' she insisted. 'Danny, I'm talking to you.'

'And I'm talking to you.' Bob said the words quietly

but so menacingly that Molly, astonished by his presumption, shut up and listened. 'I wanna know,' he went on, 'what yer thought yer was doing talking to the likes of him?'

Molly frowned; she couldn't figure out what Bob was going on about. 'How d'yer mean *the likes of him*?'

'Him.' Bob's jaw was rigid. 'A Jew.'

Molly was in two minds about what she should say: part of her wanted to shout at him, ask him who he thought he was, bossing her about, and that he could bugger off and mind his own business. But she didn't. There was something about him, something about the way he was looking at her that stopped her. She was like a rabbit, mesmerised by a stoat. It wasn't anything to do with his looks, although he was all right in that department, if not as handsome as Simon; no, it was to do with a way he had about him that both repelled and attracted her at the same time. She swallowed hard, as she admitted to herself that she was compelled by Bob Jarvis's arrogant, domineering attitude; it made him seem superior somehow, gave him a confidence that other boys she knew just didn't have.

Molly flashed a look at Liz who was silently observing the bizarre scene. Could she really let him speak to her like that in front of her friend, not to mention Danny, who'd never let her hear the end of it? And why should anyone have the right to tell *her*, Molly Katherine Mehan, who she could or couldn't speak to? But despite that, and despite the fact that she was going to meet Simon the next day, Molly didn't want to spoil her chances of going to the pictures with Bob – that was a price she wasn't prepared to pay.

'Well?' Bob demanded. 'Are you gonna explain yerself?'

47

'He was lost,' she said, sticking her chin defiantly in the air. 'Wanted to know the way to Aldgate, didn't he? So I told him. "Up there," I said. "That's the way".' She stuck her fists into her waist. 'That all right with you, is it? Or is there a law against it or something?'

Molly sneaked another quick look at Liz. Liz was saying nothing, she just looked straight ahead, wide-eyed and with a half-smile on her face: a convincing picture of pretty, if slightly daft, innocence.

Bob also lifted his chin and stood very straight, looking along his nose at Molly, weighing her up. 'So long as yer sure. 'Cos I don't want no girl of mine being mates with no Jews.'

'Bloody cheek. Who said I'm your girl, then?'

'I did.'

Molly folded her arms, then unfolded them. 'I was only telling him the way, all right?' She turned and looked sheepishly at Liz, but her friend hurriedly averted her eyes. Molly turned back to Bob; she folded her arms again. 'If it's anything to do with you.'

'That's all right then,' he said eventually.

'I am glad,' said Molly, with a cynical lift in her voice. Then she linked arms with Liz. 'So, are we going to the flicks or what?'

Bob relaxed. 'Yeah, course. You girls walk on, I've just gotta finish a bit of business, private like, with Danny here.'

Molly and Liz looked at each other and, relieved by the broken tension, they shrieked with laughter.

'Private business!' Liz spluttered.

'Hark at them,' Molly roared in response.

For all their derision, they walked on ahead exactly as Bob had told them to, so that he and Danny could talk about whatever it was that they considered so important.

Molly pulled Liz close to her. 'Yer a good mate, Lizzie Watts. Thanks for not giving us away.'

'Why should I give yer away?' asked Liz, looking back over her shoulder at Danny and Bob, who were now deep in conversation. 'Can't have blokes thinking they own us, now can we?' she added.

Molly felt herself blush. Had she really acted that stupidly? She lifted her lips into a deliberate smile. 'What, not even blokes like our Danny?'

'No good you trying to torment me, Moll,' Liz sniped straight back. 'Least I'm only getting meself hiked up with one bloke at a time.'

3

While his children were all out having a good time at
their various Saturday evening occupations – Danny and
Molly going to the pictures with Liz and Bob; Timmy
and Michael having a rowdy kick-about with the Milton
kids; Sean supposedly in the charge of his big brother
and sister – Pat Mehan had wandered along to the
Queen's, the pub at the blocked end of Plumley Street,
for a pint of best. He was standing at the little bar, his
elbows resting on the counter, staring into his glass.
Although he had never been one to waste his time, or
his money if he had any to spare, in the pub, Pat did like
to have the occasional jar and the chance of a chat and a
laugh with his friends and neighbours.

The pub hadn't begun to fill up yet. There were
just Pat, Joe Palmer standing next to him at the
counter, nursing the remains of a pint, and, in the
corner, Jimmo Shay and Albert Tucker, two of the
older residents of the street, who were playing crib as
though their lives and reputations depended on it.
The evening was still warm, but the four customers
all had their caps jammed on their heads and pulled
down well over their eyes, stocks tied tightly round
their necks, and their waistcoats, all barring the
bottom buttons, of course, neatly buttoned up, and, for
the sake of their own notions of respectability and

despite the heat of the evening, topped off with aged, threadbare jackets.

Pat drained his glass and looked up at the brightly dressed, elaborately made-up middle-aged woman who was standing behind the bar.

'Two more pints for me and Joe here, please, Mags,' he said, with a flash of his eyebrows. 'And send a couple of halves over to them two while yer at it and all, please, girl.'

Instead of rewarding Pat with her usual broad smile and a whiff of her scent as she raised her arm to pull the pints, Mags Donovan dipped her chin and began to sniffle into a frothy lace handkerchief that she pulled from her sleeve. She flapped her hand distractedly in the direction of her portly husband. 'Ask Harold, if yer don't mind, Pat. I've gotta just . . .' Her tears overcame her and, not wanting her customers to witness her sorrow, she dashed through to the back room.

Pat, never able to cope with a woman's tears, stretched his lips tightly across his teeth. 'Here, Harold, I ain't said nothing to upset her, have I?'

The publican shook his head; he looked close to weeping himself, a real oddity in such a big, usually tough-acting man. 'Don't mind Mags, Pat,' Harold said, raising an empty pint glass for Pat's approval.

Pat nodded and said, 'Two pints and two halves, please, Harold.'

Harold began to draw the beer, levering the wood and brass pump towards him in a strong, even pull. 'She's gone and got herself all worked up, ain't she?'

'How's that then, mate?'

'Well, it's our young Margaret, see. Mags can cope with the boys moving away like.' He set a full, brimming glass on the counter in front of Pat, which in turn he slid along the polished wood towards Joe. 'It's only right that boys go and live near their wives' families, no one'd disagree with that.' Harold put the second glass in front of Pat before starting on filling the two half-pint mugs. 'But, like I say, it's our young Margaret.' He slammed the first of the smaller drinks down on the bar, slopping the foaming liquid over the polished counter. 'She's really gone and broke my Mags's heart.'

Pat and Joe raised their glasses to each other in silent salute, then sipped at their beer, listening respectfully while Harold told them about his troubles – a reversal of what usually happened in the Queen's Arms.

'I suppose yer've heard all about it anyway, how she's moved all the way to bloody Dagenham.'

Pat and Joe nodded to show that they had indeed heard what had been the talk of the whole turning for weeks.

'Don't know what got into her.' Harold whacked down the second of the smaller drinks. 'What would anyone wanna go and live in a place like that for? Everyone knows it's all kippers and curtains down there. And our Margaret's always been such a down-to-earth girl. Well, before she married, she was.' Harold paused, then, sneering over the words, he added: 'Paul Monroe. I ask yer, what sort of a name's that when it's at home? *Paul Monroe*? Suppose he thinks they're too good for the East End now they've got their *bathroom* and their *inside lav*.' Harold spoke of his daughter's new living arrangements as though they might be horribly contagious.

Pat sorted through a handful of loose change that he'd taken from his trouser pocket. 'Here, Harold, have one yerself, mate. Go on.'

With his jaw set to stop himself from breaking down

in tears, Harold did his best to smile his thanks. 'Good luck, Pat.' He rang up the total on the big brass till, and slung the change carelessly into the wooden money tray. 'I will have a half with yer.'

Harold pulled his drink and then sat himself down on the high stool behind the bar that usually stood unused, and stared into the foam as though it might hold the solution to all his problems.

Pat took the two half-pint glasses over to the little round table in the corner where the elderly men were still concentrating on their cards. He put the drinks down in front of them, careful not to disturb their game.

'Aaaah! Just the job,' said Jimmo Shay, winking appreciatively. 'Ta, son.'

'My pleasure, Jimmo,' said Pat, slapping him on the back. 'And cheers, Albert.'

Albert grudgingly lifted his gaze from his hand and repaid Pat's generosity with a low growl.

Pat didn't take offence. Albert Tucker's gloom was legendary, and, considering that for the last forty-odd years he'd been married to Phoebe, a right old dragon who could turn milk sour with just one glance from her beady little eyes, no one in Plumley Street really expected anything else of the miserable old devil.

As Pat settled himself back at the bar, Joe Palmer was chuckling to himself. 'Look at them two, will yer, Pat? Yer know yer won't get no drinks back off them crafty old sods. Got rubber weskits the pair of 'em. Put their hands in their pockets and they bounce right out again.'

Pat shrugged. 'Don't matter, does it, treating 'em now and again. Don't suppose they've got more'n a couple o' coppers to bless 'emselves with, poor old buggers.'

'Don't you believe it, Pat. They're doing all right. Since

54

them two old goats retired from the market, my missus has fed the pair of 'em and their old girls. I'm telling yer, it's a fact. You know what my Aggie's like – feels sorry for every living creature, she does. If she sees a sparrow hurt she has to fetch it home and look after it, and she's the same with that little mob. She's over Phoebe's or Sooky's every five minutes with a bread pudden or a drop o' stew. No, yer don't wanna waste no sympathy on them, Pat. They do all right, you mark my words.'

Joe took a long swallow from his pint. 'Now, that poor bleeder Milton,' he went on, 'that's a different story. He needs everything anyone's got to give him, he does. Never seen a decent pair of boots on any one of them kids of his.'

'Me and Katie was saying that when we was having our tea just now. He's a poor bastard. I mean, it's bad enough for me down the docks, worrying the life out of meself about how to get hold of a few bob when I miss the odd day – and there's been more and more of them lately.'

'Yer must miss the money with a family to bring up, Pat.'

'Yeah, that's obvious, innit? But it's the other things and all. Seeing yer mates, having a laugh and that. I reckon it'd drive me mental; I dunno how he passes the days.'

'Queueing up down the bleed'n Labour Exchange waiting to be insulted, that's how,' said Harold, joining in from his perch on the other side of the bar. 'Dunno how they put up with it.'

Joe Palmer took another long swig of his beer. 'You seen him lately, Harold? Been in at all, has he?'

'No, he's not been in here for months.'

'Well, yer'd be shocked, I'm telling yer. Looks just like an old man, he does now.'

Pat tipped his head back and drained his glass. 'Drink up, Joe. Let's have another one.'

Joe did as he was told and pushed the empty glass towards Harold. 'What's all this in aid of, Pat? That'll be two pints yer've stood me.'

'Just to say thanks again for keeping our Danny on. It means a lot to me and Katie to know he's working, specially during times like these.'

'My pleasure, Pat. And don't go getting it into yer head that I'm doing him some sort of a favour. He's a fine little worker. Willing. It's good to see it in a kid of eighteen. So yer don't have to keep standing me pints. Not that I'm saying no, mind yer.' Joe laughed. 'And my Aggie thinks he's an angel, so I wouldn't dare get rid of him, would I?' He paused. 'She'd have loved a kid like him, yer know, Pat.'

Pat nodded. 'I know.' He slapped a handful of change down on the counter. 'Well, if you don't want me to buy you a pint to say thanks, I'll ask yer to join in a bit of a celebration with me instead.' Pat lowered his voice. 'Don't let on to my Katie, but I had a bit of luck yesterday.'

'What, got a tip off of Prince Monolulu, did yer?'

'Good as.' Pat held the glasses out to Harold. 'Two more in here, please, mate, and have another one for yerself.'

Harold levered himself listlessly off his stool 'Not for me, ta, Pat.'

'Well?' Joe was intrigued.

Pat couldn't hold back a smile as he recalled his good fortune. 'See,' he began, 'we had a bit of time on our hands yesterday, nothing to do again, and I thought I was gonna be well outta pocket. But we kind of fell into having a few rounds of pitch and toss with the customs blokes.' He leant over the bar to Harold. 'And you know the feeling when luck's with yer? Well, I was nearly fifteen bob up by the finish. Fifteen bob for nothing, so I thought we'd maybe up the odds a bit.' He looked over his shoulder to make sure that Jimmo and Albert weren't earwigging. Both had wives who were experts in spreading tales, and the last thing he wanted was for Katie to get wind of what he'd been up to. He dropped his voice to a hoarse whisper. 'So I said I'd take on any one of 'em. And there was one who was willing – the *only* one who was willing as a matter of fact,' he added proudly, 'who was game enough to take on Pat Mehan in a fight. Great big bleeder, he was, from over East Ham way somewhere. Right fancied his chances with me, he did.'

Harold and Joe both laughed in anticipation.

'But he weren't as tough as he thought he was. Aw no. "I could have you," I said to him, "with one hand tied behind me back." And that's exactly what I did.'

'What?' Joe nodded towards Pat's arm.

'Yep, we went behind the sheds and I took him on with it tied behind me back with a lump of rope. Two minutes he lasted.' Pat took off his cap and lifted his thick fringe of dark hair from his forehead. A deep blue stain showed through his weather-beaten skin. 'I got that and another fifteen bob for me trouble.'

Joe threw back his head with laughter. 'Don't let your Katie find out or yer'll have more than a bruise on yer crust, yer'll have a frying pan there and all.'

Pat joined in with his laughter. 'I ain't daft.'

'She's a girl, your Katie.'

'Yeah, she's that, all right, but she's got a heart of gold and all, Joe, just like your Aggie.' Pat dropped his chin and said quietly, 'Yer know what, even with all us mob to worry about she's *still* been taking grub over to the Miltons for the last couple of weeks. I reckon she thinks none of us have been noticing but I've seen her.'

'She's a rare one, that missus of your'n, Pat. I mean, Aggie's only got me and her to see to. But your Katie – I dunno how she finds time.'

Joe drained his glass and held it up to Pat. Pat hesitated for just a moment then smiled. 'Go on then, but just half or yer'll have me singing.'

Joe leant across the bar. 'Two halves, please, Harold.' He sat back, arms folded across his chest. 'It's like how she's been helping out Frank Barber with that kid of his. Aggie's been full of it.'

Pat frowned.

'He must really appreciate it, yer know. Must be murder for a geezer like him bringing up a kid by himself.'

No sooner had Harold put the two half-pints on the bar than Pat had drained his glass. He stood up, wiped his mouth on the back of his hand and started walking over to the door. Before he left he turned round to the astonished Joe. 'Thanks for the beer,' he said, his voice flat and his face drained of colour. 'I'll be getting off home now.'

Harold shook his head at Joe with a look that said: Don't ask, mate, just keep yer trap shut if you've got any sense.

As Pat stepped outside on to the street the warm evening air hit him like a wall. He stood there, breathing deeply, trying to sort out the thoughts that were buzzing around in his head. Frank Barber. Joe had said it, plain as day, she'd been helping Frank Barber. Why hadn't she said anything to him about it?

In a more rational mood Pat would have told himself that that was Katie's way: not bragging about what she was doing for people and just getting on with things. But Pat wasn't thinking rationally. The blackness of jealousy had closed his mind into a single, dark tunnel of anger, rooted in an undeniable, but never spoken fear of losing her. He had seen his mother go off so many times when he had been a child that he had absorbed the perverted lesson without ever questioning it, that that was what women did – they went off and left you, no matter how much you needed them, or how much you loved them. His mother hadn't stayed away, however. She had always come back, claiming she was sorry for what she had done. But that wasn't the truth, or so his father had hollered so loud that Pat could hear from his bedroom as he cowered beneath the blankets. The truth was that she was bored as she always was, sooner or later, by her latest man. Next there would be the screaming match with Pat's parents accusing one another of things that Pat chose not to hear, or at least not to remember, and finally his father would explode into a violent frenzy of punching and kicking, beating his wife until she collapsed from his blows, while Pat buried his head under his pillow, sobbing for them to stop.

Pat had never asked his parents, or even himself for that matter, whether it was his father's violence or his mother's straying that had come first, but he had sworn to himself that when he grew up he would never live the life that they had; when he got married he would never let his wife leave him.

He pulled down his cap and prepared himself to walk back along the road to number twelve and confront her, but what he saw going on outside their house at the other end of the street was enough of an excuse to tip his fermenting anger over into a blind rage. There was Katie, broom in hand, rowing noisily with a woman Pat recognised as coming from one of the flats in the tall three-storey houses in Upper North Street; she had the reputation for being a wild street fighter who didn't mind getting a bloody nose or a thick lip so long as she got her revenge for whatever slight, real or imagined, that she was disputing.

Usually Pat would have raced along the street and been first in the queue to support his wife, whatever the issue, against such a woman, believing implicitly that Katie could never be in the wrong. But after what Joe had just said to him, supporting his wife was the last thing on Pat's mind.

He strode purposefully towards the little crowd that had gathered round the two yelling women, his mind full of the vision of Katie smiling up at Frank Barber, the widower from across the street at number eleven. He didn't even notice the younger Miltons hanging out of their top window jeering and pelting things at the woman who had the cheek to be rowing with their friend's mum. Nor did he register that Phoebe Tucker and Sooky Shay were sitting on kitchen chairs on the pavement in front of number seven, looking, apart from the fact that they were togged out in crossover aprons and trodden-down carpet slippers, as though they were in a theatre audience watching a high drama being acted out for their entertainment.

As Pat drew nearer to the rowdy scene he began to get the gist of what the woman from round the corner was shouting at his wife; she was complaining about one of his sons.

'Your precious little Michael wants his arse tanning,

60

the rotten little bugger. Nearly ripped the sleeve right off that jacket, he has,' the woman hollered, poking her finger dangerously close to Katie's mouth. She was either very brave or didn't know that if anyone had anything bad to say about her kids, Katie Mehan had it in her to bite right through to the woman's bone.

'My Michael, you say,' said Katie, deceptively calm. Crouching forward, she circled the woman, her broom clasped in her hand as though it were an Amazon warrior's spear. 'Aw no, yer've got that all wrong.' Katie shook her head, making her halo of red waves quiver. 'I ain't having that. It's not my Michael yer wanna be after. No, if yer looking for the troublemaker, yer wanna look at yer own flaming kid. Yer've brought up a right little monster there, if yer can call it bringing him up, the way he's left night and day while you go out gallivanting Gawd knows where.'

Katie jerked her thumb at the woman's scabby-kneed child, who was wishing he had never mentioned the name of Mehan to his mother.

'It was *him* what picked on *my* boy. Michael was only protecting himself. He knows better than to start a fight, but he knows he should always be the one to finish it. Just like I've always taught him.'

Katie turned to Michael for confirmation of what she had just claimed and, as Michael was far more scared of Katie than of any kid, or any kid's mother for that matter, he nodded angelically and whispered, 'That's right, Mum. It was him what started it. Honest. It weren't me.'

The woman's nostrils flared. 'You little liar!' She looked round at her audience, making an appeal for truth, just in time to see a lump of slate being pelted along the street with considerable speed and accuracy

61

from the Miltons' upstairs window. She ducked and it fell at Katie's feet; the Miltons weren't doing too well at protecting their champion. 'Did yer see that?' the woman gasped. 'This whole street's full of bloody hooligans.'

'Never you mind no one else,' Katie snarled. 'It's me yer've got the row with, not them.'

'I wouldn't mind,' the woman roared, 'but yer've got the sodding nerve to call yerself a churchgoer. Churchgoer, my Aunt Fanny! Yer no good, the lot of yer. And if yer don't stop him now, that Michael'll turn out just like that Sean of your'n.'

Katie straightened up from her fighter's stance. 'What's this about my Sean?'

The woman again appealed to the crowd. 'What's this about her Sean, she asks.' She turned back to Katie. 'Don't make me laugh.'

For the first time, Nora, who up until now had been standing quietly observing, spoke up. 'Yer don't have to stand for that, Katie, girl,' she said, flapping her hand at the other woman. 'You get yer blouse off and paste her!'

But before Katie could follow her mother's instructions, Pat arrived on the scene. He grabbed hold of his wife's arms and hissed into her ear to get indoors.

So shocked was she that Pat would even dare treat her like that in the street, especially in front of the neighbours and her own mother, Katie followed him dumbly into number twelve.

Feeling that honour had been satisfied, the woman from Upper North Street treated the gawping crowd to a scornful smile, stuck her chin in the air and wandered off around the corner, dragging her humiliated son by the collar of the torn jacket that had caused all the trouble in the first place.

Nora, however, felt she had been cheated out of a proper end to the business. Determined to have a row of some kind or other, she stood her ground on the pavement between her and her daughter's houses, and turned her attentions to her two neighbours who were still sitting on their kitchen chairs, apparently hoping for a second act to the drama.

'And what are you two old hens looking at?' Nora demanded loudly.

Phoebe Tucker's skin was too thick for such taunts to worry her, and anyway she was too busy insulting other people to bother wasting her time being offended.

Leaning back in her chair, she addressed her companion loudly: 'Like I said, Sook, it ain't just their kids they wanna keep an eye on neither. That flaming mongrel of their'ns been doing its business all over decent people's street doorsteps again. Disgusting, I call it, proper disgusting. Mind you, what would yer expect of a family like that? Fighting in the street. Disgraceful.'

Sooky, who always agreed with Phoebe – when she was within earshot, at least – nodded sagely. 'Yer right there, girl.'

Michael looked aghast at the women's accusation. 'Our Rags never did his business on no one's steps, Nanna. Mum'd kill me if I let him do that.'

Nora very deliberately reached into the deep pocket of her apron and retrieved her purse. Taking out a couple of pennies, she thrust them into Michael's hand. 'Go and get some chips and take Timmy with yer,' she instructed her grandson. Then she pushed up her sleeves and bowled across the street to put Phoebe Tucker and Sooky Shay right about one or two things.

Inside number twelve, Katie was pacing up and down the little kitchen, trying to figure out what had got into her husband, while he sat staring at the scrubbed table top, his face fixed with hostility beneath the peak of his cap.

'Are yer gonna say something, or are yer just gonna sit there with that face on yer?' Katie demanded, spinning round to confront him.

'Yer was causing a scene in the street,' he accused her. 'And . . .' He smacked the flat of his hand hard against his thigh, 'and yer'd think there'd at least be a bit of bread and cheese on the table for a man when he gets home from the pub.'

Katie was at a loss. She started her pacing again, thinking that if she stood still she might just have to take a saucepan to her husband's thick, stupid head. He was acting like that day he had seen the feller from the market slip some extra tomatoes into her string bag; he had insulted the man, and her, by accusing him of trying to buy his way into Katie's affections with a few over-ripe vegetables. That was typical of Pat's jealousy, but she honestly couldn't think what had made him so wild this time. It couldn't really be about bread and cheese, he never got worked up over things like that. No, all that ever set Pat off was the idea that some bloke might have noticed she didn't look like the back end of a number sixty-five tram.

She took a deep breath, stopped her pacing and looked at her husband. 'Pat, yer've not long eaten yer tea. You ain't hungry. So, will yer tell me what this is all about?'

'Did I say I was hungry?' Pat shouted. 'Did I say that? No, I didn't, did I?'

Katie pulled out a chair and sat down at the table opposite her husband. She spoke as evenly as she could manage, although her mouth was dry and her hands were trembling. 'Look, Pat, I ain't having this. Yer acting like a madman. Now will yer tell me what's really up with yer?'

Pat bowed his head. His chest rose and fell as he breathed rapidly in and out. 'Forget it, all right?'

'No, Pat, that ain't good enough.'

Pat rubbed his hands over his face, the work-worn skin of his fingers catching on the thick blue-black stubble that covered his chin. 'All right, I'll tell yer. I'm worried. Satisfied? I'm worried that when I go in on Monday the work'll have dried up completely. That there'll be nothing left for no one.' He lifted his face towards the door. 'When yer see the likes of them Miltons and what it's done to them, it gets yer down. It's enough to get anyone down. Can't yer see that?'

Katie stood up again. Her hands were now shaking almost uncontrollably as she picked up her chair and slammed it down hard under the table. 'No, Pat. I won't have it. Yer lying to me. All right, yer worried about work, but we both know there's something else up with yer, don't we? And from the way yer leading off, I reckon it's another one of them bone-headed ideas yer get stuck into that thick bonce of your'n.'

Now Pat was standing too. He towered over her, but she stood her ground, fists thrust into her waist.

'Well?' she demanded.

'Yer really wanna know?'

'Yes.'

'Right, I'll tell yer. Yer was talking to Frank Barber. Joe Palmer said so, so there's no use you denying it.'

Katie threw up her hands. 'Why would I deny talking to Frank Barber?'

Pat leant forward and thumped the table top with the side of his fist. 'Because he's a sodding widower, that's why,' he bawled.

'Yeah,' Katie snapped back, 'that's right. Yer know, yer must be a flaming genius, you. His wife's dead, so *that's* what he is, he's a widower. Now why didn't I think of that?'

Pat said nothing.

'And,' Katie went on, practically vibrating with temper, 'it's 'cos he's a widower that I was asking if there was anything I could do to help with that poor little kiddy of his.'

'What's that gotta do with you?' Pat was blazing. 'He's got old girl Evans living upstairs for that.'

Katie almost laughed. 'You are kidding, ain't yer, Pat? Nutty Lil, with all her ghosts and spirits and hymn singing? Not to mention her gin. Everyone knows she's half barmy.' She shook her head in baffled wonder.

'Kate, I couldn't care less if she was Nutty Lil or Fag Ash Lil.' Pat was losing track of what had seemed like a totally reasonable argument to him as he had strode along the street from the Queen's, determined to put a stop to whatever his fevered mind had fixed upon. 'And anyway, a feller looking after a little girl like that – well, it ain't manly, is it? I don't want yer mixing with him.'

'It ain't manly?' Now it was Katie who was losing her grasp of what they were meant to be arguing about. 'What d'yer think he should do? Stick her in a home because his old woman's dead?'

Pat didn't answer. He walked over to the sink, turned on the tap and, without even bothering to take off his cap, he ducked his head under the stream of cold water.

Katie went to stand behind him. Pointing her finger at his back she yelled, 'Tell yer what, I *admire* the way he's managing, whether you think it's manly or not. And I dunno how you can have the cheek to even talk about whether I should be helping someone. You're the one who fetches home every passing waif and stray, just 'cos yer've heard some hard luck story off 'em. I've had more hungry strangers sitting down at that table over the years than I could count on the fingers of both me hands. And, as for looking after kids, how about the way you've always helped me look after our'n?'

Pat was beside himself. He ripped his soaking wet cap from his head and dashed it to the floor, then he snatched up the little jug of daisies that Katie had put on the window ledge over the sink and threw it as hard as he could across the room. It smashed into the drawer of the painted dresser, sending pieces of jug, flowers and water flying everywhere.

'Don't you understand nothing?' he bellowed, twisting round to face her. Grabbing her by the tops of her arms, in a grip that burnt her flesh, he shook her as if she were a rag doll. 'He's a man, Katie. And you, you're a woman.'

Jerking her head up, Katie looked him in the eyes and said very slowly and deliberately, 'Take your hands off me, Pat. Now.'

He whipped his hands away from her, and held his tightly clenched fists stiffly by his sides. From the murderous look on her husband's face, it would have been understandable if Katie had backed out of the room, made off hell for leather down the passage, and then run into the street screeching for help. But that wasn't Katie Mehan's way.

Instead, she stood there, slowly looking her husband up and down. 'I'm not putting up with this, Pat Mehan,' she said. 'I love yer, yer know that, and yer should never doubt it. But I'm telling yer this for nothing, I ain't having this performance no more. This is yer last chance. Yer *very* last chance. I know yer've got a lot on yer mind

67

over work, but that ain't no excuse. If yer don't do something about this jealousy, I mean it, Pat, it'll be the end of us. I'll leave yer. 'Cos I ain't gonna wind up a punchbag like yer mum did. Even Father Hopkins himself couldn't stop me.'

The tension in Pat's face crumbled away as he slumped back down into his chair and crashed his elbows on the table, covering his face with his hands. His big labourer's shoulders began to shake. 'I'm sorry, Kate. I'm sorry. I'd never hurt you, I swear.' His words came in short bursts as though he couldn't catch his breath. 'Yer know what I get like. And, with everything else being the way it is, I just can't help meself. I don't mean to . . .'

With an exhausted sigh, Katie walked over to the table, sat down beside her husband and reached her arm around him. Pat turned to her and buried his face in her shoulder. As he wept noisily into her blouse, Katie patted his back and rocked him as though he were a huge overgrown child.

'We'll have to sort something out, Pat,' she said, as much for her own benefit as his. 'Yer do see that, don't yer? This can't go on.'

Pat lifted his face to look at her. His eyes were red and watery. 'I know.'

Katie tried to smile. 'Yer a great daft 'apporth. Come here.' She brushed his hair away from his forehead and frowned at the deep blue bruise, wondering for a moment who he had been fighting and if it was anything to do with Frank Barber, but he looked so pathetic, she couldn't bring herself to challenge him – not for the moment, anyway. She took his face in her hands and gently touched her lips to his.

With a careworn sigh of relief, Pat folded his arms round her, pulled her close and kissed her on the mouth.

Desire overcoming his anger, he stood up and took her by the hand. 'Coming to bed?' he asked her, his voice low and gruff.

Katie pulled away. 'Not just now.'

His face hardened again. 'Are you refusing me?'

'No, Pat, I ain't. And, if yer'd have given me a chance before yer jumped down me throat, yer'd know that I was gonna say I'll wait down here for Molly, Danny and Sean to come home, before I come up. But you, of course, have to jump in with both feet. And, if yer think we can sort this out by just falling into bed together, then I don't reckon yer thinking straight. Don't you realise that's the last thing I feel like?'

'What, got yer mind on someone else, have yer?'

'Do you really think that, Pat? D'you really think I'd even dream of *looking* at someone else?'

'When yer acting like this, why shouldn't I?'

Katie's mouth fell open; she genuinely didn't know what to say.

But then neither did Pat.

They had rowed over his jealousy plenty of times before, but it had always been Pat complaining that she didn't realise how her good looks and her friendliness could give men the wrong impression if she wasn't careful; he had never gone as far as accusing her of actually being interested in someone else.

After what seemed like an eternity of silence with the two of them staring at one another, Pat stormed out of the kitchen, along the passage and stood, panting at the bottom of the staircase. Michael and Timmy were sitting halfway up the stairs, stuffing themselves with greasy chips and pieces of vinegar-soaked crackling from a cone of newspaper.

Timmy smiled at him. 'Wanna chip, Dad?'

'Get into your nanna's. Go on. Now!' Pat bawled at the top of his voice as he shoved his sons out of the way, and took the stairs two at a time.

The boys didn't need telling twice. They launched themselves off their backsides, scarpered out into the street and dived into the safety of their nanna's house before their mother had a chance to come after them as well.

But the whereabouts of her two youngest sons was, unusually, the last thing on Katie's mind that evening, as she sat at the kitchen table, listening to Pat crashing about above her head.

When he had quietened down and all she could hear was the occasional creak of springs from the bedstead, she got up and filled the kettle. The evening was still warm and, with all the bad feeling, the kitchen felt like it was closing in on her, but she couldn't face sitting out in the street with her mum, not knowing that all the neighbours must have heard every shaming word of what had just gone on. So, after she had made herself a pot of tea, Katie unlatched the back door and propped it open with the chalk model of a Scottie dog that Sean had so proudly presented to her after winning it on the hoopla at the Blackheath fair last August Bank Holiday.

He had always been such a good kid, she thought to herself, as she dragged one of the kitchen chairs out into the little yard. She just didn't know what had got into him lately. All she wanted was for her kids to be happy, but as much as she hated to agree with the snipe-nosed old harridan from round Upper North Street, Sean was getting himself a reputation – but only for being a bit sullen and having a bit too much lip at times, she was sure. He wasn't a bad kid, not deep down. She wouldn't have anyone say that about him.

She sat there smoking and drinking tea, looking up at the cloudy night sky, wondering when her three oldest children would eventually get themselves home. According to the clock on the mantelpiece, it was getting on for a quarter past ten and she had told them not to be in too late because of Mass in the morning. She tried to convince herself that she had nothing to worry about, that Molly and Danny were old enough to make sure the three of them got in at a decent hour, but it was no good. She had to admit things weren't as wonderful as she had tried to kid herself. Fretting about what Sean was up to wasn't the half of it; what was on her mind more and more nowadays was being short of money, not knowing whether she could make ends meet and panicking if one of the little ones grew out of yet another pair of boots before his older brother was ready to pass his down.

As she drained the first cup of tea from the potful she had made, and went in to get a refill, Katie stared down at the worn patch of lino in the kitchen doorway. She had scrubbed it so often that there was practically no pattern left; but she knew it was no good even thinking about buying any more. She'd just have to carry on keeping clean the raggy bit that she already had.

She stirred a spoon of sugar into her cup.

Women's work, she thought to herself, they say it's never done. Well, whoever *they* were, they had got it just about right as far as she was concerned. Cup in hand, Katie examined herself in the sparkling glass of the overmantel. Thirty-seven years old. She supposed she didn't look that bad for her age, not too bad at all, considering, but the lines were beginning to show, and the red hair that had always been her glory was definitely starting the gradual sad fading away to what

71

she knew would one day be like her mother's now dull auburn, a colour that always made Katie think of a red lampshade with its bulb turned out.

She tipped her head to one side and examined her profile. Her chin was still firm and her skin as clear as someone's ten years younger might be, but, whatever she looked like, tonight Katie Mehan felt like an old woman.

She raised her eyes to the ceiling, imagining her husband lying there, his arms flung above his head as usual, his handsome face dark against the snowy white cotton of the pillow slip. He was a good-looking man all right, she thought. And, while her looks might be on their way to getting past their prime, he was getting more beautiful every day; if anyone should be jealous ... She checked herself, that wasn't a sensible way to start thinking; but no one ever said that life made any sense, or that it was fair.

Settling herself back down on her chair in the back yard, Katie wondered what her mother had looked like when she was younger. Katie could only remember her as looking almost the way she did now, and she was, what, in her late fifties? She was still a fine woman, there was no denying that, but some women of that age, or rather ladies, Katie corrected herself, the ones she saw in the papers and on the newsreels, those with their fur coats and their shiny earrings, and servants to run around after their every whim, they looked years younger than Nora, almost as young as Katie, in fact. But then they never had the worries that the likes of her or her mother had had to contend with lately.

As she sipped her tea from the thick-rimmed china cup, Katie found it hard not to wonder what her life would have been like if she had been born to money, privilege and ease, instead of to the stress and the work that made up every minute of every day of her life recently.

She hated letting herself think that way – it wasn't like her to be self-pitying, she had always been such a contented woman, happy with her life and her family. But just for a moment she wondered, crossing herself hurriedly and flicking her eyes heavenward for forgiveness as soon as she had, what her life might have been like had she stayed single, and not had a husband or kids to drive her to distraction.

4

After the few hours of sleep she finally managed to
snatch, Katie Mehan could barely rouse herself when
the alarm went off at nine o'clock the next morning. She
reached out from under the covers and groped around
before finding the button on top of the offending clock
and gave it a good solid smack to shut it up.

She flopped back on to the bolster and groaned:
Sunday morning. Why didn't she just turn over and go
back to sleep? No, she argued with herself, she had
always gone to eleven o'clock Mass in the past and there
was no good reason for her doing otherwise today. A
late night spent rowing first with her husband and then
with the three supposedly most grown-up of her five
children for getting in late wasn't any excuse.

Anyway, in not much more than an hour's time, her
mum would be standing on the street doorstep all ready
and eager to get off to church, not only to worship but
also to catch up on the chat and news with all her friends
in the neighbourhood. And then there were Katie's two
youngest – they'd be standing there with their nanna,
all scrubbed and polished ready to face their mother's
neck and ear inspection. And, of course, there were
Molly, Danny and Sean; after her stern words to those
three last night, they would be sure to be ready soon'
after the little ones, if not before. And even if it weren't

75

for all of them, there would be Father Hopkins expecting her . . .

. This time Katie groaned more loudly. Everyone expected so much of her; sometimes it made her feel worn out just thinking about all the responsibilities that people seemed so keen to heap upon her, never once asking whether she could do with a bit of a rest herself. Not that she would want to sit about doing nothing, but a bit of consideration would be nice now and again. She sighed, wondering how it had ever come to this. It wasn't five minutes ago that she was a young woman, now here she was, thirty-seven years old and feeling more like a hundred and seven.

Still half asleep beside her, Pat moaned softly and slung an arm out over his head. 'What time is it?' he murmured.

'It's nine o'clock,' Katie answered stiffly. 'I'll make us some tea.'

Pat rolled over on to his stomach and threw his arm across her. 'Don't get up yet, Kate,' he whispered into her ear. 'How about a little cuddle first?'

Katie pulled away from him and the smell of stale beer that soured his breath. 'There's no time for that,' she said, turning her back on him and throwing off the covers.

Pat rolled on to his side and moodily dragged the sheet up over his shoulders.

Katie could feel the tension building between them again. 'I'll go and make that tea,' she said. 'And boil some water for yer wash and shave.'

As she swung her legs on to the now threadbare rug that she and Pat had been so proud of making together when they were first courting, Pat circled his arms around her waist and held her back. 'Please, Kate,' he whispered urgently, 'not yet.' He buried his head in the back of her hair. 'Yer waist's as tiny as it was when yer was a young girl.' He nuzzled into her neck. 'I love yer, Katie.'

Katie twisted round and kissed him on the top of his head. 'Yer soft, you are.'

Pat pulled her down on top of him. 'I didn't mean to upset yer yesterday, yer know.' He was looking up at her, his pupils so wide that his already dark eyes looked black.

Katie smiled down at him, her expression gentle and loving, hiding her troubled thoughts. Last night had scared her. Usually the kids being a bit late wouldn't have mattered that much – she'd have given them a good tongue-lashing, they'd have behaved like angels for a few days, and it all would have been forgotten. But things were different last night. The kids were getting wilful, less easy to control; and what with Pat's outburst . . .

Katie, always so strong and capable, hated to admit it, but last night she had actually begun to feel sorry for herself and that made her panicky, scared, as though she were no longer in control of things. Maybe it was just being short of money that was getting to her, like it was getting to everyone lately. But no, it was something else, much as she tried to deny it, even to herself.

Still outwardly smiling, Katie smoothed her husband's hair back from his forehead. 'Look, Pat, I wanna say I'm sorry and all, about what happened between us last night. But we're both tired out and what with yer work being the way it is, and the kids playing up like they was two-year-olds . . .' Katie paused, she didn't know quite how to say it but she knew she had to, it couldn't be avoided any longer, the one thing that, if she were to have any peace of mind, she had to get off her chest.

Seeing the concern in her face Pat pushed himself up on his elbows and gently stroked her face. 'What is it? Tell me, love, what's up?'

Katie let out a long slow breath. 'Yer see,' she began.

'What? Has someone said something to yer, or done something to one of the kids? Katie, tell me.'

Katie shook her head. 'No, it's nothing like that, Pat.' It was now or never. 'Look, I know it shouldn't be on me mind all the time, Pat, but when I wouldn't, you know, come upstairs with yer last night—'

'Katie?'

She closed her eyes and said it: 'Pat, I'm still young enough to get in the family way again and I don't reckon that'd be such a good idea at the minute.'

'Would it be such a terrible thing if yer was to have another child with me?'

Katie threw up her hands in exasperation. 'I *knew* I shouldn't have said nothing. I knew it. Now it's come out all wrong.' She rubbed her face with her hands. 'Yer know I didn't mean it like that, Pat.'

'Do I?' Pat dropped back on to the pillows and threw his arm across his face.

'It's knowing we wouldn't be able to afford—'

'Don't bother with no tea for me,' he interrupted her loudly. 'I ain't gonna go to Mass. I'm going back to sleep.'

'Can't we try and talk to each other without rowing, Pat? Please?'

He ignored her.

'Pat,' Katie was pleading with him, 'can't yer see? This is where it's all going wrong. We've gotta talk. But what with everything else on our plates we've just stopped having time for each other.'

Pat sat up with such force that Katie backed away.

78

'No time for each other? Yer having a joke, ain't yer? Every time I try and get near yer, yer just make another stupid excuse.'

'Forget it,' shouted Katie, and stomped off downstairs to make herself some tea.

Katie ducked down to check her hat in the dressing-table mirror. As she adjusted the pin, sticking it more firmly through her thick wavy hair, she caught Pat's reflection in the glass as he lay there, still as a slab of marble. Pulling on her cotton summer gloves, Katie sat down on the edge of the bed and leant forward to kiss her husband on the cheek. But Pat pulled roughly away from her.

'There's a cup o' tea for yer there on the side,' she said, determined not to let Pat hear she was upset. 'Make sure yer drink it before it gets cold. I'll be back straight after Mass to see to the dinner. The veg is all peeled ready and the meat's in on a low light so yer'll have nothing to complain about there, will yer?' She stood up. 'I'll see yer later on.'

Katie flounced out of the room closing the door noisily behind her.

Downstairs, Nora was waiting outside by the street door, just as Katie had expected. Danny was standing by his grandmother's side, fidgety and chewing on his bottom lip.

'Look, Mum,' he said, 'if Dad don't have to go to Mass, then I don't reckon I should have to neither.'

Nora shoved her grandson hard in the side. 'You just be quiet, Daniel Mehan,' she hissed, 'talking to yer mother like that. I can't believe it.' She wagged her finger up into his face. 'A boy your age kicking up such a great big fuss. Whatever next?'

Katie looped her handbag over her arm and stuck her hands on her hips. 'And how do you know yer father ain't coming to Mass with us?'

'I should think the whole flaming street knows,' said Danny, immediately realising he'd been too cheeky for his own good, but in for a penny; he stuck his hands deep into his pockets. 'You could hear you two shouting right through the wall next door in Nanna's.'

Before Katie had the chance to tell her son to button his lip, she was distracted by the sound of the upstairs window of number twelve being shoved open with a determined slam.

Tousle-haired and grim-faced, Pat stuck his head out. 'I heard that, Danny. Now you listen to me, boy. You just watch yer mouth and do as yer mother says. Yer gonna go to Mass and that's the end of it.'

While Katie, Danny and Nora stared up at Pat, Molly came running down the stairs of number twelve, skipped over the step and out into the street beside them.

With a furtive glance up at her angry-looking dad, Molly smiled and said, 'I'm just popping into Nanna's to round up the young 'uns.' She dodged round her brother and disappeared in through the open door of number ten. After the trouble the night before, Molly had resolved to be the perfect daughter. She knew that if she wanted to meet Simon that afternoon – and she really was looking forward to seeing him – she had to make every effort to get back into her mother's good books, or she would be banned from going out all together, let alone be given permission to go off to meet a boy she barely knew.

Pat, however, didn't seem very impressed with his daughter's perfect behaviour. 'In and out, back and forward,' he complained. 'This family gets more like a flaming circus act every day.' Ducking back inside, he closed the bedroom window behind him with another sharp slam.

Nora turned her attention back to her eldest grandson, glaring belligerently at him for daring to defy his mother. 'See what yer've done now, Danny?' she fumed. 'Sure I thought it was only Sean, with his body growing faster than his brains, who'd speak to his mother like that. I reckoned a nearly grown-up lad like you would know better.'

While Danny, full of embarrassed rage, snorted and shuffled around on the pavement, Molly stood in the passage of number ten, hollering up her nanna's stairway. 'Two minutes, I'm warning yer, you three. Then Mum's coming in after yer.'

Sean appeared out of the bedroom he shared with Danny. He stood there on the tiny landing at the head of the stairs, facing Michael and Timmy's room, fiddling with his shirt cuffs, pulling them down so that they showed, just right, under his jacket.

Molly frowned. 'I ain't never seen that shirt before, Sean. New, is it?'

Sean shrugged and came lolloping down the stairs towards her, his gangly, adolescent limbs seeming to have minds of their own. 'Might be,' he said dismissively.

'So where d'yer get it then?'

Sean pushed his sister out of the way. 'Get yer nose out, Moll, can't yer?'

'Mum'll bleed'n kill yer if yer've been thieving,' Molly hissed under her breath, careful not to let anyone else hear her.

'What's going on in here?' Nora was suddenly in the doorway behind Molly.

'Nothing, Nanna,' Molly assured her.

'There'd better not be,' said Nora. 'I don't want no trouble starting in this house.'

'Honest, Nanna, it's nothing. I'm just trying to shift the two little 'uns. Come on, you two,' she shouted up the stairs. 'And don't start, or I'll save Mum a job and come up and skin the pair of yer meself.'

Timmy immediately appeared on the landing and came running down the stairs. His ginger curls were plastered to his head with water and his knees were red and glowing from where Nora had taken the flannel to them while he was trying to eat his breakfast. 'I'm ready, Moll,' he said, 'but our Michael's got the bellyache. Real bad, he is.'

'Michael,' Nora called, stepping into the passage, 'come down here if yer poorly, darling, and let yer nanna have a look at yer.'

Michael came staggering out of the bedroom he shared with Timmy. 'I ain't kidding, yer know, Nanna. I really have got a headache and I feel all horrible all over.'

Nora nodded. 'So it's a headache *and* a bellyache yer've got, is it? Now that does sound bad.'

Michael flashed a look of contempt at his little brother. 'I told yer to say it was me head, Tim. Don't you ever listen?'

Timmy opened his mouth, ready to protest, but Molly whisked him outside to join their mother and brothers in the street, leaving their grandmother to deal with young Michael.

'So, it's a bit of both yer've got, is it?' Nora said. She climbed halfway up the stairs to where her grandson was standing, unsteadily clutching at the banisters. She looked really concerned as she placed the flat of her hand against his forehead. 'Yer head and yer belly.' She nodded again and then clapped her hands triumphantly as though she had solved a great puzzle. 'It's the collywobbles yer'll be having. I'm that sure, I'd lay money on it. And what do you think, Michael? Do you think that's what it might be?'

Michael agreed eagerly, as the thought of spending a Sunday morning tucked up in the big iron bed, maybe flicking idly through some old comics, stretched before him like a blissful dream.

'So you wait here, my little love, and I'll just nip down to the kitchen and fetch me bottle of jollop. Then you can have a few big tablespoons before we go to Mass.' Nora walked slowly back down the stairs and along the passage towards the back kitchen. But she stopped abruptly, turned her head and looked up at her open-mouthed grandson. 'Oh yeah, and I'm thinking that a few glasses of liquorice water wouldn't come amiss neither. Clear yer system right out, that will. Terrible thing if yer system's clogged up.'

Michael came down the stairs two at a time. 'No, Nanna, honest, I feel much better now. Look.' He began running up and down on the spot, flinging out his arms like they were made to do at school during the dreaded PT lessons.

'Praise be,' said Nora, clasping her hands together and rolling her eyes heavenwards. 'It's a miracle, sure it is. Just you wait till Father Hopkins hears about this.' She gripped Michael's ear firmly between her finger and thumb. 'Now, let's get moving, eh, Michael, 'cos we don't want to be late to share the good news of such a wonderful event, now do we?'

'No, Nanna,' gasped Michael and, freed from his grandmother's clutches, he ran out into the street and took his mother firmly by the hand. 'I'm ready, Mum.'

Katie cast a critical eye over her children and her

mother, unaware of the little melodrama that had just been enacted in number ten.

Satisfied that they were all booted and suited in their Sunday best, as was only fitting for decent, respectable people going to church, she nodded briskly. 'Right, you lot, let's be off.' And, with Michael still clasping her tightly by the hand, Katie led the family procession out of the turning, round the corner and into Grundy Street.

Danny and Sean loped along behind their mother and Michael, with Timmy bouncing around between them, chatting and asking non-stop questions. Last in line came Nora and Molly; Nora preferred it that way as it meant she could keep an eye on what was going on.

Nora patted her granddaughter's arm that was linked though her own. 'So, we're not calling for Liz this morning? Not fallen out, have you?'

'No. Her auntie and cousins are coming over for their dinner later, so she had to go to nine o'clock with her mum.'

'Good,' Nora whispered to her. 'Now, let them rush off in front. We'll walk nice and slow, just so long as I can keep my eye on those boys, and that'll give us a chance for a little chat. So, tell me all about this boyfriend of yours.'

'What boyfriend? I ain't got no boyfriend.'

Nora stopped dead in her tracks and narrowed her eyes at her granddaughter. 'Molly Katherine Mehan, do you really think I'm as green as I'm cabbage-looking? I've seen how yer've been growing up lately, so fast I'm losing track almost. A real young lady now you are. Just look at yer, with that haircut of yours and that look in your eyes. I know there's a feller around, my girl. Yer can't fool yer old nanna.'

Molly smiled. She was right, she never had been able

84

to keep secrets from Nora. They began strolling along again.

'So?'

'Well, I'm sort of seeing Danny's mate. Bob Jarvis, his name is. He's a new bloke Dan's been hanging around with. He paid for me to go in the flicks last night, and I'm gonna see him again next Saturday. Nice, he is, really nice. Sort of exciting.'

Nora patted her arm approvingly. 'Glad to hear it. I wouldn't want my best girl seeing someone who wasn't nice and exciting, now would I?'

Molly dropped her chin with uncharacteristic coyness. 'And there's another boy, Nanna. I'm gonna see him this afternoon, I hope.' Her shyness forgotten, Molly glared at Sean who was slouching along in front of them, kicking stones viciously across the street. '*If* Mum lets me out after us getting in so late last night. I could kill that Sean. It was all his fault, yer know, Nanna. I wouldn't dare tell Mum on him, but me and Dan had to spend ages looking for him. He's a right flipping nuisance, he is.'

'Never mind Sean, there's not much yer can do with lads of his age except wait and hope he'll grow up and out of it. No, I'm more interested in this, or should I say *these* two young men of yours.' Nora raised her eyebrows questioningly. 'So, yer serious, are yer, about either of 'em?'

Molly didn't even consider the question. 'No, Nanna. It's nothing like that. You know me, I'm not the sort to get serious.'

Nora looked relieved. 'Well, thank the Lord for that. And I'm pleased to hear yer stringing two of 'em along at the same time.'

'What? Stringing 'em along?' Molly was shocked by

her nanna's brazenness; she wasn't sure whether she was being broad-minded or just plain barmy. Her grandmother was in her fifties after all, and Molly knew that people could be a bit eccentric as they got older. 'I'm not *stringing* either of 'em along. We're just friends, that's all. The way yer talking yer make me sound terrible.'

As they paused on the kerbside for an elderly man to wobble past them on his bike, Nora put a finger to her lips. 'Don't take on so much, Molly, girl. I only meant that there was no hurry for yer to go throwing yerself at the first feller what comes along.' They hurried across the street. 'You want to have a life before you settle down with some lucky feller, don't yer?'

Molly shrugged non-committally. 'S'pose so.'

'See? I'm right. There's no hurry, is there?' Nora stopped again.

Molly was getting impatient with all this stopping and starting; they'd be late if they weren't careful and then her mum would never let her go out this afternoon and Simon would be left standing there like a lemon and he'd never want to see her again. 'Come on, Nanna,' she urged her.

'If you just let me have my say first. This is important. You must promise me, Molly, before yer go settling down, yer make sure yer've found yerself the right one. If yer like, I wouldn't mind giving them the once-over to see what I think of 'em.'

Molly glanced anxiously along the road. Her mother and brothers were already in Canton Street and had nearly reached Saint Mary and Saint Joseph's Church. 'Please, Nanna. Not now.'

'But yer will remember, Molly, won't you?' Nora insisted. 'Promise. Yer must be sure. No matter how mad in the head and sick in yer stomach you are for the love of him, you will make sure he's the right one?'

Molly put her head on one side and looked at her nanna. It wasn't like her to be so serious. 'What, yer don't want me to make a mistake like you did, Nanna?' Molly asked softly.

Nora snorted scornfully. 'Mistake? Sure I never made no mistake. My Stephen was a good man. A rare man. The best there was and the best there is.'

With all the stories she had heard over the years about her grandfather, Molly was confused.

'A good man?' she asked incredulously, her mum and Mass temporarily forgotten. 'What, walking out on you when you was six months gone carrying Mum, and then turning up every few years out of the blue if he just happened to be passing, or was on the tap for a few bob?'

Nora fiddled around with her hat. 'You listen to me, Molly, and you pay attention. I've more good memories from the times I've spent with your grandad, God love him, than most women ever have from a lifetime with a dozen men.' Then with a lift of her chin, she added, 'And haven't I got your mother to show for it? God love her, as well.'

Molly shook her head in wonder; no one could ever say that Nora Brady wasn't one to come up with the surprises.

Nora smiled into the middle distance. 'And she's got your grandfather's lovely red hair. A real Irish beauty, so she is.' She reached out and touched her grand-daughter's glorious auburn waves. Tipping her head critically she said, 'Just like you, my love. Shame our Danny got your father's dark mop.'

Molly laughed, despite her concerns about ever getting her grandmother to start moving again.

Nora ran her hands over her hips, smoothing down her lightweight summer coat. 'Yer know, I always reckon that it was having had just the one baby that kept me so young-looking. I mean, look at the other women round here in their fifties. Battered old cows the lot of them.'

Molly's hand flew to her mouth. 'Nanna! Someone'll hear.'

'Well,' Nora said, leaning close to her granddaughter, 'they don't get married for real love, do they? They get hiked up with the first feller who comes along just 'cos they think that's what they should do. Then they turn into brood mares, popping out a sprog a year till they're collapsing with it.'

Molly felt the flush rising in her cheeks. 'I can't believe yer talking like this, Nanna.'

Nora winked and slipped her arm back through Molly's. 'Well, don't tell yer mother, will yer? Now, are yer coming or what? The last thing yer need is to be late for Mass. Then she definitely won't be letting yer out so's yer can go and meet yer fancy feller.'

As usual when the service was over, the congregation, including Nora and Katie, spilled out through the big wooden doors and then milled around outside, exchanging news of all the doings of the past week.

And, Nora thought to herself, as she kept a diligent eye on her daughter, there was one member of the congregation who, if she wasn't careful, would become the sole topic of interest for the meaner-minded gossips, stirrers and troublemakers. Whatever had got into her? There, in front of everyone, bold as brass, and despite what her husband would say if he found out, Katie was standing chattering away to Frank Barber, the widower from number eleven who had unwittingly caused all the trouble between her and Pat the night before. Nora really couldn't figure out what her daughter thought she was up to.

As far as Katie was concerned, it was quite simple: she would not be told by Pat, or by anyone else for that matter, who she could or could not speak to. And anyway, she had reasoned when Frank had come up to her in the church porch, what harm was there talking to the man when all he was doing was expressing his gratitude for a bit of help she had given him with his poor motherless child? Wouldn't any decent neighbour do the same?

But, if she was pressed, even Katie would have admitted there was something else that kept her standing there with Frank Barber: it wasn't only *what* he said, thanking her for her help, she liked the *way* he said it. It was the first time in years – apart from when Pat was feeling amorous, and that didn't count – that anyone had treated her like a woman. Frank talked to her in a way that Pat seemed to have forgotten about, a way that made her feel as though she was another adult, rather than just a wife and mother of a clutch of increasingly unruly kids. She was flattered by her quietly spoken neighbour's attentions, and she heard herself offering to help him again in any way she was able.

It was easy making excuses for what had happened between herself and her husband: they had both been so busy and preoccupied, they were worried about work and money, the kids were driving them barmy – but, all that apart, there really was no excuse for her and Pat forgetting how to be nice to one another. She so wanted someone to be nice to her. And that's what she felt, smiling up into Frank Barber's sad, hazel-coloured eyes – that here was somebody who was being nice to her, and not just for what she was doing for him, or because she was someone's wife, mother or daughter, or even because he wanted to make love to her, but just because he seemed to like her for who she was, herself, Katie Mehan.

She thought she could float away on his soft voice as he talked to her, that she could forget that she was someone whose fine red hair would soon be fading, and who felt as though she had the weight of the world on her shoulders. In fact, she was so deep in conversation with Frank Barber that, until he interrupted their conversation, Katie hadn't even noticed the arrival by her side of Father Hopkins.

'I've been hearing some stories about your boys, Mrs Mehan,' he said in a voice that, like Nora's, still held more than a trace of his native Irish brogue. 'Your Sean in particular.'

Katie smiled. 'Young lads, eh, Father?'

The priest, accustomed to his reprimands, no matter how slight, being taken with rather more seriousness by members of his congregation, was stunned into momentary silence by her casual attitude.

Katie turned back to Frank. 'I mean, what would yer do with 'em, eh?'

Frank laughed, a soft, throaty chuckle. 'Be easier if they played hopscotch and two balls like the girls, I reckon, Kate.'

'Yer right there,' she agreed. 'Better than being out fighting. I mean, look at your little Theresa. What a sweetheart. Now look at them two rogues of mine.'

Michael and Timmy were in the middle of a surging, rolling heap of boys, punctuated by flying fists and feet, not caring that the dusty patch of scrubby grass and weeds which surrounded the church was supposedly holy ground.

'Mrs Mehan— ' Father Hopkins intoned the words with great solemnity.

'They're like a barrow load o' monkeys, ain't they?' Katie broke in.

Father Hopkins put on his fiercest expression. 'I suppose you don't think there's anything wrong with boys roaming the streets and terrorising poor old women with their noise and their fighting?'

In complete contrast to what Father Hopkins would ever have expected from such a devout parishioner, Katie very calmly put her hands on her hips and asked him, 'Are you saying my lads are like that pack of monsters from over Stink House Bridge, Father? Because that's a serious thing to say to a woman about her children.'

The red-faced priest tried to stand his ground, but his tone betrayed the fact that he knew he had lost all authority. 'I don't think I said that now, Mrs Mehan.'

Frank Barber smiled, his open, gentle face giving out reassurances that there was no need for any of this. 'They're just a bunch of healthy kids, showing off their high spirits after sitting so nicely while you talked to us all this morning, Father Hopkins. And a very interesting sermon it was and all, if yer don't mind me saying.'

Before Father Hopkins had the chance to begin questioning Frank Barber to check if he really had been listening to his words of wisdom, Nora, frowning so hard her eyes had almost disappeared into her head, had decided it was time that she joined the three of them.

Molly groaned as she watched her grandmother's determined progress. 'Don't start chatting with Father Hopkins, Nanna, please. We'll never get home at this rate and I'm starving.'

'You just get the boys rounded up while I go and fetch your mother,' she called to her without turning round.

Knowing that there was no point arguing with her nanna, Molly weighed in to the still brawling bunch of kids and grabbed the first Mehan ear she could reach.

Michael squealed from the pain and the indignity. 'Oi, leggo o' me ear'ole. That bloody hurts, that does.'

'And yer arse'll hurt a lot more if Mum hears yer using that language,' Molly hissed into his burning ear.

'But, sis,' Michael complained, pointing accusingly at a bedraggled-looking boy of about ten years old, 'that Bobby Leighton's nicked me ciggie cards.'

Bobby's eyes bulged at such injustice. 'You little liar, Micky Mehan. I never nicked 'em. You give 'em to me fair and square.'

'You're the bloody liar! They was meant to be swapsies. Now come on, give me what yer owe me or give 'em back.'

Molly grabbed any cigarette cards from the grasp of the unsuspecting bystanders. Holding up her hand to silence their indignant protests, she formed the cards into a neat pack, licked her thumb and dealt the first card off the top.

Studying the picture then turning it over, she said threateningly, 'Right, I'm gonna divide these out, so yer wanna keep quiet or I might make a mistake, mightn't I? Now, let's see. Whose is this Don Bradman?'

A grubby hand shot up, declaring ownership.

'Right.' She handed it over. 'Dixie Dean?'

While Molly was sorting out the rightful owners of the treasured cards, Nora concentrated on sorting out Katie. 'Come on, girl,' she said, hoisting her bag up her arm. 'Time we was going.'

'Do what?' she asked absently, still smiling at Frank,

'not seeming to care that she sounded uninterested in what Nora was saying.

'Now, Katie.' Nora glared pugnaciously at Frank. 'Yer husband's expecting yer home to do his dinner, and I'm sure that Father Hopkins has plenty he has to be getting on with.'

The priest decided to cut his losses and took Nora's words as his cue to shuffle away and try to exercise his authority more productively on less forceful members of his congregation.

'Sorry, Nora,' Frank said. 'That was me going on. But I just wanted to thank Katie for all she's done for our Theresa recently. It ain't been easy for me since my Sarah . . .' He looked over to where his little girl was watching Molly hand out the cigarette cards.

Nora lifted her chin and stared along her nose at Frank. 'That's our way,' she said, 'being neighbourly,' and she hooked her arm through Katie's and unceremoniously tugged her away. Looking over her shoulder, Nora called to Danny and Sean who were lolling against the wall. 'Come on, you two, we're going home for a bit of dinner.' She flashed a look at Frank who had gone over to his daughter and was retying her hair ribbon. 'Yer father'll be waiting for us. And Molly, make those young 'uns get a move on.'

At first, as Katie was marched by her mother back towards home at double speed, not even pausing to cross themselves at the big wayside statue of Christ on the cross on the corner of Upper North Street and Canton Street, she didn't say a word, she was steaming with humiliation at being pulled away by her mother as if she were a little schoolgirl who was late going home for her tea. But, by the time they were almost at the corner of their turning, Katie could stand it no longer. She dragged Nora to a halt beside her, shoved her hands on her hips and demanded, 'So, are yer gonna tell me what that little performance was all about?'

With a hasty glance towards her grandchildren, who were still dawdling along behind them, Nora leant close to her daughter. 'Didn't I warn you about geeing up that man of yours? He won't take it, yer know, carrying on like that in front of everyone. And at church too. And on a Sunday.'

'Mum, just leave off, can't yer? Saying things like that. You should be on *my* side, not encouraging his stupid jealousy.' Katie looked anxiously up and down the road. 'And keep yer voice down. Someone'll hear yer if yer ain't careful.'

'And if they do, is there something you'd be ashamed of?'

'I'm not putting up with this.' Katie strode off, swinging her arms furiously.

'I'd watch meself if I was you, Katie,' Nora called after her.

Katie spun round and confronted her mother. 'I don't believe this. It's like being under flaming guard. You know your trouble, Mum? I never realised it before, but I reckon you've got a worse imagination than Pat.'

'And you, my girl,' countered Nora, as she turned the corner into Plumley Street, 'I reckon *you've* got a guilty conscience.'

5

Sunday dinner in number twelve had been a much quieter affair than usual, with no happy laughter or even a bit of playful bickering. Instead, the atmosphere was nastily touchy, with everyone, apart from young Michael and Timmy, seeming to be either brooding about something or else ready to boil over into a row. Even an inoffensive remark about the tastiness of the carrots and a simple, polite request for more gravy were met with scowls and grunts. To make matters worse, the warm, sunny weather had turned hot and muggy, with heavy clouds hovering in the distance, threatening to move closer; the stormy atmosphere making the kitchen feel more sultry and crowded than ever.

So it was with a sense of relief, rather than a pleasant feeling of comfortable fullness, that everyone left the table, and with it a hefty portion of Nora's usually fought over fruit pie still untouched in the dish – a previously unheard of event in the Mehan household.

When his mother had offered the pie round for the second time, Michael was sorely tempted to take another helping, but, in a rare moment of good judgement, he had decided that it was best to shake his head with a polite, 'No thanks, Mum,' as all the others had done. But, the sight of the gloriously sticky pie being put away in the food safe worried Michael's sense of what was right, and it would play on his mind like a guilty secret until he could pilfer it later on.

Fruit pie, or any other food, was the last thing on Molly's mind. She had barely noticed eating anything. All she could think of was how she was going to get out of the house to meet Simon Blomstein. With the mood her mum was in, she dreaded even mentioning that she had plans to go out for the afternoon. She was bound to have something that Molly had to do instead: an errand that suddenly had to be run or a job that couldn't wait. And then there was her dad, she sighed to herself. And her nanna. They were usually easy to get around, but with their current frame of mind they could prove as difficult as her mum. Molly just couldn't figure out what had got into them all and had spent the whole meal fretting about what she was going to do.

But Molly had been troubling herself unnecessarily about her mum. As soon as the clearing up was finished, Katie, without saying a word to anyone, carried one of the kitchen chairs out into the back yard and got stuck into tackling a pile of mending as though her life depended on it.

Molly was surprised to find that she didn't have to worry about her dad or her nanna either. Pat took himself off to the front room, supposedly for a look at the paper, but more likely for a Sunday afternoon doze, while Nora, with a whispered warning to the youngest two about behaving themselves and not upsetting their mother, went across the street to check on what tales Phoebe and Sooky were peddling between them. She was all too aware of how quickly the neighbourhood grapevine could work, and the idea of those two telling tales about her Katie and Frank Barber had worked her up into a real froth.

That only left Molly's brothers to mess things up for her, but not one of them appeared to give a tuppenny damn about what she was planning for the afternoon, so it was with real relief – and a stomach full of butterflies – that Molly ran upstairs to her bedroom to get herself ready for her outing.

Molly had the luxury of a whole room to herself. Liz Watts, the last of her family still to be at home with her mum and dad, was the only other girl of her age Molly knew who didn't have to share a bed, let alone a room, with a gaggle of younger brothers and sisters. Even though Molly's room was the little one at the back that overlooked the yard and faced the back of the flats above the shops in Chrisp Street, it could have been as small as the toot cupboard under the stairs and have faced a bare brick wall for all she cared. It was the privacy that Molly treasured.

Occasionally, one of the boys would complain about Molly's privilege, but Nora would inform whichever of her grandsons was moaning that he was lucky to be sharing two bedrooms between only the four of them while she slept downstairs in the front parlour. And, if they didn't stop their whining, they could all pile into the back room of number ten while she took the large front bedroom which was, after all, hers by right, and how would they like that? Just the thought was usually good enough to stop their griping.

Molly closed her bedroom door and sat down at the little dressing table her dad had bought her when times had been a bit easier. He had got it from a second-hand furniture man who traded under the arches near Club Row, and Molly had nearly fainted with joy when he had brought it home on a borrowed handcart. Second-hand it might be, and it wasn't even particularly pretty, but it was hers, and Molly kept it polished with the care she would have lavished on a rare antique. Molly had learnt well from her mother to keep her things nice and to be proud of what she was lucky enough to have, but though she had always kept the mirror shining, she hadn't spent very much time actually looking at herself in the glass before. She had been too busy raking the streets with Danny or fooling around with Liz, but she felt differently now. Today her reflection was a thing of intense interest.

Molly leant forward and examined her face for flaws. She had a look about her that was difficult to put an age to, and an air of someone who seemed to know about things, which, combined with the energy that was bursting from her, made her into a more than averagely attractive young woman, although she certainly wasn't aware of the fact.

She leant closer to the mirror and stared. She supposed that all the strange new things she had been feeling lately meant that she was growing up. It was like when she and Liz had both suddenly decided to have their hair bobbed, a daring decision made on their way home from work one Friday, which had caused ructions in both households, the lopping off of their long hair being seen as too adult a decision for either to take without first getting permission. The girls had both been thrilled with the results, but Molly wasn't so sure now. She liked the way the thick auburn waves framed her blue eyes, but she would have liked to have scooped her hair up into a ribbon, the way she used to, and have it falling in curls around her shoulders. Still that was her – making wild decisions then regretting them afterwards. It was no good moping about it, and it was no good sitting there staring either. If she didn't get a move on she'd be late.

Molly opened the bottom drawer of the dressing table and took out a little flannel bag from beneath the pile of clean underthings. With a quick look towards the still closed door, she opened the pouch and took out a tube of lipstick and a box of Phul Nana face powder. She and Liz had treated themselves to the illicit cosmetics in Woolworth's a couple of weeks before, and considering the fuss about their up-to-date hairdos, both girls had wisely chosen to hide their newly purchased make-up. But they had experimented with it in secret, creeping up to Liz or Molly's bedroom whenever they could. They hadn't quite got the hang of making themselves look like Merle Oberon yet, but they were definitely getting better at it.

With a slightly unsteady hand, Molly slid the lipstick from its case and spread a thin layer of red across her mouth. Not satisfied with the results, she tried to straighten up the wobbly line, rubbing at the worst bits with her finger and then dabbing a generous amount of powder over the resulting pale pink smudges. She narrowed her eyes and studied the effect.

With a sigh she took her hankie from her dress sleeve and wiped the whole lot off again, then hid the make-up pouch and the stained hankie back in the drawer – another bit of hand washing she'd have to do before her mum noticed. She needed a lot more practice before she could present her sophisticated new image in public, so, until then, the world would have to brave Molly Katherine Mehan as she was: red-haired, bare-faced and freckled. And with a growing store of secrets in the bottom of her dressing-table drawer.

Since they were old enough to whisper behind their hands, Molly and Liz Watts had always shared secrets such as the make-up, and now they were sharing another, far more grown-up one. While Molly had told her nanna, maybe a little recklessly she now thought, that she was seeing two boys, only Liz knew who they both were, and she had promised not to tell anyone. Molly definitely didn't want anyone, particularly Danny, to find out about Simon Blomstein. She just knew her brother wouldn't approve of him, and could imagine how bonkers he would go if he discovered she was seeing what he'd call a posh sort of bloke – meaning one whom he thought had it easy in life because he had an uncle with a bit of money who'd give him a job whether he deserved it or not. To make it worse, the job was what Danny would consider soft sort of work, where you used your brain rather than your muscles. One of the reasons Danny grafted so hard for Joe Palmer was that he'd never have anyone saying he was soft or a sponger; a man should earn his living, not have it handed to him on a plate.

But there was something else Molly feared Danny would disapprove of, and it had a lot to do with how Bob Jarvis had acted when he'd seen her speaking to Simon: good Catholic girls definitely weren't meant to go around with Jewish boys . . .

Before she let her mind begin leading her along that thorny path, Molly stood up. It was nearly twenty past two according to her tinny little bedside clock, and if she didn't get a move on it wouldn't matter who approved or disapproved of who or what, she'd be so late that there would be no meeting at all. Simon would have turned right round and gone home again.

As Molly neared the corner of Preston's Road and Poplar High Street, the place where she had agreed to meet Simon, all sorts of doubts began to flood into her mind.

Usually so confident and full of herself, Molly began to feel sick. Suppose she didn't recognise him? What would she do? She had this vision of a bloke of about nineteen, maybe twenty, with dark eyes and dark hair, but that could be a lot of people. And then say she didn't like him? Or say he was a murderer, or one of those blokes who lured young women into the white slave trade just like old Phoebe Tucker and Sooky Shay were always going on about? But, worst of all, there was the awful possibility that he wouldn't turn up at all and she would be left standing there like a lemon, with passers-by knowing full well that she'd been stood up and she'd have to go through the humiliation of strangers feeling sorry for her.

She now felt so confused that she didn't know whether the thought of Simon turning up was worse than the thought of him not being there, nor could she decide whether all this going out with boys was worth the bother. And then there was Bob Jarvis and Danny and what they'd have to say if they found out. She wasn't exactly Bob's girl, but she had sort of started seeing him, and he was Danny's mate. And he had paid for her to go to the pictures and she was seeing him again next Saturday. And she did really like him.

'Hello, Molly.'

Startled to hear her name, Molly collided with a middle-aged couple who had been strolling towards her. 'Sorry,' she mumbled in apology and then, with her nerves sending her blood beating in her ears, she turned to see who had spoken to her. She could hardly bear to look. Was it him?

She knew immediately that it was. And she also knew that he could never be a mad axeman, or a kidnapper waiting to pounce on her and ship her off to some sheik's harem in the moonlit sands of a faraway desert – he was far too handsome. Maybe it would have been a bit of all right if he had planned to whisk her off somewhere on the back of a camel; he was smashing.

'Hello, Simon,' she said, her voice cracking slightly. 'I ain't kept yer waiting, have I?'

'No, of course you haven't. It's me, I was worried I'd be late, so I got here a bit early, that's all.' He laughed. 'I must've been here for half an hour. I reckon all the passers-by thought I'd been stood up.' He paused. 'But I didn't care, I didn't want to risk missing you.'

Molly lowered her eyes; she could feel him looking at her. 'That's really nice of yer. Thoughtful.'

They stood there for a moment, Molly peering up at him through her lashes, thinking how good-looking he was, and he smiling down at her as though they had known each other for ages.

Simon suddenly grinned, showing teeth more even than Molly had ever seen before, and as white as his stiff shirt collar that contrasted so handsomely with his olive skin. 'I ran all the way,' he said with a throaty chuckle. 'I've only just about got my breath back.'

Molly felt herself blush. She wasn't used to such consideration from anyone, let alone a boy. Her mouth felt dry and she had to swallow before she could speak. 'Yer must've fagged yerself out.'

Simon shrugged amiably. 'I'm all right. I keep fit with all the running around I have to do for my uncle.'

Molly nodded feebly, unsure as to what to say next – not a usual problem for her.

Simon didn't seem to notice her rising panic and continued to speak easily. 'Much of a walk to this foot tunnel, is it?' he asked.

Molly's surprise made her forget her nerves. 'Ain't yer never been through it before?'

'No, and I've never been to Greenwich either. I've only lived in the East End for a few years. I used to live in North London with my aunt, but when I left school I needed a job so I came to live with my uncle's family in Whitechapel.'

'You ain't got a mum or dad, have yer?' The idea of being an orphan intrigued Molly; hers was a romantic image of foundlings and mistaken identities that she'd got from the cinema and from reading penny romances.

Simon stared down at his feet. 'They died when I was a baby. There was an accident.'

Molly reached out, and before she realised what she was doing she was holding Simon's hand. 'I'm sorry, I should learn to mind me own business, shouldn't I? I've got such a big mouth, every one says so.'

He raised his eyes to meet hers. 'No,' he said, 'you haven't got a big mouth. I think you've got a lovely mouth.'

'Blimey, now *that's* something no one's never said to me before.'

'I can't believe that.'

'And I can't believe we're standing here in all this dust and muck when we could be walking through the grass in Greenwich Park.' Molly began running along Preston's Road, pulling Simon behind her. 'Move yerself then, there's a number fifty-seven coming along. That'll take us right down to the bottom of the Island. It'll be worth the tuppence each to save our legs for hiking up that great big hill. You just wait, you ain't never seen nothing like it. Nothing in yer whole life.'

Just fifteen minutes later Molly was leading Simon down a winding iron staircase and into the mouth of a big, tiled pipe of a tunnel that took them right beneath the bed of the Thames and across to Greenwich on the south side of the river.

As they emerged from the lamp-lit mustiness of the foot tunnel into the strong summer light of the riverside, the far horizon to the west was growing heavier with storm clouds and the afternoon heat was becoming even more stickily oppressive, but Molly didn't notice either; all she was aware of was that she and Simon were still holding hands.

Fascinated, Simon looked back across the river and then along the bankside. Piles of boxes and pallets were waiting to be loaded or shifted into the warehouses, carts and trucks that crowded every available inch of space. Even on a Sunday afternoon the bank was bustling with people and activity, and on the river itself there were boats and barges, skiffs and tugs, all bobbing up and down in the wake of the paddle steamers, carrying crowds of laughing day-trippers up river towards Westminster and the elegant delights beyond, or down river to the estuary and the less sophisticated pleasures of Southend-on-Sea.

'I can't believe we've only come across the river,' said Simon, shaking his head in wonder. 'All this.'

'Wait till yer see the park,' Molly said, again hauling him along behind her. This time she led him through dingy side streets lined with soot-stained terraced houses. 'Yer'll love it. There's views that'll take yer breath away.' She glanced sideways at him, her eyes sparkling with excitement. 'All over London yer can see – miles and miles and miles. Yer feel like yer standing right on top of the world.'

Practically every hot step they took from the river to the park, there was something that Simon either wanted to stop to admire or to ask Molly questions about. Most of the time she didn't know the answers, particularly those about the big buildings that Simon said he was sure must be something to do with royalty and that he intended looking up in some book or other when he got home. She had never known anyone before to be so interested in everything and anything that presented itself. All Molly wanted to do was enjoy the fresh air, lick the ice-cream cone that Simon had brought her from the stop-me-and-buy-one man on his trike, and just bask in the pleasure of Simon's company. But, if that meant listening to him going on about buildings and kings and queens, then that was all right with her. He could have been talking about how his uncle's printing machines worked for all she cared, just so long as he carried on holding her hand and smiled at her whenever he caught her eye.

When they reached halfway up the hill, even with all her energy, Molly was exhausted by the heat and the climb. 'Come on, let's have a sit-down,' she said, jerking her head towards a huge chestnut tree. 'I'm flipping tired out. And I'm so hot.'

They leant their backs against the hard, knobbly trunk and stared down the hill towards the river, watching it sparkle, darkly silver, in the few starkly etched rays of sunlight that were managing to find their way through the now almost completely flat, leaden grey sky.

'You always like this?' Molly asked, concentrating on sucking a drip of the now liquid ice cream that was seeping through the hole she had bitten in the end of her cone.

'Like what?' Simon asked, squinting his eyes as he tried to focus on her face in the dappled shade.

'Sort of, I dunno, nosy like me, I suppose. But not about people like I am. About things and about what's going on and that.'

'Don't you want to know about things?'

Molly considered for a moment as she ran her tongue along the sweet, rough pattern on the side of the cornet. 'Never really thought about it to tell yer the truth. I mean, I've always wanted to know about what's going on in Plumley Street.' She looked round at him. 'That's where I live, off Chris Street, with me family. And about me mates, of course – I wanna know how they're getting on. And there's the warehouse, you know, where I work. But all that's always been, sort of, enough for me to think about. I suppose I've never really had the need to know much more about anything else. The rest of the world kind of passes me by.'

She crunched the last of her cone and licked the remaining drips from her fingers. 'My dad's interested in things. He's in the union down the docks and he reads the paper from front to back and back again. And he's always telling me to be quiet and stop chatting so's he can listen to the news on the wireless – we was the first in our street to get one.' She shrugged. 'Maybe I'm just stupid, eh?' she added, beaming at him.

This time Simon didn't return her grin. 'No, you're not stupid, Molly, you're lucky,' he said. 'Not needing to worry about things and having friends to care about. I envy you.'

Molly sat up straight. 'What, you ain't got no friends?'

Simon plucked a blade of grass and pulled it between his teeth. 'I've moved around my family so many times, so often, I've not been anywhere long enough to make any. Not really.'

Molly sprang to her feet and held her hand out to

him. 'Well, yer've got yerself a friend now,' she said, surprising him with the strength of her grip. 'Come on. On yer feet. Now we've had a sit-down I'm gonna take yer to the top of the hill and show yer the best view of London yer've seen in all yer life. And yer can get that collar and tie off and all. Yer look like a turkey cock how red yer've gone.'

The rest of the afternoon passed in an easy blur of talking and laughter, with Molly doing most of the talking and each of them having a fair share of the laughs. And when Simon checked his watch after the first fat drops of stormy rain began to fall, Molly was thrilled to hear that it sounded like genuine regret when he said they should be thinking about getting home.

They ran, holding hands, down the grassy hill back towards the river, Molly refusing Simon's jacket, clutching her hat in her hand, not caring what happened to her hair.

'I love the rain,' she shouted, lifting her face to the sky, as the thunder began to rumble in the distance. 'My nanna used to sit on the street doorstep with me on her knee and tell me that the raindrops hitting the tarry blocks was soldiers marching up and down the street to keep me safe from the storm.'

'I feel I know your family after all you've told me about them,' Simon panted as he strained to keep up with her. He was fit but Molly seemed to have enough energy for two as she surged on ahead, looking like she wouldn't stop until she reached the river bank. That was why he was so surprised when she stopped dead and turned to face him.

She looked mortified. 'I've talked too much, ain't I?' She dropped her chin and tutted angrily to herself. 'Dad's always telling me to slow down and think before I open me gob.' She lifted her eyes and looked at him. 'I'm sorry,' she said pitifully. 'It's just me. I can't help meself.'

Simon gently wiped a raindrop from her cheek. 'You've nothing to be sorry about.' He touched his lips to the end of her nose. 'I've never been happier.'

This time Molly definitely didn't stop to think what she was doing. She threw her arms round his neck and kissed him smack on the lips, right there in the park in front of anyone who cared to look. Then, wide-eyed with horror at what she'd done now, she burst into nervous giggles and began running again towards the foot tunnel.

Simon caught up with her just as she ducked inside the dome-topped entrance building. He backed her against the wall. 'Did you mean that?' he asked.

She nodded up at him, closed her eyes and lifted her face towards his.

'Good,' he whispered.

They stood there, folded in each other's arms until a loud chorus of whistles made them spring apart.

A row of tousle-haired, scabby-kneed boys were staring at them with undisguised curiosity. 'Cor, I thought yer was eating each other for yer tea,' one of the scruffy kids piped up, to the evident delight of his mates.

'Yeah, making a right meal of it,' offered another.

'Clear off!' Molly yelled.

'Here,' yet another butted in, bouncing his half-deflated football aggravatingly close to her feet. 'I know you. You're Micky Mehan's big sister, ain't yer?'

'Never heard of him,' said Molly sharply, gulping at the terrifying visions of what her mum would do to her if she found out that Molly had even been holding a boy's hand, let alone kissing one she hardly even knew. And in public, during broad daylight.

'Yes you are,' the boy persisted, still bouncing the ball at her. 'Yer Molly Mehan.'

Before he realised what was happening the boy was suddenly being hoisted by his ear, and almost off his feet, towards Simon. 'Oi!' he squealed. 'Leave us alone, you, or I'll tell me dad of yer. He'll bash you up, he will.'

Simon bent forward and looked the boy directly in the eye. 'The lady said she doesn't know you,' he said in a low, threatening whisper. 'So, are you going to run off with your little friends and be a good boy or do you want me to give you something to really cry about?' He let the child go and stood up straight. 'Well?'

The boy rubbed his ear sulkily. 'Come on,' he said to his mates, making his way towards the iron stairway that led down to the tunnel. 'I'll have me own back on him, you just see if I don't.'

As the last and smallest of the boys filed past Simon and Molly with a defiant scowl and a quick flash of his tongue, Simon grabbed him by his skinny shoulder. 'Hold it, you,' Simon said.

'What?' Now he was separated from his friends, the child's rebelliousness was forgotten completely. Looking up at Simon with big, frightened eyes, he said plaintively, 'It was them, mister, it weren't me. I never meant nothing. Honest.'

'I know,' said Simon gently. He took a threepenny bit from his trouser pocket and put it in the astonished boy's grubby hand. 'Here, you and your friends buy yourself some sweets.' He watched, a faint smile playing on his lips, as the now completely confused child, clutching the reward for he wasn't sure what, ran off to tell his mates about their good fortune.

When Simon turned back to Molly, his own smile vanished. 'Molly? What's wrong? You're not crying, are you?'

Molly shrugged, willing herself not to let the tears escape from her eyes. 'No. I'm sorry, Simon, I just don't want yer getting the wrong idea, that's all. I ain't ashamed of kissing yer or nothing but it's me mum and dad. They'd kill me if they found out.' She drew her bottom lip between her teeth. 'I suppose I didn't want nobody getting the wrong idea 'cos I ain't the sort of girl who usually does this sort of thing. I dunno what got into me.'

'I know,' said Simon, gently running his fingers through her thick auburn waves. 'Your hair,' he said softly, 'it's like flames.' He touched his lips to her forehead. 'Come on.'

They walked slowly, not saying much, hand in hand, back through the tunnel. When they reached the other side of the river, despite the rain that was now coming down in sheets, Molly still didn't want to hurry herself or even wait for a bus that would get them home more quickly. She knew she had to get back sometime, her mum would be bound to start wondering where she was, and she would have more than a little explaining to do when she did get home – especially now that she was soaked right through to her underwear – but she didn't want their parting to come a moment before it had to. It would be all too soon anyway, because, unspoken though it was, they both knew that Simon would not be walking Molly all the way back to Plumley Street.

Molly had never met anyone like Simon before; being with him made her feel happier than she could ever remember. No, she corrected herself, not happier exactly; her family made her happy in their own special, noisy, rumbustious way. And being with Bob made her happy too; in fact, even though she had bristled every time he had been bossy and arrogant, which had been quite often during their evening together, she had actually been thrilled that he had cared enough about her to bother to tell her what to do. But being with Simon was, well, it was different. As they walked along in easy silence, she tried to work out what it was. It eventually dawned on her: Simon was treating her like she was special just because she was her, Molly Katherine Mehan, and not, as Bob had made her feel, that she was someone he wanted to own and make her into someone else, someone he would prefer her to be.

It was scary when she thought about it, someone liking her for who she was, when he really didn't know that much about her. But she knew herself all right, and knew that she could be exactly what her dad called '*a right little madam*' when she got a mood on her, and that was something she would hate Simon to see. She wanted Simon to think she was perfect, and there'd be a fat chance of that if he saw her bawling at her brothers at the top of her lungs, or shinning up over the wall at the end of the street, or worst of all, if he saw her actually fighting with Danny. She felt herself going red with shame just at the thought of it.

'Are you sure you won't take my jacket?' Simon asked her. 'You're looking a bit flushed, I'd hate you to get a fever.'

'I'm as tough as old boots, me,' Molly said, shaking her heavy wet hair away from her face and trying to let the rain cool her burning cheeks.

'I don't believe that for a moment,' he said.

They had just reached the point where Manchester Road became Preston's Road. They both knew that they would soon be making excuses as to why they had to go their separate ways from the corner of Poplar High Street, the place where they would be in increasing danger of people they knew seeing them together, and not just little kids with footballs who could easily be accused of making up stories for mischief.

Paying no heed to the teeming rain, Simon stopped and turned Molly to face him. 'I'm sorry, Molly, but I won't be able to see you all the way home. All right if I leave you at the corner up there? I hate to do this, but I hadn't realised how late it was getting.'

Saved from having to make up a story of her own, Molly smiled happily at him. 'I reckon I can manage to find me own way from there, 'cos I ain't exactly a delicate little flower, yer know,' she said, unconsciously echoing her brother Danny's sarcasm. 'I told yer, tough as old boots, me.'

'No matter what you say about yourself, I think you're wonderful.'

'Blimey,' she answered for want of knowing what else to say.

'So, before we both catch our deaths,' he said, putting his hand in the small of her back and guiding her forward. 'What time shall we meet next Sunday?'

'Yer wanna see me again?'

'Yes,' he said simply.

She stopped and looked at him. Hurriedly banishing any thoughts of what Bob Jarvis would have to say if he found out about all this, she blurted out, 'And I'd really like to see you again and all.'

'We could go to Victoria Park if you like. I could take you on the boating lake. Show you my muscles.'

'I reckon that'd be smashing.'

They stared at each other for a long moment, then

Molly turned her head away and said nervously. 'Look, don't bother walking any further with me. I ain't got far to go. Just leave me here. I know yer've gotta be getting home yerself, and, I don't wanna sound like a little kid or nothing, but my dad, he really is ever so strict.'

Instead of thinking, as Molly had expected, that she was daft, Simon just laughed. 'Sounds like my uncle.'

'Honest?'

He laughed again. 'Honest. And that's why I didn't mind when you pretended you were someone else to those boys. I knew how you felt. And I understand about having to keep things from your family sometimes.'

'Really?'

'Really.' Simon took his handkerchief from out of his pocket and rubbed it over Molly's hair. 'And if you're going home we'd better get you dried off a bit. You look a real sight with your hair plastered flat to your head.'

Molly pulled away from him.

'Sorry, you say you're the one who opens her mouth without thinking. That came out all wrong. What I should have said was that you look a really beautiful sight. And I'm honoured to be your secret.'

Simon shoved the wet handkerchief into his pocket, and, with a brief touch of his lips to her cheek, he sprinted off along Preston's Road.

Molly stood and watched until he had disappeared round the corner into Poplar High Street.

Then, with a soppy smile on her face, she began to walk slowly home; her soggy hat in her hand, her dripping wet cardigan sagging from her shoulders and her shoes squelching every blissful step of the way.

113

6

By breakfast time the next day it would have seemed to an outsider that, superficially at least, most things in the Mehan household were back to normal, and that it was just another summer Monday morning, with squabbles and smiles in about equal proportion. But it wouldn't have taken a very close inspection to realise that all those sitting around the kitchen table were wrapped up in their own concerns, and it would have been clear to anyone that something or other was going on.

For a start, Pat had left for work even earlier than usual, Katie not even having realised he had gone until she woke up to find the cold cup of tea he had brought her on the bedside cabinet. And then there was Katie herself – she might have been blustering around as though it was a normal Monday morning, but she was preoccupied, hardly bothering to tell anyone off for their bad manners or for taking liberties with one of the others, as she usually did. And if she had been taking more notice, Katie would have had a word or so to say to her daughter, for Molly was acting decidedly shifty. Molly kept flicking furtive glances at her family, convinced that at any minute her nanna would come in from next door and start blabbing – *why* had she told her? – or that any one of the others sitting around the table would somehow guess what was going on inside her head, and would blurt out to the rest that Molly had a terrible, guilty secret: she had two boyfriends at the same time!

If any of them had been interested enough to try to see into Molly's mind, it certainly wouldn't have been Sean. He was sitting there, slumped in his chair, self-absorbed, mopey and uncommunicative, behaving like a typical fourteen-year-old, in fact.

Unusually, Michael and Timmy were keeping just as quiet as Sean that morning, but they were far more content with their lot. They were happily taking advantage of their mother's rare preoccupation, by not eating any more of the dreaded porridge that had in the past only been inflicted on them as an occasional economy measure, but during the last few months had become the family's breakfast staple. One bowl of the stuff was definitely more than enough for either of them.

The porridge was also the reason for Nora's absence; since the sad day of the regular introduction of the awful sludge to the table of number twelve, she had taken to having a lie-in until half past eight and only then, when she was sure the so-called breakfast had been finished, would she come in from next door to help her daughter with whatever chores were to be tackled that day.

Even Danny, who was ordinarily as reliable as the kitchen clock, had altered his routine that morning. As soon as he was washed, dressed and shaved – strictly speaking, and dark as he was, shaving was still only a twice-weekly affair for him, but he had taken to going through the daily masculine ritual of it lately – Danny had nipped round the corner to Chrisp Street to buy the early morning paper.

Katie had protested that he shouldn't be wasting money like that, and that his father would be bringing in the *Star* after work if he was so desperate for a read.

But Danny had insisted that he was only taking an interest in things as his dad had told him, and that Katie should be pleased instead of complaining.

Too distracted to bother to argue with her eldest son, or even to tell him off for being so saucy, Katie had let him go and waste his money, and now he was sitting there at the table, head buried in the paper as though it had been his breakfast habit of a lifetime.

He didn't realise how fortunate he was, sitting there safely hidden behind the news, for Katie, to the alarm of her two youngest, was holding up the porridge pot to offer round the grey goo for a third, threatening time. To their almost overwhelming relief, the boys were saved from having to eat any more of the horrible muck by an unexpected rapping at the front door. It was a surprise to everyone, not only because it was barely eight o'clock, but because whoever it was hadn't just walked in along the passage with a cheery 'Don't worry, it's only me' as regular visitors did.

Katie put down the pan on a square of folded newspaper, put there especially to save the table top from burns, and pointed to Molly. 'See if any of this lot wants any more before them two little 'uns dive in and scoff the lot, will yer, love?'

As her mother checked her hair in the overmantel mirror and then went out to the passage to see who was there, Molly tapped Danny's newspaper, lifted the big wooden spoon from the pot, and pointed it at him, letting it drip with glutinous porridge.

Looking round to make sure that his mum wasn't within earshot, Danny shook his head firmly. 'No fear, Moll. What d'yer think I am? Just look at it, it's like flipping cement. Now, if it had been a nice bit of streaky, or a couple of slices of black pudding . . .'

'How about you, Michael? Tim?'

Wide-eyed, they both shook their heads as firmly as their big brother. 'No thanks!' they said in unison.

'Mum must think we're barmy,' added Michael, made brave by his mother's absence, 'if she thinks we'd eat any more of that dog poop than we have to.'

'Hard times is hard times,' said Molly, dropping the spoon back into the pot with a shudder of distaste. 'Now come on, you lot, let's get this cleared away and save Mum a job.'

Sean shoved his chair back and stood up. 'If yer so keen, you do it.'

Before Molly had the opportunity to protest, Sean had snatched the surprised Rags from under the table, where he had been hoping that someone might slip him some unwanted morsels, had tucked the little dog under his arm, and was out in the yard, clambering up and over the back wall.

'You little sod,' mouthed Molly, as he disappeared from sight. 'And where d'yer think yer taking that flaming dog?' she hollered.

While this was going on at the back of her house, Katie was standing at the street door, smiling encouragingly at Mrs Milton, while silently cursing her kids for showing her up in front of a neighbour with all the row they were making.

'Why don't yer come in for just a minute, eh Ellen?' she said invitingly. 'There's a pot of tea just been made, and it'll only go to waste.' She raised her eyebrows. "Cos by the sound of it in there, the kids'll be off out any minute.'

'That's very nice of yer, Kate, but I've only come over to return yer stewpan. It was ever so good of yer. Ta.'

'Don't be daft,' said Katie, doing her best to smile

convincingly at the pathetic little bundle that the hollow-eyed woman was holding in her arms. The baby looked nearly as poorly as its mother, as it screwed up its drawn little face and let out a high, thin cry. 'Yer can say what yer like, Ellen, I ain't taking no for an answer. And I just can't wait to have a cuddle of this one.' Katie jerked her head along the passage towards the kitchen. 'Come on.'

'It ain't that I don't wanna, Kate,' Ellen said wearily. 'I'd love to sit down and have a cuppa with yer, but yer know how things are. I wouldn't be able to ask yer over mine. Yer've been so good to us, I'd hate yer to think I was mumping.'

'Whatever gave yer that idea?' said Katie, hoping she sounded more enthusiastic than she felt. Reaching out, she took the baby from its mother's arms and strode purposefully along the passage, knowing that Ellen Milton would be dragging herself along behind her. The baby was only three months old and wherever it went, so would the little scrap's mother. Katie looked over her shoulder and, sure enough, there she was.

When she reached the kitchen doorway, Katie saw Molly was about to scrape the remains of the porridge pot into the bucket that Nora kept by their back door to collect scraps for her chickens. 'Moll,' Katie snapped. 'Leave that.'

Molly straightened up. 'I was only going to—'

'Never mind you was going to, you and Danny get yerselves off to work, and you two little 'uns, you get yerselves out in the fresh air, look how pasty-faced yer looking. Go and get some sun on them knees o' your'n.'

Seeing the determined look on their mum's face, and more than happy to escape both the porridge and the screeching baby, they all did as they were told. As they filed past out into the passage, they all mumbled good morning to Mrs Milton and then hurried past as quickly as they thought their mother would consider polite in front of company.

Timmy, who was the last to make his escape, was hoiked backwards by his collar. 'Hang on, you,' said Katie. 'Where's our Sean?'

'He's gone out already, Mum.'

'All right,' said Katie letting him go. 'And no fighting. Right?'

Katie held the baby tightly to her shoulder and pulled out a chair for her neighbour. 'Right, that's that mob out of the way. School holidays, eh? They'll be the finish of me, I swear they will. Tell yer what, if them old schoolmarms had kids at home to put up with, they'd soon have 'em back in class. Still, thank Gawd we've got a bit of time to ourselves, eh?' Katie was carrying on patting the baby's back and jiggling it up and down, but there was no distracting the poor little thing. 'Mum might pop in later,' Katie said brightly, trying to pretend that the yelling wasn't piercing her eardrums, 'but no one else'll disturb us. You take her a minute, love, and I'll get us that tea.'

As Katie handed the baby back to its mother, she saw a look of quiet desperation cloud Ellen's haggard face. 'Me milk's nearly dried up,' she said, her voice barely more than a whisper. 'I dunno what I'm gonna do.'

'You just sit there a minute.' Katie went over to the stove and lit the two front gas rings. She put the kettle on one set of jets and held a slice of bread carved from the remains of a loaf on the end of a toasting fork over the other.

'You ain't making none of that for me, are yer, Kate?'

'Course I am. Us mums need a bit of something before we start grafting for the day.'

'But—'

'No buts.' Katie blew on the toast to put out a flame that had caught the corner of the thick hunk of bread. 'There, stick some marg on that and get it down yer. And yer can give that precious bundle back to me.'

Katie took the baby from her exhausted neighbour and pulled the cover back from the child's angry, contorted little face. 'I bet this one'd go mad over a sugar tit,' she said. 'All right if I do her one?'

Mrs Milton nodded weakly. 'Ta. It might quieten her down a bit.'

'It ain't that, is it, darling?' Katie cooed at the infant as she sat at the table and crossed one leg over the other. Then she lay the shrieking baby on her lap, its head supported in the crook of her knee. 'I just wanna give her a little treat, don't I, sweetheart?' With the practised hands of a mother of five, Katie took a clean handkerchief from her apron pocket, then she scooped a spoonful of marg and a spoonful of sugar into the centre of the cloth, kneaded the two together with the back of the spoon, rolled the hankie tight and, with the baby cradled in her arms, offered the cotton teat to its bawling, puckered mouth. At the first taste of the sweet concoction the baby, forgetting its fury, fastened its lips hungrily around it and her little body relaxed into easy, rhythmic sucking.

'There,' said Katie, touching the back of her finger to the child's cheek. 'That's better, ain't it, little 'un? Now, let's make me and yer mum a drop of tea before that kettle boils its head off.'

Half an hour later, when Katie's mother had come in to help her daughter start the laundry, Ellen Milton became flustered and, for fear of outstaying her welcome, wanted to leave immediately. But Katie would only hear of Ellen going if she agreed to allow Katie to top up the remaining half-pot of porridge – the breakfast that Molly had almost sacrificed to her grandmother's ever greedy hens – with a couple of big dollops of condensed milk, and pour it into a clean basin so that Ellen could take it back home for her kids.

Despite all Ellen Milton's protestations that she couldn't possibly, Katie Mehan, as usual, refused both to take no for an answer or to listen to any thanks. In Katie's understanding of how the world turned, there was no need to thank a neighbour for lending a helping hand. As she saw Ellen and her now peacefully sleeping baby to the door, she looked across the street to number eleven, Frank Barber's place, and thought about how trying to help him had caused so much trouble, but she quickly dismissed the thought from her mind. Pat would have to sort himself out about his jealousy; he might have a lot of worries, but so did she, not the least of which was all the washing she had to do. There were piles of the stuff, and that was more than enough to occupy any woman's mind on a Monday morning.

Nora rested the copper stick across the tin bath full of rinsing water and rubbed the back of her suds-covered hand across her forehead. 'It's no good, Katie, love,' she puffed, arching her aching back. 'There's not enough soap left to wash another single sock, let alone the rest of these sheets. And we could do with some more Reckitt's blue and all.'

She stepped out of the little lean-to scullery that housed the copper, the tin bath, the rubbing board, the mangle, and all the other paraphernalia associated with washday, and wiped her hands dry on her crossover apron. 'Is Michael or Timmy around? One of them can run over to the shop and get some.'

Katie took the dolly peg from her mouth and stuck it firmly over the wet pillow slip, anchoring it securely to the line. 'No, leave 'em, Mum. I'd rather go meself.' She looked over her shoulder at Nora. 'They're all right out there playing. Yer know what they're like once they're indoors. They'll be under our feet and we'll never get done.' She squinted up at the clear, summer sky. 'It'd be a pity to waste this lovely sunshine.'

She bent down and picked up the blue-rimmed, white enamelled bowl that had held the wet washing ready for pegging, and handed it to her mother to put in the scullery ready for the next lot of rinsed, blued and mangled laundry.

'I'll be two minutes.' Katie untied her damp apron and threw it over the line to dry out while she was gone, then fetched a chair from the kitchen. 'There y'are. Take the weight off yer feet for a bit.'

'What weight, yer saucy mare?' said Nora happily, as she dropped down gratefully on to the chair. 'I'll have you know I'm the weight today I was on the day I married your father.'

'Must have been a big frock,' laughed Katie.

'Yer not too big for a slap, yer cheeky madam,' grinned Nora. 'I'm still a fine figure of a woman.'

'Fine figure of two women, more like,' Katie said, skipping neatly over the back step and into the kitchen, well out of reach of her mother's raised hand. 'Anything else we want, Mum?' she asked, checking her hair in the glass.

'Two bob's worth of five-pound notes,' called Nora, closing her eyes and tipping up her face to be warmed by the blazing sun.

While Nora dozed contentedly, her mind filled full of glorious childhood visions of green Irish fields and fishing boats bobbing in the harbour, Katie walked to the blocked off end of the street, then stopped to examine a cardboard box outside the shop.

It was full of men's slippers and had a notice pinned to the side, explaining that they came in size seven only but would stretch with wear. For a brief moment, Katie considered buying a pair for Nora, but the moment soon passed; new slippers were a luxury for times easier than these. But slippers weren't the only things piled on the pavement outside Edie and Bert Johnson's shop to tempt her. There was a towering stack of galvanised buckets, just one of which would make emptying and filling the zinc bath easier than the leaky effort she had to make do with on bath night. Then there was a double row of wooden boxes full of fruit and vegetables, balanced on barrels brimming with pigeon and hen food; and a regiment of different length mops and brooms that would help her whisk her way through the never-ending housework in half the time.

But even these attractions only gave the smallest clue to the astonishing amount and variety of goods actually sold by the Johnsons. Once across the threshold, it would have taken a determinedly difficult shopper whose needs could not have been met. As Katie stepped inside the dark interior, her nostrils twitched in recognition. There was the sharp odour coming from the big cans of disinfectant vying with the robust tang of the huge wheel of crumbly, mature cheddar; and then there was the musty aroma of teas, competing with the mouth-watering saltiness of delicious boiled ham ready to be carved into great pink slabs straight from the bone for those who could still afford the occasional luxury. All these were mixed up with other less assertive, yet still identifiable scents and smells that, when they were all added together, made up the familiar, scintillating combination which not only made Katie's nose tingle, but her mouth water.

Her eyes had to become accustomed to the gloom inside the crowded little shop, but she didn't have to focus to know that in front of her would be the dark, polished wood counter on which packets of this and tins of that stood in artfully displayed pyramids, alongside the proudly presented china stand which held the damp muslin-covered slabs of best butter. And behind the counter, reaching right up to the ceiling, were the shelves jam-packed with everything from packets of corn plasters and boxes of liver pills, to jars of red and yellow sugar-coated pear drops and of dull orange barley sugar twists.

In front of the counter were yet more goods: glass-lidded tins of biscuits; drums of chick meal, wrinkled beans, split peas and dried lentils – supposedly for soaking to stretch a stew to feed a family, but, during the annual fad for pea shooters, just right for ammunition. And finally, as familiar as any other fixture in the shop, there stood Edie Johnson, with her hair caught up in a neat knot on top of her head and her customary, pure white, thick cotton apron stretched tight across her broad middle, presiding over all of it, ready to serve her customers and to pass the time of day with them.

'Morning, Ede,' Katie said with a smile.

'Morning, Kate.' Above Edie's head, a curling flypaper dangled like a forgotten Christmas decoration, but anyone who knew her wouldn't have to examine it to know that it would only recently have been hung there; being a stickler for what she referred to as 'hygienics', Edie changed her flypapers more regularly than was strictly necessary, and was proud of it.

'Bert's out the back boiling some fresh beetroot – lovely and sweet, they are. Good price and all. Want me to put a few by for yer, Kate?'

'Lovely,' said Katie, with a nod.

'Right, I'll call in one of the kids to fetch 'em for yer when they're done.'

'Save a couple for me and all please, Edie. Beetroots're my Bill's favourite. Lovely in a nice sandwich with a slice of corned beef.'

Katie turned round and smiled again. Peggy Watts, Liz's mum from number nine, had just come into the shop.

'All right, Peg?' she asked.

'Not so bad, Kate,' said Peggy, settling herself on the chair by the counter.

'Now,' said Edie Johnson, 'apart from the beetroots, what can I do for yer, Kate?'

'Bar of laundry soap, please, Ede.'

Edie busied herself wrapping the heavy slab of soap in a sheet of newspaper.

'Honestly,' said Katie, 'I dunno where the flaming washing comes from. If I didn't know better I'd swear my Pat was taking it in from the neighbours to earn a few bob on the side.'

'It's them four boys o' your'n,' said Edie, handing Katie the soap. 'I'll bet they're murder to keep in clean clothes.'

Katie rolled her eyes in agreement. 'Yer can say that again. But, honestly, my Molly's the one lately. Wears something a couple of times and then expects it to be washed.'

'Typical of girls that age,' said Edie, smiling fondly. 'They're growing up, so they wanna look their best, don't they? Yer can't blame 'em, can yer? Yer know what it's like.' Edie had no children of her own; some said it was because of the poor health suffered by her husband, Bert,

126

who, when he was no more than a boy, had been invalided out of the army after being seriously injured in the trenches in France. Others said it was Edie's problem as, although she was still a relatively young woman, they reckoned that she had had trouble 'down there' for years. But, whatever the reason for her having no children, Edie Johnson looked on the youngsters of Plumley Street with probably more indulgence than their own, more realistic mothers.

'Yer right there, Edie, if my Lizzie's anything to go by,' said Peggy. 'You should hear her. She ain't stopped talking about your Danny lately, Kate.'

Kate looked sceptical. 'Our Danny and your Liz? Daft. They're more like brother and sister, them two.'

Edie chuckled. 'More like brother and brother the way your Lizzie carries on at times, Peg. Frock tucked in her knickers and up and over that wall again she was on Saturday night. I don't reckon she realises what a good-looking girl she's turning into.'

'I think she does, Ede. Honestly, they grow up that fast nowadays. I didn't have a clue when I was sixteen.' Peggy turned to Kate. 'Ain't yer noticed nothing different about your Danny? He goes all soft when he talks to our Liz.' Seeing the blank look on Katie's face, Peggy jerked her head towards her, while saying to Edie, 'I reckon she's in a right dream, don't you, Ede?'

Katie frowned. 'What?'

Edie folded her arms and said wistfully, 'It must be hard for yer Kate, bringing up a growing family like your'n, wondering what they're all up to all the time.'

'Maybe I should be taking a bit more notice,' Katie said, her voice subdued.

'Leave off, Kate,' said Peggy, flapping her hand. 'No one's trying to have a go at yer or nothing. Yer've got more than enough on your plate without finding yerself even more things to worry about. If Danny and Liz wanna see each other, I dunno about you, but I couldn't be more pleased. He's a good boy. Liz'd have to go a long way to find one as nice. When yer see some of the hooligans round here, I reckon yer've done a right good job bringing him up.'

Katie shrugged non-committally, obviously not convinced by her neighbour's attempt to reassure her. 'I just feel that I have to keep running just to stay on the spot lately. D'yer know what I mean?' She picked distractedly at the corner of the newspaper wrapping the soap. 'My Danny's growing up and I ain't even noticed.' Katie let out a long slow breath. 'Some flaming mother I am.'

'I've spoken out o' turn,' said Peggy, standing up and putting her hand on Katie's arm. 'Don't take on, girl. It's easier for me. For a start,' she said, trying to sound jolly, 'yer know how girls talk more about that sort of thing.' She smiled at Edie and sat back down on the chair. 'Can't stop 'em once they've started. And then I've only got the one at home to worry about while you've got five still, and Lizzie's hardly a baby no more, is she?'

'Don't matter how grown up they reckon they are,' said Edie. 'And no matter how many smart haircuts they get, they're still kids, ain't they?'

'I ain't so sure about that.' Peggy leant forward in the chair and said in a loud whisper, 'You should hear the questions my Liz's been coming out with.' She looked round, checking for eavesdroppers. 'All sorts, she's been asking about.'

'What?' asked Edie, momentarily forgetting her 'hygienics' and resting her elbows on the polished counter.

'You know.' Peggy nodded wisely. '*Things*.'

Edie nodded back at her. 'Aw. *Things*. That'll be her age and all.'

Now Katie looked really depressed. 'I'll have to find time to have a little talk with my Molly. She was really sensible when I told her about her, you know . . .' she nodded downwards ' . . . her monthlies. But that's as far as I got. Gawd knows what sort of ideas she's got in her head about the rest of it. I ain't really explained much at all.'

'She's a good girl,' said Edie comfortingly. 'She won't let yer down.'

'I know,' said Katie, 'but I'd still like to feel that I could talk to her. I know my mum did her best with me but I was so dim. Yer wouldn't believe some of the ideas I had.'

Peggy grinned. 'Yer wouldn't believe some of the ideas my Bill had when we first got married.' She pressed her lips together to stop herself giggling. 'Practically needed a target, he did.'

The three women burst out laughing at the thought of Bill Watts looking for the bull's-eye, but, at the sound of someone else coming into the shop, they stifled their laughter and turned to see who it was. And they were all glad they had; it was Phoebe Tucker, Plumley Street's answer to the bush telegraph.

Phoebe knew, or at least claimed to know, just about everything that went on, with whom, how and why, and more often than not, why it, whatever *it* was, shouldn't have happened in the first place. And, even if she didn't know, she'd make it up anyway, because she could never let old Sooky Shay, her next-door neighbour, get the idea that she had more information about someone or something than she herself did.

Phoebe stood in the shop doorway eyeing her three neighbours suspiciously. As usual she had a lighted cigarette stuck in the corner of her mouth, slippers with the backs trodden down on her feet, and, even in the summer, fire-scorched, blotchy legs. With a great display of daintiness, Phoebe dotted her cigarette ash into her apron pocket, coughed bronchially and stepped inside. 'I heard yers laughing,' she said accusingly, 'from right outside.'

'It's this smashing weather, Phoeb,' said Edie, with a wink at Peggy. 'Makes us feel like youngsters again, don't it?'

Disappointed with the dead end, Phoebe tried another approach. 'I see you had that Ellen Milton at yer street door this morning,' she said to Katie.

Katie put her soap on the counter, leant back, folded her arms across her chest and looked Phoebe up and down. 'Yeah, that's right. So?'

'It's good of yer making time for the likes of her.' Phoebe smiled insincerely, showing her uneven teeth made brown by strong tea and even stronger tobacco. 'And yer seem to be finding plenty o' time for that Frank Barber and all.'

Katie shuffled her feet and paused just long enough to alert Phoebe to the fact that she might be on to something. 'So?'

'Well, I think it's very good of yer.' Phoebe flashed a look at Peggy and Edie, gauging their reactions. 'What with him being a widower and everything.'

To keep herself from wrapping her hands around Phoebe's crepey neck, Katie snatched up her soap from the counter. 'If people spent more time helping others than they did gossiping,' she said through clenched teeth, 'I reckon the world'd be a sight better place.'

Phoebe smiled triumphantly. 'I only speak as I find,' she said. Having finished with Katie, she now launched into an attack on Edie. 'Here, it ain't true what they've been saying, is it?'

Edie rolled her eyes heavenwards. 'Probably not,' she said wearily.

It wasn't clear whether Phoebe was ignoring Edie's sarcasm or whether she was oblivious to it. Either way, she wasn't put off. Brushing roughly past Katie and practically knocking Peggy off her chair, Phoebe thrust her heavy, drooping bosom across the counter and hissed at Edie, 'I've heard tell how Aggie Palmer's gonna be working in here.'

Edie looked down her nose defiantly at Phoebe. 'Yer know, for once something yer've got to say about someone actually is true.' She looked to Peggy and Katie, wanting the support of their understanding before carrying on. 'My Bert, he's been a bit peaky, finding things hard. So I asked Aggie if she fancied doing a few hours for me.'

'No!'

'You got any objections, have yer, Phoeb?'

'You do know her old man's half pikey, don't yer?'

Edie threw up her hands in wonder. 'Gawd above, yer don't say so, Phoeb. And there was me thinking he was the Prince of Wales. Now I've gone and wasted all that money on buying meself a tiara for nothing.'

Before Phoebe had a chance to think of a reply, Katie had tapped her on the shoulder.

The old gossip twisted round to face Katie. 'What?'

'I'd watch me mouth if I was you, Phoeb,' Katie said. 'Joe Palmer's been good to my Danny and I won't hear nothing said against him. All right?'

Phoebe's wrinkled face broke into a victorious sneer. Looking from Peggy to Edie and then back to Katie, she said with slow viciousness, 'Yeah, he's kept him on and all, ain't he? Wonder how yer got him to do that? Funny how all these blokes—'

'You what?' Katie demanded.

Peggy grabbed her arm. 'Ignore the old trout, Kate, she ain't worth it.'

Katie shook off Peggy's hand, and in a menacing gesture, uncharacteristic of her usually dismissive attitude towards the spiteful elderly woman, she held a shaking finger really close to Phoebe's puggy little nose. 'Yer wanna remember how that girl brings them dinners over to you and Albert, you wicked old cow. If it wasn't for Aggie Palmer yer wouldn't have nothing to stick in that wicked gob o' your'n or to fill yer rotten, fat belly.'

Phoebe gulped and, with primly pursed lips, stepped backwards, pressing herself tight to the counter to avoid Katie's threateningly close hand. 'What's that gotta do with you?'

'Nothing. But yer wanna watch yer mouth. They're good, decent people. Yer should be grateful to 'em, not running 'em down.'

'They shouldn't give us nothing if all they want is thanks,' Phoebe snapped cockily. 'That ain't the right way to go about things.'

Katie was trembling with fury. 'Aw, but it's all right you taking their grub so's your old man can spend every penny he gets down the pub or on the dogs, is it?'

'Do something, Peg,' Edie mouthed.

Peggy nodded. 'Come on, Kate,' she said. 'This won't get the washing done now, will it, girl? Yer know how Nora likes to get it all done before dinner time. I'll bet she's going spare over there waiting for yer.'

Katie took a deep breath and straightened up. Then keeping her eyes fixed on Phoebe, she took her purse from her skirt pocket. 'How much do I owe yer, Ede?'

'Don't worry about that now,' said Edie, obviously relieved that Katie wasn't going to let fly in her shop. 'Yer can settle up with me later on, when I send the beetroot over with the kids.'

Katie nodded. 'Ta,' she said, then turned on her heel and began walking stiffly out of the shop with Peggy steering her forward.

'Aw, so she gets tick, does she? What makes her so bleed'n special?'

Peggy only just avoided being walloped by Katie's elbow as she spun back round to confront Phoebe. 'You old bag!'

'That's nice talk, I don't think. Churchgoer and all.'

Edie ran her hands over her face. 'Phoebe, do us all a favour. Shut up, will yer?'

A small door at the back of the shop opened and Bert, Edie's husband, stuck his head through.

'Hello, ladies,' he said, smiling pleasantly, obviously unaware of what he was interrupting. 'Just wanted to let you know, Ede, them beetroots'll be cool enough to handle soon.' He limped through the doorway, dragging his game leg painfully behind him and leant against the counter next to his wife. 'I've just gotta nip over to see Arthur Lane a minute, about a bit of business. Won't be long, love.'

Bert, a gentle, unassuming man, was totally innocent as to the new ammunition he had just handed to Phoebe. He winked affectionately at his wife, lifted the flap in the counter and hobbled his way out of the shop.

Open-mouthed, Phoebe moved with surprising speed over to the shop doorway and watched him as he made his way slowly across the street to see Arthur Lane.

Lane was a moneylender and, so it was rumoured, a

fence, who lived with Irene, his brassy, much younger wife, over the road at number six, between the Queen's, which was important and big enough to have two numbers, and the Palmers at number eight.

With a look of undisguised glee, Phoebe walked back over to the counter. 'Going over to see Laney, eh? What a pair they are. I was saying to my Albert, I wouldn't be surprised if him and that so-called wife of his was living over the brush. I mean, she turned up there a bit sudden, didn't she? Right out of the blue. And I never heard nothing about no wedding. And she must be, what, at least half his age? Dirty old bastard.' She peered up into Edie's face. 'So what's your Bert doing going over there then?'

Gasping at her neighbour's audacity, Katie went to say something, but Edie stopped her.

'It's all right, Kate. I can handle this.' Edie stepped round from the other side of the counter and stood very close to Phoebe. 'Not that it's anything to do with you, or anyone else for that matter, Phoebe Tucker, but my husband, God love him, is in a lot of pain, and he's going to see how much Arthur Lane can get him on his old dad's gold hunter watch, so's he's got a bit of spare cash should he ever be lucky enough to find a doctor what can do something for him. If that's all right with you, of course. 'Cos I'd hate to think we was doing something yer didn't approve of.'

Phoebe wasn't one to be distracted by something as simple as another human being's misery. 'Selling his watch, eh? Bad leg? More like times not being so good in the shop, if you ask me. But it's yer own fault. It's giving the likes of her too much credit,' she said, jerking her head towards Katie who was still standing in the doorway. 'And talking about Laney's "wife",' she went on, with a disapproving shake of her head, 'have yer seen her lately? I dunno, young women today.' She turned and looked Katie up and down. 'They're all the same. No self-respect, see. All dressed up like bleed'n ham bones, they are. It's like that frock she had on the other day – tits hanging out all over the place they were. It fitted where it bloody well touched. And I do hear talk,' she said, lowering her voice, 'as how someone saw her going into that Married Women's Clinic what them posh old tarts have set up near the Town Hall. Not that I reckon she *is* married but . . .' she gave an exaggerated shudder of distaste, ' . . . using things to stop babies. Whatever next? It ain't natural, I'm telling yer. No better than she ought to be, that one, just like that Mrs Fortune from round by the school. I mean I ain't never seen someone bring home so many so-called uncles to meet their kids. I ask yer. Want a good larruping from their old men, the pair of 'em. And then there's—'

'See yer, Edie,' said Katie. 'Coming, Peg?'

'Oi!' bawled Phoebe. 'I was talking.'

'Aw, was yer, Phoeb?' Katie said contemptuously. 'Sorry, I thought it was yer guts rumbling.' With that, she and Peggy walked out of the shop.

Phoebe was livid. She ran to the door and shouted after them, 'And the way your two girls have been getting 'emselves done up, them and their haircuts. Disgusting, that's what it is. Girls their age! White slavery, that's what'll become of them, I'm telling yer. I've said it often enough. White slavery. My granddaughter'd never be seen dead got up like them two. Never. She's been brought up right though, she has.'

'If she only knew half the stories going round about her darling granddaughter, eh, Kate?' Peggy whispered.

'Yeah, but I'll bet none of them stories are true,' said

135

Katie shaking her head. Then added with a chuckle, ''Cos, although yer'd never believe it, Peg, there's actually people what get pleasure from spreading lies and gossip.'

They were still chuckling, as much from relief to be away from Phoebe as anything else, when they reached Peggy's house at number nine. Katie went to cross the street over to hers, but Peggy stopped her with a touch on her arm.

'I really will be glad if our Liz takes up with Danny,' she said, ''cos, much as I hate to admit it, Kate, Phoebe's right about one thing: girls are a right worry, ain't they?'

'I know I got meself all worked up just now, Peg, but I don't think we've really got nothing to worry about with *our* kids.'

'No, I ain't saying we have, but it's who they get mixed up with, ain't it? I don't wanna sound like Phoebe, spreading stories, but did you hear they found another baby dumped in the lake over Vicky Park? Some other poor cow what got caught out and couldn't manage.'

Katie sighed. 'How do they get 'emselves in that state, eh girl?'

Peggy shrugged. 'Ain't too difficult, I don't reckon. That's why I hope something does come of this business with my Lizzie and your Dan. Least I won't have to worry about who she's out with, will I?'

Katie smiled reassuringly. 'And I hope so too, Peg, I really do. And not just 'cos I'm right fond of your Liz, but 'cos I feel for you and all. Having to see yer little girl turning into a young woman must be so hard. I'm just glad my Molly ain't started getting herself involved with no blokes yet. I've got enough to worry about indoors, more than enough, without any o' that lark.'

7

While Katie and Nora were getting on with the rest of the washing in the back scullery of number twelve, Molly was busy getting on with her job at Terson's, the tea blenders near the docks where she worked with Liz Watts.

Katie and Nora's work might have been heavy and boring, but at least the two women could take breaks if they felt like it; and even though Katie wasn't exactly in the mood that day for having a laugh and a joke as she usually did with her mum, she could still stop for a while, in between the pounding and boiling, the rinsing and wringing, mangling and pegging out, just to enjoy the sun on her face. But where Molly and Liz worked, there was no such luxury: every action was dictated by the need to keep up with the team.

Each team was made up of six girls, sitting three aside along a wooden workbench. The first two girls held empty paper packets under the metal funnels, collecting pre-weighed amounts of tea as it was shot down from the room above. They then banged the bottoms of the packets on the bench, tapping down the loose leaves, before passing them on to the next pair of girls, whose job was to stick down the top flaps and then gum on the labels. The last pair of girls parcelled the packets into six pound stacks on the wooden pallets, which were then collected by the young men who rushed in and out carrying the tea away to the store room or to the loading bays, where the delivery men waited by their vans.

It wasn't only the speed of the machinery and the pressure of doing piece work – when slowing down meant letting down your other team members – that dictated the working conditions at Terson's Quality Teas, it was also the noise. With the whirring and shushing, clanking and banging, tapping and scraping, constantly barraging them, it was no wonder that they rarely stopped to chat, or rather to yell above the racket, with the others. There wasn't even any point trying to peer out of the skylights to admire the summer sky, as the years of tea dust had darkened the mean little windowpanes to a uniform brownish grey.

But the work gave the girls a lot of time to dream and, unsurprisingly, Terson's didn't figure in many of their fantasies, most of which, if Molly was anyone to go by, figured some sort of escape from the monotony of packing tea. Molly had said it to Liz more than once, if it hadn't been for the just about passable wages – which included the bonuses that meant working even faster than the break-neck speed that Mrs MacKenzie, the stern-faced overseer expected of them – Molly would have told old Terson exactly what he could do with his tea packets, *and* she would have smiled as she said it. But her mum had come to depend upon Molly's money to supplement the ever-dwindling family kitty.

It was all very well for the older women, some of whom looked even more ancient than old Terson himself, going on about what a privilege it was to work there and what big money they had earned in the good old days, but that was all before Molly and Liz's time. In more recent years, what with unemployment being the way it was, Terson had been able to cut the bonuses with impunity, again and again, until now it had to be an exceptional week for them to earn more than two pounds for the boring, repetitive, mind-numbing work. And so it was with the usual weary relief that the girls heard the whistle go for knocking-off time and they each hastily gummed on their final and most lop-sided label of the day.

As they queued to file past the tight-lipped overseer for the regular, humiliating check to ensure that none of them was pilfering Mr Terson's precious tea leaves, Molly bent forward and whispered into Liz's ear, 'Look at that old mare. Yer'd think it was her bleed'n tea the way she watches us. Right flaming bundle o' laughs, ain't she?' Molly shoved Liz forward. 'Now yer know what people mean when they say how lucky we are being in work. It's having her moosh smiling down at us like our guardian angel that makes it all worthwhile.'

Liz stifled a giggle. 'I reckon it gets more like one of them holiday camp places every day. Yer know, I can't wait to get here of a morning 'cos it's such a pleasure seeing her happy face.'

They took another step closer to Mrs MacKenzie and Molly held her hand up to her mouth to muffle her words. 'There's no other answer, Liz, we'll have to get ourselves a couple of rich old boys to take care of us and give us a life of luxury like what we deserve. Then we can toss flipsy to this old bat and spend our days eating bags of sweets and listening to the wireless.'

Liz rolled her eyes heavenwards. 'Aw yeah, brilliant idea, that's just what yer need, Moll, another bloke on the firm. What, ain't two enough for yer?'

Molly curled her lip. 'Yer as clever as old Dick's hatband, you are.'

'Yeah, yeah,' nodded Liz at the familiar saying. 'I know, and that went round twice and still wouldn't tie.'

It was almost their turn to parade past Mrs MacKenzie and her scrutinising stare. They watched as she assessed the hapless worker in front of them for any sign of criminal activity involving tea leaves.

'Imagine what her old man's like,' hissed Molly under her breath, tipping her chin towards the overseer. 'Fancy, you know, having to do it with her. Mind you, perhaps his eyesight ain't very good.' Without missing a beat, Molly treated the overseer to a sweet smile and a dazzling display of teeth. 'Night-night, Mrs MacKenzie. See yer tomorrow.'

Liz too smiled at the would-be exposer of tea thieves, before turning to Molly and groaning wretchedly, 'Don't, Moll, yer making me feel sick.'

The girls rushed into the changing rooms and tore off their hated overdresses and cotton hats that looked more like pancakes than headgear. Then they were free.

Safely outside of the factory, they leant against the high, blank walls and lifted their faces to the sun.

Liz's eyes sparkled mischievously beneath her heavy blonde fringe. 'Would yer really do it, Moll? Like that Irene did?'

'What you on about now?'

'Would yer marry an old boy like Laney just 'cos he had a few bob?'

Molly pushed herself away from the wall, tossed back her head and clasped her hands to her chest. 'Maybe she loves him, Liz.'

'Yeah, some hopes.' Liz nodded good night to one of the other girls who was rushing off to get her tram. 'Loves his wallet, more like.'

Molly screwed up her nose. 'Can you imagine what he looks like in his vest and pants with that big belly of his hanging over the elastic?' She clapped her hand over

140

her mouth. 'Say you had to kiss him!' she mumbled through her fingers.

Liz winced as she dug around in her bag for the toffees she knew were in there somewhere. 'Euuurr! Do us a favour, Moll,' she said, handing one of the sweets to her. 'And she's right pretty and all, ain't she, that Irene? Lovely clothes. And I don't suppose she's much older than us two neither.'

Molly chewed thoughtfully. 'I wonder what she's like.' She screwed up the toffee paper and flicked it into the dusty gutter. 'You ever talked to her?'

'No.' Liz shook her head. 'She says good morning and that to me mum, but I don't think she really talks to anyone proper, like. No chatting or nothing.'

'I wouldn't mind talking to her, yer know, Liz. See what she's like.'

'What, to get a few tips?' chuckled Liz.

Molly didn't join in with her laughter. 'No, to see how hard yer'd have to be to do something like that. To not care what anyone else thought of yer, no matter what yer did.'

'I think yer wrong there, Moll. I reckon she does care. That's why she don't talk to no one; she's too ashamed. I mean, you ain't gotta be a flipping genius, now have yer? Everyone knows why she's with him.'

Molly linked her arm through Liz's and they began walking home. 'And I know something and all, Liz, and I'll tell yer it for nothing. I'd rather be totally, completely, stony, boracic lint, than marry a bloke what I didn't love. Loving him'd be everything for me, no matter who or what he was.'

Liz pulled her arm away from Molly and began running along ahead of her friend. 'So, that's what yer doing, is it?' she called over her shoulder, a broad grin lighting up her face. 'Yer trying out all the blokes yer can get yer hands on, so's yer can see what one takes yer fancy before yer say "I will".'

'You wait and see, Lizzie Watts, I'll wind up with the best-looking geezer yer've ever seen in all your life,' Molly yelled, taking up the chase. 'And I'll really love him, and he'll really love me and all.'

'What? Only the one?'

'Yer just jealous 'cos they can't resist me!'

Out of breath from running in the afternoon heat, Liz stopped, turned round and waited for Molly to catch up with her. 'Have yer, you know,' she puffed, 'let either of 'em kiss yer yet?'

Molly cocked her head to one side and thought for a moment. 'Might have done,' she said casually. 'In fact, I might have kissed both of 'em. Right smack on the lips. Mmmmwwwaaa! Just like that.' Then she ran off, giggling and swinging her bag, leaving Liz standing there, open-mouthed and speechless.

Ten minutes later, Molly was walking into the kitchen of number twelve.

'Hello, love,' said Katie, looking up from the saucepan she was stirring. 'You're home early.'

'Yeah,' panted Molly, 'me and Liz wound up running all the way home.'

'What, in this weather? I dunno where you kids get yer energy.'

Molly joined her mother at the stove and looked down into the pot. 'That looks nice,' she said, not sounding very convincing.

'I know it's sausage stew again,' Katie said, 'but what with yer dad's work being the way it is . . .'

'Remember when, every Monday, we used to have the

142

cold meat left over from Sunday with mash and pickles for our tea?' Molly said longingly. 'I couldn't half go that now, Mum.'

'We're lucky to have food on the table at all,' Katie snapped.

'I didn't mean—'

Katie let the spoon drop into the pot and then rubbed her hands over her face. 'I know, darling, and I didn't mean to have a go at yer. Look, while we've got a bit of peace and quiet, you put the kettle on while I go and fetch in the last of the washing, and then we can sit down and have a little talk before the others get in. Just the two of us. How'd that be?'

Molly picked up the kettle, took it over to the sink and turned on the tap before she answered. 'If yer like,' she said warily.

She frowned as she watched her mum go out into the back yard and start unpegging the sheets. This was all a bit ominous, she thought. It wasn't like Mum to be so formal about things. It wasn't the way things happened, not with the Mehans. If someone had something to say they just went ahead and said it, or, more often than not, they shouted it so that they could be heard over the row being made by all the others. There was none of this sitting down and having talks over the teacups. What on earth was going on? Surely that kid with the football who saw her with Simon hadn't split on her?

Katie came back into the kitchen and dumped the dry washing on to the table next to a pile that had already been neatly folded. Without saying a word, Molly picked up one of the sheets and held out an end to her mother, then they began silently folding the sheet side to side then end to end. They worked their way through six sheets and a stack of pillowcases before either of them said a word.

It was Molly who spoke first. 'Is something up, Mum?'

'This lot'll keep me busy ironing tomorrow,' Katie said, briskly scooping up the now teetering pile of laundry from the table and carrying it through to the front parlour. Unlike some women, Katie was never content just to run the dry sheets back through the mangle again to smooth out the creases. She liked doing things properly, even if it did make more work.

'That kettle boiling yet?' she asked as she reappeared in the kitchen doorway.

'Yeah. I've made the tea.' Molly carried the pot over to the table. 'Now are you gonna tell me what's up, Mum?' She sat down and, with a silent promise that she would go to confession at the very soonest opportunity, she added as airily as she could manage, "Cos I can't think of anything I'm meant to have done.'

Katie reached out and touched her daughter's freckled cheek. 'Daft, you ain't done nothing, babe. I just thought we could have a chat, that's all.' She lowered her gaze, suddenly apparently fascinated by the worn wooden surface of the kitchen table. 'You know how worried and busy I've been lately what with one thing and another,' she went on. 'I feel terrible that I ain't had a chance to spend no time with me best girl.'

Molly couldn't figure out what her mum was leading up to, but at least it didn't seem to be anything to do with Simon Blomstein or even Bob Jarvis. 'I know yer've been busy, Mum.'

Katie smiled wistfully. 'Yer a good kid. I just want yer to be happy, and safe, and healthy, and all right. That's all I've ever wanted, for you lot to be happy. I'm sorry I don't have more time to, you know . . .'

'I know,' said Molly, not having a clue as to what her mum was going on about, but she had the feeling that if she kept agreeing with her then she wouldn't go far wrong. 'I'll be all right, Mum.'

'Will yer? Will yer really? You are happy, ain't yer, Moll?' She nibbled at her bottom lip. 'And yer won't get yerself in no bother or nothing?'

'Me?' Grabbing her cup by way of a distraction, Molly gulped down a mouthful of the scalding tea. 'What sort of bother would I get in?' She had, in a wild, fleeting moment almost added that she might be seeing two boys at the same time, but if anyone was going to get themselves into bother it would be their Sean not her, but she had immediately, and wisely, thought better of it. She swallowed another burning mouthful of tea instead.

Katie reached across the table and took Molly's hand in hers. 'I don't mean it would be your fault, Moll,' she said. 'But yer not a little girl no more, are yer? Yer sixteen years of age, and that's why I think it's time we had a talk about things.'

A flash of horrifying realisation came over Molly as she at last cottoned on to what her mother was hinting at. It was not going to be *a* talk, it was going to be *The Talk*. She didn't want this, she really didn't; it had been embarrassing enough when she had sat in Liz Watts's bedroom while Liz had whispered, goggle-eyed and half disbelieving, all the information she had gleaned from her own mum about 'things' and what sort of trouble a girl could find herself bringing home if she wasn't careful and didn't respect herself.

Molly withdrew her hand from her mother's and fiddled with her now half empty though still steaming cup of tea. 'Mum,' she began nervously, 'I don't think we need to have this little talk.'

'Aw?' Katie snapped. 'And why's that then? You're not telling me . . . You haven't—'

'No, Mum,' Molly interrupted her, something she wouldn't normally dream of doing, but she was scared that if she didn't say something quick, then not only would she have to go through the embarrassment of The Talk but that her mum might somehow guess from her reaction that she had actually been kissing a boy. 'It's nothing like that. Honest. It's just that, well, Lizzie's already had this sort of talk thing with her own mum, like, and well . . .' She shrugged. 'Then Lizzie sort of told me.'

Katie sighed loudly. 'Hearing it from yer mate. I feel so guilty.'

'Do yer?' Molly was now really puzzled. She'd have thought her mum would have been glad they didn't have to go through all the details.

'I didn't want it to be like this,' said Katie, getting up from the table and going over to the stove. 'I wanted it to be, I don't know, special. Just between us. See, I love your nanna, Molly, but she never got round to telling me nothing. It was all right for her, being brought up in the country; I don't suppose she thought. But I was that ignorant when I met yer dad. And I didn't want it to be like that for you.'

Listlessly, she picked up the wooden spoon from the pot. 'Still, this won't get no boots mended, will it? I'd better get on with this before the boys and yer dad are in with their tongues hanging out, ready for their teas.'

Molly felt confused; not only had she upset her mum, but she was shocked to discover that she felt sorry for her as well. How could she feel sorry for her mum, who was always so strong and capable, and the one who everybody turned to if they needed help?

'Can I do anything for yer, Mum?' Molly asked quietly.

'Yer can mix up a bit of flour and water thickening

and then—' Katie began, but was interrupted by a commotion outside in the passageway. 'What now?'

Timmy and Michael came spilling into the kitchen accompanied by a furious bashing on the street door.

'There's some old girl to see yer out there, Mum,' said Timmy, 'and she's got the right hump.' With that, Timmy and Michael slipped through the back door, ran out into the yard and scrambled over the wall, well away from whatever it was that was going on out the front.

'Katie Mehan!' a woman's voice bellowed along the passage. 'Are you coming out here to face me or have I gotta come in there after yer?'

'For Gawd's sake,' said Katie. With dead-eyed, practised accuracy she aimed the long-handled wooden spoon into the greasy bubbling stew, untied her apron and hung it on the nail behind the kitchen door.

The bellowing started up again.

'All right,' Katie shouted back, 'hang on, will yer? I'm coming as fast as I can.'

Molly followed her mother from the kitchen, waiting halfway along the passage while Katie went to the street door to find out who it was who wanted her so urgently.

On the step stood Timmy's so-called 'old girl', a woman in her early thirties; she had her chin in the air and her arms folded aggressively across her chest.

'Hello, Vi,' said Katie to the woman, who came from nearby Ida Street. 'What can I do for yer?' Katie was trying to sound pleasant, as she had the uncomfortable feeling that this was going to be something to do with one of her boys and that it wasn't going to be about their doing anyone a good turn.

'What can yer do for me?' asked Violet incredulously. 'I'll tell yer what yer can do for me. Yer can explain why I've just had my Percy come home and tell me he ain't got the money from pawning his dad's suit this morning, that's what. And, while yer at it, yer can tell me how I'm gonna get through the week till pay day without it. So go on, clever, tell me that if yer can.'

Katie frowned. 'I'm sorry about that, Vi, but what's it gotta do with me if young Percy ain't got yer pledge money?'

Violet said nothing, she just threw her hands up in wonder.

'I could lend yer a couple of bob if yer like,' suggested Katie. 'I ain't got much but yer welcome to what I have got, if yer really short.'

'Of course I'm sodding short!' bawled the woman at the top of her voice, bringing both Phoebe and Sooky out on to their street doorsteps as if they were the mechanical figures on a town hall clock that had just struck one. 'And it's all your bleed'n Sean's fault. As if yer didn't know.'

'I'm sorry to disappoint yer, Vi, but I ain't got the foggiest what yer on about.'

'He's been down the wood yard again, ain't he? With that sodding mongrel o' your'n.'

Katie looked over her shoulder to see if Molly maybe had any idea as to what the woman was talking about, but Molly only shrugged and shook her head in reply. Katie turned back to face Violet. 'So it's our *dog's* fault your boy's not got the pledge money?'

The woman gasped in exasperation. 'No, I never said that, did I?' she hollered. 'It's your Sean taking bets on how many sodding rats the flaming dog can muller. And my stupid bastard, Percy, lost all the pledge money to your conniving little cowson and that bloody louse-ridden hound o' your'n.'

'Bets? Our Sean?' Molly stepped out of the house on

to the pavement next to her mum, who was slowly rolling up the sleeves of her blouse. 'I don't think so.'

With two Mehan women to contend with, Violet suddenly seemed less confident about her accusations.

Katie flicked a glance at her daughter. 'Our Sean's got no money for gambling.'

'That's right, Mum,' agreed Molly. 'He ain't.'

'Aw no?' said Violet, taking a strategic step backwards before she continued. 'Well, that ain't the half of it. There was fighting and all. Wound up a full-scale battle, it did, over who owed who what. That rotten toerag o' your'n can't even take a bet honestly. Dustbin lids, sticks – terrible fight there was. And my Percy's got a right shiner to show for it, and all.'

Nora put her head round the street door of number ten. 'You all right out there, Katie, girl?'

'No, not really, Mum. Violet here reckons our Sean's been causing trouble.'

Nora folded her arms and strolled menacingly towards the woman. 'I can't see our Sean being in no trouble, Vi. Sure, he's an angel of a boy, so he is.'

'And you can keep out of it,' said Violet, backing away further still. She pointed accusingly at Nora and said to Katie, 'And another thing, you ask that mother o' your'n why your two youngest never went to school the Friday before last.'

Katie looked at Nora. 'Mum?'

Violet nodded vigorously. 'I saw her. Coming out of the flea pit with 'em, she was, bold as brass, right in the middle of the afternoon.'

'Mum?'

Nora jerked her head towards the woman. 'Not in front of strangers, Katie, if yer don't mind.'

Katie nodded for Molly to go indoors, grabbed her

mother by the arm, yanking her inside the doorway of
number twelve, and then flapped the woman away. 'I've
no time for all this, Violet. I'm busy getting me husband's
tea ready. And so should you be.' With that she slammed
the door firmly in the woman's face, leaving her to
Phoebe and Sooky, who, if they were on their usual form,
would no doubt let Violet give her complaints a good
airing, and add a few of their own for good measure.

With the door safely closed against prying eyes and
ears, Katie turned on Nora, her voice quaking. 'Even
you, Mum, even you're a bloody nuisance to me. How
could yer?'

'Talking like that to your own mother,' said Nora
indignantly, 'and such language. Whatever next? And
anyway, what's wrong with my boys having a little secret
with their nanna? They was breaking up from school
that afternoon anyway, so what did they miss? Nothing,
that's what.'

Katie was speechless. She covered her face with her
hands and took long, deep breaths, trying to calm herself.

Nora signalled urgently with her eyes for Molly to
say something.

'You know what the boys are like, Mum,' Molly said
hurriedly. 'Don't blame Nanna. They'd lead a saint
astray, them pair.'

Nora nodded victoriously. 'And so they would, the little
devils. Especially the age they're getting to. Look at
Sean.'

Molly gestured for her nanna to keep quiet before she
made things worse, then guided her mother gently back
into the kitchen. 'They'll all grow out of it soon enough,
Mum. Remember how cheeky our Danny was? He drove
yer barmy.'

'It don't have to be like this.' Katie slumped on to one

of the hard kitchen chairs. 'You was a real good little kid when you was their age, Moll,' she sighed. 'Never lied or got into trouble. Nothing.' She glared at Nora who was nosing around the stove, inspecting what her daughter had made for their tea. 'Won books for good attendance at school and all, yer did. And as for secrets, this family's never had no secrets from one another. Never.'

Molly swallowed; her mouth felt as dry as if it had been filled with sawdust from the butcher's shop floor. Visions of Simon kissing her hard on her mouth came so vividly into her mind that she was sure her mum could see them, just as though they were being projected on a screen at the pictures.

But Katie was too worn out with everything else that was going on to notice her daughter's discomfort. 'Yer know,' she said, staring down at the table, 'I never used to feel like this, but I feel like I'm ninety years old lately.' Katie pulled away as Nora tried to put her arm round her shoulders in a gesture of reconciliation. 'If only that father of your'n was more help instead of moaning and shouting at me all the time. God alone knows what'll happen to this place while me and your nanna are down hopping.'

Molly had never heard her mother talk that way before. Never had she said a bad thing about Dad; she'd shouted at him, yes, but never criticised him behind his back.

'Yer know how he's worried about work and all the blokes down the docks getting laid off. He does what he can, Mum.'

Katie looked up at her daughter with such fury in her eyes that Molly felt as though she had slapped her. 'And so do I, but I don't complain, do I? I just carry on and manage the best I can. I'm fed up with him moping about. Where's the life he used to have in him, eh?' She paused and then added quietly, 'What's happening to this family? One minute it's tearing kids' coats off their backs, then it's taking money off 'em for bets.' She got up from the table and took her apron down from the nail. When she'd tied it round her waist she dug around in the pocket and pulled out her handkerchief and an envelope. She dabbed at her eyes, blew her nose loudly and then waved the envelope in the air. 'I got this, this morning. Our hopping letter.'

'That's nice,' said Molly warily.

'Yeah, it is,' sniffed Katie. 'I can't tell yer how glad I'll be when September comes so I can get away from here.' She grabbed the wooden spoon from her mother's hand and began viciously poking at the bubbling sausage stew. 'More's the pity I'm not going by meself.'

'Sure, yer don't mean that do yer, Katie?'

'No, course not. I'm sorry, Mum. I'm just all wound up like a clock spring. I don't know what I'm saying.'

Nora pointed her finger at Molly. 'And don't let me catch you upsetting your mam like that again.'

'Nanna!' Molly was indignant. 'It weren't nothing to do with me.'

'And don't you cheek me neither, miss,' said Nora. 'Now, you can make yer mam and me a nice cup o' tea. Or better still,' she added, smiling winningly at her daughter, 'perhaps yer mam'd like yer to fetch us both a little drop o' something from over the Queen's to steady our nerves.'

8

It was Saturday evening, and, in just a few hours' time, Katie, Nora and the two youngest boys would be leaving Plumley Street to make their way to London Bridge Station. There they would buy their cut-price tickets for the hoppers' special train, which would carry them away in the pre-dawn half-light, to the hop fields in the heart of the Garden of England.

Pat was sitting outside on the back kitchen step busily nailing Blakeys to the soles and heels of Timmy and Michael's boots, making them ready for the wear and tear of racing around the countryside. Pat knew the sort of punishment a pair of boy's boots could suffer down in Kent. He had climbed more than his fair share of trees and had forded enough streams during his own boyhood years, when he had gone with his mum on the annual cockney pilgrimage.

The sound of Pat laughing out loud to himself, as he remembered all the strokes he had pulled as a lad in his efforts to get out of helping his mum strip the hop bines, made Katie look across at him in surprise. It made a welcome change; there hadn't been much laughter in her kitchen during the past few weeks.

'What's tickling you, Pat Mehan?' she asked, squinting down at her youngest son's head as she inspected his scalp for nits.

'Just remembering going hopping when I was a kid,' said Pat, as he expertly fixed another metal crescent moon to the heel of one of the boots that was more patch than original leather.

'Nice to hear yer in such a good mood,' said Katie, smiling to herself as she got on with her job of searching through Timmy's head.

Like most East End mums, Katie had, over the years, become something of an expert on nits. She knew all about having to make sure they never got a hold in her family, even if she couldn't stop one of the little ones sometimes coming home from school a bit cootie.

She sat on a kitchen chair, with Timmy held tight between her knees on the floor in front of her, his head bent forward over a sheet of newspaper, while Katie went through every strand of his hair looking for signs of the dreaded head louse. She was using the fine-tooth comb that, if the boys saw her with it before she'd grabbed hold of them, was the signal for them to leg it as fast as they could, and to lie doggo until either she had forgotten all about it, or she was too busy torturing some other poor victim.

But this time, Timmy hadn't done a runner; he knew that it was all part of the preparations for hopping, and if he wanted to go to Kent it was no good his trying to get out of it. It still didn't make it any less painful or stop him moaning and complaining, even though he knew his mum would give him a sharp tap on the side of the head with the metal nit comb, making it twang against his ear as she told him to be quiet and to stop being such a baby.

Having his hair wrenched out by the roots wasn't the only reason that Timmy, in any other circumstances, would have had to feel humpy. The humid weather seemed set to go on and on, and had started to get people down. It was the beginning of September and yet there was no sign of a break in the hot, sultry sunshine, not even a shower to bring a hint of relief from the dusty heat that had at times become almost unbearable.

It was so uncomfortable, in fact, that although Timmy and Michael were meant to be going back to school on Monday, Katie for once had no qualms about what stories Pat would have to tell the school board man about their absence. This year, she was more than happy for him to say that his wife had taken their boys down to the green countryside of the Kent farm, where she and her own mum had been going since Katie herself had been no more than a babe in arms.

As for Timmy, with the prospect of running wild in the woods and fields instead of having to go back to school before him, it could have been thick fog and snowing for all he cared. Head torture apart, he certainly wasn't complaining.

Sean would usually have been as excited as the little ones about going hopping, but this year he just wasn't interested. Like Molly and Danny, it was the first time that he wasn't going with his mum and his nanna to Kent, and, no matter how hard Katie tried to persuade him otherwise, he wouldn't budge. She promised him that she would try to get him a few hours' work from the farmer pole pulling in the hop gardens, but he still wouldn't listen. He was convinced, or so he told her, that he had more chance of finding a job at home in Poplar, because all the hop-pickers' unemployed husbands would be sure to have asked the farmer about any work that was going and, with that sort of farm work at least, a man was paid for what he did rather than according to his age.

Katie had tried not to show it, but she'd been hurt

when he said he wouldn't be going with her. Still, she knew that with his attitude lately, arguing would get her nowhere except into yet another shouting match. And, as she was doing her best to make it up with Pat before she left, the last thing she wanted was for Sean to start leading off and causing yet more rows. All that apart, it didn't make it any easier for her to stop worrying about him. It would have been different if, like Danny and Molly, he had a job to go to: a proper reason for staying at home with his dad. Deep down, Katie felt that Sean was making excuses, that there was some other reason he didn't want to go with her, but what could she do about it?

As Katie twisted Timmy's head round to the light so that she could see better, she sighed, thinking about how quiet and empty the hop hut would seem without the bickering and laughter of her three eldest children. Still, she couldn't tie them to her apron strings for ever, and, with a flash of her old optimism, she told herself that she had every right to be proud that the three of them were at least trying to make their own way in the world. And she'd be bound to see them at the weekends when all the men and the grown-up children travelled down to the hop and fruit farms to visit their mums and their grannies. Maybe Sean would surprise her and bring some good news down with him about finding himself a job. She had always said that better times were just around the corner, and with the way things were going, she could only hope and pray that they were.

She gave Timmy's hair one final, punishing rake-through and then patted him on top of the head. 'Right,' she said brightly. 'That's you all clean and paid for. Now go and call yer brother in for me. And if he says "in a minute" tell him I'll be out after him.'

With his agonies over and the happy prospect of his brother having his turn to come, Timmy scampered from the room and started hollering for Michael.

Katie heard Michael shout back from the street, then the sound of the boys running along the passage towards the kitchen.

Michael stuck his carrot-topped head round the kitchen door. His expression froze when he saw the comb in his mum's hand.

'Down here, Michael,' she said, pointing her thumb to the space between her feet.

Before Michael had a chance to either do as he was told or to kick up a fuss, Timmy came dancing into the room and jigged around in front of his brother. He poked out his tongue, stuck his thumbs in his ears and wiggled his fingers. 'Nerr, nerr, nerr-nerr, nerrrr. Mine's a-a-a-ll do-o-o-ne!' Timmy mocked.

'You little—' Michael began, furious at being duped into coming indoors for this.

But Michael never finished cursing his brother. Katie stood up, grabbed hold of his collar and was hauling him over to her chair before he realised what was going on.

She shoved him down on to the lino in front of her. 'Such a fuss for a boy of your age. What an example in front of yer little brother.' She jerked her head over to where Pat was still tapping away at the boots. 'And what'll yer dad think of yer?'

'Mum!' Michael moaned, shrinking his head down into his shirt. 'Don't. Yer hurting me.'

'What, d'yer wanna show me up?' Katie asked, parting his hair as she set about her examination. 'Yer know them snotty-nosed home-dwellers all think we're lousy.' She glared at the still grinning Timmy. 'And you, young man, you can get next door into Nanna's and take yerself

157

up off to bed for a few hours' kip before we go.'

Timmy was indignant. 'But it's not right dark yet, Mum, and all the other kids are still playing out.'

'If all the other kids stuck their heads in the gas oven, would you?'

Timmy opened his mouth and closed it again. He knew he was beaten. His mother did it every time, saying things like that, things that he could never quite figure out what they had to do with what he was saying. Things that he never knew how to answer. He turned, neck hunched into his drooping shoulders, and made his way slowly from the kitchen.

'Night-night, baby,' jeered Michael. 'Make sure the bogey-man don't get yer.'

Michael was silenced by his mum stinging his ear with a quick swipe of the comb. 'That's enough of that,' she said briskly. 'And you, Timmy, you can come and say goodnight to yer dad before yer go.'

Timmy slouched back into the room and over to the back doorstep where Pat was sitting. 'Night-night, Dad,' he mumbled.

'Night-night, God bless, son,' said Pat, ruffling his youngest boy's hair. 'Here. Hang on.' He leant back and dug his hand deep into his trouser pocket and pulled out a handful of coins. He sorted through them, picked out a shiny sixpence, held it out to his son and winked. 'There's a sprazey anna for yer. You treat yerself when yer away, but not all on the first day, eh? Don't want yer getting the bellyache from too many sweets or yer mum'll be after me. Now go on, do as yer mum says and get in next door for some kip.'

'Cor, ta, Dad.' With his eyes gleaming at his good fortune, Timmy waved the sixpence in his brother's face and then skipped out of the room.

'Don't forget yer prayers,' Katie called after him, without looking up from her search through Michael's hair. 'That was good of yer, Pat,' she added gently. 'But yer don't wanna go spoiling him.'

'I can't help the way I am, girl,' said Pat. 'I care about me family, and I don't reckon yer can spoil no one by loving 'em.'

Katie's hands suddenly stopped their exploration of Michael's scalp.

'Right,' said Michael, trying to scramble to his feet. 'That me done and all?'

'Eh? No, no.' Katie sounded preoccupied. 'I was just thinking.'

With a loud sigh, Michael dropped back down on to his bottom, gritted his teeth and waited for the dig of the comb. But it didn't come. Instead his mum started talking again.

'Yer a good man, Pat Mehan,' she said.

Michael groaned quietly with embarrassment. He hated it when his mum and dad acted all soft. He'd thought that they'd got over all that, now they'd started rowing with each other all the time, but here they were, at it again. He was just glad that they were indoors and none of his mates could hear.

'And I'm a lucky man and all, being married to you, Kate.'

'Yer will look after yerself when I'm away, won't yer, Pat?'

'Course I will.'

'Yeah, course he will, won't yer, love?' said Nora, stepping into the kitchen. "Cos yer a good 'un, aren't yer, Pat? I've always said so.'

'Just what I was saying meself, Mum,' Katie agreed, smiling up at her mother.

'Hello, Nanna,' said Michael eagerly, knowing his grandmother was always a potential accomplice in any battle against other adults.

'Hello, me little darling,' said Nora, winking at her grandson. 'And how are you?'

'I think I'm really tired, Nanna,' Michael whined, playing his trump card in his efforts to escape the nit comb. 'I reckon I should go in next door to bed.'

Nora raised an eyebrow. 'Really? Well, that shows what a grown-up lad you've gotten to be, now doesn't it? Ten years old and yer taking yerself off to bed without being told. Soon as yer mam's finished, yer can go right in.'

'Cup o' tea, Nanna?' said Michael, trying another, less promising, tack.

'No, yer all right, Michael. I just popped in to let yer mam know that I've put young Timmy in my bed instead of upstairs in your room,' she paused for effect, "cos the poor little mite seems worried about some old bogey man what someone was scaring him with. I wonder where he got them silly ideas from, eh?'

Michael ducked his head, but was still caught by the inevitable sting round his ear.

Nora folded her arms and looked wistfully at the wall that divided her kitchen from her daughter's. 'Yer should see him in there, all propped up on my feather pillows, looking though a comic, he is. With that little angel face of his, he looks like a baby prince in a fairy tale, sure he does.'

Michael snorted derisively at the image conjured up by his grandmother, but was soon hushed by another crack of the nit comb.

'Sure yer don't want no tea, Mum?'

'No, thanks, Katie, or I'll be in and out to the wotsit

160

all night. I just wanted to say me goodbyes to Molly and the boys.'

Katie glanced over at the clock. 'They shouldn't be long. They said they'd make sure they'd be back nice and early to see yer.'

'Good, good.'

Pat hoisted his big, muscled frame from the step in one easy movement. 'There,' he said, holding out the two pairs of boots for everyone to see. 'That's done.'

'A good job jobbed,' said Nora, nodding her approval. 'Now, Katie, I won't leave Timmy next door by himself. Will yer send the kids in to me when they get home?'

'Course I will.'

'Right.' Nora went over to Pat, reached up and touched his bristly cheek. 'You're a good feller, Pat Mehan, and there's not many as can say that about their daughter's husband.' She dropped her hand but still looked up into Pat's dark brown eyes. 'I'll see yer in a while, but I'll leave yer for now with yer wife.' She turned and held out her hand to her grandson. 'Come on, Michael. Nanna'll finish scalping yer next door.'

Knowing his nanna's more lax attitude towards nits, Michael was up and out of the door with a hurried, 'See yer later,' before anyone had the chance to change their minds.

Nora followed him at a still lively, but slightly more dignified pace, leaving Pat and Katie in the kitchen by themselves.

'Tea?' asked Katie, carefully screwing up the newspapers to make sure that no creatures, if there were any, could escape into her clean kitchen.

'I thought we might have a glass of something,' said Pat. 'There's that quart bottle of light ale I brought back from the Queen's last night and never started.'

'That'll be nice. Ta.'

Katie shoved the newspaper into the bottom of the rubbish bucket outside the back door, and sat herself at the kitchen table, while Pat poured the foaming ale into two thick glass tumblers from the set Katie had bought in Woolworth's at a time when sets of glasses hadn't been an unthinkable luxury.

'Shall I take yer a chair out the front?' Pat asked, handing her her drink.

'How about if we sit out in the yard instead?' Katie felt oddly shy with her husband. It had been so long since they had been nice to one another, what with all the money worries and the bad atmosphere since he had flown off the handle about her helping Frank Barber, she didn't quite know how he'd take things.

She smiled with relief when Pat said, 'Good idea, girl,' and, with one hand, grabbed the back of two of the bentwood kitchen chairs and lifted them out over the back step.

Katie took off her apron, hung it on the nail behind the door, went outside and sat down in the warm night air. She sipped at the tepid beer and looked round the dusty little yard with the patch of scruffy pot marigolds that had grown there since she had helped Molly plant them when she was a toddler. It really wasn't like her, but Katie found herself at a loss as to what to say.

'Penny for 'em?' Pat said, stretching his long legs out in front of him.

'Eh?' she answered, surprised by the sound of his voice. 'Sorry, I was miles away.'

'Worrying about what we'll get up to while yer down hopping?' he asked with a chuckle.

'Yeah, that's right.' Katie nodded and took another mouthful from her glass. 'Especially our Sean.'

'He'll be all right. I'll ask around again next week, see if anyone's heard of anything going. And, who knows, he might be in luck. The way they're laying off all the older lads, they might be after a bit of cheap young labour.'

Katie sighed. 'Wonder if Mr Milton's got himself fixed up with anything yet.'

Pat shook his head. 'No. Joe said he saw him lining up outside the labour exchange again on Thursday. Arse practically out of his trousers, poor feller. Said he looked too weak to do anything even if there was a job for him.'

Katie stared down at the pale golden foam on top of her beer. 'I know times are hard, Pat, but we should be grateful, yer know. We've got so much when yer see how other people have to manage.' She hesitated, then added quietly, 'That's why I always do what I can for other people. It seems only right. And I know how yer get, Pat, but honestly, I never meant to upset yer about Frank Barber. I really was only helping him with his little girl.'

Pat didn't answer, he just lifted his glass and silently swallowed the rest of his beer.

'I don't wanna start nothing with yer, Pat, I just wanted to clear the air before I go.'

When he still didn't respond, she stood up and went inside to fetch the bottle from the kitchen. She refilled Pat's glass, draining out the last drop, stood the empty by the back door, ready for someone to take back to the Queen's, and then sat down again. 'I'd better get meself shifted soon,' she said, 'or it'll be time for us to go and I won't have nothing ready.'

'You sit there for a while, girl,' Pat said. 'I'll help yer in a minute.'

Katie ran her fingers through her thick auburn hair, pulling it away from her face and neck. 'It's that hot, I

163

don't think I could sleep tonight even if I had time.'

'Kate,' Pat said.

'Yes, love?'

'I'll miss yer, yer know.'

Katie reached out her hand and stroked the back of her husband's great rough paw. 'I know,' she whispered.

Pat stood up, took his wife by the shoulders and pulled her towards him. Leaning back against the door jamb, Pat kissed her urgently. 'Katie,' he gasped, tipping back his head, 'please, let's go upstairs.'

Katie nodded and reached up to kiss him again. Their lips had just touched, when they heard Molly's voice calling from the passage. 'We're back, Mum. And even our Sean's on time.'

Pat let his hands fall to his sides.

'I'll make it up to yer, Pat,' Katie whispered. 'When yer come down and see us. I promise, I will.'

Sunday had come at last – just. It was half past two in the morning and Joe Palmer was manoeuvring his pride and joy – a recently purchased flat back truck – out of his yard at number eight Plumley Street.

He pulled up on the corner outside the Mehans', where Katie and Nora were waiting for him with all their gear packed in the two tea chests and assorted bundles and parcels that were piled up around them on the pavement.

'I knew we should have got Joe to take us all the way by lorry,' Katie was saying to her mum. 'I dunno why I let them boys kid me to go by train. What we gonna do with all this lot at the other end if the farmer ain't there with his wagon? We'll never be able to hump it all the way to the farm by ourselves.'

'He'll be there, Katie,' Nora assured her. 'Don't you go worrying yerself about that. Sure doesn't he need his hops picked? And what would the feller do without us to pick 'em for him?'

'I can still drive yer if yer like, Kate,' said Joe, jumping down from his cab and going round the back to let down the tailboard. 'Don't make no difference to me.'

Katie looked anxiously at Pat as he clambered up on to the back of the truck. 'What d'yer think? Should Joe drive us all the way?'

Pat shook his head as he took the first of the tea chests from Joe. 'Yer know the boys'd be choked if they didn't get their train ride.'

Katie's frown softened into a smile. 'Yeah, I suppose yer right.' She turned to Joe who was swinging another parcel up to Pat, and her smile broadened into a grin. 'It's your fault, Joe Palmer,' she joked. 'If yer didn't let 'em hang around that yard o' your'n and have goes in yer truck all the time, they'd have been making me promise to let 'em go by flaming lorry.'

Aggie Palmer, her hair in metal curlers, was leaning out of the upstairs window of the flat she and Joe lived in above the yard, watching them load up.

'You sure yer don't want Joe to take yer, Kate? I don't mind.' She started laughing. 'Keep him down there with yer for the picking and all, if yer like. Your Danny can do all the work here and I'll have a rest from Joe's snoring.'

'Cheeky mare,' laughed Joe fondly, handing the final parcel up to Pat who stacked it with the other luggage hard up against the back of the cab. 'Right. That's that lot done. Now, let's be having the passengers.'

'No!' shouted Nora, making everyone jump. 'Sure, how can I go when I don't know what I've done with me handbag?'

'Mum,' Katie shushed her, looking anxiously up and

down the street at the curtain-shaded windows. 'Yer'll have everyone awake.'

'Well,' said Nora, 'I need it.'

'Why? We ain't going to church, we're going hopping.'

Nora leant close to Katie, scowling at her daughter's foolishness. 'Sure, hasn't it got me penny policies in it. I want to make certain that Pat pays 'em for me while I'm away.' She looked over her shoulder to check that no one could hear her private business. 'What would it look like if something happened to me and I couldn't even pay for me own funeral and I had to be buried on the parish?'

'Mum! Don't go talking like that.'

Nora straightened her already upright frame until her back was like a ramrod. 'It's all arranged,' she said proudly. 'I've told the insurance man to come of an evening instead of in the afternoon.'

Nora turned round and spoke to Molly, who was standing hollow-eyed with tiredness, her coat thrown on over her nightdress for modesty's sake, waiting to wave goodbye. 'Would yer do a favour for yer old nanna?' asked Nora needlessly.

'Course,' yawned Molly.

'Go inside and see if yer can find me handbag for me, love.'

Stifling another yawn, Molly nodded and began to move slowly towards her nanna's house next door.

'And send them boys out here and tell 'em to fetch the dog and all, while yer at it, please, love,' Katie added.

Timmy and Michael appeared on the doorstep. They had slept in their clothes so that they would be ready for the early start, and, as they staggered out on to the pavement, it showed. With their creased shorts and shirts and their hair standing on end like cock fowls,

166

they looked like two bundles of rags ready to be sorted through on a toot stall.

'Muuuum,' wailed Michael, rubbing his eyes. 'Molly's gone and dragged us out of Nanna's bed, and she's really hurt me.'

'Don't you dare start,' said Katie, wagging her finger at him. 'It was you two what wanted to go on the hoppers' special in the first place. Now go and get Rags, and make sure he's done his business before we get in Joe's truck.'

Michael made no attempt to move, he just stood there looking dejected.

Timmy appeared every bit as dishevelled as his older brother, but he was wide awake. 'I'll go and fetch Rags, Mum,' he said, taking a running kick at a stone, sending a satisfyingly bright spray of sparks from his boot as the Blakeys made violent contact with the pavement. 'Cor, look, Mick,' he said, the dog forgotten as he experimented with different effects. 'It don't half look good in the dark.'

'It won't be dark for much longer,' said Joe, squinting at his pocket watch. 'And trains don't wait for yer, yer know. Now are you lot coming or what?'

As Katie busied herself with fussing around the boys: first chasing them indoors to get Rags, and then settling the three of them on an old blanket on the back of the truck, Molly was searching for her grandmother's handbag. She eventually appeared in the doorway, holding it aloft.

'There y'are Nanna,' she said, handing over the battered brown bag. She lowered her voice. 'It was out the back in the lav.'

'Thank you, darling,' said Nora with a grin. She sorted through the papers that were its only contents and set about issuing Pat with instructions as to how he was to make the payments to the insurance man.

Pat was perfectly familiar with the bowler-hatted, bicycle-clipped Mr Randall, who, being the nearest thing to a professional that most of the neighbours ever saw, spent much of his time touring the area on his sit-up-and-beg bike, dispensing wisdom as to the state of the world, writing letters explaining school children's absences, and even settling disputes. But it still took Pat a while to assure his mother-in-law that he had managed to grasp the principles involved in paying her weekly premium. When he finally succeeded, he turned his attention to saying goodbye to his wife, while Nora turned her attention to her granddaughter.

'See anyone last night?' she enquired. 'A feller maybe?'

'Nanna,' protested Molly, pulling her coat primly round her shoulders, 'keep yer voice down, can't yer? Everyone'll hear yer.'

'Not if yer don't go shouting yer head off with yer complaints, they won't,' said Nora with a sly grin. 'Now, come on, you can tell yer nanna.'

Molly swung her shoulders from side to side. 'I might have done,' she said, staring down at her bare feet.

Nora's grin broadened. 'Nice is he? This one?'

'Yeah. He is. Bit sort of bossy sometimes. He likes to sort of take control. But I don't mind 'cos he's really, you know, a bit of all right.'

Nora's grin disappeared. 'Jesus, Mary, Joseph!' she exclaimed. 'I never thought I'd hear a granddaughter of mine say a thing like that.'

'Like what?' Molly demanded indignantly. She could have kicked herself; why had she said that?

'Like yer don't mind him being a bit bossy, that's like what. For God's sake, girl, where will that lead yer, eh?'

Remembering the need to keep her voice down, Molly moved closer to Nora and said almost inaudibly, 'We're

168

'all different, Nanna. And we all like different things.'

'Not that different, I hope,' said Nora sharply. 'You wanna watch yerself, my girl. A feller telling my granddaughter what to do. Whatever next?'

'But I didn't say that, did I?'

'Didn't yer? That's what I heard.'

'No. And anyway, he's a mate of our Danny's, and he wouldn't let no one take a liberty with me, would he?'

'He'd better not.' Nora was bristling.

Molly chewed at her lip, trying to decide whether what she was about to do would get her out of the mess she seemed to be in, or whether it would make it a million times worse. Stupid as she thought it might be, her impulsive nature got the better of her. 'Can I tell yer something Nanna? *Without* yer raising yer voice and shouting and going barmy?'

Nora said nothing, she merely raised her eyebrows imperiously.

'Know that secret I told yer, Nanna? The one I told yer to keep to yerself?'

'When have I ever not kept a secret yer've told me?'

Molly knew that her nanna had never let her down, but she also knew that this was one secret that she really didn't want to risk her spilling to anyone, and she knew how impetuous her grandmother could be – didn't everyone say that that was where she got her own wild nature from? But she plunged in regardless, wanting to make it clear to her nanna that she wasn't a fool letting boys use her. 'Remember that other boy I said I liked and all? The one that I was going to see?'

Nora's grin returned.

'Well, I'm sort of, well, still seeing him and all.'

Nora was triumphant. 'Two fellers still on the go, eh? That's more like what I want to hear from my Molly.'

'Sssshhh, Nanna! I told yer, it's a secret.'

Nora spat on her palm and held her hand out to Molly. 'Still our secret,' she reassured her granddaughter. 'Now, tell me all about it, but be quick, or that lot'll be dragging me on to the back of that lorry and I'll be going mad with not knowing till I see yer next week.'

'I'm seeing him this afternoon,' Molly whispered. 'His name's Simon. And I think he's smashing.'

Nora let out a contented sigh. 'Two fellers, eh? Must be, what, a month yer've been seeing 'em now?'

Molly nodded. 'Yeah,' she said, unable not to look pleased with herself.

'Maybe I should meet 'em when I get back? See what I think of 'em both?'

Molly gulped. She really hadn't thought this through. 'Well, I might not still be seeing 'em, Nan. I might—'

Nora shook her head and pulled her handbag further up her arm. 'Like I told yer before, you just make sure yer keep 'em both on a string till yer know what yer want, darling,' she said wisely. 'Sure, God didn't give us our good looks for us to just throw ourselves at any Tom, Dick or how's yer father who comes along and flashes a smile and waves a handful of ten-bob notes in our face.'

Molly's mouth dropped open. Even by Nora's standards that was a real piece of don't-do-as-I-do-but-do-as-I-say double-talk. Everyone in the family knew that that was exactly what Nora had done when she had run off and married Stephen Brady, a chancer from Cork City, with roaring good looks and an even more impressive line in Blarney. He had whisked Nora away from under the very nose of a decent farming lad from Wicklow – to whom she was engaged to be married – and had brought her over to London, *and*, so the story went, before he had even made an honest woman of her.

170

But even if Molly had been bold enough to argue the point with her nanna, she had missed her chance. Phoebe and Sooky had appeared on the scene and, even with the amount of indignation Molly felt, there was no chance of her questioning her grandmother's integrity in front of anyone, let alone those two old gossips.

They came strolling across the street as though it was the middle of the afternoon. Both were dressed up in coats and hats, and were being followed, somewhat grudgingly it looked, by their hapless husbands, Albert and Jimmo, who were struggling to carry an assortment of bundles wrapped up with bits of knotted string and creased brown paper.

With a sour-faced silent gesture, Phoebe directed Albert to hand her parcels to Joe Palmer and then for Jimmo Shay to do likewise.

'What's all this about?' asked Joe. His question wasn't strictly necessary, as he knew all too well what it was about.

'Yer going to London Bridge Station, ain't yer?' snapped Phoebe accusingly.

'Yeah.'

'Well, so are we.'

'So you ain't going with that lot from Chris Street in the back of Neaves's van, then?'

'Does it look like it?'

'No.'

'That's right. We thought we might as well go on the train for a change. So get that lot stacked on the back of yer motor, Joe Palmer. Proper mind, we don't want nothing broke. And yer can keep it away from that tripe hound and all.' She sniffed and glared through narrowed eyes at Rags and the boys, who peered back at her from under the blanket on the back of the truck. 'Then yer can give me a hand up as well. And yer do know a woman o' my age'll have to be travelling up in the cab, don't yer?' She jerked her head towards Nora and Katie. 'Not on the back with that mob. The screws in me knees wouldn't take it.'

'Screws in her neck more like. Look at her, just like Boris Karloff in that Frankenstein film,' said Michael, leaning over the side of the lorry; his cheek earning him a grin from his dad and a quick flip round the ear from his mum.

Joe didn't bother to argue with Phoebe, he just beckoned to Pat to help him load up. As they slung the parcels on to the back of the truck, Joe had a look of complete resignation on his face, but he was muttering darkly to himself. 'Just five minutes and we'd have been away and these two old trouts would've had to have gone in the back of Neaves's van with that lot from round the corner. I *told* 'em to hurry up, but would they listen? No. Now they're gonna be stuck with 'em on the train, and serves 'em bleed'n right and all, if you ask me.'

Phoebe, arms folded, stood herself on tiptoes and cast a critical eye over Pat and Joe's loading techniques, making several suggestions about rearranging things, which they pointedly ignored. But Phoebe wasn't one to put up with such disrespectful behaviour. 'Look at that Joe's face, will yer? Miserable bastard,' she said loudly, jabbing her finger at him. 'Yer can see he hangs his fiddle up when he gets home.'

Molly rolled her eyes at Nora. 'Yer've struck lucky, Nanna. You and Mum're gonna have Phoebe and Sooky bending yer ear'oles all the way down there.'

'We can handle them, love. Sure, we won't even notice the battered old cows.' But Nora had spoken too soon.

Phoebe had repositioned herself, this time in front of

Katie. 'I'll bet that Frank Barber'll miss you,' she said, with a nasty smirk on her face. 'And all the – what is it yer call it now – *help*, what yer've been giving him.'

Nora stepped between her daughter and her vicious-tongued neighbour. 'Yer lucky my son-in-law wasn't standing here to listen to yer filthy tongue,' she fumed.

'It don't matter, Mum,' Katie said coldly. 'Ignore her. She ain't got nothing better to do with her time.'

Phoebe turned to Sooky. 'Just look at these two, Sook,' she said, tipping her head towards Nora and Katie. 'Stop a clock, their faces would.'

Nora and Katie seethed at the insult but both knew that they couldn't start anything, not with Pat around. They'd have to bide their time.

Molly wasn't feeling quite so controlled about it all, and it was only Joe Palmer insisting that if they didn't go there and then, he would go back to his bed and the lot of them could walk to London Bridge Station for all he cared, that a row was prevented from breaking out.

The indignant-looking group clambered on to the truck, called a chorus of tense goodbyes and waved stiff farewells to their loved ones as Joe, with not inconsiderable relief, pulled away out of Plumley Street.

'Just say one word about being tired or cold, Michael Mehan,' Katie warned her son through gritted teeth, 'just one word, and, I promise, I'll skin yer.'

When Pat came home from work to Plumley Street the next evening it felt strange, cold: his kids weren't playing out in the street, the house wasn't full of the noise and the bustle of women talking and laughing while they got the tea ready, and Rags wasn't jumping all over him, begging Pat to scratch him behind his ears. Even though he should have been used to it by now – Katie went to

Kent almost every autumn, after all – the house, as he stepped inside the passage, had an emptiness that would never seem right to him. And, though it was hard to admit it, he knew why. It reminded him too much of when he had been a little kid himself, and he had come home from school and his mum had been missing yet again. Young as he had been, he had known she had gone off with some new man, and would be away until she got fed up with him and was ready to come home and face the rows and the violence which would inevitably start . . .

He tried to bury those memories somewhere deep inside him, to stop them hurting him, and usually he succeeded, but at times like this when he felt so alone, no matter how hard he tried, he couldn't stop them rising to the surface to torment him. It was just like the blackness that overwhelmed him whenever he saw Katie talking to another man. He knew it did no one any good, but he just couldn't help himself.

He looked around the empty kitchen and rubbed his hands roughly over his face, dragging his fingers down his weather-beaten cheeks. With his wife miles away from him, and after the day he had had at the docks, Pat Mehan was feeling not unclose to weeping.

He walked over to the tap and filled the kettle. He'd have a cup of tea. That would make it feel a bit more like home. He took off his cap and flicked it on to the draining board. Immediately he checked himself – Katie would never have allowed that if she was there – so he picked it up and took it out into the passage and hooked it on one of the coat pegs in the glory hole under the stairs.

Then he went back into the kitchen, sat down at the table and set about rolling himself a cigarette, while he

174

waited for the water to boil, and thought about his day.

Even for a Monday it had been dismal down at the docks, but usually, no matter how quiet things had been, Pat managed to get at least a couple of hours' paid work under his belt. He was a stevedore who was well-respected by men and management alike, known for his reliability, his strength and his willingness to have a go at any job no matter how demanding; and he had always made sure that the union, regardless of how tough their demands, had played fair with the governors, and they had always looked after him in return. But not that day. It had been dead down there, and even Pat had been told, sorry, there was nothing doing, they might as well all go home.

He had been so fed up that he was tempted when one of the other blokes, whose wife had also gone hopping, had asked him to go for a few jars rather than straight home to their empty houses, but had decided against it. Not only were visits to the pub something he couldn't afford if he wasn't earning even a few hours' pay, he had his Molly, Danny and Sean to think about. Pat might have been a big, powerful-looking man, but he cared as passionately about his children as he did his wife, and he wasn't ashamed of it either. In fact, he was one of the only men ever to have been seen pushing a pram along Plumley Street, he had been that proud of becoming a dad. So, it was with no excuses that he had said thanks all the same, but not today, to his workmate's offer, and had taken himself off home to make a start on the tea.

It wasn't only that Pat felt responsible for his children, he was also keen to see that they were eating properly, so he could reassure Katie, when he saw her at the weekend, that her precious chicks were having at least one decent meal a day. He knew what youngsters could be like, and he knew how Katie worried about them. In fact, if he had had a few bob to spare he would gladly have bet it all that Sean would have gone through the whole day with nothing more passing his lips than the two slices of bread and scrape he'd shovelled down himself at breakfast time.

Pat looked over at the gas stove. The kettle was steaming like a train. He ground out his dog-end in the pickle jar lid that served as an ashtray, took off his jacket and rolled up his shirt sleeves. He'd have a cup of tea later, when he had got himself organised. It shouldn't be too difficult making a bit of tea for his three eldest, he'd had some practice over the years seeing to his own supper when Katie and the kids had been hopping, after all. Admittedly, in the past, he only had himself to see to, and had tended to stick to bread and cheese or visits to the eel and pie house or the chip shop, but Katie had left a list of instructions and enough stuff in the larder to get them through the first few days so they wouldn't have to resort to eating cold food or fish and chips just yet awhile.

Unfortunately, Pat was a willing rather than a skilful housekeeper and when Danny and Molly came home from work they found him in the kitchen surrounded by every saucepan, pot and dish they owned, and enough sausages, mash and fried onions to feed at least a dozen people. Even when he had dished up their helpings and had put a pile on to a plate for the absent Sean, there was still a mountain of it left over.

Pat scratched his head and stared at the heaped up plates. 'I can't think where all this came from,' he said. 'I didn't think I was peeling that many spuds.'

'I think yer must've used up the whole week's worth,' grinned Molly, sprinkling salt over her mound of food.

'D'yer reckon?' Pat frowned at the drifts of peelings snaking all over the draining board. There had been no instructions on Katie's list about how many potatoes he should peel, just 'enough for the four of you', it had said. What was that supposed to mean?

'Look, when we've had ours I'll nip over to Mrs Milton's with the rest. Them little 'uns of her'n won't let it go to waste.'

'Right. Good girl,' said Pat, handing Danny a plate piled so high it was more like a serving dish than a single portion. 'Get that down yer, son.'

'Ta,' Danny said flatly.

Pat sat down at the table with his own equally enormous supper, picked up his fork and pointed it at his son before digging it into the mashed potato. 'You're quiet, Dan. Nothing wrong at work, is there?'

'No. Nothing's wrong at work. Not exactly.' Danny cut into one of the shiny, dark brown sausages, making it pop as the skin split, sending a spurt of hot grease into the air. 'I was thinking about something I saw in Joe's evening paper just now.'

Pat swallowed his food and nodded approvingly. 'Been reading the paper, have yer? Good on yer. So, what was it yer saw?'

Danny took his time answering; it was as though he was weighing up the best way to put it. 'It's all this stuff . . .' he began slowly, drawing his fork backwards and forwards through the mass of potato his father had presented to him.

'What stuff's that then, son?' Pat encouraged him.

'This stuff about how Hitler's meant to be treating Jews so bad. And how he's meant to be a warmonger. I can't believe how they're trying to make him sound such a villain.'

Molly flinched as Pat smashed his knife and fork down on the table, sending the salt pot flying and the mustard jar crashing to the floor and spinning off across the lino. Hurriedly she scrambled under the table as much to get out of the firing line as to retrieve the condiments.

'*Sound such a villain*?' Pat echoed his son disbelievingly. 'Are you off your head, boy? Are you a *complete* idiot?'

'No, I ain't,' said Danny defiantly. 'Everyone knows Hitler's the best thing what could have happened to Germany. He's gonna sort that country right out, you just see. They'll all be in work over there, and everyone'll have plenty. And what'll be happening in this stupid country? We'll have nothing, that's what. Right laughing stock, we'll be.'

'I can't believe this – a son of mine talking like them no-good bastards what stand on street corners, giving out them stinking leaflets. What yer gonna do next? Start smashing old people's windows?'

Molly gently put the mustard jar and salt pot back on the table and sat down. She picked up her knife and fork, but she didn't start eating again, she was too engrossed by her brother arguing with their dad in a way she would never have believed he would dare.

'You reckon you know it all,' Danny went on aggressively. 'Well, if you're so clever, how comes yer doing so bad for yerself? Couldn't even get yerself a few hours work today, could yer?' He leant back in his chair and smirked. 'And you reckon *I'm* the idiot.'

Pat clenched his fists so tightly that his knuckles stuck out sharp and white against his sun-tanned skin; he was struggling against an almost irresistible urge to raise his hand and strike his son hard across the face. He closed his eyes and, in a voice trembling with temper

178

said in a barely audible whisper, 'Gawd, I wish yer mother was here to sort you out. I can't trust meself to keep me hands off yer, yer stupid little sod.' He opened his eyes, shoved his chair back and stood up. 'I'm going out for a drink and some fresh air.'

Pat must have said he wished Katie was at home in Poplar at least a hundred times during the first week that she was away in Kent. Not only because he was missing her – and he was, badly – but also because he needed her to help him sort out the nonsense that Danny had got stuck in his head. And Sean needed something more than the talking to that he could give him as well. Pat genuinely hadn't realised just how much work it took to keep the kids in order. Whenever there was any trouble with them, Katie and Nora put it down to their age, but that excuse – and it *was* an excuse Pat was convinced, because he was never like it as a boy – could only really apply to Sean. Danny was eighteen, a young man, not a kid, and he definitely should have known better by now. Pat just counted himself lucky that at least there were no problems with Molly, or he really wouldn't have known what to do then.

Actually, Molly did have problems, but she was a bit more skilled than the boys at hiding the fact from her dad.

Molly was becoming increasingly troubled that things weren't going how she had planned. She had presumed that her dad would be going down to Kent to see her mum and nanna and the little ones at the weekend, and that she would be left at home with the boys, probably on the understanding that she cooked their meals and kept the place in order. Then she would have the freedom to meet Simon and Bob and to come home whenever she

179

felt like it, the idea behind her plan being that it would be the perfect opportunity to get to know them both a bit better and to decide which one she preferred. It had been all very well at first, seeing the pair of them, but things were becoming a bit complicated. She didn't like lying, well, not lying exactly, but having to cover up all the time was against her usually open nature, so she had decided that she would sort it all out once and for all. But it hadn't turned out like that.

Come the first weekend of her supposed liberty, her dad had plans of his own – and unfortunately they involved her. Pat had supposed that, unlike the performance he had with the boys, having to issue threats, in order to get them to go with him, Molly would be thrilled at the prospect of getting away from Poplar and spending Saturday and Sunday in the countryside with her mum and nanna. But it hadn't worked out like that at all.

All of his three oldest children, Molly included, had made his life such a misery, particularly during the return journey and for the five days afterwards when their mother wasn't around to hear them, that, come the second weekend, Pat had turned up outside Katie's hop hut alone. He was worried enough about how he was going to tell her that he had only had two days' work again, without bothering himself with those three and their moaning. But Katie had dismissed his money worries with a flap of her hand and a sharp telling off about his overreacting as usual. No, she was far more exercised with what her absent children were getting up to. The more she thought about it, the more frantic she became, until she finally worked herself up into a real lather, demanding to know what he had done to make them want to stay away, and yelling at the top of her voice about her husband's irresponsibility in leaving her babies to fend for themselves.

Pat didn't have the inclination, or the energy, to row about it, and had half-heartedly retorted that they were big enough and ugly enough to look after themselves. He thought it wise not to mention that he had had just about enough of the three of them and he was delighted that they had stayed back in Poplar. All he did add, and it was the truth, was that Molly had said she wanted to stay at home to clean the house out from top to bottom as a surprise for her mum's homecoming, when hopping finished at the end of the next week. What he omitted to tell his wife was that their precious daughter had said she would do the housework as a way of saying she was sorry as she had been such a little mare to her dad about not going to Kent with him.

But when Pat arrived back in Plumley Street on Sunday evening, there was no sign of Molly or the house having been given even the briefest flick over with a duster, let alone the thorough going-through with a mop and bucket that she had promised. Nor was there any sign of Danny.

The only person who was at home was Sean; he was sitting in the kitchen, picking at a hunk of unappetising-looking bread and a piece of greyish cheddar that was more rind than cheese. He appeared totally unaware of the fact that he was surrounded by flies and the debris of what looked like every drink and meal the three of them had eaten since Pat had left for Kent late on Friday night.

Pat exploded with anger about the state of the place but Sean had nothing to say in his or anyone else's defence. He just got up, leaving his bread and cheese on the table, and disappeared out of the back door and over the yard wall.

181

When Molly eventually came home, Pat was standing at the sink wringing out a dishcloth. He glanced over at the clock on the mantel shelf. It was a few minutes off a quarter to ten.

With very controlled movements, he folded the cloth into a neat rectangle and draped it over the now shining single brass tap. 'Well?' he asked, turning to face his daughter. 'What's yer story?'

Molly's face flushed scarlet. 'I went to the park with me friends. I didn't expect yer back till later.'

Pat still sounded calm. 'Yer was in the park till this time of night?'

'I didn't realise how late it was. Yer know what it's like when yer get talking.'

'And how about the promise yer made about doing out the house? A way of saying yer was sorry, wasn't it?' He leant back against the sink and folded his arms across his chest. 'D'you know how long it's taken me just to get this kitchen straight? It'd be nice, wouldn't it, for yer mother to come home to this pigsty next week?'

Molly, if it was possible, went even redder. She pulled off her hat and threw it on the table, then took down her mother's apron from the nail behind the door. 'I'll do the front room and passage now and I'll do the rest every evening after work,' she said, tying the strings tightly round her waist. 'I really promise, Dad.'

Pat filled the kettle and set it on the stove. 'So, who were yer with? And don't tell me Lizzie, 'cos I went over the Wattses' to see if yer was there.'

Molly dipped her chin. 'I met a boy.' Was she stupid? Why had she told him that?

Pat smacked his hand hard on to the draining board. 'You just wait till yer mother hears about this.'

'She was my age when she was seeing you.' Molly

gulped; why hadn't she just kept quiet?

'But she didn't lie to her mother about what she was up to, did she?'

Molly said nothing.

'Now, who is this boy? Do I know him?'

What could she say? Molly had seen Bob Jarvis the night before and had then spent all Sunday with Simon. Her throat was so dry she could scarcely get the words out. 'Just a boy. I only just met him with some girls from work and we was all talking and . . . You know.'

'Are you lying to me, Molly?'

'No, Dad.' Molly snatched the broom from the corner by the hearth. 'I'll get started on the front room.'

'No, you don't . . .' Pat began.

Molly was sure that it must have been her silent prayers, because at that very moment, when she was sure her dad was prepared to throttle the truth out of her, they heard the front door crash back on its hinges and the sound of someone stumbling along the passage.

'What the bloody hell's happening now?'

Danny appeared in the doorway. He had an idiotic grin on his face. His usually neat collar was awry, his dark curly hair looked as though it'd been combed with a lavatory brush and there was a smear of blood at the corner of his lip. The stench of stale beer and tobacco was all about him.

Pat ran his hands through his hair. 'Thank Gawd yer mother ain't here to see this,' he said distractedly. 'Now, get out of my sight, the pair of yer. I'm gonna kip in next door, and when I come in here tomorrow morning, all I can say is that you two had better be ready for work, and this place had better be in a state fit for decent people.'

Molly waited for the sound of her nanna's street door

being slammed shut, then she hauled her brother up the stairs and shoved him on to her parents' big double bed. Then she ran back down to the kitchen to get a bucket in case Danny was ill in the night.

As she pulled off her brother's shoes she had two reasons to be grateful for the state he was in: not only had he taken his father's attention from what she had been up to, but he was in no condition to ask her any awkward questions either. With a bit more luck, if she got stuck into the cleaning now and made sure that she had a decent breakfast on the table first thing, her dad would calm down a bit and she would have had the chance to get her story straight.

Danny suddenly opened his eyes. They were bloodshot and puffy from drink. He blinked slowly, then grinned. 'I've been out with Bob,' he slurred. 'Me best mate, that feller.'

Molly didn't say anything, but was thankful for the information; now she wouldn't make the mistake of saying she was with Bob Jarvis when her dad asked. She wiped the blood roughly from Danny's lip with her hankie, then pushed him on to his side as she struggled to get him out of his jacket.

'Thinks the world of you, Moll,' Danny mumbled, barely audible from where Molly had turned his face into the pillows. 'He's been telling everyone that you're his girl.'

Molly cringed as she visualised what Danny would have to say if he found out she was two-timing his mate. She rolled him on to his back again.

'There's a bucket by the side of the bed,' she said to him, folding his jacket.

As she put it down on the brocade-covered stool, she looked at the collection of framed photographs of the family that her mother displayed so proudly on her dressing table. Molly felt her cheeks burning again as a pale, monochrome image of her mother smiled out at her with such tenderness and love. Molly swallowed hard, determined, dreadful as she felt, that she wouldn't cry.

She closed the door to her parents' bedroom and stood on the dark landing. Everything was such a mess. Why hadn't she done what she'd been planning for weeks? Why hadn't she sorted it all out when she'd had the opportunity?

She knew why: she didn't want to. She liked them both, Simon and Bob. How could she be expected to make up her mind when they were so different?

There was Bob, so arrogant and full of himself. He didn't seem to care what she thought about anything, but he could thrill her with just a look, and when he actually touched her . . . She shuddered with pleasure at the memory of his fingers playing up and down her cheek.

And then there was Simon, so gentle and kind. He was interested in everything she had to say, and he wasn't exactly slow when it came to kissing either.

She went into her own room and closed the door behind her. She couldn't even think about starting the clearing up now. No, she'd have a good night's sleep and then she'd get up really early and start on the housework tomorrow first thing. That's what she'd do.

She let her clothes drop to the floor where she took them off, tugged her nightgown roughly over her head, then climbed between the sheets and pulled the eiderdown up under her chin.

With a slow sigh, she closed her eyes and reassured herself that things had a way of sorting themselves out. They always did. Everyone knew that. Didn't they?

9

Since Katie had come home from hopping, the atmosphere in number twelve Plumley Street had been going from bad to worse; as the days grew shorter so, it seemed, did Katie's temper. She really was beginning to feel desperate. It was as though she was not only losing control of herself – moaning and shouting all the time – but also of her family.

The situation had become progressively worse since that first Sunday afternoon when she had arrived home in Poplar with a bit of money in her purse, her head full of stories from Kent, and happy plans as to how she would make them all laugh with her tales. She was going to have them in stitches over the things that Phoebe and Sooky had got up to, make them gasp at all the strokes that Timmy and Michael had pulled, and have them giggling, and a bit shocked, at the scrapes Nora had wound up getting herself involved in. But Katie quickly realised that her homecoming wasn't going to live up to her expectations. Instead of the gales of laughter and spluttering, disbelieving chuckles she had hoped for, she was met instead with solemn faces, and a whole series of feuds, battles and sulks, most of which she couldn't understand, even though they were going on under her own roof.

There was Pat and Molly: they had been rowing over

something or other that had left them barely able to look at each other, let alone speak, but neither of them would tell her what it was all about. Katie had decided to ask Danny what was going on, but he was never around long enough for her to corner him; he was either out with Liz Watts, which seemed fine with everyone, thank goodness, or he was disappearing off with his new friends, which definitely wasn't all right with Pat. The very mention of Danny's pals set Pat's teeth on edge; again no one was prepared to explain why. And as for Sean, he still hadn't found himself a job and was acting just as rudely as before, but, if it were possible, he was being even more secretive about where he took himself off to all the time and was more cranky than ever when confronted.

Then there was the money Katie and Nora had earned hop picking. Instead of being able to put it by for Christmas, as they usually did, they soon realised that every penny of it was needed to make up the housekeeping. Pat hadn't been exaggerating the problem after all; the reality of the slump was now biting deep, snapping away at even supposedly indispensable workers like him.

To put the tin lid on the whole sorry mess, the very day after Katie had got back, Frank Barber had come over to see her. Unluckily he had chosen to turn up at the house before Pat left for what he had convinced himself would be another pointless journey to the docks.

Frank had come to ask Katie if she would do him a favour. He knew how busy she was, but someone had given him a winter coat for his little girl, and, if it wasn't to drag round her ankles like a pair of drawers with no elastic, it needed altering. He had been going to ask

Peggy Watts, he explained to Katie, but she had done so much for him lately, he didn't like to impose on her again – not for a while anyway. Katie had told him not to worry, it was no problem at all, and she would willingly do what she could with the coat as soon as she had a spare moment.

Pat had said nothing while Frank Barber was in the kitchen talking to his wife, he just carried on staring into the mirror by the sink, shaving his chin and neck with slow deliberation, swishing the soapy razor around in the basin of hot water. But once Frank had left, the flare-up came. Pat had barely started shouting at Katie when everyone else in the kitchen – Rags included – made a hasty exit.

'That bastard must've been hanging out of that window of his just watching for yer to get back home,' Pat hollered, dashing his razor into the sink.

Katie folded the child's coat over her arm, and took it over to the dresser, brushing past Pat without a glance or even an excuse me. 'Don't be so pathetic.'

'Well, *you* tell me how else he knew yer was back.'

Katie turned round and looked at him. Very calmly, she said, 'Are yer gonna stop shouting at me?'

'I don't believe this. Yer actually gonna start having a go at me?' He jabbed himself hard in the chest.

She shook her head. 'I don't think it'd be worth it. Yer never listen.'

Pat loomed over her, but, big as he was, Katie refused to be intimidated; she stood her ground. 'I must have been stupid,' she said, looking up at him. 'I couldn't wait to get home to yer. I honestly thought yer'd be right pleased to see me.'

'Well, I was, wasn't I?' Pat was now shaking with temper. He grabbed her, his big docker's hands circling

189

the tops of her arms. 'What d'yer think we did upstairs last night? D'yer think I could do *that* if I wasn't pleased to see yer?'

She tried to pull away from him but his grip was too tight. 'Yer talking rubbish, Pat.' Her voice wasn't as steady now; he was really hurting her.

'Talking rubbish, am I?'

'Yeah.' She made another, tremendous effort and pulled away from him, stumbling backwards into the dresser, knocking Theresa's coat to the floor. She bent down to pick it up, then held it in front of her like a shield. 'I told yer once before, Pat, if you *ever* raise your hand to me, I'm leaving yer. I mean it.'

His face contorted with dark fury. 'You gonna leave me, are yer? Well, perhaps it should be me what leaves you.' He smacked the flat of his hand hard against the wall. 'I mean, why would yer want me round yer? I talk rubbish, I can't earn enough to pay you yer wages, and let's face it, yer wouldn't miss me, now would yer? I mean, yer'd have plenty of bastard company.'

He shoved past her, stormed out of the kitchen and along the passage.

Katie stood there, stunned. Had she gone too far this time? Why hadn't she listened to her mum? She threw the child's coat on the table, snatched up the packet of sandwiches she had made, and ran after him. 'Pat,' she called, 'stop. Come back. Please. Yer can't go out without drinking yer tea.'

He grabbed hold of the door latch, waited a moment, then looked over his shoulder at her. Tears were running down his cheeks.

Katie held up the sandwiches to him. 'Yer left yer dinner on the table,' she whispered.

He turned his back on her, stepped out of the house and slammed the door in her face.

It was a frosty, Saturday morning in December, with only nine days left before Christmas, but Katie wasn't exactly in a festive mood. Stern-faced and silent, she was clearing away after breakfast, stacking the dirty bowls on to the scrubbed wooden draining board ready for washing up.

Katie Mehan's family had always been everything to her, and yet most days lately she felt as though she was in the middle of a battle ground with her as the enemy. In fact, bitterly cold as the weather had turned, Katie was so fed up that, more than once, she'd wished she could have gone back to Kent, to have been miles away from the whole rotten lot of them; she would have preferred to freeze in the mean little corrugated iron hop hut than have to keep putting up with all this.

Although the meal was over, everyone else in the family, excepting Nora, who was having her usual lie-in to avoid the dreaded porridge, was still sitting around the table. And from the look of them, nobody felt inclined to move, for despite the mood in the kitchen being decidedly chilly, compared to the icy weather outside, at least the range kept the room warm.

Molly, however, knew she really should make an effort and get up off her backside a bit sharpish and help her mum before she was asked. Still having failed to do what she knew she really should – choose between Bob and Simon – Molly had enough potential trouble brewing without adding to it by being lazy, further antagonising her mum and risking being kept in over the weekend. That was a complication she didn't need. So Molly hauled herself up from the table and went over to the sink where

Katie was digging away at the porridge-encrusted bottom of the big black enamel stew pan.

'Shove over, Mum,' Molly said. 'I'll do that.'

'I'd rather yer went down Chris Street for me,' said Katie wearily, her words coming out in jerks as she dug at the pot.

'Course,' Molly said, putting on a smile. 'I'll get Liz to come with me, we'll get it done in no time. And tell yer what, we'll take them little ones with us and all. Get 'em out from under yer feet for a couple of hours.'

'I ain't going shopping with no girls,' Michael sneered indignantly.

'Good,' puffed Katie, still trying to loosen the hardened oats. 'That means you and Timmy can go and fetch the coke from Levens Road for me. We're down to the last few bits and I don't want that Kitchener going out in this freezing weather.'

'Aw, Mum!' Michael wailed. 'Yer know I hate going down Levens Road.'

'Cheek yer mother and yer'll be sorry,' said Pat, snapping his morning paper back into a neat fold. Just because he and Katie weren't exactly on good terms, didn't mean he'd tolerate the kids being lippy to their mother.

Michael paid no heed to his father's warning. 'Why can't Sean do it?'

'Because she didn't ask me, that's why,' Sean snarled.

'Who's *she*, the cat's mother?' Michael replied, adding a curl of his lip at his big brother for good measure.

Michael would have been better served keeping his eye on his dad, because then he might have dodged in time to avoid Pat's hand as it flicked across the table and caught him squarely on the ear.

Molly rolled her eyes at her mum in a gesture that

she hoped would unite them against all the male bickering that was going on, then she turned to face her brothers and proclaimed nobly, 'I'll get the coke for yer, Mum, when I've finished the shopping.'

Katie frowned at this sudden spate of goodwill. 'What you after?'

'Do I have to be after something, just 'cos I've offered to run a couple of errands for yer?' Molly asked without a trace of shame.

Katie was going to reply that from her experience lately it seemed more than likely, but she was interrupted by the kitchen door being opened and Nora walking in.

'For goodness' sake,' Nora said, throwing up her hands in a dramatic double wave. '*I'll* do it. *I'll* go to Levens Road for yer.' She sat herself down at the table and weighed the teapot, checking if there was enough left in it for a decent cupful. 'Yer do know I could hear all yer rowing from next door, don't yer? And me doors and windows are all shut tight against the cold. Thank God yer live on the corner and have got no next-door neighbours but me.' She emptied the grounds from Timmy's cup into the saucer then filled it with tea for herself. 'Now, how much will yer be wanting, Kate?'

Katie gave a warning glare at Michael. 'You don't wanna be pushing that old pram full of coke round the streets, Mum. Michael's gonna do it.'

It wasn't Michael who protested this time, it was Nora. 'I'm in me fifties, me girl, not in me nineties.'

'I didn't mean nothing like that, Mum. I just thought—'

'I know what yer thought, yer thought that I'm incapable. What d'yer want, for me to wind up all old and bent like Phoebe and Sooky? Old and cranky before

193

me time? Creeping about next door like an old crone? That suit yer, would it?'

Katie slapped her dishcloth into the basin of water, sending a shower of greasy bubbles splashing up into the air, then spun round and addressed her suddenly quiet and attentive family. 'For Christ's sake,' she yelled, 'what's wrong with everyone in this house? Can't we stop rowing and squabbling and going on at each other for just five minutes? Can't we have our breakfast in peace? Maybe talk to each other instead of screeching at the top of our lungs? Be like normal people?'

Molly held out her hands to the two youngest. 'Come on, Michael, Timmy. You two are coming with me to get the shopping. Now.' She grabbed hold of their wrists in a tight, relentless grip then nodded at Sean. 'And you,' she said, 'if yer've got any sense, yer can go and fetch the coke for Mum. And without being asked again.'

Sean let out a loud puff of air. 'Not me,' he said and was gone from the kitchen, off down the passage and out of the front door.

Molly turned to Danny who shook his head and shrugged. 'Sorry, I've gotta see someone.'

Pat very deliberately and very noisily shook out his paper before rolling it into a tight cylinder and whacking it down on the table. '*I'll* get the sodding coke,' he said, shoving back his chair. 'Happy?'

Katie said nothing as she turned back to the sink to get on with the washing up, but she listened to Pat as he stomped out into the passage and then swore angrily to himself while he fought through all the old shoes and coats and boxes and bags that filled the toot cupboard under the stairs, struggling to drag out the old pushchair from all the accumulated junk.

Michael went to say something but Nora shook her

head, warning him to be quiet. 'You lads had better run back in next door and get your coats and mufflers,' she said to her grandsons. 'It'd freeze the drippings off yer nose out there.'

Despite their disinclination to go shopping with their sister – they could just guess what their friends would say if they saw them – Michael and Timmy had the sense to hurry off to get their things. They were back in less than two minutes and while Katie went over what shopping was wanted with Molly, the boys stood with their backs to their nanna while each of them went through the humiliating process of being 'got ready' to go out.

First they had their coats pulled on over the already thick layers of shirts and coarse, hand-knitted jumpers, then Nora wound each boy's bulky scarf tightly around his neck, before crossing the scratchy wool over his chest and finally fastening the ends tightly behind his back with a safety pin. She then jammed each boy's cap hard down over his ears, so he could barely see out from under the peak, and leant back to appraise her work.

'Right. Off yer go,' she said to the two squat bundles that only moments before had been a pair of lively, slightly skinny boys. 'Yer ready for anything now.'

'I'd be better off in longs,' grumbled Michael, in what had recently become his ritual whine about being too old for short trousers.

'Go 'way with yer,' roared Nora, pinching him affectionately on the little bit of cheek that still showed between his scarf and cap. 'Sure, yer barely out of calico gowns with lace frills on. Now kiss me and yer mammy byebye or Molly'll be fed up of waiting for yers.' As she leant forward and kissed the now puce-faced Michael, she slipped a coin into his hand. 'Don't tell yer mam,' she whispered with a wink, 'but tell Molly there's a good show on at the flea pit that you and young Timmy might like to see this morning while she does the shopping.'

Molly was surprised at the sudden change in Michael's attitude as he practically dragged her into the passage to get her coat, then steered her out of the house and raced across the street to number nine, where he hopped around impatiently as they waited inside the doorway for Liz Watts to put on her outdoor things.

It all became clear when Michael whispered to her about the money. Molly was relieved. She had only said she'd take them with her so they'd be far enough away to ensure that they wouldn't upset their mum; the last thing she had actually wanted was for them to be trailing along after her moaning and fighting all the time.

As they left the boys to join the rowdy gaggle of youngsters queueing outside the flea pit for the Saturday morning programme that promised two films, a newsreel, the weekly serial and a cartoon, all for a threepenny ticket, Liz didn't seem unhappy either.

'Good, now we can have a chance to talk without them two earwigging,' said Liz, slipping her arm through Molly's as they walked back towards Chrisp Street market.

'If this is gonna be about what I think it is, Lizzie Watts, yer can save yer breath.' As she spoke, Molly looked fixedly in front of her, spurning Liz's every attempt to catch her eye. 'I have enough of you going on every day on the way to and from work without having it at weekends and all.'

Liz yanked Molly to a rough halt, making her face her. 'What exactly d'yer reckon I'm gonna say then, Moll? What is it yer don't wanna hear, eh?'

Molly pulled her arm away from her friend and stuck

her hands into her waist, not caring that she was blocking the pavement and causing passers-by to step into the busy traffic on the East India Dock Road. 'You know very well. It's all I hear from yer. Yer've turned into a proper nagging old bat. I dunno how our Danny puts up with yer.'

Liz took a deep breath, linked arms with Molly again and led her gently but determinedly on. 'The way yer acting, Moll, yer'd think I was enjoying it. D'yer really think I wanna waste me time going on and on at yer?'

Molly shrugged non-committally.

'Course I don't, and you know it. It's just that I'm worried about yer. This Bob and Simon business, it's getting ridiculous. Yer've been playing this game for nearly six months now.'

She felt Molly stiffen beside her.

'I know yer think it's nothing to do with me, but yer me mate, and I care about yer. I just don't wanna think of yer letting either of 'em . . . well, let's put it like this, I don't want yer to let either of 'em take yer for a mug 'cos then yer'd be in a right state, wouldn't yer, with two of 'em to sort out?' She paused then added quietly, 'Yer won't, will yer, Moll? 'Cos the way yer acting I ain't sure what to think no more.'

'I ain't stupid, Liz, no matter what yer think. And I mean it, I honestly don't know why yer keep going on about it all the time.' She shrugged casually. 'Me nanna thinks it's all a bit of a laugh.'

Liz was stunned. 'You told yer nanna about 'em?'

'Yeah. She's known for ages.' She paused then added pointedly, 'She won't split on me.'

Liz shook her head in wonder. 'When yer say yer told her about 'em, did yer tell her *all* about 'em?'

'What you on about now, Liz?'

'Well, neither of 'em's a Catholic for a start, now is he? I'd have thought that that might be a little point yer might not have felt like mentioning.' Liz shook her head again at the very idea of what she was about to say. 'I can just imagine how yer mum'd be if she found out.'

'Just leave off, can't yer, Liz?' Molly snapped angrily. 'I ain't exactly planning on marrying either of 'em, now am I?'

'There's no point shouting at me, Molly.'

'Nanna's even said she wants to meet 'em,' Molly added with tight-lipped defiance.

'I just hope yer know what you're doing, Moll, that's all.'

Without any notice, Molly's mutinously aggressive expression was suddenly transformed into a broad, self-satisfied smile.

'I don't see anything to laugh about.'

'Don't yer? Well, do yerself a favour and have a look at his boat.' She nodded along the street at Danny who was walking towards them from the Barking Road. 'He looks even humpier than you, and that's saying something.'

They waited on the corner of Chrisp Street – Liz straight-faced and Molly grinning – for Danny to reach them. When he did so, he bent forward and pecked Liz on the cheek; neither of them smiled. Molly on the other hand laughed out loud.

'Blimey, what a pair. You just suit one another, you do. Miserable buggers.'

Still Danny didn't smile. 'Good job some of us take the world seriously, Moll.'

Molly's eyes widened and she spluttered all over him. 'Hark at you. You've changed your tune lately, ain't yer, Dan? Taking the world seriously, my eye!'

'It wouldn't hurt if you was a bit more serious at times, Moll,' Liz said, clasping Danny's hand.

'Lizzie's right,' Danny agreed. 'I was only thinking that meself. The way you act – I dunno, it ain't right.'

'What?' Molly didn't understand.

'It's like with Bob,' Danny said. 'There's a good bloke yer've got there, but the way you fart about, it's a wonder he can put up with yer. It'd be a shame to lose him 'cos yer was always playing the fool. Blokes like him don't take kindly to having their girl making a show of herself.'

'I don't believe this. What, am I on trial for smiling or something?'

'Just don't mess Bob around, that's all. He's a mate, a good mate. And, like I said, I don't want yer upsetting him. Gawd knows why, but he really likes yer. He likes yer a lot. All right?'

Molly flashed a worried glance at Lizzie. She hadn't said anything to Danny about her seeing Simon, surely? Her friend's stony stare was giving nothing away. If Liz had already split on her, Molly knew there was nothing she could do about it; but if she hadn't – and Molly hoped and prayed that was so – then Molly definitely wasn't going to give her the opportunity to say anything now.

'Come on, Lizzie,' said Molly hurriedly, pulling her away from Danny. 'We've gotta go.' She held her basket up to show her brother. 'We've gotta get all this shopping done for Mum, and then go and fetch the boys. And we don't wanna take all day about it, now do we?' She dragged Liz towards the market. 'Some of us take our responsibilities seriously. See yer later, Dan.'

Molly and Liz did the shopping in, what was for them, record time, and in almost complete silence. Molly was too busy worrying whether Danny knew about Simon to bother herself with browsing around the market, cracking jokes with the stall holders. She desperately wanted to know if Liz had said anything to him, but Liz was her best friend, so how could Molly ask her that? It would be like accusing Liz of letting her down, of splitting on her.

It was obvious to Liz that there was something up with Molly, but she thought it best to keep quiet and wait for Molly to speak when she was ready, otherwise Liz might go and say the wrong thing. Knowing Molly as she did, Liz knew she was quite capable of flying off the handle and making a loud, crowd-pulling scene right there in the packed market, in front of everyone, and Liz, coming from a much quieter lot than the Mehans, couldn't cope with that sort of thing.

It wasn't until they were almost back at the pictures to collect the boys, that Molly eventually spoke.

'Have you mentioned anything to our Dan, Liz? Anything, say, like about me seeing Simon? Anything that would, you know, make him wild with me?'

'So that's what's up with yer.' Liz turned to face her friend. 'Molly, I'm yer mate, ain't I? I'd never do anything I thought would hurt yer or get yer in trouble. Yer know that.'

Molly shrugged, ashamed that she had even said it. 'I just thought, sort of, well, what with you and Danny getting so close lately, yer might have mentioned it, like.'

'Molly, I ain't said nothing. Not to no one.'

'Well, what was Danny going on about then?'

'You know how Bob feels about yer, Moll. Right stuck on yer, he is. And Danny's his mate. You know how fellers stick together.'

'He wants to mind his own business.'

'That ain't the point, is it, Moll? The point is what you think yer up to and whether yer can handle all this, 'cos, d'yer know something, I don't think yer can. I think yer getting in a right mess, and yer won't admit it to no one, not even yerself, 'cos yer such a stubborn cow. You always have been. And if you ain't careful, yer gonna find yerself in so deep, you ain't gonna be able to do nothing about it.'

'Shut up, can't yer, Liz. I wish I'd never said nothing.'

'So do I,' Liz snapped back at her.

They walked the rest of the way to the flea pit in an even uneasier silence. To make matters worse, when they got there, the boys weren't waiting outside as arranged.

'Well, this is fair, innit?' fumed Molly, looking up and down the street for any sign of her two little brothers. 'This'll all be Michael's fault. Yer can't trust that little sod as far as yer can throw him. Always up to something. I'll skin him when I get hold of him. I swear I will.'

While Molly worked herself up into a knuckle-whitening temper, Liz did something more practical.

Grabbing hold of a startled-looking boy as he stepped out of the darkened cinema into the bright December sunshine, Liz stared down at him. 'You seen Timmy and Michael Mehan?' Her intentions might have been sensible, but, unlike Molly, she wasn't used to dealing with youngsters, and the child, terrified that he would somehow be involved in whatever no good the Mehans were up to this time, gave a single turn of his scrawny body and wriggled easily out of her grip. He would have made a clean escape, had it not been for Molly's more experienced hand reaching out and snatching hold of his collar.

'Not so fast, you,' she told him, giving him a shake for good measure. 'Now, let's start again, shall we? Have you seen Timmy and Michael Mehan?'

He knew when he was beaten. 'Micky's fighting in the lavs,' he answered sulkily, his shoulders hunched up round his ears.

'He's what?' demanded Molly.

'With that kid from Upper North Street again.' The boy flinched, half expecting Molly to clout him one for being the bearer of bad news, but, much to his relief, she let him go.

The girls didn't say anything to each other. They just stormed straight inside the cinema through the filthy, fingerprint-smeared, glass panelled doors – it wasn't called the flea pit for nothing – dumped their shopping at the feet of the elderly, scruffily uniformed commissionaire with an order to keep an eye on their bags, and headed for the foul-smelling men's lavatories at the front of the tatty little auditorium.

Inside, a gaggle of boys was standing by the single cracked sink cheering, as Michael and his adversary pummelled and kicked one another around the wet, tiled floor.

'Right, you lot, out!' commanded Molly. 'And I mean the lot of yer.'

The fight halted immediately, as did the roaring of the audience. As one, the boys made for the safety of the door.

'Not you, Michael Mehan,' boomed Molly, blocking his way. 'Or you,' she said, pointing at Timmy who was sneaking forward behind the crowd. 'Stop him, Liz.'

When all the others had left, Molly and Liz frog-marched the two boys out of the lavatory, through the musty aisles of the cinema and out into the street, collecting their shopping as they went, without a word to, or from, the doorman.

They didn't notice, but the elderly man treated them

to a smart salute; minding shopping bags was a small price to pay for being saved the job of emptying the cinema of a bunch of over-excited, toffee-covered little boys, determined to lie low until the next house began.

Squinting in the bright winter sun, Molly ran her hand distractedly through her hair. 'Will yer look at the state of yer, Michael. As if Mum ain't got enough of the hump with us all as it is. And fighting in front of Timmy and all.' She rapped her knuckles on his skull. 'Whatever's got into that stupid head o' your'n?'

'You wouldn't wanna know if I told yer,' shouted Michael defiantly. 'And anyway, Timmy was telling me to. Bloody girls, yer don't know nothing. Nothing.'

'Well, I might be a girl, but I know something. I reckon Mum's had enough of you two. And I tell yer what, I think she should put the pair of yers in one of them homes, that's what. That'd teach yer. And, when I tell her what yer've been up to – and I just might, yer know – well, I wouldn't bank on getting nothing on Christmas morning, either of yer.'

The thought of a toyless Christmas made Timmy burst into self-pitying tears.

'Aw, shut up can't yer?' Molly shoved a handkerchief at him. 'What a flaming day.'

'It was over you anyway,' said Michael, with a recklessness he immediately regretted.

'Do what?' Molly grabbed him by the shoulders. 'How d'yer mean, *over me*?'

He'd done it now, he might as well tell her everything. 'He reckoned he'd seen yer. With a boy. Over Greenwich. And he said yer was kissing him. In front of everyone. So I bashed him up.'

'And I told him to and all,' wailed Timmy, wiping his

snotty nose on the back of his arm, leaving a silvery trail on his sleeve. 'They was laughing at yer, Moll. And saying things. I didn't understand 'em, but Michael said they was rude.'

Molly looked at Liz, silently asking with her eyes if she was really hearing this.

Liz rolled her own eyes in reply then turned to Michael. She flashed him a winning smile and asked softly, 'It was that kid from Upper North Street yer was walloping, wasn't it, love?'

Michael nodded miserably. 'Yeah. I hate him.'

'Fancy you listening to stories like that,' she went on. 'As if your Molly'd be daft enough to go kissing boys right in front of anyone, especially the likes of him.'

Molly felt herself flush crimson as Michael thought about what Liz was saying; his usually cheeky face was pulled into a tight frown of concentration.

After what seemed to Molly like an age, he said, 'But he's said it before. And he said it was true.'

Liz laughed lightly as though it were all one big joke. 'Course he did. He was trying to get yer at it, wasn't he? Yer know what he's like. Little sod.' She brought her hands together in a loud clap. 'Here, tell yer what, I bet if you and Timmy promise Molly that yer'll both be good and that yer'll say no more about it, I'll bet she won't say nothing to yer mum about yer fighting. And yer know what that'll mean, don't yer?'

'We'll get our Christmas stockings?' sniffled Timmy, his big blue eyes wide and watery. 'And we won't go to no home?'

Liz ruffled his red curls. 'Yeah, that's right, darling, course it does.'

'We won't say no more, will we, Mick?' Timmy said anxiously.

Michael nodded grudgingly. 'I was only doing it for you, Moll,' he muttered.

'That's all settled then,' said Lizzie, handing some of the smaller bags to Michael and Timmy. 'Now come on, yer can help us carry this shopping home. Yer mum'll be wondering where we are.' The boys took their loads and walked ahead, whispering to one another so that Molly and Liz couldn't hear them.

'Ta, Liz,' said Molly, letting out a long slow breath as she heaved the heavy bag of potatoes on to her arm. 'I really thought I'd had it then. Yer know, my life is definitely getting too complicated for my liking.'

'Well, you're the one who knows what to do about it,' Liz replied wearily.

'To be truthful, Liz, I've known I've gotta finish with one of 'em for ages now, 'cos yer right what yer said before: if I don't, I'm gonna get meself in all sorts o' trouble.'

'How, Moll?' chipped in Michael, stopping and looking over his shoulder, his nosiness overcoming his common sense that had told him to keep his head down and his mouth shut. 'How yer gonna get yerself in trouble?'

He ducked just too late.

Molly might have done better to have tried slapping some sense into herself rather than into her little brother, because that night when she met Bob, just as she had done every Saturday for nearly six months now, all her good intentions went straight out of the window.

Her plan, worked out in her bedroom while she was getting ready, was to tell Bob she wouldn't be able to see him for a few weeks. She would then say the same thing to Simon the next day. Her idea being that she would find out which one she missed the most, and that would

205

be the one she really wanted to go out with. Simple. But when she saw Bob she forgot all about her plan.

The trouble was, he hadn't only smiled at her in the special way that he had when they met up that night, he had also told her what he was getting her for Christmas.

Bob had paid for her, Molly Katherine Mehan, to have a proper sitting at Griffiths', the portrait photographer's studio in Armagh Road. Then, to top it all, he had said that he wanted her to have her photo done, so that he could show everyone a picture of her, his girl, then they could see for themselves how beautiful she was. After that, she could hardly tell him she didn't want to see him for a while, could she? She didn't even slap down his hand, as she usually did, when he cupped it over her breast while they were kissing and cuddling in the back row of the pictures. And she was glad she hadn't . . .

That night, as Molly turned off her little bedside lamp, pulled the covers up over her shoulders, and closed her eyes, she could still feel Bob's hand caressing her. Even though she was alone, she smiled shyly at the thought of it; no one had ever done that to her before. A wave of pleasure flooded through her body.

She sighed with contentment: her worries were over. Why shouldn't she go on seeing the pair of them, she reasoned to herself, if nobody found out and nobody got hurt? Liz had sworn she hadn't said a thing to Danny, and Nanna always kept her secrets. And anyway, if things ever did become difficult, or maybe if Bob wanted to see more of her – and who could say he wouldn't now that she had let him touch her like that – she could always tell Simon that she couldn't see him any more.

And the way she was feeling about Bob right now, it wouldn't be much of a hardship dumping Simon.

The next morning, Molly was up and dressed for Mass before anyone else was even awake. Bob Jarvis wanted a photograph of her because she was beautiful and he wanted to show his friends!

She felt so full of herself: happy and glad to be alive. She was bubbling over with energy and had peeled a saucepan full of potatoes and had almost finished preparing a basin of sprouts by the time the others dragged themselves, yawning, into the kitchen for their breakfast.

As far as Molly Katherine Mehan was concerned, all was right with the world, and, amazingly for once, it seemed that the rest of her family felt the same way. Sean, of course, was a little bit humpy, but the others were as chirpy as a cage full of canaries.

Molly smiled to herself as she pulled on her coat and hat ready to leave for Mass; she had known there was nothing to worry about. Things really did have a way of working themselves out for the best.

When they got home from church, the improved mood, even more remarkably, continued.

As the family sat round the kitchen table waiting for Pat to get home so that they could eat their Sunday midday meal together, Katie sang to herself. Taking a dish full of crispy golden roast potatoes from the oven, she didn't care that she didn't have a huge joint of sirloin to carve up for her family, there were plenty of vegetables to fill their plates and to stretch what meat they did have. She was just pleased as punch that, for whatever reason, things seemed to be like they used to be: the little ones chattering away and laughing, Molly having a joke with Nora, Danny with his nose stuck in the paper – at least he wasn't moaning! – and Sean playing with Rags, teasing him with a block of wood on a piece of string. Katie presumed it was the Christmas spirit getting into everyone; even the most miserable of souls couldn't resist Christmas.

As she put the roasting dish on to the table, Pat arrived home, looking tired out but happy, and red-cheeked from the cold December air. He hadn't been to Mass with them, but had been pushing his way though the crowds in Club Row, as he did every year, in his search for bargain bits and pieces to put in his family's Christmas stockings. As well as the bags full of secret things he was carrying, he had a huge aspidistra in an elaborately painted china art pot propped in the crook of his arm.

He bent down and, putting the enormous plant on the table in front of where Katie was trying to dish up, he kissed her noisily on the forehead.

'I was gonna save this for Christmas morning, darling,' he said, pointing proudly at the glossy, dark green leaves, 'but I didn't think I could hide it from yer.'

'I think I might just have noticed it,' grinned Katie, peering through the foliage at her family. 'But yer shouldn't have wasted yer money on me.'

'What's the loan club for if it ain't for splashing out at Christmas?'

Pat kissed her again, this time gently on the tip of her nose, making Timmy and Michael slide under the table with embarrassment, then disappeared upstairs on the pretext of putting his coat and cap away in the wardrobe, which was something he never did, so everyone, except young Timmy, knew he was actually hiding their presents.

Katie continued dishing up slices of greasy, stuffed breasts of lamb that she had spent the afternoon before boning out, rolling and tying with lengths of string.

'Cor,' said Pat, coming back into the kitchen, settling himself at the table and pulling his plate towards him. 'I could smell this right upstairs. Handsome.'

'When yer was upstairs hiding our presents, d'yer mean?' beamed Michael.

Timmy frowned at his brother then turned to his dad. 'What's Michael mean, Dad?'

Pat looked puzzled. 'Dunno, little 'un.' He turned to Michael. 'Presents, yer say? How d'yer mean, Michael? Father Christmas is the one what does all that.' He held his hand to his face, hiding his eyes from Timmy and then winked at Michael. 'Ain't that right, son? Ain't that what yer mean?'

Michael copied his father, hiding his face from Timmy and winking broadly, something he had only recently learnt how to do without holding his eyelid down with his finger. 'That's right, Dad. I was only having a laugh.'

Timmy looked relieved; he didn't even lose his happy smile when Sean tutted bad-temperedly at all the foolishness, but at least, Katie was glad to note, he had the decency not to say anything and ruin it for Timmy.

Surprisingly, it was Danny who infuriated Katie, by spoiling the happy atmosphere.

Timmy had just done as his mother had asked, and had said grace, remembering to speak nicely and not to sniff once, and Pat had commented on how lucky they should count themselves to have a good meal on their table and a loving family to share it with during times that were still hard, if not worse, for so many.

'Lucky?' Danny said, shaking his head as though his father was an ignorant child who knew nothing of the

209

world. 'How can yer say we're lucky? We're having to struggle every single day just to try and keep things together. What sort o' luck d'yer call that?'

Pat finished chewing his mouthful of lamb, then said slowly, 'We're more fortunate than most round here, son.'

'What, you only working every other day, *if* it's a good week. You call that luck?'

Nora nodded and crossed herself. 'We should thank God for what we have, Danny. Sure, have yer seen the look of that poor Mr Milton?'

'Huh!' sneered Danny. 'Bring it on 'emselves, their sort.'

Katie stopped eating and stared at her son. 'Would you get on with that dinner?'

Pat was frowning. ' "Their sort"?' he said, as much to himself as to Danny.

'Yeah, their sort. The sort what won't help 'emselves by getting up off their lazy . . .' Danny nearly said arses, but changed his mind. ' . . . backsides and get things moving. I've said it before but people are too stupid to listen. We wanna start copying Germany or this country'll never get back on its feet. They'll have everything, and what'll we have? Nothing, that's what. And unless we do something about it soon, that's all we'll deserve and all.'

Pat wasn't sure where to start; not only was his son talking the rubbish he knew drove his dad to distraction, but he was interrupting the Sunday dinner after his mother had gone to so much trouble for them all. And she had been so happy. It was for Katie's sake that Pat did his best to control his temper.

'There's proper ways for people to go about getting what they want, boy,' he said.

Danny threw up his hands. 'That's exactly what I

mean. We've been sitting back for too long. Things have gotta change in the East End. We've let 'em get away with it for too long. We've gotta act. Now.'

Katie was more than ready to put in her own two penn'orth to the argument, whether it meant spoiling the Sunday dinner or not, but Pat beat her to it.

'Exactly how d'yer mean?' he asked.

'There's plenty can be done.'

Sean, without saying a word, stretched his arm out between Danny and his dad and reached for the potatoes.

Pat pushed the pan roughly towards Sean with the back of his hand, as he continued to speak to Danny. 'What sort of things? Having another general strike, maybe?'

'Do me a favour,' Danny sneered contemptuously. 'You and yer union meetings. What good does all that do? Proper action, that's what's needed. Real politics. Getting rid of the people what cause all the trouble in the first place.'

'And what people would they be then?'

'Scum.'

Slowly, Pat put his knife and fork together on his plate. 'I asked yer what people yer meant. Yer wouldn't mean the people they write about in them leaflets, would yer? The leaflets what them no-good filth hand out about Jewish people?'

Danny lifted his chin and looked challengingly at his father. 'I bet you ain't even seen 'em. That's you all over, that is, talking about things yer know nothing about.'

'And what you're talking about ain't nothing to do with no politics, boy.'

'Ain't it?' Danny asked insolently. 'What would you know? You don't know nothing. I've been talking to a bloke who knows more'n you'll ever know.'

Katie could hold her tongue no longer. 'Danny! That's enough. That's no way to talk to yer father. I won't have it. Especially at me own table.'

'No, yer all right, Katie. Let him speak,' Pat insisted, still sounding calm. 'I'm interested in hearing what he's got to say.' He held out his hand, gesturing for Danny to speak. 'Well? Come on then, who is this bloke who knows so much?'

All eyes were on Danny. 'That don't matter,' he said, smiling knowingly. 'What matters is that I'm seeing things straight for the first time.' He gave a sneering little laugh. 'I thought yer'd be pleased. It was you what always wanted me to take an interest in things. So I have, and now I'm just speaking out about what's right, that's all.'

Michael opened his mouth to say something, but Nora stopped him; she jabbed her finger towards his plate. 'Just eat,' she said under her breath. For once, Michael was sensible enough to do as he was told.

'I'd be right interested to know what yer've got to complain about.' Pat was leaning right across the table. 'Joe Palmer's done you proud. He's given yer every opportunity a young feller could want. He's made himself a good business out of carting, even during hard times like these, and if yer play yer cards right and keep yer trap shut so that yer can learn something from someone with a bit of sense, yer might be able to do the same one day.'

Danny leant back in his chair and folded his arms defiantly across his chest. 'I've been thinking about turning me job up, if yer must know.'

'You *what*?'

'I don't like the idea of working for a didicoy.'

Pat whacked his hand down on the table, making them

all flinch, but no one except Danny said a word. They just listened, shocked at what they were hearing as, eyes shining, Danny launched into a speech about what was wrong with the East End and how it was all the fault of people he described as 'filthy outsiders'.

What Danny said was completely at odds with everything that the Mehan children had been brought up to believe in by their parents and their nanna, but it was the way in which he was speaking that really bewildered them all. He was talking as though he had learnt a speech in the schoolroom, repeating it as though it was the five times table. But his words were nothing to do with how many fives made fifty; these were words of hatred.

Molly felt sick; unlike her dad, she knew exactly from whom Danny, the brother she had always idolised, had got these terrible and frightening ideas. They were all too familiar. She could hear Bob speaking in her head, as clearly as though he were standing there next to her, when he had accused her of speaking to a Jew; she could feel his hands gripping her, hurting her . . .

Nora couldn't care less where her grandson had got his ideas from, she just knew she had to make him shut up. 'You,' she shouted, standing up and pointing at Danny, 'are a complete disgrace to yer mother's table.'

Danny lowered his gaze, unable to face his grandmother, but his words were still defiant. 'I'm only saying what I know's true.'

'True?' demanded Katie. 'I won't have this sort of talk in here. And yer won't be giving up no job neither. D'you hear me?'

Danny shrugged moodily.

'And another thing, what's all that about the Miltons? You know better than to turn on people, especially people what ain't as fortunate as yerself. Us Mehans help people, we don't kick 'em when they're down.'

'Yeah, Dan,' Michael butted in, his mouth full of potatoes and gravy. He gave a sly sideways grin at Timmy, who was sitting next to him, wide-eyed with alarm, wondering if this latest scrap would mean that Father Christmas's visit would really be cancelled this time. 'Just think,' Michael went on, nearly bursting from the effort of stopping himself from laughing out loud, 'how Phoebe Tucker always goes on about how Mum helps Mr Barber.'

Pat shoved back his chair and stood up. 'I'm going over the Queen's. I've had enough.'

Katie glared at Michael, then at Danny. She could have bashed their heads together. If Pat reckoned that he'd had enough, how did he think she felt? But she didn't want any more trouble, not at Christmas, so instead of hollering at her husband, she said quietly, 'How about yer meal, Pat?'

'I ain't hungry,' he said stiffly, pulling open the kitchen door and letting in an icy blast from the passage. 'You go and find one of yer friends from round the church to give it to. I'm sure they'd appreciate it more than me.'

Forgetting her resolve to keep the peace, Katie hollered at him as she chased him out into the passage, 'And who did you have in mind, eh?'

Pat didn't answer; he pulled open the street door, slamming it back on its hinges.

'I'm talking to you, Pat!'

He turned round very slowly and looked at her. 'I can't take much more, Kate,' he said slowly.

'*You* can't?' she shrieked. 'I've had it with you. You and yer accusations. D'you know something, it'd be your fault if I ever did go off with someone, 'cos you'll drive me to it, the way you're going.'

'You bitch,' he breathed.

'Don't you *dare* speak to me like that.'

'When yer say things like that? Why shouldn't I?'

''Cos if you do, you can get out.'

'I'll do exactly that if you push me any harder, Kate, I swear I will.'

'Well, go on then, bugger off!' screamed Katie at the top of her voice. 'Yer've threatened it enough times lately. Why don't yer just do it?'

When Katie came back in the kitchen, Michael giggled nervously, nudging Timmy in the ribs to join in.

Katie turned on Michael. 'And as for you!'

'Me?' asked Michael, a picture of puzzled, injured innocence. 'What have I done?'

'You're old enough to know better, that's what.' Katie bit the inside of her cheek, doing her best not to cry in front of her children.

Timmy wasn't so successful in hiding his tears; his bottom lip trembled as his mind whirled, and he tried to think of something, anything, that might salvage the situation and guarantee his Christmas stocking being filled.

'Now, all of yer, get on with yer dinner,' sniffed Katie, waving her fork at her children.

'It's lovely, darling, just right,' said Nora gently.

They ducked their heads and returned quietly and without appetite to their food, but the silence was shattered as Timmy, an idea suddenly coming to him as to how he might take his mum's mind off the row, yelled excitely, 'I never give yer this!' He leant back in his chair and dug deeply into the pocket of his shorts. 'I

215

forgot. It's been in me pocket for ages and ages.' He handed her a screwed up piece of paper across the table.

'What is it?' asked Katie.

'I dunno. Teacher give it to me.'

'When? When did you see your teacher?'

Timmy couldn't think back beyond what he had been doing that morning. 'I ain't sure.' He frowned with the effort of trying to remember. 'It must have been before we broke up.'

'Course it must, stupid,' sneered Michael. Then a horrified look of realisation came over his face. 'You big girl,' he hissed at his brother. 'That was when the nit nurse come round the school, wasn't it? I told yer to chuck it away. I told yer.'

'Timmy?' Katie confronted him. 'Is this true?'

'Yeah,' Timmy nodded gloomily as he too realised what he had done: his hoped for distraction from the row had become just another nightmare. 'I'm cootie. She said I had to have me head shaved, but I run off while she wasn't looking. And 'cos it was the last day—'

Timmy never had the chance to finish his tale of how he had escaped the nit nurse's clippers.

'Right,' said Katie, snapping into action, 'dinner's over. Molly clear that lot away. And you two,' she pointed at Timmy and Michael, 'yer not going out to play, right. Yer gonna help me fill that bath up and I'm gonna scrub yer from head to toe and I'm gonna go through every one of them red curly hairs o' your'n with that steel comb.'

Sean couldn't be bothered to sit through any more of this; without saying a word, he stood up, tucked Rags under his arm and walked out of the back door. Timmy started crying again and Michael, looking as though he was ready to kill his little brother, was whispering something threatening to him under his breath. Molly and Nora began clearing the table. Only Danny sat still, apparently calmly finishing off his lamb.

'That'll be mixing with them Miltons,' he said, sopping up the fatty gravy with a piece of dry bread. 'Dirty buggers, they are. Yer can see how they live. Just like pikeys. And I'm sure that Milton's a foreigner.'

Katie sighed, a mixture of tiredness, anger and sadness almost overwhelming her. She had been hoping, praying, for a nice quiet Sunday and it had seemed, for just a while, that she was going to get it. She had been so confident that Pat had got over all his nonsense about Frank Barber at last, and that maybe even Sean was beginning to grow out of the miserable, horrible phase he had been going through. But now, without warning, Danny had caused all this – Danny, whom, out of all of the boys, Katie had thought would never cause her any trouble.

She stood up and took her apron down from the nail behind the door. 'You seem to have forgotten, Danny,' she said, her tone cold as ice as she wrapped the strings twice around her and tied them in a tight, waist-pinching bow, 'yer own grandparents were foreigners. People in trouble they were, and made welcome in this country when they needed a place to go to.'

'They wasn't foreigners,' grimaced Danny. 'Them Jews, they're the foreigners.' He looked about him, gesturing with his hands as though he were addressing a meeting. 'Ain't none of you lot heard how they treat decent English girls what work for 'em in them sweat shops? They want kicking out of this country, the lot of 'em.'

'They pay good money, so I've heard,' Nora answered. 'Me too,' said Molly, quietly.

Danny opened his mouth to speak, but Katie would have no more of it. She slammed her hand down on the table. 'Just shut up, can't yer? All of yer. And you, Danny, you get out of my sight before I do something I'd regret.'

'I'll be glad to.' He scraped his chair back across the lino. 'I wanna be with people who talk sense, not through their arses.'

Katie dropped her chin, but she just didn't have the energy to reply. She waited until she heard the front door slam, then said with as much dignity as she could muster, 'Timmy, you help Molly and your nanna with that clearing up, while I fetch the bath in from the yard.' She pulled open the back door, ignoring the freezing wind. Looking over her shoulder she added, 'And don't get yer head near yer sister's, we don't want her getting 'em and all. And you, Michael, you can get out here and chop some kindling for the copper.'

Katie dragged the big tin bath inside the kitchen and manoeuvred it past the table, positioning it in front of the Kitchener. Then she straightened up, tucking a curl of her thick auburn hair behind her ear.

'Why can't we be a family like we used to be?' she asked. 'I know times are hard, but ain't that all the more reason to stick together?' She snatched up the kettle from the stove. 'Let's get to the tap, Mum,' she said to Nora, reaching across her. 'I mean, just look at them Miltons. What have they got? Nothing. Potless. But you don't hear them rowing all the time, do yer?'

'They had the school board man round before we broke up,' Michael piped up as he came back into the kitchen carrying a bare handful of sticks that he held out to his mum for approval. 'All staying off school again, they was.'

Katie set the filled kettle back on the gas stove and, taking the kindling from Michael, she shook her head

218

disgustedly. 'Don't you start sounding off like Danny. The only reason them poor little devils never go to school is 'cos their boots're always in pawn.' She carried the pathetic bundle of sticks over to the back door. 'I'm going out to light the copper now and when I get back in here I don't want another word out of any of yer 'cos I mean it this time, any more rows and all the bits you was gonna get for Christmas are going straight over to the Miltons. This is yer last chance. Yer very last chance.'

As she pulled the door to, she said to herself, 'Now there's a bunch of kids who'd appreciate getting something for Christmas, let alone the stuff this lot expect.'

She shivered and pulled her cardigan round her shoulders as she ducked inside the little flagstoned scullery and bent down to set the wood under the copper. It felt cold enough for snow. 'It's my fault,' she went on to herself as she fiddled with the matches. 'I've ruined them kids o' mine.'

Later that afternoon Molly gingerly opened her bedroom door and poked her head out on to the narrow landing.

Hardly daring to breathe, she listened for sounds from her parents' room. She couldn't believe how long it had taken them to stop shouting at each other after they had gone upstairs, when her dad had got back from the pub.

For a while she had really thought she would have to miss seeing Simon, and just leave him standing waiting for her outside Stepney East Station. But, if her dad's snores were anything to go by, they had exhausted themselves at last, and were having a Sunday afternoon sleep.

Molly was just about to close her bedroom door and

sneak off when a loud crash at the back of the house made her nearly stumble backwards down the stairs.

'What the hell was that?' she whispered to herself. She threw down her bag on the floor and crawled across her bed to look out of her bedroom window. She pushed the frame up to the top of the sash and stuck her head outside into the cold air.

'I might have known it was you two,' she said at the sight which confronted her – Timmy and Michael climbing out of the back bedroom window of their nanna's house on to the ice-covered, corrugated iron lavvy roof.

'Yer'll wake everyone up in here. And yer'll be skinned alive when Mum catches yer.' Remembering she was dressed to go out, Molly whipped off her hat and hid it behind her back. 'Yer know she told us all to stay in our rooms till tea time.'

Michael grinned saucily. 'We won't tell on you if you don't tell on us.'

'What d'yer mean, tell on me? Yer cheeky little bugger!'

'Here, listen to her language, Tim,' grinned Michael. 'Mum'd love that, and she'd love yer sitting in yer room with yer hat on and all. Or maybe yer was thinking about going out somewhere?' With that, the boys waved to their sister and skidded down the lavvy roof on their backsides, and disappeared over the wall.

Molly could have spat; that bloody kid from Upper North Street, had he seen or said something else?

Whether he had or not, it was too late to worry about that now; if she didn't get going right away she might as well not bother going at all. Without even stopping to check in the glass if it was straight, Molly stuck her hat back on her head and rushed down the stairs. When she eventually arrived at Stepney East Station, Simon was standing there waiting for her, shivering like a half-set jelly. She looked round to make sure that there was nobody passing by who knew her, then she pecked him hastily on the cheek.

'It was easier meeting in the summer, wasn't it?' she said, clapping her gloved hands together. 'One of us is gonna freeze to death at this rate.'

'I know a way to keep warm,' said Simon, his dark eyes shining out from beneath the snap brim of his hat.

She raised an eyebrow. 'Aw yeah, and how's that then?'

He laughed ironically. 'It wouldn't be my first choice, but how about if I take you for a slap-up tea.'

Molly sighed and clutched her heart dramatically. 'I suppose that'll have to do.'

They didn't link arms as they walked off in the direction of Aldgate, where they knew they would find plenty of cosy little coffee shops and cafés open on a Sunday, but walked along side by side. They never discussed it, they just had the awkward understanding that they kept their distance when there was any chance of being seen by anyone they knew.

That afternoon, as they had done so many times before, they talked almost non-stop, pausing only to swallow cup after cup of stewed brown tea to wash down thick sandwiches of hot salt beef and mustard, and quivering slabs of sultana-dotted cheesecake. They always had so much to say to one another, that the hours just slipped away, and, all too soon, it was time to go.

As Simon walked Molly back towards the corner where he would leave her, they were still talking.

'You've given me so many things to think about, since I've met you, Simon,' she said. 'And you always give me the feeling I wanna know more.'

Simon smiled. 'I'm glad.'

'Some people . . .' she began, thinking of the scene around the dinner table, with Danny shouting the odds, and about what Bob would have to say if he could see her now. 'Some people say some really stupid things. But I reckon it's not always because they're bad. I reckon sometimes it's because they've just listened to the wrong people and haven't had the chance to know any better. I reckon anyone could learn to think the right way if other people took the time to explain things to them, don't you?'

Simon nodded. 'I *think* you're right. But in the end, we all have to make up our own minds about things, no matter what other people say.'

She thought for a moment. 'I've been thinking about joining the library in Poplar High Street. There's some things I wanna get straight. To understand more.'

'Good idea. I was going to join one myself but my uncle stopped me. He won't let me use the public library.'

'Why not? You love reading. That's what gave me the idea to join.'

'My uncle says the books are contaminated,' Simon said sheepishly. 'You know, not knowing who's been touching them.'

'He sounds a bit barmy to me. Or a right snob more like.' Molly stopped in her tracks and her hand flew to her mouth. 'I'm sorry, me and my big gob. That just sort of slipped out.'

'Don't worry. Anyway you're right.'

'What, he's barmy? Or he's a snob?'

'Let's just say he's not barmy. And he's not really a snob either. He just has very set ideas about what's right and he sticks to them. He likes things to be the way he thinks they should be.'

'What, like Jewish boys having Jewish girlfriends?'

Simon laughed sardonically. 'Come on, time's moving on.'

He placed his hand on Molly's arm to guide her forward, but she didn't budge. Instead, she dipped her chin and said quietly, 'I do love being with yer, yer know, Simon.'

'I'm glad.'

'But . . .'

'But?'

She lifted her eyes and looked directly at him. 'Do you honestly think we can go on like this?'

'I knew this would happen.' He pulled off his hat and ran his hands distractedly through his hair. 'I suppose I should just be surprised it's taken this long. Look, Molly, I'm not making any excuses for my uncle, it's just that I owe him so much. I don't know what would have happened to me if his family hadn't taken me in.'

'Yeah, I know.' Shivering, Molly pulled her collar up around her ears. 'And that's why it's never gonna work, is it? He's never gonna approve of me in a million years.' She hesitated, half turned away from him. This was her chance to sort it all out. 'I don't think I should see yer any more, Simon. I mean, there's people round here who don't like what we're doing, people who stop us from even having a cuddle, 'cos we're scared they might see us. People who could hurt yer, Simon.' She started sniffing. 'I couldn't bear it if anything happened to yer.'

'Molly, don't, please.' He looked up and down the cold street. In the miserable half-light of the late winter afternoon he could see that apart from the two of them and a man rushing past with his head down against the icy wind, it was deserted.

Simon swallowed hard, pulled Molly towards him and kissed her full on the mouth.

Molly reeled backwards. 'Blimey.'

Simon looked grave, not at all like a young man who had just acted so impetuously. 'Now, is there anything else you feel you're missing out on when you're with me?'

The tears spilled from her eyes as she whispered, 'The other night, I dreamt me and you was dancing. We was twirling around and around. In front of everyone. And we didn't care who'd see us.'

He took out his handkerchief, wiped her face dry and then kissed her eyelids. He laughed mirthlessly. 'I make you cry and, pathetic as it sounds, I can't even dance.' He stuck his handkerchief back in his pocket. 'In fact, I'm totally useless to you.'

'Don't say that. Please.'

He pulled her close to his chest again. 'Then say you won't leave me, Molly.'

'No,' she sobbed. 'I won't leave yer. I don't reckon I'd know how to.'

He closed his eyes and let out a loud sigh of relief. Then he held her away from him. 'Come on. We really had better be going.'

They walked along the icy street, clasping each other's hand as though that was the way they always walked along together.

'Least it ain't boring,' she said, blinking back her tears and trying to smile at him. 'I mean, how many girls have got a secret boyfriend?'

Simon squeezed her hand. 'Wouldn't you rather have a nice, easy, boring boyfriend you could take home to tea and go dancing with?'

'No fear,' she sniffed. 'I think it's the worst thing in

the world being bored. All our family's the same. It's our wild Irish blood, see?' Tears were running down her cheeks again. 'None of us ever really thinks things through. We just jump in with both feet. Trouble is, sometimes we're in too deep before we realise it.'

They were still holding hands as they reached the corner of Stainsby Road, where Simon was going to leave Molly. But instead of the whispered goodbyes and the promises to meet next week that she had expected, Simon grabbed her roughly by the arm, and dragged her back against the wall. 'Look at that!' he gasped, pointing along the street.

Smoke was pouring out of the windows of one of the houses. People were milling around outside, shouting, panicking, giving orders and crying out. Someone had organised a chain of buckets to try to quench the flames but they seemed to be having little effect.

A woman was pointing to the upstairs and screaming, 'Help her, someone! Help her! She's only a kid!'

Simon ripped off his overcoat and hat and thrust them at Molly.

'What yer doing?'

'Someone's got to climb up there, and none of those seem very keen.'

'I'll help yer.'

'No, Molly. Stay here. Please, I mean it. I need to know you're safe. I can't be worrying about you as well.'

'All right.'

'Promise?'

She nodded, kissed him hurriedly on the lips, then watched as he ran along the street towards a group of men who were arguing loudly about how best to reach the upstairs rooms.

She honestly intended to wait there as he had asked, but the feeling that she shouldn't be letting him take such a risk by himself got the better of her. She had to do something to help.

With Simon's coat flapping around her legs, she ran over to a huddle of women who were standing across the street, opposite the house.

'Can I do anything?'

'Do?' one of the woman snapped at her. 'Shoot that bastard landlord, that's what yer can do. That girl's gas stove ain't been working right for weeks, has it, Flo?' she said to the woman next to her. 'But would he do anything about it? Course not. Yet what d'yer think would've happened if she hadn't paid her bloody rent, eh? I'll tell you, he'd have been round here a bit sharpish then all right. And had her right out on her ear'ole. Now her little kiddy's up there in all them flames.'

'Look,' shouted the woman called Flo. 'That feller. He's only climbing up the drainpipe. That'll never hold his weight.'

Molly looked on in horror as she saw Simon, his shirt sleeves rolled up above his elbows, inching his way up from the downstairs window ledge, the rusty-looking pipe his only support.

He had reached a join in the pipe, just above the street door, when another man scrambled on to the window ledge behind him and started shouting.

'We don't need the likes of you helping decent people like us,' he hollered, dragging Simon backwards by his trouser leg. 'Now, get down, Jew boy, and clear off back where yer come from.'

Molly could hardly believe it as the woman standing next to her joined in. 'Yeah,' she shouted, 'piss off out of it, Yiddle. We don't need the likes of you round here helping us.'

As Simon dropped on to the pavement, the man who had dragged him down turned to face the others. Molly shrank back against the wall. It was Bob Jarvis.

'Let's get some decent Englishmen up here,' ordered Bob, obviously not intending to climb the pipe himself.

Molly turned her back on the scene and ran, head down, back to the far end of the street where she hid round the corner like a criminal, and waited as Simon made his way back to her, accompanied by a barrage of humiliating catcalls and foul language.

Her decision had really been made this time. Molly was no longer seeing two fellers. She might have let Bob Jarvis touch her in a way that she had never let anyone else touch her ever before, and he might have been Danny's friend, but he was no longer any friend of hers.

She supposed she should have felt more relieved.

10

Christmas Eve had come at last; it was still perishing cold, but instead of the snow that the two youngest Mehans had longed for, the big day had brought only freezing fog, and now, at just an hour before midnight, the temperature had dropped even lower.

In the kitchen of number twelve, totally against the usual way of things, Timmy and Michael were arguing with their mum that, at such a late hour, they really should be next door in their nanna's, all tucked up in bed.

Katie would hear none of it.

'It's no good you going on, Michael,' she said, pulling on her coat over her thick woollen dress. 'Yer gonna be in this pageant, the pair of yer, and that's the last I'm saying on the matter. Now, come on. Have yer got yer word sheets?'

Michael nodded defeatedly, then turned to his equally dejected-looking brother. 'I told yer to say you had the bellyache,' he hissed at Timmy. 'Now all the kids are gonna see us and laugh at us.' He shrugged into the oversized topcoat he had recently inherited from Sean. 'And don't come running to me when they start on yer.'

'Least the narrator don't have to wear a stupid costume,' Timmy sniped back at him. 'Look at me. I look like a right big girl.'

Michael looked Timmy up and down. 'Yeah, yer do.'

'Well, I think yer look gorgeous. Don't you, Pat?' Nora sighed happily, admiring her grandson's outfit that she and Katie had cobbled together from a threadbare tea towel and an old dressing gown they had borrowed off Harold from the Queen's Arms. 'Fancy, a grandson of mine playing Joseph in the nativity play. And on Christmas Eve, in front of everyone! I'm that chuffed I could burst, so I could.'

'Yer look the proper part, son,' said Pat stiffly, ruffling his youngest child's hair.

'Yer right, Pat, he really does,' said Katie, flashing a sideways glance at her husband.

Pat turned away from her and started talking to Michael.

Katie was getting really cheesed off with his attitude. Since their row last week, instead of getting over it as he always did, Pat had been so cold with her. No matter how she tried to jolly him along, he just nodded or grunted in reply. He was talking to all the others well enough – maybe not so much to Danny – but he treated her as though she wasn't even there half the time. Still, this feeling sorry for herself wouldn't do, she had other things to worry about.

Picking up her handbag from the dresser and checking she had enough change for the collection in her purse, Katie gave her family a final once-over, then said briskly: 'You all look right smart, the lot of yer, but we'd better hurry along now or Father Hopkins'll wonder where we've got to.'

With her best hat pinned to her mass of auburn hair, Katie held her head high, and linked her arm decisively through Pat's. 'Ready?' she asked, defying him to say otherwise.

He nodded, but his arm felt rigid to her touch.

She would just have to make the best of it, she decided; if he wanted to play silly beggars, that was up to him.

And so, Katie and Pat led their family in straggly procession out of the house and round the corner into Grundy Street, where they joined the stream of people making their way to the Midnight Mass being held at Saint Mary and Saint Joseph's Catholic church.

As they crossed over Upper North Street into Canton Street, Molly swallowed hard, her mouth dry as she recalled the scene when she had stood, just around the corner from there, watching Bob Jarvis attack Simon as he had tried to rescue the child from the burning house. Could it really have only been just a week ago?

The fire and the successful if dramatic rescue of the little girl had been practically all that anyone had been talking about during the last few days. All sorts of stories and speculations about what had happened had been passed around – most of them by Phoebe Tucker – that Molly knew to be exaggerated or plain lies, but she had said nothing. She wasn't even supposed to have been out of her room last Sunday afternoon, let alone out in the street watching a Jewish boy her mum knew nothing about trying to climb up a drainpipe.

But, for the moment at least, Simon wasn't on the top of Molly's list of worries; like her mother, she had more pressing concerns, although Molly's were rather more troubling than whether the boys would remember their positions in the play. Molly was fretting about Bob Jarvis.

It had been easy enough getting Danny to give him a message explaining that she couldn't see him this week, what with all the things her mum needed help with, it being Christmas and everything, but she wasn't looking forward to telling him that she had no intention of seeing him ever again. She felt stupid now, ashamed even, that it had taken so long for her to admit to herself that Bob Jarvis wasn't a bloke to be messed around with. In fact, if she was totally honest, she reckoned Bob Jarvis was a bloke to be scared of.

By the time they reached the church, Molly's nerves were so on edge that she almost leapt in the air when she felt someone slip their arm around her waist.

'Look at these lot, will yer?' the person breathed angrily.

With a gulp of relief, Molly recognised her nanna's soft Irish brogue.

'I don't know,' Nora went on, 'heathens most of them. I mean, when did you last see *her* at Mass?' Nora pointed at a flushed-looking woman who was propped unsteadily against the church wall. 'Not once in a blue moon, that's when. And from the state of her, I can guess where she's been all night before she got round to dragging her fat carcass over here.' Nora turned to her daughter and jerked her head towards the church doors. 'Come on, Katie, let's get inside, love, before this lot nabs all the best seats.'

Nora, her elbows stuck out like the spikes on Boadicea's chariot, pushed her way through the crowd, making a path so that her daughter's family could follow her with a bit of dignity.

As usual, Midnight Mass was packed; there were those who, like Liz Watts's family, attended church regularly, only missing Mass under extreme circumstances. Then there were Nora's heathens, the complete non-believers, straight from the surrounding pubs who thought attending Midnight Mass and watching the local kids perform their nativity play was as traditional a part of Christmas as hanging up the stockings and getting in the crates of light ale for a knees-up with the neighbours. And then there were the occasional churchgoers who, according to Nora, were the worst of all. At least the heathens weren't hypocrites, they were just there out of some sentimental notion of what Christmas was all about, but the occasionals, the ones who only turned up for festivals and holy days of obligation – Nora, if she had her way, would have banned every one of them from the church, and consigned them all to an eternity of the tortures of purgatory.

But once inside, safely settled in what she considered her rightful place in the front pew, Nora forgot all about her inconsistent neighbours as the atmosphere of the church took effect on her. The sight of the children, looking deceptively angelic in the soft, transfiguring shimmer of candlelight, as they took their places around the little wooden crib, built especially for the occasion by Bill Watts, would have brought a lump to the throat of even the most hardened of sceptics, but for Nora, having her grandchildren taking leading roles in the pageant, was as close to heaven on earth as she could imagine.

The magic worked on Molly too; all visions of Bob Jarvis melted as Michael began retelling, in a high, quavering voice, the age-old story of the holy birth. And when Timmy, playing the part of Joseph, led his tiny Virgin Mary from inn to inn, only to be turned away, Molly had tears running down her cheeks.

Katie had determined to keep her chin in the air and her eyes dry, until the service was over at least, but when the little ones began to sing 'O Little Town of Bethlehem', she practically snatched Pat's big white handkerchief from him, pretending she needed to blow her nose.

Even Danny and Sean couldn't conceal their pride when, with hardly a stumble, Michael finished reading the final words off his card. Sean really felt like clapping but knew his mum wouldn't approve in church, so when his two little brothers paraded back to join their family for the final part of the service, he treated them both to a rough punch in the shoulder by way of congratulations instead, and shoved up to let them sit between him and Molly.

The two little ones sat there as good as gold, right up until the final blessing, then they were up on their feet and ready to flee. Not only were they keen to get home – it was as good as Christmas itself once Mass was over – but they wanted to escape having to run the gauntlet of jeers of the kids who had not been in the play. It took all of Molly's strength to stop them sprinting off down the aisle.

'Now we're for it,' Michael hissed at his little brother. 'I told yer to run when we had the chance.'

But instead of the expected telling off, Katie smiled benignly at them. 'Why don't all you kids get off home?' she suggested. 'Me and yer nanna . . .' She flicked her eyes sideways at Pat and saw he was smiling too. ' . . . and yer dad won't be long, we'll just have a word with Father Hopkins.'

The little ones didn't need telling twice; they clambered over Molly's lap into the aisle and were off like a pair of escaped convicts, closely followed by Sean and Danny.

Katie held out her arm to her mum. 'Coming?'

Nora shook her head, and grinned shrewdly at her daughter. 'No. You go with your husband and say your good nights to Father Hopkins. I'll be out to join yers in a minute. I just want a few quiet moments.'

Molly stood up to let her parents pass, then went to join them in the aisle, but Nora pulled her back down into the pew. 'No, you wait here with me, love.'

'All right, Nanna,' Molly said, settling back, not really understanding what was going on.

Katie looked up at Pat; he was smiling down at her, a genuine, warm smile, not the sort of expression you flashed out of habit or good manners. Happier than she had been for a week, Katie took her husband's arm and let him lead her outside to where the priest would be holding court.

Molly sat by her nanna's side and waited. When the church was empty and the sounds from outside were muffled by the heavy oak door, Nora lowered herself on to her knees and nodded for Molly to do the same.

'All I ask,' Nora whispered under her breath, her eyes fixed on the stained-glass window above the altar as it glowed in the flickering candlelight, 'is for my family to be as happy as they are tonight. That their differences stay settled, and their love for one another never leaves their hearts.'

Satisfied that she had only asked for what was fair, and that there had been no selfishness in her request, Nora pulled herself to her feet. 'Come along then,' she said to Molly, ushering her into the aisle where Nora joined her. They both crossed themselves and then began to walk out of the church.

Just as they reached the door, Nora stopped, turned round, bobbed down, crossed herself again and mumbled quietly to herself, 'And God bless and protect my Stephen, wherever he might be.'

Then she straightened up, took a deep breath and steered Molly out of the door into the freezing night air. She stood on the step looking round to see who was still in the churchyard; Katie and Pat had already gone.

'Right, my love,' she said, buttoning her coat up to

her chin. 'This is as good a time as any. I want to talk to you about these young fellers of yours.'

Molly hesitated for a moment, then said quietly, 'There's only one now, Nanna.'

'So, yer've picked at last. Good. Good.'

Molly shrugged shyly. 'Yeah, I suppose I have.'

'Well, I think it's about time yer let yer old nanna have a look at him. If you've found happiness you make sure you grab it by the tail, girl.'

'Do you believe that, Nanna? No matter what?'

'I do.' She held out her arm to Molly. 'Come on, you can tell me all about him on the way home.'

Molly didn't move from the steps. 'Nanna,' she said. 'I'd love yer to meet him. But . . .'

'Sure, he's not got two heads, has he?'

Molly said nothing.

'He's not married?'

'No!'

'So what's so wrong with him that yer keep him hidden away from us all? Or is it that yer ashamed of us, maybe?'

'Nanna, you know I'd never be ashamed of me own family.'

'I'm glad to hear it.'

'Nanna.'

'Yes?'

'Simon's Jewish.'

'I see.'

'Is that all yer gonna say?' Molly could have cut her tongue out; why had she told her? Her nanna always had that effect on her; because of the way she carried on, with all her joking and fooling about, she made Molly forget that her grandmother was one of the grown-ups – one of the ones with the power to spoil things for her.

'Yer mother isn't gonna be best pleased, yer know.'

'Nanna, please, don't tell her. I know yer mean well, but don't. Promise. I don't care if yer tell me off; if yer tell me I'm gonna rot in hell even, but don't tell Mum. She'll make me give him up, I know she will.'

Nora reached out and lifted Molly's heavy curls away from her forehead. 'What d'yer think I was praying for back there, eh? I'll tell yer. I prayed that my family would be happy. And I know your mother, whenever she puts her hands together, prays for just the same. And this young feller, he makes you happy, doesn't he?'

Molly nodded miserably.

'So what more could she want?'

'For him to be Catholic.'

'I'll get round her.'

'No, Nanna, please!' Molly begged her. 'Don't go spoiling things for me. If you tell Mum—'

'Now would I do anything to hurt my best girl?'

'But—'

'But nothing. Now come on, let's get ourselves off home and on the way I'll tell yer all about how I fell in love with the biggest rascal in Cork City, God love him.' She squeezed Molly's hand. 'Don't you go fussing and brooding. It'll be all right. I'll find a way to *make* it all right.'

'But you have to promise you won't say nothing to Mum unless you ask me first.'

'Course I do. Now, I had gone into Cork City with me mammy, your great-grandmother, buying things for me trousseau, when who should come riding past with a donkey cart and a bowler hat perched over one eye, but the most handsome man I'd ever laid eyes on . . .'

As they walked along and Molly listened to her nanna beginning the familiar story of how she was stolen away from right under her fiancé's nose by the charming

Stephen Brady, and how love conquered all, Molly began to feel slightly more easy about having told her nanna. Maybe she had done the right thing after all. Maybe her nanna would be able to help her.

It didn't seem to matter to Timmy and Michael that they had been in bed for only a few hours, and that they had been warned for months now not to expect too much in their stockings – the loan club money could only go so far – it still wasn't quite light when they were up, dressed and down in the front parlour of number ten, shaking their nanna awake and pleading with her to come in next door to number twelve to see what had been left for them under the tree.

Nora wasn't the type who needed very much persuading when it came to having a bit of fun, and she was as keen as the boys to get Christmas started.

Pulling her coat on over her nightdress – she could get herself all done up as befitted such an important day later on – Nora called upstairs to Sean and Danny that if they wanted any breakfast they had better get themselves in next door to their mother, because that's where she and the little ones were off to, and, she added at the top of her voice as she was willingly dragged outside into the freezing early morning air by her two young grandsons, she wished them both a Happy Christmas.

Timmy jammed his hand through the letter box, impatiently fishing around for the key on the piece of string, while Michael urged him to hurry up and let them inside.

With the door open the boys plunged head first into the passage like a pair of greyhounds leaving the traps, yelling a discordant chorus of greetings to their sleeping parents and sister. It was only their nanna's iron grip on their shoulders and her warning that they had to wait for Molly to come down, that prevented them from rushing straight into the front room and ripping their way through their stockings.

They didn't have long to wait; Molly appeared almost immediately on the little landing at the top of the stairs.

She might have been half asleep and, at almost seventeen years of age, hardly a little girl any longer, but she seemed as keen as the boys, and came skipping down the stairs as though she was the same age as Timmy.

Kissing her grandmother, Molly whispered, 'Thanks for being so kind about it all, Nanna.'

Nora chucked her under her chin and whispered back, 'If yer love him and he makes yer happy, there'll be a way, you just see.'

Then Molly threw her arms around her brothers and wished them all a Happy Christmas, poked out her tongue, ducked round them and into the parlour and made straight for the Christmas tree.

The stubby, sparsely needled fir might have been barely half the size of the ones that Molly remembered from previous Christmases standing there in pride of place in the corner, by the fire, but she still thought it looked wonderful, covered as it was in the sparkling glass and wooden decorations that came out year after year from the glory hole under the stairs. Next to it, in a big heap, were all the stockings, actually old ticking pillow slips, just waiting to be investigated.

Molly dived in and pulled hers out from the pile. She was already nibbling carefully at a segment of tangerine – a fruit to be savoured not rushed, she always thought, as it had the very smell of Christmas about it when you stuck your thumb into the shiny peel – before the boys and Nora had even found theirs.

By the time Katie had joined them, and Pat had gone next door to fetch Danny and Sean, who without their dad dragging the bedclothes from them would probably have slept right through their Christmas dinner, never mind the presents, the front room floor was covered with discarded boxes and paper, orange peel, nutshells and little clockwork toys.

Nothing in the room had cost very much – there hadn't been much money to spend – but everything had been given with love and with a lot of thought.

Nora gave silent thanks that her prayers had been so clearly answered when even Sean entered into the spirit of things and presented both her and his mum with a box of lace-trimmed hankies each.

When Molly saw the pleasure on her nanna's face as Katie kissed Sean and thanked him, she knew she had done the right thing when she had nipped out into the passage to slip to Sean, as he had slouched in from next door, the hankies she had bought for him to give them. She smiled happily to herself; it was the thought that counted after all.

But as Molly unfolded the brown paper bag that her mum had used as wrapping for her present, she stopped smiling and wondered what sort of thought her mum had had in mind exactly when she had gone out to get this for her. It was a Tangee lipstick. Molly felt her cheeks flush.

'Mum?' she said, keeping her back to Pat so that he couldn't hear her. 'What d'yer get me this for? Yer know yer said I ain't to wear no make-up yet.'

Katie, kneeling in front of the fire as she fed the flames with shattered nutshells and abandoned wrappings, looked over her shoulder. She was grinning. 'I ain't silly, Moll. I've seen yer hankies.'

Molly flushed an even hotter shade than the lipstick as she pictured the cosmetic-stained handkerchiefs she thought she had been laundering in secret.

'Yer hand washing ain't very good, yer know, Moll. I'll have to give yer some lessons.' Katie swept the hearth clean with the little broom and shovel from the companion set and then pulled herself to her feet. 'That shade'll suit you much better with your red hair,' she whispered. Taking her daughter's face between her hands, she kissed her tenderly on the cheek. 'Just don't let your dad see yer with it on, that's all.'

'Door,' shouted Michael, making no effort to move from his pile of treasures on the hearth rug, as someone rattled noisily on the letter box.

'I'll get it,' said Timmy, eager to try out his skills on his pair of the wooden stilts that Pat had made for him and Michael.

'It's for you, Mum,' Timmy said as he tottered unsteadily back into the room. 'These're much better than them tin can and string ones what Danny made me. Can I go out and try 'em in the street?'

'Just you wait here while I go to the door, Timmy,' said Katie, edging past him. 'And yer can go out when I get one of the others to keep an eye on yer.'

'Mum!' Timmy whined.

'One minute!' she answered, holding up her hand to show she meant it.

Katie was surprised to see Frank Barber standing on the doorstep. Pulling her dressing gown modestly round her, she smiled pleasantly. 'Merry Christmas to yer, Frank.'

'And Merry Christmas to you and all, Katie.' He held

out a parcel wrapped in a sheet of greaseproof paper that, from the look of the grease spots all over it, had probably seen earlier service wrapped around a piece of cheese from the corner shop.

'What's this?' Katie asked, taking it from him.

'A little gift. To show our appreciation, like.'

'What for?'

'For altering that winter coat for Theresa and for making her angel outfit for her. She'd never have been able to be in the nativity play if you hadn't have done that.' He paused, embarrassed. He stared down at his boots and added in a low voice, 'I was so proud to see her standing there in church last night. And I know my Sarah would've been and all,' he crossed himself, 'God rest her soul.'

'But yer can't afford to go wasting yer money on me, Frank. I know how hard things are.'

'It didn't cost me nothing,' he said with a self-deprecating shrug. 'I made it for yer.'

'Yer didn't!' Katie unwrapped the paper to reveal a rough carving of the head and shoulders of a tiny winged cherub. 'It's lovely, Frank. Really smashing.'

'D'yer really like it?'

'Yeah, I really do. Ta.'

'Katie? Who's there?' they heard Pat call out from the front room.

'It's me, Pat,' Frank called back. 'Frank Barber. Happy Christmas to yer, mate.'

Pat appeared in the passageway. He didn't acknowledge Frank. 'You wanna get yerself in the kitchen and get that leg of pork in, Kate, or we'll have no dinner.'

Frank nodded. 'Yeah, I wasn't thinking. Sorry, don't let me keep yer. I know how busy yer must be with a family to see to and everything.'

Timmy wriggled his way past his dad and tapped Katie on the back. 'Mum, can I try me stilts out now?'

'Don't interrupt when grown-ups are talking,' snapped Katie.

'I'll be off then,' said Frank with a smile.

'Right,' said Pat.

Before Frank had the chance to say anything else, Pat reached round Katie and shut the street door on him.

'So can I, Mum?' Timmy persisted.

'Be quiet, can't yer? Don't keep going on all the time.' Katie pushed past her son, then stomped along the passageway and into the kitchen, her dressing gown flapping around her. 'Don't yer know I'm too busy putting the flaming pork in the oven to talk to no one?'

Pat followed her, angrily demanding to know what she thought a wife *should* be doing on Christmas morning if it wasn't cooking the dinner for her husband.

Timmy followed them both, sulkily dragging along his stilts behind him.

In the kitchen Nora had already positioned herself at the sink, head bowed, quietly cleaning and peeling the vegetables.

Katie strode over to the table and began taking her temper out on the leg of pork. She slashed furiously at the skin, cutting long, deep scores with the vicious-looking carving knife and then rubbing handfuls of salt into the surface.

Pat stood next to her, his arms folded, opening and closing his mouth as though he wanted to speak but couldn't quite make up his mind exactly what he had to say.

It was Timmy who actually did say something.

'It's miserable enough in here,' he said, his bottom lip

quivering, 'with everyone having a go at everyone else all the time. But I bet it's even more miserable over Mr Barber's house. Just them two, with no mum or nothing. I'd hate that, if one of you was dead.' He looked up at his parents with his big blue eyes and said earnestly, 'I'm glad yer me mum and dad, even if yer do shout at me. But I like it best when yer friends like yer was this morning.'

Pat and Katie glanced at each other, but both hastily averted their eyes.

Nora didn't look round, but just carried on with her peeling and scraping into the sink. 'Out of the mouth of babes,' she said. 'Isn't that what they say? And d'yer know, I think they might be right.' She dropped a peeled potato into the basin of water on the draining board, carefully selected another, then went on. 'I've never interfered with you two, it's not my way.' Now she did turn round to face them. 'But, for God's sake, it's Christmas Day. A bit of peace and goodwill wouldn't come amiss now, would it?' Having said her bit, Nora returned to her vegetables.

The room was silent for what felt like an age before Pat spoke. 'Mags and Harold have asked us all down the Queen's tonight,' he said quietly. 'For a bit of a jolly-up, like. Apparently Mags is a bit choked, what with her young Margaret staying down Dagenham way in her new house and not coming home for her dinner.'

Katie nodded non-committally. 'That so?'

'She said yer not to go to any trouble getting yerself dressed up or nothing. It won't be nothing fancy, just the neighbours getting together.'

Michael suddenly burst into the kitchen from where he had been hiding in the passageway, listening to his mum and dad, gauging the atmosphere before he asked if he and Timmy could try out the stilts yet, but the thought of going into the pub later on was far more intriguing. 'And us?' he asked eagerly. 'Can me and Timmy go to the Queen's and all?'

Pat looked at his wife. 'Katie?'

Katie looked at Pat, holding his gaze for a long moment. 'Yeah, why not? Sounds good, I reckon.'

When they led their family along the road to morning Mass, Katie and Pat wished all their neighbours a Happy Christmas almost in unison. They helped one another to the tastiest bits of crackling when they had their dinner; practically came to blows over their both wanting to do the washing up – almost delegated it to Molly and Nora – and then decided to do it together.

And at the Queen's that evening, the conciliatory mood between them continued. Although Katie sat with the women while Pat stood up at the bar, they kept glancing across at each other, raising their glasses and mouthing silent toasts. Not only were they both determined to enjoy themselves at the knees-up that Harold and Mags had been kind enough to invite them all to, but, as Timmy had made them realise in his own childish way, they should count their blessings.

Their parents' commitment to goodwill seemed to be contagious: Sean, Michael and Timmy had actually joined Albert Tucker and Jimmo Shay at one of the little round tables to play cards for matchsticks without being threatened into it. Pat wasn't sure whether it was the Christmas spirit his boys had in them or the bitter shandy he had slipped them when he thought Katie hadn't been watching, but whatever it was, as he sipped his beer up at the bar, he was proud to see them spending time with the two sour-faced old curmudgeons. And he was proud to have his other son, Danny, standing up at the bar with him, talking with all the men.

Danny had been dancing with Liz Watts to the old-fashioned medleys that Sooky Shay was bashing out on the piano, but Liz had got fed up with the sight of her mum grinning at them both.

She knew exactly what was going through her mum's mind: Peggy was making plans for her and Danny's wedding. Even though Liz protested endlessly that she and Danny were just good friends, Peggy would hear none of it. So, as much as she loved dancing with Danny – he was really good at it – Liz could stand her mum's leaden hints no longer, and had cut off her nose to spite her face. She had gone to sit with the women after packing Danny off to the bar with his dad.

She watched him standing there, chatting away and laughing with all the men. There was her own dad, Bill, Bert Johnson, Joe Palmer and Harold. The only men from the street who were not in the Queen's that night were Frank Barber, Mr Milton and Arthur Lane.

Frank had thanked Harold and Mags for inviting him but his little girl was exhausted, what with all the excitement of Christmas and being in the nativity play the night before and had fallen asleep straight after her tea.

Then there was Mr Milton; welcome as he and his family were, no one had actually expected them to turn up. And as for Arthur Lane, according to Phoebe Tucker he had been spotted the night before, leaving the street in a cab with Irene, who had herself all done up like a dog's dinner. Not only that, but they had got the driver to carry out a set of *matching* suitcases, something unheard of in Plumley Street and as sure a sign of criminal activity as having on a striped sailor's shirt, a

246

face mask, and a bag marked 'Swag' slung over your shoulder. It was obvious, wasn't it, Phoebe said to anyone who would listen, how else could someone in the East End afford a set of matching bags? And as for that Irene, she had only had the cheek to wish Phoebe a Merry Christmas, but Phoebe, being a decent woman, had, of course, turned her back on the little madam, and slammed the door in her face.

The women of Plumley Street, including Nutty Lil – who by the way she was dressed up, complete with tinsel ribbons in her wild grey hair, could have stood in for the Christmas tree fairy without the need for rehearsal – were divided into two groups. They were either standing around the piano, swaying and singing along to Sooky's enthusiastic if somewhat hit and miss playing of all the old songs, glad to be away from Phoebe's trap for five minutes, or they were out the back of the pub, helping Mags cut piles of sandwiches, using up the enormous goose that a customer from the market had given her and Harold in exchange for a few bottles of light ale, when he hadn't been able to sell the bird off last thing on Christmas Eve.

Also dotted around the pub in variously sulky and jolly huddles were assorted relatives of the Shays and the Tuckers. Both families had invited their elderly aunts and uncles to spend Christmas evening with them, but Phoebe had persuaded Sooky that, like her, she should refuse, and make them all come to Plumley Street. After all, neither of them wanted to miss anything that might go on in the Queen's, *and* the grub was free.

Molly and Liz had gone into the back kitchen to help Mags and Edie Johnson from the shop make the sandwiches, soon getting into the rhythm of buttering the bread, covering it with layers of sliced goose and topping it off with a good sprinkle of salt and pepper.

Molly paused for a moment, butter knife poised in the air. 'Liz,' she said softly.

Liz, her tongue stuck thoughtfully between her teeth, looked up at her friend. 'Yeah? What?'

'Ssshh,' Molly warned her, flashing her eyes at Edie and Mags who were across the other side of the kitchen, arranging wallies, pickled onions and cabbage in big glass bowls. 'It ain't for everyone to hear.'

'Is something up?' Liz whispered.

Molly shook her head hurriedly. 'No. No, course not. It's just that . . .'

'What?'

'I've decided I ain't gonna see Bob Jarvis no more.'

'Aw, Moll, are you sure? I thought it was Simon yer was gonna dump. We've had some right good laughs going out together, the four of us. And yer was really keen on him.'

'Keep yer voice down, Liz, please.' Molly lowered her chin. 'It's just, I don't like some of his ideas. All right?'

'Danny won't be very happy about it, yer know.'

'I think Danny'd do well to think about whether he should stay mates with him and all.'

'How d'yer mean?' Liz didn't like the serious direction this seemed to be taking. 'Moll? Will you tell me what yer getting at?'

'This ain't the place, Liz, and it certainly ain't the time.' Molly jerked her head towards Mags who was coming over to the girls with a bowl of pickles. 'I've said too much already. I just ain't gonna see him no more. So let's leave it at that for now, all right?'

Mags put the bowl down on the table. 'Blimey, look at you two. Cheer up, girls. I thought I was meant to be the one with the hump.' She put her plump, perfumed arms round their shoulders, pulling them close to her. 'Listen, I know we've had a few hard Christmases round here, but look at all this grub we've got to share. We should be more than happy. Tell yer what, let's share our good fortune and all, eh? You two put plenty of that nice white breast meat on a plate and cover it with a cloth and I'll run it over to the Miltons later on.'

'Righto, Mags,' said Molly, chastened by the thought of how the Miltons must be suffering.

'Then when yer've done that, perhaps yer can carry them sandwiches yer've made through to the bar. I don't want them blokes guzzling all that beer on empty bellies or we'll wind up with 'em all wanting to up one another.'

'Some chance of that,' laughed Edie, joining them at the table. 'If they've stuffed a dinner down 'em like my Bert did, I reckon they won't be able to hardly move for a week, let alone have a fight.'

As the girls went to carry the plates of sandwiches through to the bar, Liz paused at the kitchen door. 'Look, Moll, before anything else gets said, I wanna say this one thing, all right? It's hard for me, being pulled between you and Danny. I don't wanna fall out with either of yer, specially not over no bloke.'

Molly pushed open the door with her foot and stepped into the bar. 'There's no reason why we should fall out, is there Liz?'

Danny reached right across the bar and snatched one from the tottering pile of sandwiches that Liz was balancing precariously on her plate. 'You two fall out?' he said, through a mouthful of goose and bread, catching the end of their conversation. 'Never! Still,' he added with a wink, 'I suppose there's gotta be a first time for everything, eh, girls?'

Liz glanced sideways at Molly, then looked at Danny

and said with a smile, 'Mind yer business, nose ointment. This is girls' talk.'

He winked at Liz again and finished the rest of his sandwich in a single bite.

The girls went over to the piano to start offering round the sandwiches.

Katie took one, but Nora refused with a wave of her hand, she couldn't sing and eat at the same time, and having begun a rip-roaring rendition of 'The Wild Rover' – the song that after a few glasses of stout she always claimed was her favourite – she wasn't about to stop.

She had just launched into the final chorus of, ' "So it's no, nay never. No never, no more, will I plaaaay the wild rover..." ' when someone tapped her on the shoulder.

Nora stopped singing and spun round, ready to give whoever it was a piece of her mind for interrupting her song like that, but instead, much to the surprise of everyone, she stood there for a moment, open-mouthed, looking at the tall, slim man with the mop of thick, grey-tinged red curls, then threw her arms round his neck and planted a kiss on his smiling mouth.

Then she slowly turned back to face her daughter, and, with her chin held high and a grin spreading right across her face, she said to Katie in a loud, triumphant voice: 'I don't suppose yer remember him that well, do yer, darling? But this here's the handsomest man that ever came from Cork City.'

'Mum?' Katie grabbed hold of the piano for support.

Nora clapped her hands together. 'Sure, isn't it Stephen Brady himself? Isn't it yer father come to see us?'

11

It was late Friday afternoon, the end of the first really nice spring day of 1934, and it seemed that many of the residents of Plumley Street were determined to make the most of it, sitting outside their houses, enjoying warming their bones after the long cold winter they had all had to endure.

At one end of the street, Nora, Katie, and Peggy Watts from over the road, were sitting on kitchen chairs they had parked on the pavement between numbers ten and twelve, catching up with the bits of mending and knitting that seemed so much less of a chore now they didn't have to do them indoors in the gloom of artificial light.

At the other, blocked end of the street, Edie Johnson was also outside, but she was standing on her chair. Balancing precariously on her stout legs, she was giving her shop window its first thorough clean of the year. She had caught a shocked glimpse of the state of the glass when the spring sunshine had filtered through the grime that had accumulated there during the wet, foggy winter, and had decided to do something about it there and then. Bert had tried to persuade her to leave it, telling her that when his leg was feeling a bit better he would do it for her, but Edie had refused, insisting that he had enough to do, before getting on with the job herself. She had refused his offer very gently; her Bert

251

was a proud man and she knew that his injury from the Great War was not only a constant source of physical pain to him, but also of regret, as it meant that he could not do what he thought was a fair share of the work it took to run the shop, and that hurt him almost as much as his damaged leg.

Next door to the shop at number three, there was no sign of Mr and Mrs Milton; they weren't outside the house enjoying the sunshine, nor was there any clue as to whether they were at home, as the front room curtains were tightly drawn even though it was still broad daylight. But in the gutter outside the house, there was plenty of evidence of the Milton kids. Barefoot and dressed in an ill-fitting assortment of hand-me-downs supplied by Katie and the church jumble, they were playing with Timmy and Michael at a complicated game involving stones and bits of knotted string.

The youngsters and their doings were being closely observed by Phoebe Tucker. She was just waiting for any behaviour that could in any way be described as a nuisance, so that she could knock on the Miltons' door or go over to the Mehans' to complain about them. She was accompanied at her post outside number seven by Sooky Shay, who had fetched her own chair from number five next door.

The two women, with their shoulders hunched and eyes narrowed, were like a pair of dusty old crows, as they sat there in their dark frocks, their crossover aprons, rolled down stockings and ever-present slippers, drinking tea and smoking foul-smelling roll-ups. The pair of them disapproved of just about everybody and everything, but they saved their most spiteful venom, as they gossiped and chattered, for their husbands. But Albert and Jimmo were used to it and, as soon as they saw their wives setting their kitchen chairs on the pavement, they made themselves scarce by sloping off to Ricardo Street to pass an opinion on an old pal's newly painted pigeon loft. If they had have hung around, they knew what they were in for: Phoebe with her talent for conjuring jobs out of nothing, would have them limewashing their backyard walls, or replacing the putty in the front windows, or some other such nonsense just to get them at it, while she and Sooky supervised and complained and told them how useless they both were.

Further up the street, Frank Barber had come home early when he'd been told there was nothing down the docks for him. He and Theresa were in the back kitchen, getting their tea ready. Frank had, as usual, offered to share their meal with Nutty Lil from upstairs, but, also as usual, she had merely shaken her head and carried on singing her hymns in her high warbling falsetto.

Frank felt bad that Lil would never accept his invitation to eat with them, but he knew she got by well enough and he would never intrude. But that didn't get away from the fact that he would have liked to have done something for her, if only because he felt it would have made up in some way for how good people had been to him since he had lost his wife. Sarah Barber had died less than an hour after giving birth to their baby son. Their little boy had survived for just a few moments longer. It had been a terrible time, but it would have been a whole lot worse without his neighbours; he wouldn't even have been able to go to work if it wasn't for Peggy Watts from next door, keeping an eye on little Theresa when she came home from school until he got in of a night.

Back on the other side of the street, next door to Nora's, Joe and Aggie Palmer were out in the yard. The yard took up the whole downstairs of number eight, as well as a narrow strip of ground that ran along behind the Lanes' house and the Queen's Arms. Joe had finished work for the day, but he was still busily polishing his precious truck, while Aggie fussed around with her hens and rabbits, and Duchess, the little grey pony that she had persuaded her husband not to part with, even though she no longer earned her keep since Joe had bought the truck and his haulage business had gone motorised.

Joe often joked with Aggie that she and her menagerie were taking up more and more of his yard every year, and how it was all because she preferred pottering around with her dumb creatures to being stuck upstairs in the flat with dusters and floor polish. But Joe would never really have complained about her. Aggie was everything to Joe, and if she had wanted the whole of the downstairs and the upstairs rooms as well turned into a farmyard, he probably would have gone along with it. He loved her, not just because she was a kind, caring woman, but because she was the one who had convinced him that he could make something of himself. Aggie had taught Joe to read and write; she had shown him that he could settle down and earn a bit of respect from decent neighbours; and had made him see that he didn't have to stay an illiterate tearaway all his life. When he thought back to what he'd been like as a kid, and how his life could have turned out, Joe Palmer had every reason to be grateful to his beloved Aggie.

Next door to the Palmers was number six, a house that looked as lifeless as the Miltons'. But the Lanes certainly weren't hiding themselves away. They had arrived home very publicly in a cab less than an hour ago, having been out all day. From the posh names on the armfuls of boxes and bags that the cabbie had helped

Arthur carry indoors, it was obvious that they had been on a huge shopping spree up West. Or at least, that's what Phoebe had reported to Sooky when she had fetched her kitchen chair out to join her. Sooky had lapped up Phoebe's lurid description of Irene's painted face, and joined in her spiteful laughter when Phoebe bragged about how she had turned the other way when Irene had waved to her.

They were all still outside when, at just gone a quarter to six, Pat appeared from round the corner.

'Hello, love,' he said, bending down to peck his wife on the cheek. 'All right, Nora? Peg?'

Katie looked up at him, shielding her eyes against the final, slanting rays of the afternoon sun. 'Hello, sweetheart, you're home early.'

Pat nodded. 'Yeah, it's been a bit quiet at work again today. Well, more than a bit quiet, to tell yer the truth; there was a bit doing for me and another couple of the chaps, but not enough. Not nearly enough. Still . . .' He pulled off his cap, stuck it in his pocket and asked his usual question. 'Where's the kids? What they been up to today?'

'Danny's just rushed in from work, got ready and rushed out again. With Peggy's Liz,' Katie added with a knowing smile at Peggy.

'For a change!' Peggy joined in.

'And our Molly got in – when was it, Mum, five minutes ago? Then she was straight out again and all.'

Nora shook her head. 'It was less than five minutes ago. I'm surprised yer missed her, Pat.'

'Right hurry she was in and all. Her and Danny both didn't bother with nothing to eat.'

'Yer can't tell 'em,' said Peg, squinting at her knitting as she counted the rows.

'Where was she off to this time?' asked Pat, leaning back against the sun-warmed bricks and rolling himself a cigarette.

'Going to meet some friend or other, from the tea factory, I think she said, didn't she, Mum?'

Nora said nothing, she just carried on with her darning.

'She was in that much of a rush,' Katie went on, 'I never really caught what she said.'

'How about our Sean? If that ain't a silly question.'

Knowing that Sean wasn't exactly an easy topic of conversation for her neighbours lately, Peggy went to stand up. 'Time I was going, I reckon,' she said cheerfully.

'No, Peg, yer all right.' Katie sighed. She leant back in her chair and spoke softly, so that Phoebe and Sooky couldn't make out her words from across the street. 'He went off early this morning, just after you left yerself, Pat. To see this bloke from Stepney who he says has been paying him to do these odd jobs, whatever they might be. Mind you, at least he's got a few bob in his pocket. Even left a dollar on the kitchen table for me before he went out.' Katie shook her head wearily. 'I don't even like to think what he's up to.'

'Don't worry yerself, Katie, girl,' Nora said airily. 'He'll be doing a bit of labouring for someone. I told yer, worrying's no good to yer.'

'It's all right for you, Mum—' Katie began.

'All right, all right,' Pat interrupted her. 'Don't get yerself all worked up. You know what lads of his age are like. Slippery as eels, the lot of 'em. Never know what they're up to. Like yer mother says, he'll be doing a bit of labouring for someone what don't fancy paying a grown man a full wage.'

Katie shrugged. 'Maybe.'

'And he's never brought no trouble home, now has he? That's what yer wanna be thankful for.' Pat licked the cigarette paper and stuck the finished roll-up in the corner of his mouth. 'Now, where are them two young 'uns of our'n?'

Katie pointed across the street with a lift of her chin. 'Over there with the Milton kids.'

Peggy smiled wistfully. 'Look at 'em, love their little hearts. Happy as pigs in muck playing with your two. They're poor little so-and-sos. Ain't got ha'penny to bless 'emselves with. Never have nothing, but they don't complain.'

Pat held up the coil of thick, tarred barge rope that he had looped over his arm. 'This'll please 'em. I fetched it home so's they can all have a game with it.'

'I wondered what yer were thinking of doing with that,' said Nora. 'I thought yer might be planning to string up the rent man from the lamppost.'

Pat laughed. 'Not a bad idea, Nora, but I think it might be better if I tie it round the lamppost and make a swing out of it for the kids. Remember how we used to when we was little, Kate?'

'Are you crackers?' Katie was on her feet. 'Tying it to the lamppost? What, d'yer want 'em to go hanging their flaming selves? That'd be nice, wouldn't it? Me having Ellen Milton over here shouting the odds that we've strangled all her nippers to death.'

'We never come to no harm playing with ropes when we was kids,' said Pat. He shook his head at Nora for putting such a stupid idea into his wife's head. He sounded and looked hurt; he and Katie had been getting on so well lately, but here she was, throwing his surprise for the kids back in his face, and in front of people too.

'Yer just don't think, do yer, Pat.' Katie looked at

Peggy then at Nora, appealing to their better, female, sense. 'Men,' she tutted, 'they just don't see no danger, do they? Hopeless.'

Neither of the other women said a thing; they knew better than to interfere in a disagreement between a married couple.

Katie turned back to her husband. 'It's just like them stilts yer made at Christmas for our Timmy and Michael.'

Pat flicked his cigarette butt into the gutter and pushed himself away from the wall. 'I thought they really liked 'em,' he said flatly.

'Yeah,' agreed Katie. 'Course they do. 'Cos they're rotten dangerous and they worry the life out of me every time they go out on 'em. I can't count how many times they've nearly broke their flipping necks on 'em. Flaming things. Might as well give 'em a carving knife to play with – and a saw and all while yer at it.'

Pat stared down at his boots. 'It must be me, I reckon. I can't do nothing right. It's like down the docks; I've had a right pig of a day. I was trying me best to explain to the blokes, as honest as I could, that there just weren't enough work for everyone again. And what do they do? They all act like it's my bloody fault. Now I come home, just trying to do something nice for me kids, and *you* start on me.'

Katie felt her cheeks grow warm. She bowed her head for a moment and looked through her lashes at Peggy and Nora who were pointedly concentrating on their handiwork. Then she looked up at her husband again, her angry scowl softened into a smile. 'Hark at me, leading off. I'm sorry, Pat,' she said, knowing how he hated having a show made of him in front of anyone. 'I'm really sorry. It must be all this sunshine getting to me. We ain't used to it, are we?' She reached out and

258

touched him on the cheek. 'Why don't yer go down the Queen's and treat yerself to a drink? I wasn't expecting yer in so early so I ain't even got yer tea on yet.'

'My Bill's had a walk down there, Pat,' Peggy said pleasantly. 'He'll appreciate a bit of company.'

'I could go a pint,' Pat nodded, glad of a reason to get away. 'Is Stephen about? I'll see if he fancies a quick one and all.'

Katie sat down abruptly, snatching up her darning from her chair. 'I dunno where he is,' she answered tartly. 'Yer'll have to ask Mum. Not that I suppose she knows either. Right man o' mystery, he is.'

Nora rolled her eyes at Peggy Watts, who held up her hand and shook her head as much as to say, 'Don't involve me, Nora,' and got on with her knitting.

Nora thought for a moment, then looked up at her son-in-law. 'You go and enjoy yer drink, son. When Stephen turns up, I'll send him down to yer.'

'Okay, Nora. I'll just give the boys their rope first.' He raised a questioning eyebrow at Katie. 'If that's all right with you.'

'Just tell 'em to be careful, eh, Pat?'

Pat had been over at the Queen's for less than ten minutes when Stephen Brady came haring round the corner and skidded to a halt in front of Nora, Katie and Peggy Watts. He might have been getting on for sixty years of age but he was still as lithe as a fit forty-year-old.

'Yer'll never guess what,' he gasped, his usually soft Irish brogue made raucous with a combination of breathlessness and enthusiastic glee.

Katie sat stony-faced, not charmed in the least by such behaviour, but Peggy smiled, amused by his childlike excitement, and as for Nora, she beamed with proud pleasure at her husband's high spirits.

'And what's that, that I can't guess, me darling?' Nora asked him.

'Up the road,' he said, bending forward and grasping his thighs as he tried to steady his breathing. 'There's something right peculiar going on, Nora. Yous'll never believe it; yer'll have to come and see for yerself.'

'Peculiar eh?' Nora said, impressed by the idea. 'Now calm yerself down, Stephen, and tell us all about it.'

'There are these men,' he said, jerking his thumb over his shoulder towards the end of the street, 'on the corner of Guildford Road. By the pub there. Yer know where I mean? It's by—'

'Yeah, yeah, we know, we know,' Nora interrupted, impatient to hear his story.

'Well, I'm telling yer, yer'd not believe it unless yer saw it with yer own eyes. A barrel organ, they've got, and they're singing and they're dancing, and aren't all the kids from round there sitting along the kerb and clapping and laughing, and the fellers from the pub are throwing pennies and—'

'What's so special about that?' Nora butted in again, disappointed that her husband's story was so ordinary.

Stephen leant close to them and put his hand to his mouth. 'Sure,' he whispered, 'aren't they all dressed up as ladies? With frocks, lipstick, the lot!'

Nora burst out laughing. 'That'll be the Nancy Boys or the Jazzers, yer daft eejit.'

Now it was Stephen who was disappointed. 'So they're nothing special then, these Nancy Boys and Jazzer fellers?'

'Course they're special,' Nora reassured him. 'Don't the kids just go crazy for 'em. Tell yer what, why don't yer take Michael and Timmy round to see 'em? They'd love it.'

Momentarily unsure as to whether Nora was just humouring him, Stephen stared uncertainly at his wife, but he quickly recovered and was off across the street to tell Timmy and Michael the good news. He asked the Milton youngsters if they'd like to go too, but, like wild animals scared by a predator, the hollow-eyed, scrawny-looking kids shook their heads and scampered off along the passageway of number three, calling behind them that their mum had told them to stay close to the house.

'I didn't mean to frighten yer mates, Micky,' said Stephen.

'That's all right, Farvee,' Michael answered in the matter-of-fact tone that only a child familiar with such deprivation could use. 'They ain't got no money or nothing so their mum and dad don't let 'em do nothing 'cos, you know, they can't give nothing back and they'd be right embarrassed. See?'

Stephen nodded. He saw all right, of course he did. As a little boy his parents had taken him to live in Cork City, escaping from a starved and barren part of the west coast of Ireland, where the success or failure of the potato crop had meant the difference between whether a family would have enough stodge to fill their bellies, or would fade away to life-sapping sickness.

'Come on then,' he said, 'we'll tell yer mates all about it later. And, I know what, when we get back, I'll buy yers a farthing's worth of odds from Edie and Bert's to share with 'em. How'll that be?'

'That'll be smashing, Farvee!' Timmy was almost beside himself. Not only was his granddad taking him to see the Nancy Boys, but he was buying him and his mates a bag full of all the bits from the bottoms of the

261

sweet jars that Edie poured into a special jar she kept on the side of the counter by the till. 'I hope there's plenty of pear drop crumbs in it.'

'Don't you go spoiling yer teas,' said Katie, obviously not quite so impressed with her father's promises. 'And you be careful, Timmy, and keep hold of Michael's hand.' She was still hollering instructions after them as, stern-faced, she watched her two youngest sons disappear around the corner into Grundy Street, dragging the heavy, tarred rope behind them, trotting to keep up with the man they had so easily come to call Farvee, but who she still could not bring herself to call Dad.

'It's amazing having that man back with me,' Nora sighed contentedly, folding her arms across her aproned chest. 'Yer know, it feels like only yesterday . . .'

'He ain't changed a bit, Kate,' Peggy said, peering closely at her knitting, as she tried to hook up a dropped stitch. 'Still a good-looking man. I remember when I was what, about eight years old, must it have been, Nora, when we first moved here?'

Nora considered for a moment. 'I reckon you was about that,' she said. 'Yeah, I'm sure, 'cos what, I'm nearly eight, nine years older than Peggy, ain't I, Kate?'

Katie nodded stiffly. 'That's about right.'

'Yeah, that is right,' said Peggy. 'Me dad was still alive, God rest his soul, so I must have been about that age.' She let her knitting fall into her lap. 'I used to watch your dad, Katie, as he strolled along to the Queen's of an evening.' She laughed at the memory. 'I loved my dad, no one could have loved a man more, but he wasn't a match on Stephen when it came to having a bit of style and swagger. He was a dandy, that man.'

'Yer must have a flaming good memory,' Katie snapped, roughly shoving the sock she was mending into

262

her apron pocket. 'He was only here five minutes before he buggered off, leaving Mum six months gone and no one to turn to.'

'Yer mustn't blame him,' Nora said defensively. 'He was only a boy himself. And anyway, he used to send me money whenever he could find work.'

Katie stood up. 'If it hadn't have been for my Pat's mum and dad, me and you would have starved and you know it. Now, I'm going in to make a cuppa tea. Want one, you two?'

'Yes please, love,' said Peggy quietly.

Nora waited until her daughter had gone indoors. 'Yer know, Peg,' she said reflectively, 'my Katie's a clever girl, always has been. But she doesn't understand about her dad and me. And she never will if she won't listen.'

Nora shifted in her chair, all too aware of Phoebe and Sooky sitting across the street, straining their ears to twig what was going on. 'When we came over from Ireland, a pair of kids we were. No idea of the world or what we should do or what anything meant. We was just trying, trying our best to make a life for ourselves and the baby I was going to have.' Nora dropped her chin, suddenly fascinated by a loose thread on her apron. 'Yer know, I wish Katie would just try and forgive him, Peg. Call him Dad maybe. Just for me. But it's as though she's so set on what she thinks is right, that that's it. She'll not bend an inch. It's like the way she was talking about Pat's parents like they was saints. Yes they helped us, they helped us a lot, but she knows as well as us what went on in that house between those two. What with Pat's mum off with the fellers and his dad mad blind with jealousy.' She lifted her head and turned to Peggy. 'Everyone has their problems, Peg, don't they? She should see that, surely?'

Peggy nodded. 'We all have our problems all right, Nora.' She finished the row she was on and then folded the knitting round the needles before sticking the points into the fat ball of wool. 'Look, I know your Katie ain't a little girl no more, but she's still your baby, Nora, and yer know how kids get with their mums, even at her age. Stubborn. And they think feelings haven't been invented until they have 'em 'emselves. They can't understand that their mums have feelings and all.' She hesitated. 'Or that they have needs. If yer know what I mean.'

Nora sighed loudly. 'Aw, I know what yer mean all right there, girl.'

They sat there in silence for a while, watching Phoebe and Sooky whispering behind their hands and pointing occasionally across at them. Neither Peggy nor Nora bothered to speculate as to the object of the old women's gossip. It was bound to be something bad about someone or other. Then Katie came back out, carrying a battered tin tray with three cups of tea on it.

'Give us that here, love,' said Nora, standing up and taking it from her. 'Now you sit down and drink yer tea and tell yer mum why yer looking so fed up.'

Katie sipped at her tea. Determined as she had been not to say anything – she had always prided herself on sorting out her own problems – it all suddenly came tumbling out. 'Look, I know it's hard for everyone, all this worrying about work and money all the time, and I know we're better off than we might be if Danny and Molly weren't both earning, even if they are fetching in kids' wages and eating like adults. But it's the way things have got so much worse lately. It's like nothing goes right – nothing.'

Peggy swallowed her tea, almost scalding her throat

264

in the process, stood up and said, 'This sounds like family business to me. I've gotta be getting off anyway.'

'No, Peg. Please,' Katie said, touching her arm. 'Sit down. I could do with you two telling me if I'm just letting things get to me.' She laughed mirthlessly. 'Maybe it's me age. Maybe I'm going a bit doolally, eh? But it was like with Pat just now and that stupid rope. I shouldn't have had a go like that. He's as good as gold to me, that man, and I have to start hollering at him.'

Peggy exchanged a brief knowing look with Nora, and then sat down again.

'See, part of it's all this bad feeling between Danny and Molly. It's really been upsetting me.' She glanced sideways at her mum. Katie was sure Nora knew what was going on – she was always whispering to Molly about something or other lately – but there was no getting anything out of her, no matter how hard Katie tried. 'I don't know if Liz has mentioned anything, Peg, but the atmosphere round that table in there when the pair of them do decide to sit down and eat with us, well, yer could cut it with a flaming knife. Danny's only gotta look at her the wrong way and Molly's up in the air like a flipping rubber balloon.'

Peggy opened her eyes wide and exhaled loudly. 'I don't like to say nothing, Kate, but Liz has mentioned that there's something going on.'

'What?' Katie was on the edge of her chair. 'What is it?'

'Look, all I know is my Liz was saying the other night how she feels torn between the pair of 'em. Don't know what to do for the best, she don't. But as to what it's all about, she ain't said, and that is the truth, girl. I really don't know. And, to be honest, I didn't think it was my place to ask. I reckon she'd have told me if she thought she could.' Peggy patted Katie's hand. 'But yer don't wanna worry yerself, Kate. Yer know what kids are like, rowing one minute and then best mates the next.'

'But they ain't babies no more, Peg,' Katie said bleakly. 'Molly's seventeen and Danny ain't far off nineteen. And anyway, all this is hardly a five-minute wonder, is it? It's been going on since Christmas time.'

'Well, if that's all yer've got to worry about,' said Nora, leaning back in her chair and folding her arms, 'I think yer should count yerself a lucky woman.'

'Thanks, Mum,' snapped Katie. 'Yer making me sound a right idiot, like I'm worrying over nothing.'

'Well, what have yer got to worry about that's really so terrible?'

'D'yer want me to list all the things I've got on me mind?' Katie stuck out her hand and began counting them off on her fingers. 'There's Sean up to Gawd knows what. There's the little 'uns growing up into a world where it don't seem there's gonna be no future for no one.' She dropped her hands and leant forward, looking directly into her mother's face. 'You tell me how to explain to kids about them marchers? I didn't know what to say when they asked me about that last lot, them poor buggers from Newcastle, what was staying in Poplar a few weeks back.' She leant back in her chair again. 'Then there's all the stuff on the wireless about all them horrible things happening abroad.'

'The Good Lord help us and save us, girl,' said Nora. 'Sure, yer can't go taking the troubles of the whole world on yer shoulders. Tell her, Peg.'

Before Peggy had the chance to tell her anything, Katie, quite unexpectedly, began crying. 'And you,' she snapped tearfully at her mother, 'you're worrying me to a sodding frazzle and all, what with *him* hanging around

266

the place. I know the bastard's gonna let yer down again.'

Peggy glanced across the street at Phoebe and Sooky, who were obviously enjoying every minute of this unscheduled entertainment, especially hearing Katie using bad language.

'All right, Katie, love,' Peggy calmed her. 'Don't give them old bags the satisfaction of seeing yer upset yerself. It's all this trying to make ends meet all the time. That's what it is. It's getting yer down. And Pat's a good feller, he does what he can.'

'I know he does, Peg, but it *ain't* that,' sniffed Katie. 'I'm worried what's happening to me family. I told yer.'

Nora shook her head in wonder. 'I don't know why yer just don't come out and ask me straight,' she said calmly. 'If yer must know, the boys are fine upstairs in their bedrooms and I'm just fine sharing me front parlour and me bed with yer dad.'

If it hadn't have been for Phoebe calling across the street to them, Katie would have run indoors to hide from the shame of her mother speaking like that, and in front of Peggy Watts of all people, a good Catholic woman whose daughter was seeing their Danny. As it was, Katie's embarrassment was rapidly transformed into anger.

'Getting all upset, are yer, Katie?' Phoebe shouted. She nudged Sooky and jerked her head towards Frank Barber's house on the corner. 'What is it? Not seen yer *friend* for a while? Or is it that girl o' your'n yer worried about? Been seen around with a strange boy, so I hear. Ain't from round here apparently. Very dark he is. Looks foreign by all accounts.'

'And yer'll be looking at my hand across yer face if yer don't shut up, you old cow,' Nora shouted, launching herself off her seat.

Katie grabbed her mother by the arm. 'Sit down, Mum,' she hissed. 'It'll only give her more to talk about.'

Phoebe wasn't in the least perturbed. 'And as for your young Danny, I've heard how he's spending a lot of time hanging around with that Jarvis boy and his cronies. They're the ones what give out them leaflets, so they say. Them ones that are against the Jews. I'm surprised. "Red Pat", ain't that what they call his father down the docks? And yet your Danny's hiked up with that mob.' Phoebe gave Sooky a sly grin. 'I'd have thought that would've concerned you, Peggy Watts, 'cos your girl's seeing Danny, ain't she? I mean, I wouldn't fancy no daughter o' mine getting mixed up with none of them riots they start or nothing.'

'For Gawd's sake shut your flaming gob, Phoebe.' It was unusual for Peggy to raise her voice, but anyone talking about her Liz was pushing their luck too far.

'See, Sook, they don't like the truth, some people. But let 'em put that on their needles and knit it.' Phoebe was suddenly on her feet, pointing animatedly to the end of the street. 'And what's this coming along? Will yer look at the state of him? He's been up to no good, you mark my words.'

The new object of Phoebe's attention was Michael. He had just turned into Plumley Street; head bowed, shoulders stooped, and his clothes soaking wet. As he squelched towards her, Katie could see he had bits of twig and weed in his hair.

'You was meant to be watching the Nancy Boys,' said Katie in a slow measured tone, as she rose from her chair.

'We was,' he said sheepishly. 'At first, like.'

'So tell me – I'd love to know – where'd yer go afterwards?'

Michael shrugged and breezily raised his hands, every movement leaving a wider puddle of evil-smelling water at his feet. 'Nowhere really.'

Katie went to grab him by the shoulders but had second thoughts when she caught a whiff of whatever was dripping from him on to the pavement. 'Michael, I am losing my temper. *What* exactly have yer been up to?'

'Give the boy a chance.' It was Stephen. He had just appeared with Timmy, who was grimly gripping his grandfather's hand; both of them were as soaked as Michael.

Katie was momentarily speechless; she flapped her hands ineffectually at the gall of the man. When she had finally composed herself enough to speak, she said weakly, 'You just shut up. Do you hear me? Shut up.' She poked herself rhythmically in the chest as she said each word: 'I am talking to *my* son. The son that I bothered to stay around to bring up.' She turned her finger on Michael, waving it in his face. 'I know what yer've been doing, you've been swimming down that Cut again, haven't yer? When I told yer yer wasn't even allowed *near* there.' She jerked her thumb at Stephen without looking at him. 'And he took yer, didn't he? There's no point lying to me, Michael.'

Stephen winked supportively at his grandson, egging him on; he was lucky that Katie never saw him.

'We was only jumping off Stinkhouse Bridge, Mum,' said Michael in a bored, matter-of-fact sort of way. 'Swinging on that rope what Dad got us.' He elbowed the stricken-looking Timmy in the ribs. 'It was a right laugh, weren't it, Tim?'

'A right laugh?' Katie could hardly believe her ears.

'We never meant to fall in or nothing.'

Her distaste for his foul, stinking, slime-covered clothes forgotten in her anger, Katie grabbed hold of Michael by the jacket, but she quickly withdrew her hand. 'And what's this sticking out of yer pocket? It looks disgusting.'

Michael pulled out the object of his mother's revulsion. 'It's cold fish.'

'It's what?'

'Cold fish. You know, what yer get in the chip shop from the day before. Farvee got it for us. He's gonna make me and Timmy and him some sandwiches with it. 'Cos swimming makes yer right hungry, don't it, Farvee?'

Katie took the filthy lump of fish from her son and gingerly peeled back the sopping wet batter so that she could examine the inside. Her nose wrinkled. She held it out for Peggy and Nora to see. 'Look at it. Just look. It's grey. He'd have poisoned 'em. It must be at least a week old.' Katie glared at Stephen.

Peggy was out of her depth, she really did want to go home, but as she rose from her chair, Katie would have none of it.

'No,' said Katie, 'you stay where you are, Peg. Don't let him . . .' She jabbed an accusing finger at Stephen. ' . . . drive yer away. I'm gonna get these two in the kitchen, give 'em a good scrubbing. And yes, Michael, with the nail brush. Then I'll make us some more tea.'

Stephen raised his eyebrows and tutted at his grandsons in recognition of the fact that there was no understanding women, then he put on what he thought was a winning smile and turned to face his daughter. 'So, if there's no fish sandwiches about, Katie love, is there anything else for us to eat for our teas?'

Katie's mouth dropped open at such gall. 'I can't believe you, I really can't. Yer'll get me flaming put away for what I'd like to do to you. I'd like to get my hands round that stupid neck o' your'n and—'

'Yer telling me yer've not got our tea on yet, then, are yer, darling?' Stephen said with another wink at Michael.

'That's right. In fact, there's no cooking gonna be done by me in this house tonight. None at all. So yer can just go and fetch us all some fish and taters – fresh ones, not flipping three days old. And yer wanna be quick about it and all. Pat'll be back from the Queen's expecting his tea any minute now.'

With that Katie stormed inside, dragging Michael by the ear and Timmy by the elbow. She paused in the doorway just long enough to say to him, 'You might have got round Mum, but you ain't getting round me. Now you two, in, and don't you *dare* drip on my clean floor.'

Stephen chucked Nora under the chin. 'So, that son-in-law of ours is over in the pub, now is he? Sure, I'd better go and have a quick word with him, see if it's rock or cod he'll be wanting.'

Phoebe was barely able to contain herself with delight at the spectacle she and Sooky had witnessed, and even though her neighbour could see just as well as her, Phoebe gave Sooky a running commentary on her interpretation of events.

'Look at him,' she said, nodding towards Stephen. 'Off down the pub, he'll be. He won't be getting any supper tonight, you mark my words. And as for her, that Katie, what a right madam! Always acts likes she's good enough to put ten bob on herself in the three thirty, that one. But now she's so ashamed she's had to have it away indoors. Wants to be out of sight, see. Pride comes before a fall, they say, and I reckon they've got that just about right. Like I told yer, they don't like the truth, some people. Soon as I mentioned him from the end, that

271

widower, *Frank Barber* or whatever he calls himself, she had to change the subject. Churchgoers. Don't make me laugh. And they want to keep an eye on that Sean and all. I've seen him going in that Laney's. *And* when the old man's out. That's the one they should really be worried about, if you ask me.'

Nora got on with her sewing, but all the while she listened while Phoebe rattled on. When the old gossip eventually paused to draw breath, Nora stood up.

'Peg, I don't wanna be rude, love, but I think I've heard more than enough of them two. I'm going in to help Katie with the boys. That be all right with you?'

'Course, Nora,' Peggy said, hooking her knitting bag on one arm and picking up her kitchen chair with the other. 'I'll have to be seeing to my Bill's tea before he gets back from the Queen's anyway, or there'll be another row for them spiteful old biddies to get their mouldy rotten gnashers into.'

Nora chuckled. 'What a turn out, eh, Peg?'

'Never a dull moment in this street, eh, girl?'

When Katie and Nora eventually came back outside with the boys, who were now clean, dry and looking really sorry for themselves, daylight had faded into a pleasant, early spring evening. As the streetlights had been lit, Nora repositioned her chair by the lamppost, and sat herself down to get on with her mending.

Before Katie sat down with her, she bent forward and wagged her finger close to Michael's face. 'Now, if yer don't wanna be sent up to bed without yer tea, yer can play with yer glarneys right there,' she pointed to the pool of gaslight shining on the pavement in front of the house, 'where I can keep me eye on yer.'

'Why is it me yer telling? Why don't yer tell him?'

272

demanded Michael. 'Timmy never gets told off.'

'Not that I should have to answer such a rude little boy, but it seems to me that it's always you what's in the middle of whatever's going on when there's any trouble. And that Timmy, daft idiot that he is, just follows yer.'

Unsure as to whether he should be pleased or annoyed at being identified as the ring leader, Michael merely scowled in reply, took his marbles out of his pocket and sat down heavily on the kerb.

'Now,' Katie said, hands on hips, 'where's he got to with our tea?'

Nora looked up from her darning. 'He popped over the Queen's first to have a word with Pat about what he wants to eat.'

'So he still ain't gone to get it yet, then?'

'He said he'll fetch it in a minute.'

Katie slumped down in the chair next to her mum. She felt worn out. 'The mood he's put me in, he'd just better, that's all. I dunno what he was thinking, taking 'em down there. Of all the daft, stupid, thick-headed—'

Nora dropped her sewing on to her lap. 'Katie,' she said, sounding exasperated. 'Sure, all it was was a bit of fun, girl, that's all. It's good to have a laugh, you wanna remember that. It's a while since I saw you even crack a smile across that face of yours.'

'Aw yeah, there's so much to laugh about, ain't there?'

Nora shook her head. 'Don't start on that again.'

Katie dragged her own mending from her pocket and started darning furiously. 'He'd better get back here soon, that's all I can say.'

It was nearly an hour before Stephen eventually reappeared and, from the way he was weaving along hanging on to Pat's arm, it looked as though he had spent most of that time pouring booze down his throat

273

rather than enquiring as to the variety of fish his son-in-law fancied for his tea.

As he swayed backwards and forwards in front of Katie and Nora, grinning foolishly, Stephen began a long rambling explanation as to how he had got talking with Harold and how he couldn't possibly walk out on a man who was seeking his advice on matters of great importance.

'Advice? From you?' Katie hadn't raised her voice but her manner was menacing enough to shut Stephen up immediately.

'All right, love,' Pat said, touching his wife gently on the shoulder. 'He's just had a few too many.'

'And where did he get the money from to get in that state?'

'I treated him.'

'You what? You paid for him to get plastered?'

'I think we'd better go indoors if we're gonna have a row about this,' Pat said, taking hold of her arm.

'No, hang on, I wanna get this straight. There's no work,' Katie said shaking off his grip, 'but yer can find money to buy booze for *him*?'

'All right, we're short of money, so's everyone round here. What d'yer want me to do about it, go around moaning all the time like you've started doing? Or causing rows in the street and showing you up whenever I get the arsehole about something, even if it's nothing to do with yer?'

With a sigh, Nora got up. She went to the kerb and told her grandsons to go indoors into hers. Reluctantly, for it looked as though their parents were brewing up for a really good row, they did as they were told.

'So I'm moaning all the time, am I?' Katie shouted. 'And I have a go at yer for nothing?'

'Yer wasn't listening. I didn't mean—'

'Aw yes you did, Pat Mehan; that's exactly what yer meant. Well, I'll tell yer what. I'm gonna go out and find meself a job and earn some money, that's what I'm gonna do. Then there won't be nothing for me to moan about, will there?'

'I'm the breadwinner in this house. I ain't having no wife of mine going out to work.'

'Why not?' Stephen butted in, his drunken grin still twisting his lips into a lop-sided grimace. 'Sounds like a fine idea to me.' He winked, screwing up the whole of his face as he struggled to keep one eye open. 'All the more money to spend over at the Queen's, eh, Pat?'

Pat ignored his father-in-law. 'What sort of a job could you get anyway?'

'I dunno, but there's bound to be something. Ain't it you who's always going on about women getting jobs 'cos we're cheap?' With fists stuck in her waist, Katie glared at Pat, daring him to say another word.

Stephen spoke, or rather mumbled, again. 'Isn't that our young Sean up there?'

'Stephen!' Nora warned her husband. She was too late.

'It is, look, going into that moneylender feller's house.'

Katie's eyes turned on her father. 'Eh?'

'Sean,' he repeated, 'going into Laney's. I saw him. He just jumped over the wall by the pub, and dived into number six. Like a young deer he was, real athletic, just like me when I was a young man. Now did I ever tell yers about the time I ran in that race against Micky O'Halloran on the—'

'So that's his game, is it?' Her row with Pat forgotten, Katie marched along the street and banged on the Lanes' front door.

Pat went to follow her but Nora stopped him. 'Pat,

275

don't. Let Katie sort the kids out. Anyway,' she said, jerking her head towards Stephen, 'the state that one's in, he's probably talking out of his hat. You just go and fetch a nice bit of fish for us all, and you'll see, by the time you get back, Katie will have forgotten all about her hollering and hooting at yer, and it'll be Sean what'll be copping it.' She grinned. 'Poor little devil!'

Pat ran his hands through his hair, shrugged, then, with a loud sigh, set off for Chrisp Street to fetch their supper.

The door of number six was opened by Irene, Arthur Lane's much younger, bleached-blonde wife. Katie didn't say a word to her. She just barged past her into the house, shouting at the top of her voice: 'Sean! Where are yer? You get out here, now! Do you hear me?'

'Mrs Mehan?' Irene called after her, in her girly, high-pitched little voice. 'Is anything wrong?'

Katie didn't answer her, she was too busy looking in the front room, but it was empty, so she stormed her way along the passage to the back kitchen.

There she found Arthur Lane, the despised local moneylender and, so it was rumoured, fence. Despite his very profitable services being in more demand than ever, since even the work in the docks had become so unpredictable, Lane had the reputation of wringing every last brass farthing out of anyone he could, even the most desperate of women who were struggling just to put a loaf of bread on their table to feed their children. He was sitting at the kitchen table, not wearing a shirt but he had his braces on over a baggy white vest, his big, fat belly hanging in folds over the top of his trousers.

Katie was so appalled by the sight of him – she had only ever seen him in his expensive suits or his camelhair overcoat – that she didn't even notice her son standing in the corner, leaning against the wall.

'What you doing here?' Sean asked, blowing a stream of smoke from his nostrils.

Katie blinked, as though released from a spell, turned to face her son and strode across the room towards him. She snatched the cigarette from his mouth and threw it in the fireplace.

'So, this is where you're getting yer money from, is it, Sean? You've been borrowing money from him.' She moved closer to her son, her face almost touching his. 'I hope it is just borrowing and you ain't been thieving.'

She looked over her shoulder at Arthur Lane, who was clearly interested in how Sean was handling himself, and said, very slowly, 'If you've got my boy involved in anything crooked . . .'

The contempt in Katie's voice made Lane chuckle, sending vibrations of amusement wobbling through his gut, but Irene, who had just appeared in the kitchen doorway sounded more upset than amused by what Katie had said.

'Mrs Mehan,' she squeaked, 'Sean ain't been doing nothing wrong, have yer, Sean? Tell yer mum. Go on.'

'I ain't borrowed nothing off no one,' Sean sneered. 'I don't have to, do I?'

'So where are yer getting yer money from?' She lowered her voice. 'People have started talking, Sean.'

'I'd be more worried about what they're saying about you and that geezer over the road, if I was you,' Sean said, looking past his mother and smiling over her shoulder at Arthur.

'Sean!' Irene piped. 'Don't speak to yer mum like that!'

The sound of someone else telling *her* son how to behave had Katie boiling. She raised her hand ready to slap the smirk right off her son's face, but she stopped. She wouldn't show herself up in front of the likes of Arthur and Irene Lane. 'I'll swing for you, Sean, God help me if I don't.' She paused, taking a deep slow breath. 'Now, get home with yer.'

Sean didn't move.

'Do as yer mother says,' Katie heard Arthur Lane saying behind her. 'Go on. Get yerself off home.'

As Katie spun round to tell Lane it was none of his business what her son did, Sean levered himself away from the wall and swaggered past her right out of the kitchen.

'See yer, love,' Irene trilled after him, 'and behave for yer mum, eh?'

Katie was beside herself. She launched herself across the room at Lane's wife, her fists clenched by her side to stop herself from slapping the stupid smile off of her red, painted lips. 'If yer so desperate for a bit of company closer to yer own age than that fat old pig,' Katie raged, 'yer wanna get yerself down St Leonard's Road to the gin palace. I'm sure there're plenty prepared to *pay* for the privilege down there.'

She ran out of the kitchen and along the passage.

Irene caught up with her, just as Katie was about to step out on to the pavement. 'Yer shouldn't talk to me like that, Mrs Mehan,' she said quietly. 'Yer don't understand . . .'

Katie didn't wait to hear what it was she didn't understand, she was too concerned with getting out of there and catching up with Sean before he had the chance to leg it. As she stepped out of the doorway, she looked about her to see where he had got to. She knew it: there he was clambering over the wall and escaping on to the East India Dock Road. The little so-and-so, showing her up in front of the likes of the Lanes. But before Katie made up her mind whether there was any point giving chase right away – he could be off in any direction by now – or if she should wait up until she heard him creep back into his nanna's later on and then read the little tyke his fortune, she heard her mum shouting the odds at the top of her voice.

Whatever now? Katie asked herself as she made her way wearily back towards this latest family drama.

Nora was standing on the street doorstep of number ten, apparently rowing with Stephen and a destitute-looking man who was standing, or rather swaying, by his side.

'What's all this about, Mum?' Katie asked, standing well back from the foul-smelling stranger.

Nora, her arms folded tightly across her chest, barring the entrance to the passageway of her house, jabbed her thumb at the man. 'This one here reckons, if ever yer've heard such a thing in the whole of yer life, that yer father issued him an open invitation to come and stay any time he liked. Met him in a boozer over Bow Common, if yer don't mind.'

Stephen nodded in drunkenly foolish agreement. 'That's true. Sure as I'm standing here in front of yers, I said to him, my wife is a good 'un, a real treasure of a woman. She'll not mind yer coming any time yer need a bed and a decent meal down yer. Them's exactly the words I said, weren't they?'

'They were, lady,' the man said in support, his boozy breath nearly knocking Nora off her feet.

'The silly bastard might have promised yer a night in Buckingham Palace for all I care,' Nora fumed, stabbing her finger into the man's chest. 'But so long as I'm the one what cleans this step, I'm telling yer, if yer put one foot across it I'll take the poker to yer. Now, bugger off!' With that Nora slammed her street door firmly in their faces.

Almost immediately the letter box flapped open and they heard Nora shout from inside, 'Katie? You still there?'

'Yes, Mum,' said Katie, not knowing whether to laugh or cry at this latest episode.

'Pat's gone to fetch some fish and taters for us all, so you can pass mine over the back wall and I'll feed the boys in here. It's up to you whether yer feed that drunken swine or not.' There was a moment's silence and then the letter box flapped shut again.

Stephen patted his new friend on the shoulder. 'We're all right,' he grinned. 'My little girl, Katie, wouldn't turn a man and his pal away, now would yer, darling?'

'Wouldn't I?' she said. 'Well, that's just where you're wrong.' And, with that, Katie stepped inside number twelve and, just like her mother, she slammed the street door shut behind her.

12

The fine spring weather continued with hardly a break and, by the middle of May, there was the makings of what looked like being a hot, dry summer. But while the sky was clear blue, the weather pleasantly warm and full of promise of even better things to come, the atmosphere in number twelve Plumley Street was very far from unclouded.

It was Monday afternoon and Katie was in the kitchen doing the ironing; there was a mountain of it and no one to give her a hand. Before Stephen had shown up out of the blue in the pub at Christmas, almost six months ago now, Nora would have been there in the kitchen with her, helping her daughter with all the work that it took to keep the family clean, clothed and fed. But she was too busy for all that now, what with all the time Stephen expected her to spend with him.

Katie didn't mean to be selfish, that wasn't her way, she just wished that the rest of the family would do something to make her load a little easier. She didn't even want them to do very much – just find a few minutes to sit down and talk to her, to reassure her that her fears about what was happening to them all were just silly, groundless worries, made worse by her being so tired lately; at least that would have made her feel she wasn't losing touch with them.

But, of course, like Nora, they were all too busy with their own lives to bother about Katie; she had always coped and they all just seemed to expect that she would carry on doing so.

It had been so much easier when the kids were little. The worst thing that happened to any of them then was a scraped knee or a lost football. But even Timmy, at nine years old, was no longer her baby. And that was another worry to add to the pile: the boys hadn't stopped growing just because there was less money in the house; new boots and trousers still had to be found from somewhere. The idea of getting a job seemed more and more sensible to Katie, but she knew that that was the last thing even to try to bring up with Pat. At least she was bumping along reasonably enough without too many rows with him, so why add extra needle to what was already a tough enough situation for a woman to handle?

While Katie fretted to herself in the kitchen of number twelve, as she ironed and pressed and thought about how she'd have to get a move on if she was ever going to get the tea ready, things next door were very different. In number ten, life seemed to be going along very nicely for all concerned, particularly Stephen. He had not only ingratiated himself with his wife but, with all his tales and jokes – not to mention his Blarney – his grandchildren had completely fallen for him. Every one of them loved having him there.

It was, as Katie had fruitlessly tried to point out to her mother on more than one occasion, as though Stephen Brady, the totally self-centred young villain who had abandoned his pregnant wife, had been totally forgotten, and had been replaced by Farvee, a lovable old scoundrel who could apparently do no wrong in anyone's but Katie's eyes. She had pleaded with her mother to take care and watch him like a hawk if she didn't want to be taken for a ride again, but Nora had dismissed her daughter's concerns and told her she should be more forgiving. And, every time, out came the same excuses: Stephen had been just a boy and had known no better, but he was a man now, and Nora was glad of it.

Nothing could convince Katie. She still thought he was a waste of space and wouldn't, even for her mum's sake, make the effort to call him Dad. But then Stephen did something that made even Katie grudgingly admit that she supposed there was a bit of good in everyone.

It started one evening in the Queen's when Stephen was sitting up at the bar, listening to Pat and Harold discussing how the so-called Great War was still affecting people, and relatively young ones at that – men like Bert Johnson, for instance, who was only in his early forties.

'When I went over to Edie's for me fag papers the other morning,' Pat said, setting down his half-empty glass on the counter, 'looked right upset she did. Reckons Bert's in such a bad way with that leg of his, he can't even stand on it no more.'

Harold, who was propping up the other side of the counter, gave a distressed shake of his head. 'She was telling my Mags how it's all swollen and infected again. Terrible it sounds. Poor sod.'

'It must get to him,' Pat went on, 'knowing his old woman's gotta do everything in that shop. And all he can do is sit there.'

Harold leant forward on the bar and said quietly, 'Edie told Mags she tried to get him to sit in the shop with her – at least he'd see a bit of life that way – but he wouldn't have it. Said he'd only be in the way.' Harold straightened up and moved along the counter to serve a stall holder who'd just come in for a quiet drink after packing up for the day. 'Know what he's doing?' he asked Pat and Stephen as he pulled the man a pint.

'What's that?' asked Stephen, speaking for the first time since the topic of Bert Johnson had come up.

'He's got himself stuck away in a corner of that little storeroom out the back of the shop, that's what. Sitting there by himself all day, he is.' Harold handed the stall holder his drink and took his money before rejoining Pat and Stephen.

'Sure, that'd drive a feller mad.'

'Yer right there, Stephen,' Harold agreed. 'It would. But he says at least he's out of her way. And if he hadn't had to drag himself out to the lavatory in the back yard, he reckons he would stay upstairs in the bedroom.'

The terrible thought of spending all that time alone, with no one to have a laugh and a joke with, made Stephen decide that he would do something to cheer up Bert Johnson.

So over the weeks, Bert and Stephen became like old pals. They'd sit in the shop's back room, day in, day out, playing hand after hand of cards, drinking bottles of the warm pale ale supplied by Edie, and smoking smelly roll-ups that clouded the room with a sickly fog. But as far as Edie was concerned, and despite her being a stickler for cleanliness, the two of them could have been smoking old tarry barge ropes; no matter what sort of stink they caused, she would never have complained. She was just grateful that her Bert had a bit of company to help him through his pain.

The sounds coming from the storeroom, of roaring laughter or of the two men discussing what they'd read in their morning papers, were as much a tonic for Edie as they were for Bert, and she found that she could get on with her job, serving her customers, stocking the shelves, slicing and wrapping slabs of this and that, with almost the same enthusiasm and energy as she had before Bert had finally succumbed to his injury.

A lot of the other neighbours were only too willing to help out the Johnsons, of course. Aggie Palmer, for one, had proved to be a real friend to Edie. Not only was she doing more hours in the shop than usual, but she had also persuaded her husband, Joe, that he should let her and young Danny Mehan take his truck to Pledger's the wholesaler to collect Edie's stock of a morning, before Joe and Danny started their regular day's haulage work.

Danny was a bit put out when Joe had told him about going with Aggie, and had made sure he let her and Joe know that he was only doing it for Edie and Bert. But even Danny had not been able to resist cracking a smile when, as he was carrying a carton of tinned peas into the shop one morning, he watched Edie Johnson telling his stern-faced mum that she must be really proud that her son had turned out so much like Stephen, his saint of a grandfather.

But as much as Bert appreciated Stephen's company, really enjoyed it even, after nearly a month of being stuck out the back and feeling more like a spare part than ever, it was with real excitement that he announced he wouldn't be needing Stephen to call on him for a couple of weeks, as he was hoping to go into hospital for treatment at last. Edie had heard from a customer about a doctor who had treated the woman's brother with some new surgical technique that might be of help to Bert. As soon as the woman had left, Edie had shut the shop, gone to the hospital, and had fought like a lioness protecting her cubs to get her husband an appointment to see the consultant.

When she had come home and told Bert what she had done, all he could say was, could they afford it? Even with the money he had got for his gold hunter watch from Arthur Lane, he was still worried about the cost of it all. But Edie wouldn't even let him talk about money. Whatever they had was his, whether it meant selling the shop and every stitch that Edie stood up in. All she wanted and prayed for was for him to be well again and free from his terrible pain.

It was nearly half past eight, on the first Friday morning in June, the morning that Edie was going with Bert to the hospital, and Aggie Palmer was banging on the door of the corner shop. She couldn't understand why it was still locked. She looked over her shoulder, across the street to where Danny was sitting in the truck that he had just backed out of the yard ready to go and fetch Edie's order from the wholesaler's.

'Dan, come over here a minute will yer, love?' Aggie called to him.

Danny reluctantly turned off the motor. He had been out a bit late the night before, seeing Bob Jarvis, and had a head on him that felt like he'd been bashing it against the yard wall. Having to turn off the engine and crank it back into life again in five minutes' time was just about the last thing he felt like doing.

He sighed loudly and dropped down on to the pavement from the cab. For about the fiftieth time that morning, Danny wished with all his heart that he could get another job and leave Joe Palmer and his bloody haulage business to rot. It wasn't that he didn't enjoy the work, it was the thought of working for someone who was half gypsy, a stinking pikey as he thought of him, that Danny had learnt to detest.

As he sauntered over to Aggie, hands stuck deep in his pockets, Danny had a look of total disdain on his face. He didn't mind helping out Edie and Bert, he liked them, they were decent people, but this was what he resented – being called over by Joe's wife to do her errands for her. Why should he do what the likes of her told him? What did she think he was, some sort of lackey?

'What's up?' he asked, insolently.

'See if yer can get over the side gate and have a look round the back for us, would yer please, love?' Aggie held her hand up to the glass window and peered through it, trying to make out if there was anyone in the dark interior of the shop. 'I can't be sure, but I reckon there's something wrong in there. I thought Edie would've been up for hours, knowing they was going to the hospital this morning.'

His resentment of Aggie Palmer temporarily forgotten, Danny grasped hold of the top of the gate and heaved himself up and over the fence. He landed lightly in the paved alley that ran between the shop and the Miltons' next door, straightened up and made his way round the back.

The back door, which led to the storeroom where Stephen and Bert had set up their impromptu card school, stood wide open but he knocked on the glass out of politeness.

'Edie?' he called. 'You there? It's me, Danny. Me and Aggie have come over to fetch yer order.'

No reply.

Danny stepped gingerly inside.

After the bright morning sunshine it was difficult to make out where he was treading, so he waited a moment for his eyes to become accustomed to the gloom. There was nobody in the room except the fat old tabby who

287

feasted on any mice who were stupid enough to think they could come into the Johnsons' yard. When he heard Danny come in, the cat awoke, stretched out in luxurious ease on its bed of sacks and licked contentedly at its fur.

Danny frowned. Everyone in the street knew that Edie, with her obsession with 'hygienics', never let that cat put a paw inside the storeroom. If he wanted to go indoors he had to clamber up over the lavvy roof and miaow outside the upstairs window until either Bert or Edie heard him and let him in that way.

Without another thought, Danny rushed along the passage and took the stairs two at a time up to where the Johnsons lived above the shop.

As he reached the top, he skidded on the slip mat, and slid right across the polished landing. He came to a stumbling halt outside the front bedroom door.

Like the back door, it too stood wide open.

Inside, Edie was sitting on the floor with Bert's head cradled in her lap; tears ran down her cheeks as she rocked back and forth.

Danny was back down the stairs in a flash, shouting for Aggie to come and help. His hands trembled so badly it took him what felt like hours to undo the bolts and the lock on the shop door to let her in.

'It's Bert,' he said, standing back to let Aggie dash past him. 'They're up in the front.'

'You'd better come with me, Dan,' Aggie called over her shoulder. 'I might need some help.'

Danny followed her back up the stairs, but he didn't go into the bedroom; he stood there, in the doorway, his heart racing and his mouth dry, watching Aggie kneeling on the floor by Edie, gently wiping the tears from her face.

'He was so sure this doctor was gonna do something

for him, Agg,' Edie whimpered. 'Now there's nothing no one can do. No one.'

Aggie put her arm round her shoulders, trying to comfort her, but Edie's suffering couldn't be stilled so easily.

'He fought in the war, in them sodding trenches. He was a hero. He never talked about it to no one, but he was. And is this all there is for him? Him dying like this? A cripple?' A sob shuddered through Edie's body. 'What was it all for, eh? He'd get himself that worked up of an evening when we listened to the news on the wireless. "What did I fight for?" he'd say. "All this business in Germany – did all them poor sods die in the filth and mud for nothing? 'Cos it's happening all over again."'

'Don't take on, Ede,' Aggie said softly. 'Look, why don't we—'

'It ain't right.' It was as though Edie hadn't heard her. 'Men like my Bert – no, not men, they was boys when they was fighting – they got hurt, they lost their lives, just for it all to happen again. You wait and see. I used to kid him that I thought he was wrong. I tried to keep him from getting so worked up, but he was right.' Edie bent forward and kissed Bert's uncombed hair. 'Weren't yer, love? My Bert couldn't stand the thought of it, could yer, darling? People listening to that Mosley and them Blackshirt bastards.' Aggie stroked the cold, slightly damp flesh of her husband's cheek. 'When he got better he was gonna go and sort out the no-good cowsons before any of the kids round here got hiked up with 'em. He was talking about it only yesterday, God love him.' Another sob shook through her body. 'Soon as he was better he was gonna do something. Now he can't do nothing. And if no one else takes his place, they'll

289

just be left to get on with it. That's what Bert was scared of. If no one stops 'em, there'll be another war. It'll all happen all over again.'

'You know the people round here, Ede,' Aggie soothed her. 'None of 'em's stupid enough to get took in by the likes of that lot. It'll all come to nothing, you'll see. It'll be a five-minute wonder, then they'll get some other daft idea in their heads.'

'No, Agg,' Edie insisted. 'This is different. Bert knew. He knew that these are wicked, terrible ideas, and they're gonna cause real trouble.' She began rocking backwards and forwards again, touching her lips to her husband's lifeless forehead. 'Aw, Agg, my poor Bert. My poor, poor Bert.'

Aggie looked up at Danny. Now she was crying as well. 'Go and fetch yer mum for us, eh Dan? There's a good lad.'

Danny was only too pleased to do as she asked. He hated to hear women crying, and as for having to look at a dead body, the thought sickened him. He had never seen anyone dead before, well, apart from the time when he was only a little kid, and the old parish priest had been laid out in the church in his open coffin. But, as they had all filed past, paying their last respects, Danny had had his eyes half closed and hadn't really looked at him. It had still given him the willies though. Yes, he was more than glad to be out of it, there was nothing he wanted to see in there. And as for what Edie was saying, there was nothing he wanted to hear either.

It was Friday, 8 June 1934, just a day after Bert Johnson had been laid to rest, and Plumley Street was still in a state of shocked mourning for their neighbour.

Danny was standing alone in the kitchen of number

twelve, shaving over the sink before he went out. Katie, Nora and Molly had gone over with Peggy and Liz to sit with Edie; Stephen and Pat were sitting out in the back yard of number ten keeping an eye on the youngsters, making sure that they didn't go making too much noise and show disrespect for the dead; and Sean had taken himself off out somewhere straight after he had swallowed down his tea.

Satisfied that he looked smart and respectable – just the way Bob Jarvis had told him to – Danny wiped his chin dry with the towel and then carefully oiled and combed his thick black hair away from his forehead. He peered out of the kitchen window to see if he needed to take a coat. The mourners at the funeral yesterday had witnessed the first sprinkling of rain since the drought had started all those weeks ago, but it looked like it had cleared up again.

Danny looked at the clock on the overmantel for what must have been the twentieth time since he had come in from work. He felt nervous, excited, wound up like the spring of a clockwork toy; he was going to a British Union of Fascists rally with Bob Jarvis. Bob had promised him that he would never have seen anything like it in the whole of his life, and that it would change the way he thought for ever.

Well before Danny Mehan was even within sight of the Olympia stadium, where the Blackshirts were holding their meeting, he was astonished to see just how many people were surging along the pavement heading towards the rally. The showery rain had started again, but it did nothing to discourage the people who were converging on the arena. There were thousands upon thousands of them. And, what was beginning to make

Danny feel even more nervous was not only did a lot of the people not seem to be members or even supporters of the British Union of Fascists, but a lot of them, far too many for Danny's liking, seemed to be involved in organising some kind of demonstration against the BUF. There were all sorts of people, mostly men, carrying banners and handing out leaflets denouncing Mosley and his supporters and jostling and heckling anyone they identified as a supporter of the fascist cause.

Danny was wondering whether it was such a good idea to have come along after all, and whether it might be better to turn round and go home, when someone tapped him on the back. He swung around, fists up, ready to defend himself, but instead of punching out, Danny smiled with relief and slapped the man matily on the shoulder. 'Bob!'

'Wotcher, mate!' Bob Jarvis greeted him in return. 'What d'yer think of all this scum?' he sneered as he brushed away a hand holding out a leaflet to him. 'Pathetic, ain't they?'

With his confidence increased now he was no longer alone, Danny agreed easily with Bob. 'Yeah, right, pathetic.'

'See,' said Bob, steering Danny towards the queues of smartly dressed young men pushing their way to the entrance, 'if only them mugs'd listen they'd realise what the Union could do for 'em. It'd sort out this country's work and money problems in no time. But this mob,' Bob sneered again, this time at a banner-waving girl who looked barely old enough to have left school, 'they couldn't stand the discipline what's needed.' Bob continued to push him forward. 'If this country's ever gonna be anything again we've gotta fight these communist idiots. What do they know, eh? Nothing, that's what.'

It was barely seven o'clock, still almost an hour before the meeting was due to start, but when Bob and Danny turned into Addison Road, they saw that there were already thousands of BUF supporters congregated there, waiting for the main gate into Olympia to open. As they moved slowly forward through the crush, Danny felt Bob grab his sleeve. They had stopped by a group of a dozen young men of about their own age, all wearing black shirts, armbands with the BUF insignia, and knee-high black boots.

'We'll wait here until the doors open,' Bob told him, slipping off his long raincoat to reveal that he was dressed the same as they were. Seeing Danny's look of surprise, Bob tapped his chest proudly and said, 'I'm a steward, me.'

Danny nodded, trying to look impressed, but he couldn't stop himself glancing warily over Bob's shoulders at the increasing numbers of banner-waving, anti-fascist demonstrators.

'See, Dan,' Bob went on, acknowledging his colleagues with a stiff little dip of his head, 'it's a classless brotherhood we want. And we're gonna explain all about it to everyone. Well, to anyone what's got the brains to listen.' He jerked his thumb behind him. 'Not like these red scum. All they understand is violence. We *persuade* people with our views. Then, once they've heard what we have to say, they realise we're right. That's why I'm so proud to be one of the stewards.' He puffed out his chest. 'You can set an example, see. Let 'em have a look at how decent people conduct 'emselves.' He flicked at a speck on his sleeve. 'It's just a shame your Molly never saw it that way.'

Danny, embarrassed, looked away. 'Yer know what girls are like, Bob,' he said quietly. 'There's no telling 'em. I did try and explain like yer told me.'

Bob punched Danny playfully on the arm and winked. 'Don't worry yerself, Dan. I've decided to give her another chance, ain't I? I'm gonna wear her down and she'll be going out with me again before she knows what day it is.'

It was almost eight o'clock and the meeting was due to begin. Bob and Danny, like all the young men surrounding them, were now more than ready to file into the hall, but the door still hadn't been opened. People were growing restless.

Suddenly, without any warning, a group of demonstrators surged forward waving their banners and jeering at the Blackshirts, singing 'The Red Flag' and the 'Internationale' at the tops of their voices. At that moment the doors were flung open from the inside and Bob shoved Danny forward into the mass of dark-uniformed men who, ignoring the taunts, began marching smartly inside.

Danny strained to turn round to see what was going on behind him, but he was being sucked along, dragged forward by the strutting crowd. From all the shouting and screaming he could hear, it sounded as though a real battle had broken out.

Inside the arena, Bob guided Danny towards a seat in the middle of one of the rows, where they sat down and waited.

It was a quarter to nine when the Blackshirt parade finally entered the hall.

They marched in with a strange, stiff-legged gait, waving replicas of the huge black and yellow flags of the British Union of Fascists with which the whole place seemed to be draped. The mood was already electric, but by the time the massed bands, all dressed in the same sombre uniform as the stewards, led in Oswald Mosley himself, in a blaze of sweeping lights, the whole hall was primed and set to give their leader a wild, adulatory welcome. As one, the audience rose to their feet and roared their salutations.

Mosley mounted the stage and all the arc lights were focused on him alone. He opened his mouth to speak but his words were immediately drowned out by barracking and yelling from one of the galleries. 'Fascism means war!' bellowed the groups of demonstrators who had infiltrated the meeting. 'The Blackshirts want another world war! Stop the fascists!'

Bob tapped Danny on the arm and signalled with a nod for him to watch as members of the Blackshirt Defence Corps, who had only moments before heralded in their leader, ran to the sides of the hall and began to scramble up the sloping, tiered walls to reach the demonstrators who were perched halfway up, waving their own banners across the BUF's flags and showering the people below with leaflets. The huge room erupted into a wild cacophony of shouts and yells with each side voicing their support for either the fascists or their opponents.

Danny watched, wincing at the force the Blackshirts used as they grabbed at the hecklers and dragged them to the ground before frogmarching them outside.

'I told yer,' said Bob triumphantly, 'we respect discipline. Efficiency, see? Not like them idiots. Just look at 'em. How could they even think they'd be any match for us?'

Mosley began speaking again; this time his clipped, upper-class tones rang clearly around the arena.

Danny was dumbfounded by what he was hearing – not that an obvious 'toff' should speak about the same things that Bob and his friends had been drumming into him during the last few months, he had expected that; what he hadn't expected was that Mosley was using almost exactly the self-same words.

It made Danny uncomfortable as he realised what it reminded him of: it was just like last Christmas when young Timmy and Michael had rehearsed their lines for the nativity pageant together. In the end, they had done it so often that each of them could recite the other's part perfectly without having any sense of what they were actually saying. Much as everyone had admired the kids' efforts, they really were more like little parrots than actors.

Danny glanced sideways at Bob – he looked transfixed as he sat there staring straight ahead at his leader. But suddenly Bob, Danny and everyone else in the hall swung their gaze towards the ceiling as a loud voice came from high above them in the rafters: 'Down with fascism!'

The arc lights swung around until they picked out, at what must have been a hundred feet above the agitated crowds, a man shuffling his way precariously across the narrow girders in the roof. Almost immediately, Blackshirt stewards had appeared on either side of him, making their own uncertain way across the rafters towards him.

All but one of the beams of lights were returned to the stage and most eyes in the hall refocused on Mosley, who had begun speaking again. 'It is customary at fascist meetings,' he explained, looking directly at the assembled members of the press without a trace of irony, 'for a very few people to prevent the audience from hearing the fascist case.'

Then there was a terrible crash, the sound of smashing glass and something fell from the rafters to the ground at the side of the hall. There was an instant huddle of Blackshirts around whatever it was that had landed. Nobody could actually see what it was, but the whisper quickly went round that it was the heckler who had unfortunately 'slipped'.

From the back of the arena, somebody threw something which landed close by Danny's feet; it was quickly followed by a hail of similar missiles. Danny soon realised what they were, as the air rapidly became tainted with the sickening stench of stink bombs cracking open around him.

It was enough to make the already tense atmosphere explode. Fights broke out all around the place, both in the packed galleries and on the main floor of the hall. Danny ducked out of the way as a young woman plunged past him yelling anti-fascist slogans. She was grabbed by two equally young women, both dressed entirely in black, who chopped her to the ground with the sides of their hands.

Bob threw back his head and gave a savage laugh. 'Let me introduce you to our jujitsu girls,' he crowed. 'But, good as they are, we can't leave it all to them.'

Danny looked on in horror as Bob Jarvis took a weighted sock from his trouser pocket and swung it hard against the side of a man's head as he cowered on the ground in front of him. Danny was rapidly coming to the conclusion that he had heard enough of the non-violent fascist case. It was time to go; he had seen enough, more than enough. And he had been made a fool of. All he wanted was to get out.

While Bob was busily 'explaining' his views to his unfortunate victim, Danny clambered over the back of his chair and, keeping his head well down, began to weave his way towards the back of the hall.

He took one last disbelieving look back towards the stage as he heard Mosley claiming that the brutal tactics of his henchmen and women only showed how 'very necessary the Blackshirt Defence Corps is to defend free speech in Great Britain.'

Before he turned his head away in disgust, Danny saw Bob swing the weighted sock down on to the now unconscious man who lay at his feet.

Danny felt the taste of bile rise into his mouth; he had to get out in the fresh air. Using his elbows and his shoulders, he eventually reached the double doors where, less than an hour ago, he had entered the hall so cocky and full of it all. But his way out was barred by a bizarre-looking group of men and women in evening dress. The women's clothes alone looked as though they would have cost Danny a year's wages. They were all braying and laughing as the men in their group shoved their way past the anti-fascist demonstrators, heedless as to whom they knocked down in their eagerness to get inside and to listen to their hero. It took all Danny's remaining strength to struggle past them, but he had to get out.

When he at last managed to fight his way on to the street, he found that fresher air apart, things were just as bad out there. There were lines of banner-waving demonstrators, locked in brutal clashes with club-wielding stewards dressed in the full Blackshirt regalia. Behind them were what Danny guessed must have been a couple of thousand police, mounted as well as on foot. They had their batons drawn, and made charge after charge at the fighting hordes.

Danny pressed himself against the wall and edged his way along, moving as fast as he could away from the scene of escalating madness, trying to lose himself amongst the bloodthirsty crowds, gathering to watch the spectacle.

When he finally reached Plumley Street, it was so late that even though it was a Friday night, both number ten and number twelve were in darkness. But before he went into his nanna's house to go to bed, Danny stuck his hand through the letter box of number twelve and pulled out the key. He crept inside and, as quietly as he could, he made his way upstairs.

He paused on the landing, listening for any sounds from his parents' room. All he heard was his father softly snoring. He just hoped that his mum was asleep as well, as he tapped on his sister's bedroom door.

'Moll?' he hissed under his breath as he turned the handle. 'You asleep?'

'What? Who is it?' Molly's voice was thick with sleep.

'It's me. Danny.' He sat down on the bed beside her. 'Keep it quiet, Moll, they're all asleep.'

'So was I,' she whispered tetchily, pushing herself up on her elbows. 'This had better be good, Dan.'

Danny hesitated for a brief moment then said, 'It's Bob Jarvis.'

'Not him again. I told yer, I—'

'Listen. I don't want yer seeing him.'

'I don't believe this.' Molly was now wide awake and very angry. 'You have the cheek to come in here and wake me up to tell me not to see someone who I ain't even seeing?' She poked her brother hard in the chest. 'What's up with you, Danny Mehan? You pissed or something? Or have yer just taken leave o' yer senses?'

'I mean it,' Danny said. 'I don't want yer seeing him.'

'You flaming hypocrite. Yer went barmy when I told yer I wasn't seeing him no more. Yer kept going on about what a good bloke he was. And now yer saying I shouldn't see him, even if I wanted to.'

'Look, Moll, keep yer voice down and listen. He's no good. All right? But I know he still fancies yer, and he's talking about getting yer to go back with him. I just don't want yer to let him kid yer, that's all.'

'You must think I'm a right flaming idiot. But, tell me, why should I have *you* telling me what I can and can't do?'

'I don't care what yer think about me, but please, Moll, yer've gotta listen.' Danny grabbed her hand and squeezed it. 'I'm serious. If he even comes anywhere near yer, yer to tell me. Right?'

Molly pulled her hand away from him. She had never heard her brother talk like this before. Perhaps he too had seen the other side of Bob Jarvis. 'All right,' she said quietly. 'I'll tell yer.'

'And while we're at it,' he said, standing up and moving backwards towards the door, 'any other blokes who wanna see yer. I wanna know who they are and what they're up to. All right?'

'No it ain't bleed'n all right. You reckon I've gotta report to you about who I wanna see? Yer kidding, ain't yer?'

'No,' said Danny simply. 'I ain't. I wanna know everything about any feller who so much as talks to yer.' With that, he was gone.

The next morning all of the family except Danny were sitting around the breakfast table in the kitchen of number twelve. Even Nora had come in from next door when Stephen had produced a couple of pounds of bacon from one of his mysterious sources. But the reappearance of the much-missed fried breakfast on the Mehans' table still hadn't improved the atmosphere.

'Michael,' snapped Molly, slamming her fork on to her plate, 'will you please shut yer noise for five minutes? Or d'yer want me to shut yer gob for yer?'

Michael grinned at his granddad. 'Oooo, hark at her! Wonder what's up with old Misery Guts, eh, Farvee?' He jerked his head at his pale, exhausted-looking sister. 'She's been out on too many late nights by the look of it.'

'That's enough, Michael,' Katie warned him, waving the breadknife she was using to slice up the loaf to emphasise that she meant it.

'It's a good story though, innit, Farvee?' Michael went on, completely ignoring all the threats.

'It is, it is,' Stephen agreed, putting his glasses back on to read the item from the morning paper once again.

'So did the lion eat the man all up then?' Timmy asked, his eyes wide and his mouth stuffed full of toast. 'Or did it leave bits of him?'

'I reckon there was probably bits of his uniform that the big old pussy cat would have spat out,' said Stephen after a moment's consideration. 'I mean, even a big old lion wouldn't want to eat a zoo keeper's brass buttons and his peaked cap, now would he?'

'Do we *need* to go into details while we're eating?' Katie asked, looking to Nora for support.

'Sure, leave them alone,' said Nora, smiling indulgently at her husband and young grandsons. 'It's not every day of the week that you hear about a keeper being attacked by lions while he's trying to get a visitor's hat back for him, now is it?'

'I dunno why they need to read about the flaming zoo,' said Katie, slapping down another heap of toast on the table and setting about slicing some more bread. 'It gets more like the flipping monkey house in here every day, with all the chattering and squawking what's going on.'

'It's parrots what squawk, not monkeys,' said Michael, ducking to avoid the inevitable clip round the ear for his cheek.

'Pat,' said Katie, tossing down the breadknife, 'will you tell him?'

'Do as yer mother says,' said Pat without looking up from his plate.

Just then, Danny came into the kitchen, looking even rougher than Molly.

'And what sort of time d'yer call this?' Katie enquired of her eldest son. 'Yer lucky that this lot ain't finished everything off.'

'I ain't hungry,' said Danny, dropping down on to the chair next to Sean. 'I'll just have a cuppa tea.'

'What sort of a breakfast's that when yer've gotta work this morning?' Katie wanted to know. 'And anyway,' she added grudgingly, 'there's bacon.'

'I still don't want none, and I ain't going in to work this morning.'

'What?' Now it was Pat who was questioning him. 'But you always do a half-day on a Saturday.'

Danny held up his hand. 'It's all right, I just nipped along and told Joe there's something I've gotta do.'

'Aw yeah?' Pat said suspiciously. 'And what's so important that yer gonna miss work? You sure you ain't chucked that job in, Danny?'

'No. I promised I wouldn't unless I found something else, and I ain't. Satisfied?'

'Don't you *dare* speak to yer father like that.' Katie smacked the flat of her hand round the back of Danny's head. 'You ain't too big for a good hiding yer know, boy.'

'No, but I'm big enough to ask Lizzie to marry me,' Danny blurted out.

'Eh?' Katie looked at Pat, then at Nora, then at Pat again.

'I've decided it's time I settled down. I know it won't be able to happen for a year or two yet. I've gotta lot of saving to do. But it's what I want and no one's gonna stop me. I'm going over there this morning to ask her.'

'Yer right about needing a few quid if yer gonna get hitched.' Pat was unable to resist the chance of rubbing it in that he'd been right all along. 'It's lucky yer never chucked yer job in after all then, ain't it?'

'I've been thinking about that,' said Danny grimly. 'And I realise Joe Palmer's been good to me. Put up with a load of old lip from me and all. I should be more grateful.' He paused, staring down at the table. 'I mean to make it up to him.'

Pat rubbed his hands together in satisfaction. 'He's come to his senses at last. Thank Gawd for that.'

'Not now, Pat,' breathed Katie, her eyes shining with tears. 'This is too happy a time to row.'

'So yer don't mind then?' Danny asked quietly.

'Mind?' Katie rushed to her son's side and wrapped her arms tightly around him. 'How could I mind? I'm bloody ecstatic!'

Timmy and Michael burst into giggles at their mum using 'language'.

'A wedding,' Katie went on, apparently not caring that her two youngest were now repeating 'bloody ecstatic, bloody ecstatic' over and over again. 'And not only to a nice Catholic girl from a lovely family, but from the same turning and all. What more could a mother ask for?'

'And what a great time we're going to have,' beamed Nora, 'with all the planning for the wedding with Lizzie and Peg. Sure, won't it be just great?'

Katie nodded in enthusiastic agreement. 'Just think

of Lizzie's lovely fair hair under a veil, Mum. She'll look a right picture walking up that aisle.'

Nora sighed rapturously at the thought of it. 'And won't the procession next month be good practice for the boys being pageboys at the wedding? Now we'll have *two* opportunities to get them all done up in little white satin suits.'

Michael and Timmy's giggles turned to wide-eyed expressions of alarm as the double horror presented itself. Not only were they going to be humiliated at the annual Catholic Parade, but now they were expected to make idiots of themselves at their big brother's wedding.

'Pageboys?' Michael breathed, as though he were repeating the name of the very devil himself. 'Little white satin suits?'

Nora grabbed Timmy's chubby face between her hands. 'Aw glory, won't I be proud of yers!'

Stephen grimaced and rolled his eyes supportively at the boys.

'And I know it's not for a while yet,' said Danny, beginning to enjoy himself, 'but I was hoping you'd think about being me best man, Sean.'

Sean, for all his sulky, adolescent bravado, couldn't hide his delight at being treated in such an adult way. He stood up and grabbed his brother by the hand. 'Good luck to yer, Dan,' he said, pumping his arm up and down, and slapping him across the shoulder. 'I'd be proud to stand next to yer.' Then he began laughing. 'But don't yer reckon yer'd better go over and ask Lizzie before them pair of little 'uns wind up telling her before yer've had the chance?'

Danny nodded, hesitated for a moment, then said quietly, 'I'm glad yer all happy for me. Ta.' He scratched his head shyly and added with a soppy grin, 'I'd better go and do as you say, Sean. I mean, it wouldn't do to keep no secrets from Liz, now would it?'

Molly waited until Danny had disappeared into the passage, then she stood up from the table and said stiffly, 'You lot finished with all this? I'll start clearing up, shall I?'

After the shock and sadness of Bert's sudden death, the engagement of Danny Mehan and Liz Watts was such a welcome event that it was all anyone could talk about all the rest of that day, all the next day, and even in whispers during Mass. It even eclipsed the appearance of Irene Lane paying her last respects at the funeral as the most popular topic for the gossips to chew over. Everyone seemed delighted – or at least nosy regarding the arrangements – at the prospect of the wedding. Everyone, that is, except Molly. She had been unusually quiet since Danny had made his announcement.

'I'm going up,' she suddenly announced when she had helped her mum and nanna clear away after the Sunday tea, which Liz and her mum and dad had shared with them in celebration of the engagement.

'Not going out on a fine evening like this, Moll?' Katie asked her, as she folded the table cloth that had been brought out especially. She looked over her shoulder and smiled. 'I thought you had a regular appointment of a Sunday. Didn't you, Mum?'

Nora chuckled. 'I did.' She paused and looked slyly at her granddaughter. 'D'yer know what'd be a wonderful thing?' she began slowly. 'A real dream come true for yer old nanna? I'll tell yers. If the family was blessed with a double wedding.'

Wide-eyed, Molly stared in alarm at her nanna: she couldn't give her away, she couldn't.

305

'But yer'll have to get yerself a nice young man first if I'm to have me wish, won't you, darling?' added Nora with a wink.

'Just leave me alone, can't yer?' Molly shouted, and ran from the room.

The next morning, as the girls made their way to work, Liz was so excited that she didn't seem to notice that while she chattered away nineteen to the dozen about herself and Danny, Molly was walking along beside her in stony-faced silence. It was only when they came to the doors of the factory that Molly actually spoke.

'I ain't going in,' Molly said abruptly.

'I know it's Monday and the sun's shining, Moll, but we ain't ladies of leisure.'

Molly began walking away. 'There's something I've gotta do,' she said, her steps becoming faster. 'Be a mate and tell 'em I'm ill.'

Liz stood there, stunned, watching her friend sprint off along the road.

By the time Molly reached Simon's uncle's printing works, in a narrow side turning off Cable Street, she could barely breathe. She had always been a good runner but it wasn't so much the exertion as the panic she was feeling that was making her gasp for breath.

With one hand pressed to her chest to steady herself, she patted her hair tidy with the other, and then climbed the steep flight of stone steps to the front door.

She paused, closed her eyes, crossed herself and then pulled the door firmly open. With a smile set on her lips she went up to the little glass window behind which sat a stern-faced, grey-haired elderly man, writing in a big leather-covered ledger.

'Good morning,' she said, hoping that her quaking

voice wouldn't give her away. 'I've come over from Terson's Teas. It's about the order. I'm to speak to Simon Blomstein.'

Without looking up from his ledger, the elderly man shouted, 'Simon. Out here.'

As she waited for Simon to appear, Molly felt so nervous that she was convinced she was going to faint. Then, quite suddenly, there he was, peering over the elderly man's shoulder, a look of bewilderment shadowing his dark, handsome face as he realised who it was he had been called out to see.

'I know what this is about, Uncle David,' Simon said, frantically signalling with his eyes for Molly to go outside – to go *anywhere* that was out of sight of his uncle.

'It had better not be any trouble, Simon,' David grunted in reply, still concentrating on his ledger.

'No, it's nothing,' said Simon, slipping past his uncle's chair and reaching for the door handle. 'I won't disturb you; I'll go out there and see her.'

As Simon closed the door silently behind him, David carried on with his writing.

On the other side of the door, Simon hurriedly ushered Molly outside, back down the steep stone steps, and round the corner into a narrow alleyway that ran alongside the printing works.

'What's wrong?' he asked, his eyes frantically searching her face for clues. 'Why didn't you meet me yesterday?'

Now she was actually facing him, Molly wasn't sure how she was going to explain. She dropped her chin and stood there, staring down at her feet, feeling chilled to the bone even though it was a bright sunny morning.

'You're shivering. Are you ill? Is that what you're going to tell me?'

She looked up at him and shook her head. Tears fell on to her cheeks. 'I'm sorry I didn't turn up yesterday, but it's Danny and Liz. Danny's going on about wanting to know who I'm seeing and now he's gone and got engaged to Liz and she knows all about yer. They ain't gonna have any secrets, and I'm scared she's gonna give us away. And me nanna's going on about me having to get a young man, so's I can get married. Yer uncle'd go barmy . . .' She sniffed loudly. 'I'm sorry, Simon. I can't see yer no more.'

'No, don't say that. It doesn't matter if Liz tells your brother, does it?'

'You don't know what he's been like lately. He's been mixed up with these blokes.' She wiped her tears away with the back of her hand. 'I don't think he is now, but I still don't think he'd want me seeing yer, not if he knew you was . . .' She ran her hand distractedly through her hair. 'Look, I just know he wouldn't, all right.'

Simon took out his handkerchief and handed it to Molly. She took it without a word. 'Molly, I want to see you, and I know you feel the same. It'll be all right, I know it will. We'll find a way.'

Molly gave a shuddering, self-pitying sob and Simon reached out to touch her but, at the sound of voices coming from a window high above their heads, he pulled away again.

'See,' she sniffed. 'This is what it'd always be like. We'd be hiding all the time like criminals.'

'Molly, I've got to go on seeing you.'

'But yer not Catholic, Simon.'

'And you're not Jewish.' He tried to smile. 'Anyway what's happened to the girl who said that the worst thing she could think of was being bored?'

'I've grown up since then,' she said, her voice barely

308

audible. 'I ain't a little kid playing games no more.'

'Nor am I. This is the most grown-up thing I've ever said to anyone.' He reached out and took her in his arms. 'Molly Katherine Mehan,' he breathed into her ear, 'I love you. And no one, not your brother, not your grandmother, not my uncle, not anyone, is going to take you away from me.'

13

On a glorious Sunday morning at the beginning of July,
nearly a month after Danny and Liz had announced their
engagement, a topic other than The Wedding was
occupying the residents of Plumley Street: the annual
Catholic Procession from the Church of Saint Mary and
Saint Joseph.

Katie, Nora and Molly, like many other women in that
part of Poplar, had been up since first light preparing their
houses, making sure that they were clean both inside and
out, fit and in readiness for the shrines they had been
getting ready to set beside their street doors.

Katie was giving her inside windows a final polish
before rehanging the freshly washed lace curtains, while
Molly was energetically scrubbing the pavement with a
wet, long-handled broom, and Nora was engrossed in
washing her street doorstep before she gave it a thorough
whitening – and woe betide anyone stupid enough to
put even the sight of a foot within half a yard of her
efforts, she threatened.

Nora stood up. 'Glad to see yer with the colour back
in yer cheeks, Molly love,' she said, handing her
granddaughter the bucket so she could empty the dirty
water into the gutter for her. 'Sorted out the problems
yer was having with this feller o' your'n then, I suppose?'

Molly's mouth fell open. She couldn't believe that her

nanna knew about her trying to give up Simon – nor
that she could be that indiscreet. As she looked round in
hasty alarm to see if her mum had overheard her through
the window, Molly spilt the bucket, completely soaking
her dress and legs with the mucky water that was meant
to have gone down the drain. 'Now look what yer've made
me do, Nan,' she wailed.

'I knew I was right.' Nora smiled triumphantly,
ignoring the state of her granddaughter's dress. 'Yer
can't fool yer old nanna.'

'Nanna, please, don't. Mum'll hear yer.' She lowered
her eyes. 'And yer know what she'd say if she knew about
him being . . . you know.'

Nora took the empty bucket from Molly and whispered
loudly, 'So, it's the Jewish feller still, is it? I did wonder
when yer never went out the other Sunday.'

Molly flashed an anxious look towards her mother,
who was frowning at them from the other side of the
windowpanes. 'Please, Nanna, don't do this.'

Nora bent forward, leaning close to her granddaughter.
'I've said it often enough to yer, but I really would like to
meet him one day. And I could help yer get round yer
mother. You know me, I'll be able to talk her into taking a
liking to him before she knows what's hit her. He could be
one of them Lascar fellers off the ships and she'd still love
him by the time I've finished with her.'

Molly was still standing there dripping, too
flabbergasted to know even how to begin answering her
nanna, when Katie emerged from the gloom of the
passageway. 'What's going on out here?' she demanded.
'Look at yer, yer wringing wet, yer daft mare.'

'It's nothing, Mum. Is it, Nan?' Molly said, looking
pointedly at Nora. 'Just me being clumsy, that's all.'

Nora shook her head at Molly and tutted. 'That's right,

Katie,' she sighed, 'it was nothing. Just this leggy great daughter of yours being clumsy.' She picked up her bucket and then turned to face Katie. 'Pat changed his mind yet, has he?'

'No. It's no good. He won't budge.' Katie glanced across the street to see if Phoebe or Sooky were out earwigging. But she was safe; unusually for that neighbourhood, neither of the two women's families were Catholic, so they had no reason to be up so early on a Sunday morning. 'You all reckon I'm the stubborn one,' she went on. 'Well, I'm telling yer, I reckon Pat could give me lessons. He's all right, ain't he, saying he's too busy to march with us, but he can find time to watch Father Hopkins bless our shrine. I know what's really up with him: he reckons this is all women's business.'

Pat appeared in the passageway behind her. 'I don't think that, Katie, and I never said it neither, and well you know it. What I actually said was that I had me own business to attend to – important business – so don't go telling lies, all right?'

Katie stepped out on to the pavement and turned to face him. 'So what exactly is this business that's more important than the Procession then?' Katie stuck her fists into her waist and stared at him, challenging him to answer *that* if he could.

'If yer really interested, I'll tell yer,' he answered, equally forcefully. 'I've got some of the blokes from work coming round this afternoon for a meeting, like. We wanna get things straight about how far we're gonna go if the guv'nors try pulling any more o' them strokes what they've threatened.' Pat bashed the side of his fist against the wall. 'Cutting the rates and taking on non-union men. It ain't right and we won't put up with it. But we've gotta be in agreement about any action. We can't let 'em divide us.' He paused, then looked at Katie. 'Satisfied?'

Katie knew Molly was standing there behind her, and she hated having cross words with Pat in front of any of her children, but she had set her heart on his going on the parade with her. 'You've been on the march every other year.'

Exasperated, Pat threw up his hands. 'Well, we ain't been in this much shtook every other year, have we?'

She lifted her chin defiantly. 'And yer really think it'll make any difference what you and a couple of mates decide in our back kitchen, do yer?'

'Look, Kate,' he said quietly, 'I know yer disappointed about me not going with yer, but can't yer keep yer voice down a bit? It can't be helped. A man's gotta earn a living to keep his family, and that's final.'

Ignoring his appeal to calm down, Katie, her face tight with temper, yelled, 'And you're doing such a good job of that, ain't yer? That's all you can do, ain't it, rabbit on about rights and unions and Gawd knows what else. All that old bunny really puts shoes on the kids' feet and food in their bellies, don't it? Go out the back yard and have a look, go on. I can't shut that meat safe out there for all the grub yer keep putting in it.' She jabbed an accusing finger at him. 'Yer just making excuses, Pat Mehan, that's what yer doing. Yer just don't wanna march with me. Why won't yer admit it?' Now she was in full flow, Katie wasn't concerned with whether she was being fair or making sense, nor was she about to let her husband defend himself. She barely paused for breath before continuing, 'Well, there's plenty of men round here what *will* be marching. Men what ain't scared to be seen with women and kids. Mind you, they *know* they're men. They've got nothing to worry about. They ain't pathetic excuses for . . .' As soon as the words had

314

passed her lips, Katie regretted them; immediately she came to her senses and realised where this could lead them. She held up her hand in a feeble attempt to stop whatever it was she had said from doing any harm, but it was too late, Pat's face had blanched and his shoulders had dropped.

'So that's how yer feel is it?' he said, almost to himself. 'I thought we'd got over all this.'

'Pat ...'

Nora stepped forward and touched her daughter's arm. 'Katie,' she said firmly, 'that's enough. No more.'

Katie shook her away; her hands were trembling. 'Pat, I never meant ...'

Innocently unaware of the drama that was being acted out on the pavement, Timmy and Michael came bouncing out of their nanna's house, carefully avoiding the newly cleaned step.

'Mum!' Michael yelled, his voice at full volume even though he was standing right in front of her. 'Farvee said that Dad ain't marching. Is it true? Is it?' He didn't wait for her to answer. 'So can we just watch and all? We could stay here with Dad, couldn't we? We'd be ever so good.'

It was Pat who answered his son. He spoke slowly as though he was having trouble saying the words. 'Don't be so cheeky, Michael. You do as yer mother says. Yer gonna march and that's the end of it.'

'But, Dad,' groaned Michael, 'all the kids'll be there from the other schools, all them right hard kids from round Mathias Street and Wade Street. Dad, they'll really—'

Before Michael could say what exactly it was that the hard kids would do, Nora had grabbed hold of him and Timmy by the backs of their shirts and was whisking them roughly towards number ten.

'I'll skin that Stephen,' Nora muttered darkly as she

315

hoisted them backwards. 'And I'll skin you as well, if I have to listen to any more of this nonsense, Michael.' She shoved first him and then Timmy into the passageway. 'Sure, haven't I told yer both enough times already, the parade'll be good practice for the wedding.'

With her grandsons safely, if ignominiously, out of the way, Nora turned her attention to Molly, who was standing watching her parents with a look in her eyes that made her seem more like a bewildered child than a feisty young woman who wouldn't take any nonsense from anyone.

'And you, Molly,' Nora said firmly, doing her best to keep some sort of control of the situation, 'you get in here with me. I need a hand with me jobs. And I'm sure,' she continued, flashing a meaningful look at Pat, 'that yer mum and dad have got plenty they need to do indoors as well.'

Shoulders slumped just like her father's, Molly went without protest into her nanna's, her skirt dripping around her, while her mum followed her dad into next door to finish their row in private.

Katie was almost in tears as she stood facing Pat in the kitchen. 'I'm sorry, Pat, I never meant nothing, it's just 'cos I've got meself all upset that you ain't coming, that's all. Why don't yer change yer mind, eh? Just for me. It ain't too late.'

'Why should yer want me there? I'm useless, ain't I?'

'No,' Katie snapped, her blood rising to her cheeks, 'yer just flaming stubborn.'

'*Me?* That's a laugh.'

'I suppose yer can at least manage to come to Mass with us this morning.'

'No. No, I don't think I can. I'm gonna sort out what I wanna talk to the blokes about later on.'

'You liar! You just made that up, didn't yer? Just to

get me going.' Katie circled him as he stood there by the table, clenching and unclenching his fists. 'You think yer so clever. Well, it's you what'll rot in hell for yer lies, Pat Mehan.' She stopped moving and stood there in front of him, chin in the air. 'It's meant to be Sunday,' she said, playing her final card. 'Father Hopkins won't like it, you not going to church. Especially today of all days.'

'Well, that's hard luck. He ain't got no family to feed, I have. Even if yer do reckon I'm useless at it.'

With that, Pat shoved her out of the way and threw open the back door. He looked over his shoulder and said stonily, 'Now, if I have yer permission, I'm going out to the lav for a bit of peace.'

Katie sat down and stared at the table. Why had she wound him up like that? Why couldn't she just keep her big mouth shut?

She rubbed her hands over her face. It was all her mum's fault. She was the one she'd learnt it from – opening her gob first and thinking after. She laughed mirthlessly.

'Thanks, Mum,' she said to herself.

The Sunday dinner was a very restrained affair, with the boiled bacon and pease pudding being eaten in almost total silence. Stephen had made one or two attempts to cheer things up a bit, by joshing the two youngest a couple of times, but with the threat of the Procession and the hated white satin shirts and stiffly pressed shorts hanging over them, even he couldn't raise a smile from Michael and Timmy.

As for Pat, Danny, Molly and Sean, they never said a word between them; Nora chatted a bit in a general sort of a way, and Katie complained a bit, mainly about elbows on the table and the rudeness of people who stretched across without saying excuse me to others, but there was nothing that could in any way pass for the usual mealtime banter around the Mehans' kitchen table. There wasn't even a row.

As soon as the knives and forks had been set down on the empty plates, Katie stood up. 'Me, Molly and Mum're gonna get the boys and ourselves ready and the shrine set up,' she said, addressing Pat without looking directly at him. 'So, if you can manage it, and you don't think yer mates from work'll laugh at yer if they turn up early, I'd appreciate it if yer could clear the table for me. Yer never know,' she added, glaring at Sean, Danny and Stephen in turn, 'yer might even get a bit of help from someone.' She pointed at Michael. 'You sit there while I go up and fetch yer outfits from me wardrobe. Then we'll go next door into Nanna's.'

With that, Katie marched out of the kitchen. She had just reached the bottom of the stairs when she paused, her hand hovering over the banisters. 'And, Michael, don't you dare go out that back yard and try and have it away over that wall,' she called back along the passage.

Despite Michael and Timmy's reluctance and their increasingly wild pleas for mercy, they, their mum, nanna and sister were, at Katie's insistence, amongst the first to arrive at Saint Mary and Saint Joseph's in Canton Street. But the crowds soon began to gather, and soon the churchyard and the pavement outside were packed with people eager to set off on the Solemn Procession in honour of Our Lady that was due to begin at four o'clock.

But even with all the milling about, there was still no hiding place for Michael and Timmy; Katie was keeping an eagle eye on the pair of them. It was because she was concentrating on not letting the boys out of her sight that she didn't notice Frank Barber come up behind her.

'Afternoon, Katie,' he said.

Katie turned round and smiled at him. 'Hello, Frank. Yer made me jump.'

He returned her smile and said quietly, 'I was wondering if we could join yer. It used to be, yer know, someone else who used to do all this. Theresa's mum. I just used to wait at home with the shrine.' He paused, embarrassed. 'Tell yer the truth, I'm a bit out o' me depth.'

'Course yer can stand with us. Yer more than welcome, Frank.' Katie smiled down at Theresa who was wearing the white dress and little muslin veil of a first communicant. 'It's good to see a man spending time with his child. Tell yer what, I'll see if Father Hopkins'll let us march together and all, how'd that be?'

Nora shook her head. 'I don't think I'm hearing this,' she muttered to herself. 'Won't that girl ever learn?'

Frank nodded his thanks, as Katie, her surveillance of her boys apparently no longer important, went off to speak to the priest. She was back in less than five minutes, her face wreathed in smiles of victory, with the priest by her side.

'It's all arranged,' she said. 'Father Hopkins here was keeping it a secret until the last minute but he's been planning a special treat for the boys.' Katie couldn't stop herself beaming with pride, even though she knew it was a sin. 'As a reward for all their hard work in the nativity play,' she said slowly, savouring every words, 'Father Hopkins is giving our Timmy and our Michael the honour of carrying the two ends of the big flower wreath what spells "Jesus". Right at the very front of the Procession they'll be, just behind the Cross Bearer.

And he said that we can walk along behind them, didn't yer, Father?'

Timmy and Michael were not pleased by this revelation, in fact, they were totally scandalised by the idea. Carrying flowers! It was the final humiliation. Michael was desperate; those kids from Upper North Street would never let him forget this. They'd beat him to a pulp.

'But Father Hopkins,' he said, his brain whirling with the effort of trying to come up with a plan of escape, 'don't yer think . . .' As he frantically searched about him for a scapegoat, his eyes lit on Frank Barber's daughter. 'Don't yer think it'd be really nice if Theresa carried the wreath?' Then, with an inspired afterthought, he added the whispered clincher, 'What with her not having a mum or nothing.'

Father Hopkins clapped his hands together in delight and said, 'What a wonderful child you have there, Katie.' The priest patted Michael on the head. 'I'll tell you what I'll do, young Michael. I'll let you and Timmy *share* carrying it with her. She can stand between the pair of you. Now how would that be?'

Michael was fit to collapse with the shame of it. Flowers, *and* with a girl in a white frock and veil. He would have to think of something, or he might as well go and chuck himself straight into the Cut and get it over with there and then.

Katie was obviously unaware of her son's real intention. Her face glowing with pleasure and her eyes sparkling with tears of motherly adoration, she bent forward and kissed the top of his plastered down red curls. 'And just think, Michael,' she cooed. 'Me, yer nanna, Molly and Frank'll all be walking along right behind yer. We'll be able to watch yer every step of the way.'

Nora was as horrified by all this as her grandson, but for reasons of her own. She could only wonder at her daughter's apparent death wish; she was actually going to parade around the streets alongside Frank Barber. Whatever was she thinking of?

'Won't that be cosy?' she mumbled to Katie through gritted teeth. 'I can't wait to see what Pat'll have to say when he comes out to see the blessing.'

'You really think he's gonna be there?' Katie hissed back disbelievingly, so that Frank couldn't hear her. 'Anyway, even Pat couldn't be stupid enough to see anything wrong with me walking alongside a neighbour in the Procession.'

The whole experience turned out to be even more awful than Michael had feared; if only it had rained as it had yesterday, but no such luck, the sun shone, the skies were clear, and every inch of every pavement of the route was lined with people, all eager to watch his humiliation.

And what a route it was. There was nothing discreet about the Annual Solemn Out-Door Procession. It had obviously been designed, Michael was convinced, to show him off in all his disgrace to the maximum number of people in the district.

They set off from the church in Canton Street, went through Pekin Street, then out on to the East India Dock Road. Via a long circuitous route to visit the shrines of the church congregation in every possible street, the Procession returned eventually to the church for the Solemn Benediction of the Blessed Sacrament.

Michael would have fainted if he thought he could have got away with it but, every step of the way, he could feel his nanna's, mum's and sister's eyes boring into his back. Not only was every street packed, but they

321

were all decked with bunting in the blue and white of
Our Lady and the yellow and white of the Papal flag
flapping in the gentle summer breeze – all in mockery
of Michael Mehan, the rotten flowers, his stupid white
shirt and his plastered down hair. It wouldn't have been
so bad if he could have been hidden away somewhere
near the back, but no, he had to be right up there behind
the Cross Bearer. It was mortifying.

The admiring crowds obviously didn't agree with
Michael. They bowed their heads and crossed
themselves, murmuring appreciatively, as the parade
passed by, which it took quite a time to do, because
coming up behind him, his brother and Theresa, weren't
only his mum, sister, nanna and Frank Barber, but a
whole long succession of groups and individuals all
taking part in the spectacular event.

There were men from the East End Catholic clubs,
groups and guilds, carrying flower-decked statues of
their patron saints high above their shoulders so that
everyone could see and revere them. From the bases of
the statues, ribbons and garlands stretched out to rows
of accompanying children: tiny, smiling maids of honour
in pretty pastel dresses, and not-so-happy-looking boys
in neatly pressed shorts, white shirts and coloured sashes
– who held the ends in little hands scrubbed clean by
mothers determined not to be shown up by grubby
knuckles. Then there were the acolytes, the servers, the
choristers, and, of course, the clergy, all in their starched
and laundered best. And there were the clusters of
nervous young first communicants: the girls in pure
white dresses and miniature bridal veils and the boys in
their much-hated scaled-down sailor suits or the even
more loathed white satin shorts and tops, carrying
sheaves of green wheat and bunches of grapes to

symbolise the Eucharist. The older pupils from the Catholic schools in the area marched along the edges of the Procession, their job being to keep the littler ones in some sort of order and to hold out collecting boxes to the crowds.

There wasn't even the chance that anyone might sleep through the whole thing rather than witnessing Michael's disgrace, not unless they were stone deaf, because every shaming step he took along the way was accompanied by brass bands playing dignified, but very loud religious music, their gleaming instruments shining in the hot afternoon sun, signalling their arrival, as they made their way through the dusty grime of the London streets.

Despite what Michael felt about the experience, he, like everyone else who was taking part, looked his very best. For the honour of taking part in the Procession, money was found from somewhere, even if it meant pawning the very sheets from the bed or the square of ragged mat from the front room floor.

By the time the Procession reached the top of Plumley Street, Michael was in such a daze of disgrace and red-faced humiliation that he had gone beyond trying to hatch a plan of escape. He didn't even take the opportunity to try to run indoors when the priest stopped to bless the shrine that stood between numbers ten and twelve that Nora, Katie and Molly had fixed up between them after they had finished their cleaning.

The three of them had carefully arranged the delicate lace table cloth, the sole item of dowry that Nora had brought with her from Ireland, on the gate-legged table, which usually stood under the window in Katie's front room, and had topped it off with a wooden crucifix, a plaster statue of Our Lady and the aspidistra in the elaborately painted china art pot that Pat had brought for Katie in Club Row at Christmas time. But there was no sign of Pat himself standing by the shrine, only Stephen and Danny.

'Dad'll be in the kitchen with his workmates,' Molly whispered to her mum.

Katie nodded. 'Of course,' she said, doing her best to hide the disappointment and anger that was making her mouth dry.

As they waited for the other shrines in Plumley Street to be blessed, Katie watched without really seeing as the priest crossed the road and stopped outside number eleven where Nutty Lil was standing proudly by a table with a framed print of the Sacred Heart that Frank had set up for her before he and Theresa had left for the church. Then he moved on to number nine, where Liz and Peg Watts were standing by their more elaborate efforts which involved vases of bright summer flowers that Peg had bought specially from Chrisp Street the night before. At number eight, Aggie and Joe Palmer had backed the truck into the gateway of their yard and had covered its flat back with a big white sheet, on which they had set a pair of brilliantly polished brass candlesticks, complete with burning candles, and a gold-framed picture of the Virgin Mary. Even the Miltons had done their best with a rickety table topped with a cloth and a vase of flowers given to Ellen Milton by Edie from the corner shop who, still being in mourning for her Bert, hadn't felt much like having a shrine of her own.

Not being Catholic, Phoebe and Sooky hadn't decorated outside the fronts of their houses, but like Mags and Harold from the pub, and even Irene, Arthur Lane's lairy young wife, they were outside anyway watching the proceedings. But where Mags and Harold and Irene Lane were admiring the efforts of their neighbours, Phoebe and Sooky had another purpose altogether.

As they sat by their street doorsteps on their chairs, slippers on and stockings rolled down to their knees, they were having a good eyeful of what their neighbours had on display. Their intention wasn't to praise their efforts, but to criticise them, and also to make sure that they didn't miss anything that would prove the basis of a good bit of gossip. And when they saw Katie and Frank Barber in the Procession, standing together bold as brass behind the three children carrying the wreath, while the priest walked up and down waving his holy water, they couldn't have hoped for more. That was really something into which they could sink their mouldy, tobacco-stained teeth.

'Have a look at that, will yer, Sook. They've got that fancy lace cloth out again,' Phoebe quite unnecessarily informed her next-door neighbour, who could see it for herself. 'Times is meant to be bad down the docks but she ain't had to put that in uncle's, now has she? And I wonder where she got the dough to get that wreath with what her boys are carrying and all. And can yer see who they're carrying it with? Just have a butcher's, go on. Frank Barber's kid, that's who. Them flowers must have cost a flaming fortune. Her precious Pat doing bad down the docks? Don't make me laugh. But if he is, it makes yer wonder where she got the money for that little lot, don't it? Brazen, just like that red hair of her'n. No wonder her old man's not here. He'd be ashamed to see her with her fancy man.'

It was unfortunate for Phoebe Tucker that Stephen had been following Father Hopkins and his attendants, watching him as he made his way round the shrines, and was just passing her and Sooky, when she was mouthing off about his daughter.

'Oi!' he spat into Phoebe's ear, making her almost fall off her chair.

'You talking to me, Stephen Brady?'

'Yes I am, yer wicked-mouthed old cow.' Stephen ducked down, making sure that he was hidden from Nora and Katie behind the crowd, and that he kept his voice low. He didn't want anyone else in the Procession to hear what he had to say as they stood waiting patiently at the end of the turning for the priest to do his rounds. 'I just caught you nice,' he breathed. 'And, not that it's nothing to do with either of yers, but if yer don't mind, me daughter's husband is in the back kitchen discussing business. Important business. Trying to work out ways to save decent men's jobs. Now, d'yer want me to fetch him out here so's he can hear what yer saying about his wife, yer spiteful old hens?'

Banking on the fact that she would be safe from Stephen actually clouting her, what with the crowds of people in the turning, Phoebe remained bold. Taking her cigarette from her mouth and taking her time to dot her ash daintily into her apron pocket, Phoebe looked up at him and said with a disbelieving raise of her eyebrows, 'Too busy with his work to be out here to see the Procession, is he? And him a good Catholic and all. I am surprised.'

She turned to Sooky and gave a sneering grimace, which, on her face, passed for an amused smile. Then she jerked her head towards the corner where Katie was standing chatting to Frank Barber, apparently ignoring her mum and her daughter who were on the other side of her. 'More like he don't fancy the idea of what he might see out here, if you ask me.'

326

'Well no one is asking yer,' snapped Stephen. 'The only ones who don't like what they see out here are you two, you vicious old bags. May God forgive the pair of yer.'

With that, Stephen straightened up and went back across the street to where Danny was waiting by his family's shrine. 'So what was all that about then, Farvee? You don't usually have nothing to do with them.'

'I dunno what yer talking about, Dan,' said Stephen, still glaring across at the two sniggering women.

Danny laughed to himself. 'I don't think Nanna'll accept that as much of an answer, Farvee. She was nearly breaking her neck trying to see what yer was up to.'

'Aw bugger,' cursed Stephen. 'She saw me then?'

'That's right,' grinned Danny, rocking back on his heels and giving a little wave to Liz, who was smiling at him from across the street where she was still posted by her own family shrine with her mum. 'I reckon yer gonna be answering plenty o' questions when they get back from church later on.'

'No, boy,' said Stephen, shaking his head. 'Yer nanna won't get nothing out of me.'

'A tosheroon says she does.'

'Yer on!'

Danny won his half-crown from Stephen with no trouble at all. As soon as Nora, Katie, Molly and the boys had made their way back to Plumley Street, after having gone to the church to receive the final Holy Blessing from Father Hopkins, Nora made sure that she got Stephen by himself at the first opportunity. And, despite his earlier resolution that he would tell her nothing, Stephen had soon told her not only practically word for word what Phoebe had said, but also what she had insinuated about Katie and Frank Barber.

'Right,' said Nora, pushing up her sleeves.

'Sure, yer not going out to cause a scene now, are yer, Nora?' Stephen knew only too well how the women in his family could let fly when they got into one of their moods and he hated to think he'd be the one responsible for a woman getting a bloody nose or losing what few teeth she had left, even if it was only Phoebe Tucker.

'No, I ain't going out to cause no scene,' said Nora, striding out of her kitchen. 'But,' she called from the passage, 'I'm going in next door to put that daughter o' mine right about one or two things.'

Nora tapped on the frame of her daughter's kitchen door.

From where they were sitting at the table, spreading marg on a pile of bread ready for the Sunday tea, Katie and Molly looked up in surprise.

'So what's all this knocking lark in aid of, Mum?' Katie asked, wiping her hands on her apron. 'Is something up?'

'I just wanted to be sure that I wasn't disturbing Pat and his workmates.'

Katie's expression stiffened. 'Yer all right, they cleared out as soon as we got back. Went round one of the other blokes' houses to drive his old woman mad instead.'

She started slicing angrily at the rest of the loaf, tossing each slice in Molly's direction as she cut it. 'Good job and all, if you ask me. He's still got the right hump. The boys took one look at him and they was off over the back wall like sticks a'cracking.'

Nora took a butter knife from the dresser drawer, sat down opposite her daughter and began helping Molly with the spreading. 'It's Pat I wanna talk to yer about,

328

Kate. I don't wanna speak out of turn, but yer've gotta know.'

'Shall I go in next door with Farvee?' Molly asked warily.

Nora stared at Katie, leaving the decision up to her.

'I ain't got no secrets,' Katie said primly.

Nora raised a doubting eyebrow and then looked over Katie's shoulder, checking that the boys hadn't reappeared in the back yard. Satisfied that no one except Katie and Molly could hear her, Nora continued, 'There was talk about Pat not being there this afternoon.'

'I should think there was,' Katie sniped, slapping down another slice of bread on the kitchen table. 'How d'yer expect people to act when he couldn't even be bothered to step outside the street door to see his own children in the parade?'

'But, Mum, yer know his meeting was important.' Straight away, Molly knew she should have kept her mouth shut.

'So, yer on *his* side, are yer? Typical. I'm always the one at fault in this house. I thought I could at least count on me own daughter to support me, but obviously I can't.'

'I ain't on no one's side, Mum. Yer know I ain't.' Molly dropped her chin to hide the tears gathering in her eyes, tears that were as much for the confusion and fears she felt about her own life as for what her mother had just said to her. 'I never thought I had to be. I thought we was all on the same side in this family.' She shoved her chair back, lifted her chin and looked at Katie, the tears now running down her cheeks. 'I'm going out later on,' she sniffled. 'So I'll go up to me room and start getting ready, if yer don't mind.' With that, she ran out of the kitchen and up the stairs to her bedroom.

'I think yer'll find yer arguing with the wrong ones, Katie,' Nora said flatly.

'I've gotta be grateful when they cheek me, have I?' Katie asked illogically.

'Don't be deliberately stupid, girl. If yer stopped fighting with everyone and just listened for once . . .' Nora sighed despondently. 'It's like the way yer treat yer father. Do you know that that man stood up for you out there when those two sharp-tongued old biddies from across the street were running you down?'

'So I've gotta be grateful to him and all now, have I?'

'Don't yer even want to know what they was saying about yer?'

'No. But I can guess.' She looked defiantly at Nora. 'Something to do with me standing within ten yards of Frank Barber, was it?'

'I've not lost my temper with you since you was a little girl sticking yer fingers in the jam pot, Katie, but I mean it: yer pushing me that far; yer pushing all of us too far—'

'Why don't you just leave me alone? I'm fed up with the lot of yers. I'm fed up with trying to make ends meet. I'm fed up with worrying about what the kids are up to. And I'm fed up with being told who I can and can't talk to. I'm fed up with all of it. Every rotten stinking bit of it.'

'Well then,' Nora replied, as she strode over to the kitchen door, 'I suppose yer'd better do something about it then, hadn't yer?'

The next day, Pat and Katie barely said two words to one another during breakfast. Pat didn't even ask why, on a Monday morning, his wife was all done up in her decent dress, the one she kept for church and other important occasions, the one, in fact, that she had worn yesterday for the Procession. And, when he arrived home from work much later that day, tense and weary as he usually was of late, Katie never bothered to ask him how he had got on with the meeting with the guv'nor as she always would have done in the past. But she did explain why she had been wearing her good frock.

She poured Pat his cup of tea, but instead of putting it down on the kitchen table, she said, 'Let's go in the front room, Pat, there's something I wanna say to yer without the kids hearing if they come in.'

Pat took the tea and went through to the parlour without saying anything.

She followed him in, shut the door behind them and sat down on the arm of one of the easy chairs that stood either side of the hearth. 'I've been out today.'

Pat didn't answer. He just sat down on the armchair opposite her and sipped at his tea.

'Look, Pat, I said things to yer yesterday morning that I had no right to. I know yer bringing home all the money yer can, but we need more just to make ends meet. And what with the boys growing like Gawd knows what, and food definitely ain't getting no cheaper—'

'You think yer telling me something I don't know?'

Katie put her teacup down on the hearth and bent forward, her red hair falling over her face. She rested her wrists on her knees, letting her hands dangle. 'Please, Pat, I don't wanna row. I've been feeling that rough.'

'Ain't we all? You should try doing what I have to do every day. I'm down that dock every hour God sends, waiting for them bastards to do me a favour and give me and the blokes a bit o' work just to have it thrown in me face that I'm not needed, not wanted.'

331

She lifted her face and looked directly at him. 'That's why I went and got meself a job,' she blurted out. 'In a laundry in the Commercial Road.'

'You what?'

'It's only mornings.'

'If you think I'm gonna let a wife of mine go out to work—'

Katie was on her feet. 'That's typical of you, ain't it? Yer don't care about me and my worries, all yer care about is what other people'll think of *you*, always *you.*'

'It ain't that.' Now Pat was standing too.

Katie shoved her fists into her waist and stared up at him, challenging him. 'What, frightened there might be some blokes working in the laundry, are yer?'

She turned away from him, bent down and picked up her teacup, not caring that she was slopping it in the saucer, and marched over to the door. Wrenching it back on its hinges, she looked over her shoulder and said slowly and clearly, 'All women ain't like your mum, yer know. Just 'cos she was an old—'

She didn't see Pat raise his hand, she just felt the sting as it slashed across her face.

Pat sprang back from her as though he had touched a burning ember. 'Kate, I didn't . . . I always swore I'd never . . .' He could find nothing more to say. He pushed past her, spilling the remains of her tea all over the worn runner that covered the passage floor, and slammed out of the street door, leaving Katie to clear up the mess.

It was late on a hot and dusty Friday afternoon in August. Katie was sitting with Nora on the street doorstep of number ten, staring down at the potatoes she was peeling into the bowl she had balanced on her lap.

332

'Look,' said Nora, waving her knife at Katie, 'he's sending yer money round regular, so it's not as though he's just disappeared, now is it?'

Katie said nothing. It was difficult enough sitting there, knowing she was the object of so many people's pity – 'Poor Katie Mehan, did yer hear? Her old man's left her. A right shiner she had. He must have really clocked her one' – but she couldn't let herself be kept indoors; she had to face people and carry on.

'And he's used to a clean home,' Nora went on. 'He won't be able to stand them lodgings down by the docks much longer. He'll be back.' Nora laughed unconvincingly. 'His old mum always came back. Like a regular little homing pigeon, that woman was. And he'll be just the same. You see.'

Katie was hardly listening as her mother carried on talking, doing her best to jolly her daughter along; Katie felt too exhausted to listen. She had been at the laundry for nearly four weeks now – the same length of time that Pat had been away – but it wasn't just doing the work and still having to see to the house that was draining her, it was the emotional fatigue, the agony of not knowing what would happen with her and Pat, not knowing what she even wanted to happen, and her almost complete lack of sleep since he'd been gone.

'Will yer look at them?' Nora shouted to her daughter, to make herself heard over the unintelligible calls and loudly jangling handbell of the rag-and-bone man who was pushing his handcart past the top of the turning. She waved her potato knife towards Michael and Timmy, who were racing up and down the street with a crowd of other kids from the neighbourhood. This week they were all playing at being contenders in the British Empire Games at the White City, the craze that had taken over from the last fad of playing tennis with bits of wood and an old deflated football after Fred Perry had won at Wimbledon. 'The little loves. Sure, won't they look just like little angels in their pageboy outfits?'

Stephen emerged from the passage where he had been standing behind his wife. He edged between her and his daughter, who remained sitting on the street doorstep, and leant on the wall, savouring the heat of the sun-warmed bricks. He fiddled around with his pipe for a few moments, getting it lit just the way he liked it.

'The rate that Michael's growing,' Stephen said, his pipe bobbing up and down as he spoke, 'he'll be too big to be a pageboy by the time that pair finally decide they've saved enough to get married. And young Timmy's not far behind.' He puffed thoughtfully, sending up a cloud of blue, pungent smoke. 'We never bothered ourselves with that sort of thing, did we, darling?'

Nora chuckled. 'No we did not. We got married with the clothes we stood up in. The lace tablecloth left to me by my old aunt, God bless her, was me only possession. Did we ever tell yer about that, Katie?'

When Katie didn't reply, Stephen looked at Nora and shrugged helplessly. Nora shrugged back at him.

Stephen tried again. 'Look,' he said enthusiastically, 'here's our Molly home from work.'

Katie raised her eyes and saw Molly and Liz just coming around the corner.

'Molly!' Nora called. 'Hello, me darling.'

Molly waved back to her nanna, but instead of smiling and crossing the street to see her, she paused outside number nine, listening solemnly while Liz Watts finished saying something to her.

Nora shook her head, her smiles replaced by a look of concern. 'For goodness' sake, will yer look at that girl? She looks that miserable lately. And restless! I just wish she'd settle herself. She's worrying me that much. I've never seen such fidgeting and fussing, even in a girl of her age.'

'Yer not wrong there, Nora,' said Stephen, jabbing the stem of his pipe at her. 'I was watching her yesterday.' He nodded meditatively. 'She was up and down from that table like a whore's drawers on Boat Race night, so she was.'

Nora tried tutting disapprovingly at such coarseness, but it was no good, she couldn't help laughing, Stephen had that effect on her.

'It's good to hear yer happy, Nora,' Stephen said, looking pointedly at Katie. 'It's attractive in a woman, a sense of fun. I just wish that you and that granddaughter o' mine would laugh a bit more, Kate. Just look at the pair of yers. Faces like a wet weekend, so yer have.' He suddenly flapped his hand in Katie's direction. 'Sssh, don't say nothing, here she comes.'

Katie gasped in disbelief at her father. 'For Gawd's sake, I didn't even open me mouth. It was you. And how d'yer expect us to feel?'

Nora frowned at her daughter. 'All right, Katie, I know yer've not been feeling yerself lately, but there's no need to be rude to yer dad. And anyway, perhaps yer *should* be saying something to Molly, instead of just feeling sorry for yerself all the time.'

'Hang on a minute,' she snapped. 'What d'yer mean, "not feeling meself"? Me husband's left me.'

Nora shook her head, signalling that this wasn't the time to talk about such things, as her granddaughter had crossed the street and was now standing in front of them. 'Hello, Molly, love,' Nora said, smiling up at her. 'How are yer?'

'All right, Nanna,' she answered, without any enthusiasm. She bent forward to kiss first Nora, then her mum on the cheek. Then she straightened up and kissed her granddad. 'I'm going in to have a wash. I feel like I'm lousy. It was that flaming muggy in the factory this afternoon.'

'I'll help yer fill the bath up if yer like,' Nora offered. 'How'd that be?'

'No, yer all right, Nanna. I can't be bothered with all that. I'll wait till tomorrow night and have me bath like everyone else.'

Molly gave the three of them a strained smile and went in next door. But, as she stepped inside the passage of number twelve, the thought of dragging herself out to the back kitchen just to have a wash, even though she was hot, sticky and uncomfortable, was too much for her. So, instead she hauled herself up the stairs to her bedroom, grasping the banister as though it were a lifeline. She closed the door behind her, dropped her handbag on the floor and flopped down on to the soft eiderdown. That was all she was fit for: lying on the bed and closing her eyes.

Thank goodness everyone else was outside, she thought to herself as she listened to the muffled sounds from the street below; even the idea of her mum and nanna coming indoors and talking downstairs in the kitchen was too much for her to contemplate, never mind what the boys crashing about would have done to her already jangling nerves. She had had enough noise and chattering for one day.

She sighed wearily; she knew that her friend was only trying to take her mind off things, but she was fed up to the back teeth with Liz's non-stop prattling on about wedding preparations.

Even her beloved dad staying in that horrible lodging house in Limehouse wasn't what was really upsetting her.

Molly knew she was being selfish when her mum was so distressed, but she couldn't help it. She had been over and over it all in her mind so many times that it had become almost an obsession. And still she didn't know what to do about Simon.

She loved him, she was sure of that, but she was also sure that if her mum found out about him, that would be the end of it. Catholic girls did not have Jewish boyfriends. She would never be able to be with him again, not in the way she wanted. She now realised what she had felt for Bob was a stupid, childish infatuation compared to the way she felt about Simon . . .

The trouble was, what with both Lizzie and her nanna knowing, her mum could so easily find out about him. Not that either of them would hurt her deliberately, but it was only too easy for her to imagine how they might let her secret slip.

Perhaps she should just tell her mum before anyone else had the chance. Get it over with and stop the torment.

She could just picture it: there they'd be, sitting at the kitchen table and she'd say – 'I'm sorry that Dad's still away, Mum. Aw, by the way, I've been seeing this boy. For quite a while now. Simon, his name is. What's that? Why haven't I told you before? Aw, he's Jewish, see. More tea?'

Maybe it would be for the best. Anyway, what could her mum do, kill her? She probably would, knowing her. And the fact that it had been going on for so long – a year now, when she thought about it – hardly made it any easier. It was like having a job to do and leaving it because you didn't fancy getting down to starting it, and then it got worse and worse, and bigger and bigger, and, before you knew where you were, you'd never be capable of even trying to tackle it.

Molly rubbed her hands over her face, groaning to herself, as though she were suffering eternal torment. She rolled on to her side and stared at the wall. She remembered staring at the wallpaper when she was a little girl. The big cabbage roses that she had thought were so pretty were always the last things she had seen at night before she closed her eyes and drifted off into the easy, innocent sleep of childhood, the sort of sleep that came when you hadn't a care in the world to disturb you. The roses had faded over the years and were now the palest of pinks.

Briefly her mind wandered and she imagined what it would be like to be able to afford new wallpaper – just because you felt like it. She felt a tear trickle out of the corner of her eye and run down towards her ear. But she wasn't crying for faded wallpaper, she was crying for faded dreams.

With a supreme effort, she hoisted herself up on to her elbows and sniffed loudly. She couldn't carry on like this. She had to do something, and she knew exactly what it was. She would go down to the front room, dig out the writing paper from the sideboard, and write Simon a letter, putting an end to her misery once and for all. It was either that or drive herself crazy.

As she ran down the stairs, her energy restored a little along with her decision to put her life in order, she heard voices coming from the kitchen. Thank goodness the writing paper was in the front room, she thought as she pushed open the door. She must look a right state, all red-eyed and snivelling.

'What d'you want?'

Molly froze. The angry question had hit her like a brick wall.

It was Danny. He and Liz were squashed together on one of the front room armchairs having a cuddle.

'Sorry,' she stammered. 'I didn't realise anyone was in here, Dan.'

'Blimey, Moll,' he went on, sighing dramatically, 'it's bad enough the two little 'uns peeping round the door and giggling whenever me and Liz wanna be a bit private.' He wriggled around, making a bit of space and somehow managed to shove his hand into his trouser pocket. He brought out a fistful of coppers and held them out to his sister. 'Tell yer what, Moll,' he said, with a wink at Liz, 'here's a sprazey to go to the flicks, so's me and Liz can get a bit of peace. Yer could go and see that Tom Mix in *Cement*.'

'Very funny,' snapped Molly. 'I ain't never heard that one before. How on earth d'yer think of 'em?'

Trying to regain a bit of dignity, Liz pulled her skirt down over her knees, nudged Danny hard in the side, and clambered up from the armchair.

'Why don't you leave her alone, Dan?' she said quietly, her pretty eyes flashing warnings at him. 'You don't have to be so sarcy, do yer? Can't yer see she's upset?' She went over and stood beside her friend, gently touching her on the arm. 'What's up, Moll? It's yer dad, ain't it?'

Molly shook her away. 'Yer don't have to worry yerself about me, Liz.' She stepped backwards out of the room and pulled the door shut behind her.

As she stumbled along the passage towards the kitchen, her vision blurred by yet more tears, she could hear Liz telling Danny his fortune in no uncertain terms. She gave up a silent prayer of thanks. At least Liz was still on her side and protecting her secret – for now anyway.

Molly almost skidded to a halt when she reached the kitchen doorway and saw that her mum and nanna were in there getting ready to dish up the tea.

Nora turned round to see who was there. 'Whatever's the matter?' she asked, dropping the cutlery with a loud clatter on to the draining board and rushing over to her granddaughter. 'Who's upset yer, darling?'

Molly bit her lip, not daring to speak for fear of breaking down into uncontrollable sobs. She turned round, and ran back upstairs to her room.

'I don't like it, Katie,' Nora said, looking along the passage as though she could still see her granddaughter.

'What's that then?' Katie asked as she set down the plates on the table. She didn't look up and her voice was distant.

'Molly. There's something wrong with her.'

'There's something wrong with every one of this family,' Katie said flatly.

'I don't understand you.' Nora was angry. 'The girl's got a problem and you just stand there.'

Katie spun round and faced her mother. 'I've got problems too, yer know.'

'Katie, I know yer have, love.'

'No yer don't. Yer don't know nothing.'

Nora walked slowly across the little room and stood in front of her daughter. 'You need some sleep. There's dark rings under them pretty eyes o' your'n.' She reached out and brushed a heavy stray curl of thick auburn hair away from her daughter's forehead. 'He'll be back, love. I know he will.'

14

By Sunday afternoon, Molly was glad that Danny and Liz had been in the front room; it had given her the chance to think more carefully about whether she should write to Simon after all. And she had eventually come to the decision that she shouldn't. She was still going to finish with him, but, with him meaning so much to her, she wasn't going to be a coward, she was going to tell him to his face.

But as she neared the corner of Jubilee Street, where they had arranged to meet, Molly was already worked up into a real state as to how, now the time had come, she was actually going to tell him that it was over.

She was close enough to see Simon clearly: he was standing, arms folded, watching for her to come along Commercial Road.

When he caught sight of her, he levered himself away from the wall and started walking quickly towards her, a relieved smile on his handsome face.

She dreaded the moment when that smile would vanish.

'I always imagine you won't turn up,' he began, 'like that other time.'

There, it had happened, his smile had disappeared.

'Molly? What's wrong?'

'There's something I gotta say to yer, Simon. Mind if

we go and sit down somewhere?'

'All right,' he agreed uneasily. 'Let's go and find a coffee shop.'

They walked along in the direction of Aldgate until they found a café that was open.

Already uncomfortably warm from walking in the strong afternoon sun, Molly felt as though she would melt as she stepped through the narrow doorway into the close atmosphere of the tiny crowded room. Like many of the cafés in that area, it was full of elderly men, many of them Jewish, shouting and arguing about politics and all claiming that only they had the true solution as to how to put the world to rights, while they drank their way through gallons of steaming black tea and coffee.

'I don't know if this was such a good idea,' she said nervously, realising how much harder it was going to be to talk to Simon surrounded by an audience. But he had already found them a seat.

'Mind if we share your table?' Simon asked a grey-haired man who was loudly hectoring his equally noisy companion.

The man didn't look round, he just pulled out the chair next to him and carried on speaking at full volume to the other man.

Simon beckoned Molly over from the doorway and then went to the counter to get them some tea, while she settled herself uneasily next to the man.

'Thanks,' she said quietly.

Simon gave Molly her drink and sat down opposite her. Even though the tea was scalding hot, Molly sipped at it, preferring to burn her tongue rather than use it to speak the words that she knew would choke her.

'So what is it you have to say to me?' Simon was trying

to make light of it, but it was obvious that he was worried. 'Is it about your father?'

She shook her head, her eyes fixed on the bare wooden table top. 'No. It's not me dad, it's us. I ain't gonna see yer no more.'

'No. We've gone through it all before. I've told you, I won't listen to you when you talk like this.'

Still Molly couldn't meet his gaze. 'A year we've been carrying on like this, Simon,' she told the table top. 'I don't want it no more. I wanna normal, straightforward life like Lizzie and Danny's. I wanna walk along the street and not be afraid to be seen with me boyfriend.'

Simon reached across the table and took her hand. 'Come out with me tomorrow. It's Bank Holiday, we can spend the whole day together.'

'I was gonna write to yer,' she said, as though she hadn't heard him, 'but I reckoned it'd be better if I told yer to yer face.'

'So why don't you?'

She looked up at him. 'Why don't I what?'

'Tell me to my face.'

Molly hesitated for just a moment then said, 'I ain't gonna see yer no more.'

'I'm not listening to this. I'll be waiting for you by the foot tunnel, this side of the river, tomorrow, twelve o'clock.'

'I won't be there. I—' Molly felt a tap on her shoulder. She looked round. It was the elderly man sitting next to her.

'So why're you doing this to the poor boy?' the man asked. 'Can't you see how much he thinks of you?'

Molly stood up, sending her chair crashing to the floor. 'I'm sorry,' she sobbed and ran from the café.

Simon stood up to follow her but the man stretched

across the table and pulled him down again. 'You've got a lot to learn about women, son,' he said. 'Now you sit there and finish your tea. Let her cool her heels a bit. Then go after her.' He shrugged his shoulders. 'Women, who does understand 'em? Not me. But I know it doesn't do to try and reason with 'em when they've got an idea stuck in their heads.'

'But—'

'Don't worry. You can pop round her house later on. Give her a nice big kiss.' He smiled, his old face crinkling into folds and layers of olive-coloured skin. 'And when you do, give her a kiss from me as well. She's a good-looking girl you've got there.'

Simon couldn't even begin to explain to the man how impossible any of that would be.

Molly was out of breath but still she kept running. She had to get away before Simon caught up with her. She had done it at last and she had to be strong.

She was just about to cross Back Church Lane, pausing only to glance hurriedly left and right to make sure it was safe to do so, when what she saw, at the top of a narrow alley leading behind the houses, was enough to stop her dead in her tracks. A crowd of young men were blocking the way of an elderly man, taunting him as he tried to get past them.

She watched, frozen to the spot, as one of the jeering crowd shoved the old man hard in the chest, sending him sprawling backwards along the alley. It wasn't only the brutality that shocked her, it was the fact that she recognised them as the gang that Danny had been knocking around with when he was still mates with Bob Jarvis.

One of them darted forward and grabbed the battered

shopping bag that the old man had been carrying, holding it up to his mates as though it was a glorious trophy. He looked inside it and sneered. 'Bloody muck,' he said, tipping out bagels and a jar of rollmop herrings from the bag and into the gutter behind him. 'Why can't yer eat proper food?'

Another man moved forward; with a jerk of his thumb, he signalled for the others to get back and give him more room.

'Leave him to me,' he snarled. 'The stinking old Jewish bastard.'

Without further warning, he started slamming his boot into the defenceless man's side, kicking at him with such brutality, that the elderly man's body jerked around as though he was a marionette being worked by a drunken puppeteer.

Molly could stand back no longer. She started running along the street towards them without even a thought as to what use a seventeen-year-old girl would be against a mob of frenzied thugs in a narrow alley.

But before she reached them, one of the gang had started shouting for the attacker to stop.

'Not in broad daylight!' he yelled, grabbing at the man's jacket. 'Are you barmy?' He turned to the others. 'Give me a hand to pull him off, for Christ's sake, before someone hears and calls the rozzers.'

It took three of them finally to drag him off and two of them to keep hold of him as, panting and sweating with excitement at what he had done, he strained to get back to finish off the old man.

'You bloody bastards!' hollered Molly, looking around desperately for someone to help her.

The man who had shouted at the attacker darted a nervous look over his shoulder. 'Shit! There's only a sodding girl over there been watching us. Let's get out of here. Quick, come on! Move!'

Apart from the one who had been dragged off of the old man, they all poured out of the alley and ran off along Back Church Lane in the direction of Cable Street. The attacker himself, however, was far more cool; he turned round slowly, interested to see what sort of a girl would dare challenge him.

When his eyes met Molly's it was difficult to assess which of them was the more surprised: the man when he realised that the girl was Molly Mehan, or Molly when she realised that the brute was none other than Bob Jarvis.

It took only a moment for Jarvis to regain his composure. He lifted his chin and looked down his nose at Molly. 'Ain't seen yer around for a while,' he said, as casually as though he had just bumped into her during the Saturday night Monkey Parade.

Molly didn't answer him, she simply walked over to the nearest front door and hammered on it with her knuckles, not stopping until a young boy came to see what she wanted. Jarvis was still watching her, an amused grin on his face, as she spoke to the child.

'Tell yer mum yer've gotta run down the nick as fast as yer legs can carry yer,' she told him. 'Yer've gotta fetch a copper 'cos an old man's been hurt. And make sure yer tell 'em we need an ambulance and all. Understand?'

The boy nodded, but, thrilled by the idea of a bit of excitement, he ignored Molly's instruction to tell his mother, and instead took off along the street at a gallop – the first time he had ever willingly run towards the police station in Leman Street.

'What? Turn on yer own, would yer?' Bob sneered. 'I never had yer down for that sort. If yer know what's good for yer, yer wanna clear off before the law gets here and starts asking questions.' With that he gave Molly a raised hand, stiff-armed fascist salute and trotted off after his mates.

Molly felt sick at the thought that she had once let somebody so vile actually touch her, but she couldn't waste time on self-pity, she had to help the old man.

She took off her cotton cardigan, rolled it up and knelt down beside him. Suppressing her distaste for the metallic stench of the blood that was pouring from his nose and mouth and the stale ammonia smell of urine where he had wet himself during the attack, Molly gently moved his head, intending to slip the makeshift pillow between him and the hard cobbled floor of the alley.

His eyes flicked open in terror as she touched him.

'It's all right,' she soothed him, as though she was a mother reassuring a frightened child. 'I ain't gonna hurt yer, I promise. I'm just gonna make yer a bit more comfy till the police get here, that's all.'

He screwed his eyes tight and his face contorted as a new wave of agony surged through his body.

'What's going on?' asked someone behind Molly.

She looked over her shoulder. It was a woman of about her mum's age.

'Some slag kicked this poor old man in the guts,' Molly said.

The woman shook her head. 'Bastard,' she said, picking up the discarded shopping bag and the bagels. She kicked the shards of glass from the shattered herring jar down the grid over the drain and then knelt down beside Molly. 'Aw, Gawd love him,' she said, her hand flying to her mouth. 'It's only poor old Mr Zuckerman. They've been having a go at the poor old bugger for weeks now. Been torturing him, they have.'

Mr Zuckerman groaned and a thin trickle of blood ran from his ear.

'He's in a bad way,' the woman said. 'I'll run and fetch the doctor.'

Molly took a deep breath to steady herself, then shuffled sideways on her knees so that she could rest the man's head on her lap – anything to try and ease the pain he was suffering. 'It's all right,' she said, using the hem of her dress to staunch the blood. 'Some kid's gone already.'

Molly had never seen anyone die before, but she knew, even before the policeman arrived and could confirm it, that Mr Zuckerman was dead. And she also knew what she had to do. She had been born and bred in a community where it was accepted that people didn't grass on one another, but this was different; she couldn't allow Bob Jarvis to get away with it.

When the ambulance had taken Mr Zuckerman away, and the crowd that had gathered to watch and pass comment had finally dispersed, Molly braced herself to speak to the policeman.

She not only gave him details of everything she had seen, but she also identified the person who had done it. Yes, she assured the officer, she was sure his name was Bob Jarvis, she had heard the others call him that.

When the policeman said that it was a bit strange, them using his full name, Molly had become flustered, but luckily the policeman put it down to shock, and said that who knew how thugs like that would act.

When the officer asked for her name and address, Molly stumbled over her words again in her efforts to make up something convincing. The last thing she wanted was for the police to turn up in Plumley Street asking all sorts of difficult questions. And anyway, how could she have admitted that she had once been the girlfriend of such a creature?

The walk home went by in a blur, but she was still sensible enough to know that clambering over the high wall at the end of Plumley Street, and walking past all the houses wasn't a very good idea. Her clothes, her hands, and, she suspected, her face, were spattered with Mr Zuckerman's blood, and the last thing she felt like doing was explaining to Phoebe and Sooky what she had been up to.

So she walked along East India Dock Road, ducking into shop doorways whenever she thought she saw anyone she knew coming towards her, and then slipped into Chrisp Street. Being a Sunday, there was no market and everything was much quieter than usual, so no one saw her as she darted along the alley that led from the back of the Queen's to the back of Joe and Aggie's place.

Still unobserved, she shinned up over the wall into the yard of number twelve, completing Timmy and Michael's favourite escape route in reverse. But, as she stepped into the kitchen, the sight of her coming through the back door, covered in blood, was enough to make Liz, who was doing the teatime washing up with Danny, drop the saucer she was wiping dry. It smashed on to the lino, breaking into what looked like a thousand fragments.

'Moll!' she gasped. 'Whatever's happened to yer?'

'Where's Mum?' Molly asked, dropping down heavily on to one of the kitchen chairs.

Danny grabbed her hand. 'She's up having a lay down, upset about Dad again. But that don't matter, where you hurt, Moll?'

'I ain't. This blood ain't mine.' She turned to Liz; for

some reason her friend looked as though she was about to start crying. 'Yer couldn't get us a drop o' water, could yer, Liz?'

'Yeah. Yeah. Course.'

Molly nodded her thanks as she raised the drink to her lips, then she gulped it down in one go and handed back the empty cup. 'I've just seen Bob Jarvis kill some old bloke,' she blurted out.

'You what?'

'You heard, Dan. He kicked him to death, right in front of me.'

Danny shook his head, trying to make sense of what he had just heard his sister say. 'But you ain't seeing him no more.'

'No, course I ain't. I just bumped into him.'

'I don't understand.'

'It's simple, I told yer. He kicked a bloke to death and I saw him do it. And that's exactly what I told the police and all.'

'You what?'

'You heard, Dan. I told 'em everything.'

'I don't believe you. Yer do know who yer messing with, don't yer, Moll?'

'Yeah. I went out with him, remember?'

Danny looked round at Liz, but she just got down on her hands and knees, and started collecting the shards of china in a sheet of old newspaper. 'I hope this wasn't one of yer mum's best saucers,' she said, keeping her head down.

'Bugger the saucer,' hissed Danny. 'I wanna know what she thinks she's up to.'

Molly rose shakily to her feet. 'And what should I have done, eh?' she demanded, daring him to contradict her.

350

'I think I'd have thought what Jarvis might do to me before I started mouthing off to the law.'

'Aw yeah? Your old mate Bob a bit of a nutter, is he?'

Danny didn't know what to say. Not only was he scared for Molly – he had seen what Bob Jarvis was capable of at the rally – but he was still unable to come to terms with the fact that he'd been taken in by someone who could even think of doing such terrible things. Danny was sickened by the thought of how close he himself had come to being just like Bob Jarvis. In his confused state of mind, it was the fury he felt at himself, rather than any anger he felt with his sister, that made him flare up at her.

'Yer know what's wrong with you, Moll?' he asked, his eyes narrowed. 'Yer've turned on yer own.'

Molly levelled her gaze on Danny. 'You sound just like Jarvis.'

'Running to the law.' Danny shook his head contemptuously, but he was quaking inside, thinking of what Jarvis was capable of. 'Name one family round here what don't pull some sort o' stroke or other to make a few extra coppers.'

'Are you taking the piss, Dan? I ain't talking about a bit of thieving or fencing. I'm talking about murdering a defenceless old man.' Molly turned to Liz. 'You tell him.'

'Don't look at me, Moll,' she said, putting the wrapped china in the rubbish bucket. 'I ain't getting involved.' She quietly fitted the lid back on the pail. 'I know we're mates, and I hope we always will be, but I can't take sides.'

Danny went over to the back door. He grasped hold of the frame and stared out at the dusty back yard.

'Did I hear someone break something in here?' It was

Katie; she was standing in the kitchen doorway. She looked terrible, but any thoughts of her own problems were instantly forgotten the moment she saw her daughter's blood-stained clothes. 'Molly?'

'It's all right, Mum, this ain't my blood. I saw an accident.' She dropped back down on to her chair. 'I helped an old man what had been knocked over.'

'Flaming traffic!' fretted Katie. 'Even on a Sunday. What're things coming to?' She lifted Molly's chin in her hand, checking for herself that her daughter wasn't hurt. 'Was the old boy all right, love?'

'I dunno, Mum,' Molly answered her, flashing a wary glance at Danny's back. 'I left as soon as someone fetched the doctor. I didn't want yer to worry about me being late.'

'Yer a good girl, Moll,' said Katie, going over to the sink. She ran the tea towel under the tap and then busied herself, using it to wipe away the smears of dried blood from Molly's face. 'Danny,' she snapped over her shoulder, 'whatever's the matter with you, boy, standing there staring out the back yard when yer can see the state yer sister's in? Put the kettle on, will yer, and make her a cuppa tea.'

'I was just making one, Kate,' said Liz, interrupting before Danny had the chance to put his foot in it. She picked up the kettle by way of proof and, with a shaking hand, she lit the gas and started setting out the cups and saucers. Liz was used to the Mehans hollering at one another all the time, especially since Pat had been gone, but she had never seen Danny and Molly fall out really seriously before, not like this. It made her nervous. And the thought of Bob Jarvis, and what she had now gathered he was involved in, made her feel a lot worse than nervous. She had never liked Jarvis, not after he had grabbed hold of Molly that first day they had all met up, but Danny had kept telling her that she was wrong about him, that he was a good mate, so she hadn't thought it her place to say how he had given her the creeps.

'Ta, Liz,' said Katie, examining Molly's face for any other stains. 'Yer a good girl.'

As Liz spooned tea leaves into the pot, she cast around for something to say, anything to try to lighten the atmosphere a bit, and prevent Danny and Molly starting on each other again. She dreaded even to think what would happen if they did, especially in front of their mum. What would she have to say if it came tumbling out what had really happened and that Danny had been mates with the likes of Bob Jarvis, and that Molly had actually been seeing him?

Despite her mounting panic, inspiration struck. 'I know, Moll,' Liz said, reaching up to put the tea caddy back on the dresser, 'why don't yer come out with me and Danny tomorrow? For the Bank Holiday, like. It'll do yer good, take yer mind off it.'

'No thanks,' Molly said levelly, looking over her mum's shoulder at Danny. 'I've already made plans of me own.' She gazed up into her mum's careworn face. 'You be all right if I go out, will yer, Mum?'

'Course, darling,' Katie said, wearily dropping down on to the chair next to her daughter's. 'You don't have to stay in on my part.'

The next day, after a night disturbed by nightmare visions of Mr Zuckerman dying in her arms, Molly was glad to have a reason to get up and out of the house. And, stupid as she knew it probably was, she was glad that the reason was Simon Blomstein. She just hoped

353

against hope that he would be there after what she had said to him yesterday.

But it hadn't been so easy leaving the house.

When Molly went downstairs to the kitchen to wash, Katie was sitting at the table in her night things, nursing a cup of tea. From the look of her, she had been there all night.

'You all right, Mum?'

Katie didn't look up. 'Yeah, I'm all right.'

'You sure there's nothing wrong?'

She smiled weakly to herself. 'Nothing that robbing a bank and having yer dad come home wouldn't fix.'

'I won't go out. I'll stay here with you.'

She lifted her head and looked at Molly. It took Katie a moment to focus, but as the memory of Molly sitting there covered in blood sharpened in her mind, she stood up and folded her arms around her daughter.

'I don't want you to stay with me, love. I want yer to go out and have a good time with yer friends. Try and forget all about yesterday.'

'Yer sure?' Molly asked, leaning back so that she could see her mother's face.

'Course I am.'

'But won't yer be lonely? Yer know, it being Bank Holiday and everything.'

'Lonely? With that lot next door to worry about and drive me mad?' Katie made a feeble attempt at a smile and shooed her daughter upstairs to get ready.

By the time Molly reached the entrance to the foot tunnel – fifteen minutes early but still out of breath from running all the way in the midday August sunshine – Simon was already there.

The moment he saw her, he grabbed hold of her and kissed her on the mouth.

'Simon! Get off!' Molly pulled away from him. 'Have you taken leave of yer senses?'

He stepped back from her. 'I would have done if you hadn't turned up.'

Molly smoothed her dress down as though he had crumpled it into a rag. 'Will yer just look at me.'

'You look beautiful.'

Molly glanced nervously about her. 'We'd better get going before you do something really barmy.'

He stepped to one side, letting Molly through the doorway and on to the cast-iron spiral stairway that led down to the tunnel. 'I was awake all night wondering if you'd come,' he said, as he trotted down the stairs to catch up with her.

'I didn't get much sleep either.'

'Good!'

Molly said nothing until she reached the bottom stair, then she turned round and said to him, 'I couldn't sleep, because . . .' She paused, took a breath. 'Look, come over here a minute, there's too many people about.'

They moved into a dark corner, away from the lift that was just dispatching the less energetic tunnel users into the mouth of the big pipe that would take them beneath the river.

'I didn't get no sleep 'cos, after I left you yesterday, something really terrible happened.'

'Your dad?'

She shook her head sadly. 'No,' she said quietly.

'He's still not back?'

She shook her head again.

'Let's see,' said Simon, smiling gently down at her.

'You saw what life would be like if you didn't have me around to love you?'

Molly looked away; she couldn't bear to face him when she told him what she had seen. She took a deep breath and began her story.

Only when she had finished describing the whole, horrible incident and the mess she had got herself in with the police and Bob Jarvis and her brother, did Molly look at him once more. 'Well?' she breathed, dreading, yet needing his response.

'Well,' he echoed her. His tone was measured, his face tense. 'I think they're bastards, him, Jarvis, especially. I think you did the right thing. I think you're really brave. And I know I love you more now than I ever would have thought possible.'

She bowed her head. 'Even though I used to see him when I was seeing you?' she whispered, her words barely audible. 'And even though me own brother was once one of 'em?'

'You're not seeing Jarvis any more?'

'Course I'm not. Not since Christmas time.'

'And your brother doesn't sound as though he's a bad type, not like them. He was stupid maybe, but at least he saw sense.'

Molly kept her head down. 'I still don't reckon he'd like me seeing yer.'

Simon lifted her chin with his finger, so that she had to look at him. 'I think we both know that it goes without saying, there are plenty of people who wouldn't like the idea of us seeing each other.' He held out his hand to her and laughed sardonically. 'After what you've told me, holding hands doesn't really seem so very terrible, does it, Molly?'

They walked through the tunnel hand in hand, oblivious

of the noisy families and the boisterous groups of kids who pushed past them, their manners forgotten in their eagerness to get to Greenwich and the delights of the Bank Holiday fair that awaited them on Blackheath.

As they emerged on to the south bank of the river, Simon squinted up at the bright summer sky. 'The weather looks like it's going to hold,' he said, 'so I'll tell you my plan.' He smiled and shook his head at his own foolishness. '*One* of my plans,' he corrected himself. 'I've got all sorts of others worked out, in case you don't like this one.' He scratched his head, embarrassed at what he was about to say. 'Because, Molly, I have no intention of giving you any excuses for not wanting to spend the whole of the day with me.'

Molly smiled weakly back at him. 'Yer a caution, you are, Simon.'

'That's good is it?'

'I reckon.'

He nodded. 'Well, let's see if you like my plan as much as you obviously like me. Now, you sit there.' He put his hands about her waist and lifted her easily on to the wall that ran parallel to the river bank. 'And, if you don't mind, I would appreciate your full concentration on what I have to offer.'

Molly did her best to keep her smile in place as, in complete contrast to his usually reserved self, Simon pranced around, acting the fool, doing his best to cheer her up and make her laugh.

He held out his hand and counted off the proposed activities on his fingers. 'First, we have something to eat.' He bowed in a gesture of mock formality. 'I know that you, Miss Mehan, like me, can always fit in a bit of something tasty. Then we go to the park; have a walk, maybe a sit-down.'

'And an ice cream?' she asked, helping Simon with his pretence that they didn't have a worry in the world between them.

He hesitated, considering the idea. 'We'll see,' he said eventually, then grinning, he jumped back before she could reach out and flick him round the ear. He gestured behind him with his thumb. 'Then we stroll up towards Blackheath, have a little something for our tea maybe and then . . .' he waggled his eyebrows at her ' . . . this is where I become all masterful. I show off my skills and win you armfuls of prizes at the fair. And then we wander home in the twilight, happy, contented, and, of course, stuffed full of ice cream. How about that?'

'I think that sounds smashing,' Molly said. What she didn't say was that it would need a lot more than a day out to make her feel happy and contented ever again.

But, by early evening, as they walked up the hill towards the sounds and lights coming from the fair on Blackheath, Molly had begun to relax a little. She loved being with Simon so much, and he had made such an effort to make her forget her troubles, that it was no longer so much of a pretence. She really was beginning to enjoy herself.

As they reached the edge of the temporary, miniature city of tents, stalls and rides, flanked by the show people's caravans, carts and trucks, they found themselves crossing a line where everyday, mundane reality ceased and a new reality of gaudy, heightened sensations began; a make-believe world, where, for a few magical hours, the commonplace could be forgotten.

The air was heavy with the cloying smell of hot engine oil mingled with the prickly scent of burning sugar. Every colour imaginable shimmered about them, and was reflected back from the huge gilt-framed mirrors set all around the extravagantly decorated rides. Sounds of laughter and squeals of pleasure were counterpointed by a cacophony of competing mechanical organs, churning out their jangling discordant tunes.

Digging his hand into his trouser pocket, and pulling out a handful of money, Simon ushered Molly forward on to the parched, brown grass. 'We,' he said, 'are going to spend every brass farthing I have on me. So, whatever madam wants, her humble servant will be glad to provide.'

Molly looked at him and smiled, and this time she didn't have to pretend.

'So?' he asked. 'What do you think?'

'I think I wanna do it all, Simon. I wanna have a right laugh and forget everything. Come on.'

Molly grabbed his hand, dragging him past a glittering red and gold pipe organ, with cheery, painted figures jigging and prancing to its whirling, swirling music. She guided him neatly around a huge steam engine, whose fiercely burning furnace was being fed by sweat-covered, bare-chested men wielding great black shovels so it could continue to generate the power for the rides and for the strings of bulbs draped around the stands and stalls like the loops of a bead necklace.

On they rushed, dodging in and out of excited knots of people gathered by each new wonder, until they reached the steam Gallopers, a magnificent carousel with thirty flared-nostrilled, snorting steeds pawing the air, awaiting their riders.

'This first,' she shouted above the music, steering Simon towards the glass-sided pay booth. 'I went on it once when I was little with me dad.' She paused, then added, 'I hope he comes home soon, Simon.'

'He will. Now come on.'

Before the roundabout had even come to a halt, Simon hauled Molly up the curving wooden steps after him. 'Quick, I want us to go on this one. The one with the blue saddle.'

As Molly mounted the carved wooden beast and slipped her feet into the gold painted stirrups, she felt like a little girl again, or at least, the young, headstrong girl of just a year ago, the one who would scramble over the high wall at the end of Plumley Street with the best of them, not caring about who did or didn't see her legs.

Simon grasped the thick candy-twist pole from which the horse was suspended and clambered on behind her.

They rode around and around, their hair blowing back from their faces, concentrating on nothing but the speed, and the motion, and the closeness of each other's bodies.

Molly insisted they had another two goes before she was prepared to move on to see what other pleasures were on offer.

They did it all: they whirled high above the ground on the chairoplanes; gasped for breath as they sailed back and forth on the swingboats; took pot shots at the coconut shy and the hoopla; tried their luck aiming at apparently dart-proof playing cards. Then, when they both needed a breather, they went in to see an exotically attired fortune-teller, who rather spoilt the effect of what could have been a romantic, if slightly delicate moment when her prediction of five children – two dark, three redheads – and a long and happy life of non-stop enjoyment for them both, was interspersed by her puffing continuously on a corn-cob pipe and swigging from a quart bottle of brown ale.

'If we're gonna have this houseful of nippers,' spluttered Molly, as they left the dimly lit tent, each of them aching with the effort of keeping a straight face, 'I reckon yer'd better win 'em some cuddly toys. It'll be nice for 'em, having something to play with while we're busy spending all our time enjoying ourselves.'

Stopping only to buy two lurid pink puffs of candyfloss, they giggled their way over to the shooting range, where, amidst much sticky laughter, they still seemed doomed to win none of the tawdry tat displayed so proudly by the stall holders on their prize winners' shelves.

'If you don't win me them armfuls of prizes what yer promised me, and if yer don't do it very soon, mate,' Molly warned Simon with a little prod in the chest, 'know what I'm gonna do?' She jerked her thumb over her shoulder. 'I'm gonna lug yer over there to that little stage and make yer dance with me, in front of everyone. That'll give 'em all a good laugh. Two left feet, I remember yer telling me that day.'

Simon visualised the moment, as he so often did, when he had held Molly in his arms in the middle of the freezing cold street and had kissed her. He lowered the cork-loaded rifle from his shoulder and laid it in front of him on the counter. 'If that's what you really want, Molly, I'll learn to dance. At one of those schools.'

'Daft 'apporth,' she said, nudging him playfully. 'What'd be the point? Anyway, I bet it'd take more'n a few lessons to get you dancing!' Molly held her candyfloss to one side, leant forward and touched her sugary lips to his cheek.

'Now look what I've done,' she said, seeing the sticky mark her mouth had left on his skin. 'I've got a hankie in here somewhere.'

She opened her bag and began to search through all the bits and pieces she habitually carried around with her. When she found her handkerchief, she looked up at him. 'Aw, Simon,' she said, seeing from his expression that something was wrong. 'I've done it again. I've opened me big gob and insulted yer about not being able to dance, ain't I?'

Simon shook his head; he was signalling to her urgently with his eyes that it was something behind her that was wrong, very wrong.

Molly twisted round to see what it was.

Coming towards her, no, it couldn't be – it was, it was Danny and Liz.

'Hello,' Molly said feebly, springing away from Simon as though he was emitting an electrical charge. 'Didn't expect to see you two here.'

Simon nodded, warily polite. 'Hello.'

Danny said nothing.

'Yer losing yer candy floss,' said Liz, stepping forward and lifting Molly's hand to prevent the drooping confection from slipping off the end of its stick.

'Ta.'

They stood there in edgy silence: Danny and Simon staring at each other; Liz grinning like an idiot at each of them in turn; and Molly, her eyes fixed on the discarded paper targets from the rifle range strewn about their feet by unsuccessful punters, praying that an earthquake, or at the very least a thunderstorm, would interrupt her agony.

'You wanted to go to that fortune-teller, didn't yer?' Danny said suddenly.

'Yeah,' agreed Liz, slipping her arm back through his. 'D'yer wanna go then?'

'Yeah.' Danny strode away, trailing Liz behind him like a reluctant puppy new to the lead.

'See yer,' she called, with a hesitant little wave, grimacing over her shoulder at Molly.

'Blimey,' Molly groaned, leaning back against the rifle stall. 'That's done it.'

'Are you all right?'

She shook her head. 'No. It was all just a dream, wasn't it, thinking we wouldn't worry about who sees us?'

'I've told you, Molly, you're too important to me to let that get in our way. I'll think of something.' He took the rifle from the counter. 'Right,' he said, doing his best to recapture the mood. 'I've got four corks left. Let's see about winning one of those ugly-looking dolls up there.'

Simon had just taken aim, when Molly snatched at his sleeve. 'Can we go, Simon? Now. Please?' Her voice was urgent.

'If that's what you want.' Simon handed his rifle to one of the young boys who were standing around watching the older lads shooting.

'Cor, ta, mister!' the child gasped.

'It's not what you think,' Molly said, shepherding him down an alley between two of the tents. 'I thought I just saw someone else coming towards us; someone who I definitely don't wanna see.'

In the dark shadows between the canvas walls, Molly couldn't see the strain on Simon's face, but she could hear it in his voice. 'It's time we started home anyway.'

'Yeah,' she answered dully, 'maybe it is.'

Simon stood back while she went ahead. 'I wouldn't want you to be embarrassed.'

Molly went to say something, but changed her mind.

They walked back in the direction of Greenwich Park, both of them tight-lipped and tense. The further they got from the jangling music and bright lights of the fair, the uneasier things became between them.

They finally reached the edge of the heath, and paused, side by side, but slightly apart, at the roadside, waiting for a gap in the busy Bank Holiday traffic making its way back to London from the Kent coast.

The stream of tired yet happy faces of the passengers flashing past in cars, carts and charabancs was relentless; the day-trippers' pleasure mocking Molly and Simon in their misery.

'Molly,' he said suddenly, 'why don't you just admit it? You're ashamed of me, aren't you?'

'That's rich, coming from you.' She waved her arms angrily about her, trying to get an imaginary audience on her side. 'Here he is, a bloke what's kept me a secret from his family for a year and he has the cheek to say that *I'm* ashamed of *him*.'

'Now you're talking rubbish.'

That was it; with her face flaming, Molly stepped from the pavement to get away from him. What sounded like a hundred hooters and horns screeched at her as Simon lunged forward, seized hold of her dress and yanked her back to the safety of the kerbside.

They stood staring at each other, both all too aware of just how close Molly had come to being crushed.

'You can say and do what you like, Molly,' Simon said slowly, trying to calm himself, 'but, please, don't be stupid.'

'I must be stupid putting up with this,' she sniffed.

'Right. If you're so fed up with everything, maybe we *should* break up.'

'Good. That's suits me just fine. Just fine!'

'Molly.' Simon pulled her towards him, and held her head close against his chest. 'Please,' he breathed into her hair, 'don't cry. Please.'

With the traffic roaring past, Molly and Simon never heard the steps running along the path towards them.

'Oi! You! Jew boy. Get yer dirty stinking hands off her.'

Simon blinked, confused as to who it was saying those things.

'I said, get yer hands off her.'

But Molly knew immediately who it was – Bob Jarvis. She had been right, it was him she had seen back at the fairground. Struggling to free herself from Simon's arms, Molly turned on their tormentor. 'You leave us alone, you no-good bastard.' She spat the words out at him, leaning forward, challenging him to defy her. 'And if yer don't make yerself scarce, yer gonna get nicked.'

For just a moment, the cocky expression almost slipped from Jarvis's face. 'What, Jew boy here gonna run off and tell the rozzers I've upset him, is he? Or is he gonna get you to go for him, 'cos he's pissed his pants?'

'Come on, Molly, let's go. Don't waste your breath on him.' Simon tried to pull her away. But she wouldn't budge.

'No,' she said, shaking her arm free. 'No one's going for the rozzers. They don't have to 'cos they're already looking for yer. I had a word with 'em, see.' She looked him up and down with a disdainful sneer. 'I told 'em what you done yesterday.'

'You what?' Jarvis's face twisted into a hideous mask of pure hatred.

It immediately dawned on Molly what she had just done: she had told Bob Jarvis she had grassed him. She stepped back.

He threw his head forward and spat at her feet; flashed a look of scornful hatred at them and then ran off, disappearing back into the crowded fairground.

'That was him, wasn't it? The one who killed the old man. And it was him you saw just now in the fairground.'

'I ain't gonna talk about it. I just wanna get home,' she began calmly, but, unable to bear it any longer, she collapsed into Simon's arms and sobbed into his jacket. 'What are we gonna do, Simon? What are we gonna do?'

Molly wasn't the only Mehan who was feeling at her wits' end; back in Plumley Street, in the kitchen of number twelve, Katie was feeling just as desperate as her daughter, and she was sure that if she didn't talk to someone soon, she would go mad with the strain of it all. So, with all her children out, supposedly enjoying the Bank Holiday, and Stephen over at the Queen's with Bill and Joe, Katie had asked her mum in to have a quiet cup of tea, and to take the opportunity to have a talk with her.

That had been the plan, but Katie hadn't been able to bring herself to actually say what it was that was on her mind, and was instead fussing around, filling up the kettle yet again.

'Jesus, Mary, Joseph, whatever's the matter with yer, girl? I like a cuppa tea as much as the rest o' them, but if I have to drink one more mouthful of the stuff while I wait for you to tell me that you want me to go round and fetch Pat home for yer – at last, and not before time, I might add – I swear yer'll have to pour me into me bed tonight.'

Katie turned off the tap and said bluntly, 'It ain't that. I'm expecting.'

Nora rushed over to the sink and wrapped her arms around her daughter. 'God love yer.'

Katie twisted away from Nora and fiddled around with her apron, retying the strings and straightening the shoulder straps. 'Me nerves have been that bad lately, I've not known where to turn.'

'Will yer just stop yer fretting and sit yerself down at that table?' Nora steered her daughter over to her chair and settled down opposite her.

'I love him, see, Mum,' Katie told the table, 'and I want him back.'

'Course yer do, darling, course yer do. And he'll be back now, you see. Soon as he hears the news!'

Katie wasn't listening. 'I couldn't keep pushing him away, could I, just 'cos I was scared I might fall again? And then it happened. I fell. And I'm that worried about how I'm gonna manage.' Katie wiped her eyes on the hem of her apron. 'He'll never wanna come back now. I should have gone to that Married Women's Clinic.'

'Katie, sure yer don't mean that! It's a blessing, a new baby in the house.'

'But it's bad enough as it is, what with the boys all upstairs in your'n and you having to sleep down in the parlour.'

'We'll get by. Sure one more won't even make any difference till the little love's a year old or so. And then, if we're blessed with another girl it can sleep in here with Molly, and if it's a boy we'll have to budge up a bit next door. You see, it'll be all right.'

'I don't want Pat knowing. Not yet,' she sniffed.

Nora leant back in her chair and flapped her hand at her daughter. 'Why ever not? He'll be as chuffed as a dog with two tails.'

'I want him to come back because of me, not because of the baby.'

'Katie, surely yer—'

'And I'm scared he'll make me give me job up.'

'I should think so.'

'No, Mum, I can't. It ain't gonna be easy as it is.' She hesitated. 'That's the reason I got the rotten job in the

367

first place – so's I'd have a few bob to put by.'

'Yer mean yer've not just found out?'

'No. I've known about it for a while now.' Katie stood up and finished filling the kettle. 'I'm over three months gone.' She set the kettle on the stove and lit the gas.

Nora started counting on her fingers. 'It must have been about the time yer dad was going over to cheer up poor old Bert Johnson, God rest his soul.'

'It don't matter when it was, I just don't want yer going round and telling Pat, all right?' She reached up and put the matches back on the shelf. 'I mean it. I've gotta stay at that laundry as long as I can. It's the only way.'

'No it's not. We'll manage. Sure the kids can give yer a bit extra.'

'Danny already gives me what he can, and yer know how hard he's trying to save for him and Liz. I couldn't ask him for no more. They're gonna have to wait long enough as it is. And as for Molly, hard as she works, her wages're hardly worth counting. And Sean . . . well, you know as much as I do about what he's up to and what he's got in his pocket.'

'Come on, sit down. I'll finish making the tea.'

'No, yer all right, Mum.'

'I could try and get some work, cleaning, like I used to when you was little.'

Katie poured the boiling water into the teapot and set it down on the table. 'You know there's girls out there a quarter o' your age fighting for every job what comes up.'

'But, surely—'

'But nothing, Mum. Just drink yer tea, and let's forget it for now, eh? You ain't going to work, and that's it. We've always kept yer, and nothing's gonna change now.'

Katie looked up at the clock on the mantel shelf. 'The kids'll all be home soon, and I don't think I could stand another scene.'

Less than a month had gone by since the Bank Holiday when Katie and Molly had both been so unhappy, but now, early on a grey, showery, September Saturday morning, the contrast between Molly's and Katie's moods couldn't have been more marked.

Molly was still upstairs in bed, exhausted after another bad night. Over the past weeks she had become withdrawn and morose. She was still seeing Simon, but for briefer and briefer snatches of time on a Sunday afternoon. They would meet up okay, but within minutes the strain would begin to tell and they would start sniping and picking at one another. Molly would burst into tears and swear she would never, ever see him again, and Simon would say that was fine by him. Then, come the next Sunday he would be waiting for her, not caring that he would have to go through the whole miserable process again.

Katie, on the other hand, had been up and about for hours, humming tunelessly to herself, as she pottered about the kitchen, scouring the already gleaming butler sink and scrubbing down the spotless wooden draining board. She was feeling so much better, not happy exactly – how could she be with her husband gone from the house for nearly ten weeks and the kids missing him so desperately? – but there was an optimism about her that made her feel that everything really might sort itself out after all, just as her mum had said it would. And, best of all, she had started to feel the stirrings deep inside her that reminded her so intensely of the joys of holding a newborn baby in her arms.

Maybe, just maybe, she thought, as she shook more scouring powder on to her dishcloth, the time had come for her to go and see Pat and to tell him the good news.

'Lord love us,' said Nora, throwing off her damp coat and putting down the bacon that Stephen now regularly, if rather mysteriously, provided for the family's weekend breakfasts, 'I thought it was a songbird trapped in here.'

Katie looked over her shoulder at her. 'Still got it in me, eh, Mum?' She pushed back a stray curl from her forehead with the back of her damp hand.

'So's Pat from the look of it,' Nora laughed, nodding at Katie's gently curving belly.

'Sssh!' Katie pinched at her apron with her finger and thumb, pulling it forward to make it hang more loosely over her middle. 'Keep yer voice down, will yer? There's Molly's door just opened.'

Nora rolled her eyes. 'Yer not gonna be able to keep that little darling a secret for much longer,' she said, taking a plate down from the dresser to put the bacon on.

They heard Molly come stumping along the passage.

'Hello, Nanna,' she said, brushing Nora's cheek with her lips, then going over to Katie. 'Morning, Mum.'

Katie frowned. 'Yer look whacked out.'

'I'm all right. I just didn't sleep too good.'

'Again?' Katie dried her hands on her apron, reached out and felt her daughter's forehead with the flat of her palm. 'Yer not hot or anything.'

'Don't fuss, Mum,' she moaned, dragging her cardigan round her.

'She needs a bit o' fresh air to liven herself up, that's all,' pronounced Nora wisely. 'It's being stuck in that factory all week.' She put her arm round her granddaughter's shoulders and led her over to the table.

'Made any plans for tomorrow afternoon, have yer, love? I know how yer like to get out of a Sunday.'

Molly drew away from her nanna with a warning flash of her eyes to keep her mouth shut in front of her mum.

'If yer really want some air, yer could nip over the shop for me,' Katie said, too busy rinsing the sink to have even noticed the exchange between Molly and Nora. 'I've only got a piddly bit o' lard left, and yer know how you all like a fried slice with yer rashers.'

'I'll be glad to, Mum,' Molly answered primly, with another glare of caution in Nora's direction.

Katie looked over to the clock. 'Edie'll be open by now. Take me purse, it's on the side there. And don't forget the umbrella. I don't want you catching yer death.'

With a final mouthed warning at her nanna, Molly took her mum's purse and fetched her coat from under the stairs. She didn't bother with the umbrella that stood in the old, chipped vase behind the street door. Instead she pulled the coat over her head like a hood and made a dash across the rain-slicked street.

As she stepped into the shop doorway, she shook herself like a damp puppy on to the pavement. 'Don't look like yer gonna be able to put all yer gear out today, Ede,' she said, looking up at the darkening sky.

'That's what I thought,' said Edie, coming from behind the counter and joining Molly in the doorway. She was still dressed in deepest black mourning, Bert having been dead just three months.

She peered up at the ominously low clouds. 'If it ain't cleared up by now, I don't reckon it's gonna.' She ushered Molly inside. 'My Bert always looked on the bright side, God love him,' she said fondly. ' "It'll clear up soon, girl," he used to say. And, d'you know, it usually did and all.' She lifted the flap and took up her place behind the

371

counter again. 'That's the way to be, eh? Looking on the bright side.'

'Why?' asked a gruff woman's voice from the doorway.

'Because otherwise this weather'd get yer down, Phoeb, that's why,' Edie answered her pleasantly. 'My Bert always used to say, "Look on the bright side, Ede. There's better times awaiting if only we knew it."'

'I dunno about that, I'm sure.' Phoebe brushed the rain from the shoulders of her dull black serge coat, the effort of raising her arms making her chins quiver. Then she pushed her way in front of Molly without so much as a word of acknowledgement.

Edie and Molly raised their eyebrows at one another in silent amusement.

Phoebe sat on the bentwood chair that stood beside the counter and, placing her bag between her feet, she folded her arms and settled herself back until her bulky frame found a comfortable position. She would, after all, be there for some time, as, whenever it was raining, the corner shop replaced Chrisp Street market as Phoebe's preferred place for earwigging and for the passing on of all the latest gossip.

'So,' she said, eyeing Molly slyly, 'yer dad's still amongst the missing then?'

Molly snapped open her mum's purse and slapped a shilling piece down on the counter. 'Half o' lard, please, Ede,' she said through gritted teeth.

'Yes, love,' said Edie, deliberately ignoring Phoebe's remark.

Phoebe ploughed on regardless. 'They still ain't got hold of that bloke what done in that old man down Back Church Lane. Police still looking for him, so I hear.'

Molly felt a sickly fluttering in her stomach.

'The talk is that it was that Bob Jarvis what did it.'

Phoebe thoughtfully scratched the side of her puggy, blubbery nose. 'He was some sort of mate o' your Danny's, weren't he? That's what my granddaughter told me.'

'Well, your granddaughter wants to mind her own business, don't she? Spreading rubbish like that,' Molly said, spinning round to face her.

Phoebe didn't even blink. 'Apparently no one's seen him about,' she went on, 'not even none o' them mates of his what've been causing all that trouble up Whitechapel way.' She paused. 'Beating up Jews and that.'

Molly took the lard from Edie. 'I won't bother to wait for the change now, Ede. I'll be over for it later,' she said, turning on her heel and making for the door. 'Mum said to get this straight back for our breakfast, see.'

'All right, love,' said Edie, 'see yer later on.'

It was only the memory of her Bert's belief that everyone deserved polite service, no matter who or what they were, that prevented Edie from tipping Phoebe right off the chair, putting her boot up the old cow's backside and kicking her out of the shop.

'Here's the lard, Mum, and yer purse. Edie was a bit busy so I'll fetch yer change later.'

'All right, sweetheart.' Katie slipped her purse into her apron pocket. 'But don't worry about the change, I'll send one of the boys over. You really don't look well to me. Yer proper peaky. Why don't yer go back to bed?'

'Please, don't fuss, Mum.'

Nora stood up from the table. 'I reckon it's you could do with a rest, Kate.' Much to Katie's irritation, Nora gave her a broad knowing wink. 'Sure, weren't you up with the lark this morning. Now, I'll tell yer what. I'm going to go in next door and get the boys out o' their beds, and then I'm going to make their breakfasts for them in there. And Stephen's. And you can come in for yours when yer ready. So there's no excuse for you not to put yer feet up. Right?'

'Mum,' Katie protested.

But Nora paid no heed; she peeled off enough bacon from the plate for the crowd next door and put it on another plate. 'Now, Molly, d'yer wanna come in next door with me and help me with the breakfast while yer mam has a sit-down?'

With Phoebe's words ringing in her head, Molly readily agreed – anything to escape her mother's scrutiny. 'Course I'll help yer. And Nanna's right, Mum, you've been working that hard at that laundry. You put yer feet up and have a quiet cuppa.'

Katie smiled. At least Molly hadn't cottoned on to the real reason for her having been so tired out recently. 'Fat chance of me sitting down for a quiet cuppa. But I would appreciate yer keeping that mob in there for their breakfasts, Mum. Then I can catch up with a bit o' that washing I've got piled up.' She laughed wryly. 'Washing on a Saturday, eh. I dunno, I'm working in that flaming laundry all week long and I don't find no time to do none o' me own.' She went over to the kitchen window and ducked her head to catch a glimpse of the sky between the buildings. 'Let's just hope this rain clears up.'

'There's no need to do it straight away, girl,' Nora said, taking her coat from the back of the chair and slipping it round her shoulders. 'You just sit down for a bit, and remember, when yer ready, you come in for yer breakfast. Then me and Molly'll come back in here and help yer with the washing. How'd that suit yer?'

'That'll suit me fine, Mum.'

But no matter what Katie had said, as soon as Nora

and Molly left her alone, she opened the back door and ran out in the rain to the scullery, not even bothering to put her coat on first. She always hated putting off even a little job if she didn't have to, so the sight of all that washing spilling out of the basket in the corner of her kitchen was like an accusing finger pointing at a houseproud woman like Katie Mehan.

Despite the damp, she had the fire lit under the copper and the water heating up nicely in no time. Now, all she had to do was go indoors to the kitchen and fetch the basket, put the whites in to boil, and then she could sit down and have a cuppa, while she worked out what she would say when she went to see Pat.

But Katie never got as far as the kitchen.

As she made a dash for the back door, her feet slipped from under her on the rain-spattered flagstones in the scullery doorway and she found herself hurtling forward.

She threw out her hands in front of her to stop herself crashing into the big iron-framed mangle, but it was too late. As she crumpled to the rain-sodden ground, Katie felt a searing pain, like fire in her guts, as the metal-reinforced wooden handle of the wringer rammed into her side.

The next thing she knew was her head was filled with the sound of someone screaming. At first she thought it must be her, roaring with the terrible pain, but as she slowly opened her eyes, she saw it was Molly yelling like a mad thing for Nora.

'Nanna! Quick!' she was hollering over the wall. 'Quick!'

As Nora poked her head over the wall to see what all the fuss was about, her hand flew to her mouth. 'No!' Her eyes had fixed on the dark stain spreading out on the ground beneath her daughter.

'Quick, run and tell Joe to fetch yer dad in his truck. Hurry!'

On her side of the wall Nora hurriedly dragged the tin bath from her scullery and set it on its side as a makeshift step, to help her reach her daughter. In her panic, it didn't occur to her to run round to the street door.

As Nora scrambled up the wet, slippery wall, with her dress tucked up round her thighs, and balanced unsteadily on the top, making ready to tip over into the yard of number twelve, the tin bath went crashing back onto its base, fetching Michael running out from the kitchen to check on what excitement he might be missing.

'Blimey, Nanna!' he exclaimed through a mouthful of bacon, the sight of his grandmother's unsuspected acrobatic talents making him forget both his language and his manners. 'What you up to?'

'It's all right, Michael, love,' Nora said slowly. 'Yer mam's just not very well, so go and . . .'

Before Nora could finish, Michael was hanging on top of the wall peering over at his mum lying on the ground. 'Is that blood, Nanna?'

'Get yerself indoors, Michael,' she ordered him quite unnecessarily as he ran back indoors to fetch his brothers and his grandad. 'Tell 'em to bring blankets,' she called, then swore under her breath as her knees jarred as she dropped down beside Katie.

'I'm here, darling,' she whispered, kneeling beside her daughter on the soaking wet ground. She tore off her cardigan and held it over Katie, trying to protect her from the rain. 'And Molly's fetching Pat. They won't be long.'

Katie tried to lift her head, her eyes swimming in

376

and out of focus as the pain tore through her. 'Don't let Pat fetch the doctor, Mum. Please. We can't afford it.'

A pile of blankets, closely followed by the boys, then Stephen, came flying over the wall.

Danny, ashen-faced, knelt beside his nanna as she covered his mum with the blankets.

'What shall I do?' he asked, the fear in his voice making him sound like a little kid.

'I don't know if we should move her,' Nora whispered to him.

'She can't stay out here.' Stephen ran his fingers distractedly through his hair. 'I'm gonna fetch the doctor.'

'No,' groaned Katie, and she passed out again.

Katie's eyes fluttered open for a brief moment and she whimpered as she felt herself being rolled onto her back. It hurt, it hurt so much. She could hear someone speaking. It was Molly. She was babbling away nineteen to the dozen, going on about being worried when she hadn't come in for her breakfast, and how she had gone in a truck to find someone.

Then she heard her mum speaking. 'Ssssh now, Molly,' she was saying. 'Let's just get yer mam up to her bed, eh, darling?'

Then Katie felt herself being lifted into the air.

Pat carried his wife indoors, all the while sobbing that he was sorry, oh so sorry, and grimacing with the pain that was tearing his heart out.

15

'I've lost the baby, ain't I?' Katie stared up at the ceiling, not bothering to wipe away the tears that were running down her face and into her ears. It was Sunday, almost lunchtime, and, although she couldn't remember all that had happened to her in the last thirty-six hours, she knew that she was right about the baby.

Pat took her hand. 'Yer mustn't take on, Kate, yer've gotta rest, like the doctor said.'

'It's me punishment for not telling yer. It was like lying.' She screwed up her eyes and gripped Pat so hard that her nails dug into his flesh. 'Pat. I'm so sorry.'

'It's me what's sorry, Kate. I hate meself for what I did to yer. I swear, I'll never raise me hand to you again.'

Katie rolled over on to her side. Her body shook as wave after wave of silent sobs shuddered through her.

Pat looked round at Nora, who was standing at the end of the bed; he wanted her to tell him how to help his wife, what to do, how to make it all better.

Nora sat down on the bed beside her daughter and gently patted her back. 'There, there, love, try and be brave. The kids are all outside on the landing, don't let 'em hear yer crying.' She looked at Pat, sitting there helplessly, his head buried in his hands. 'Come on now,' Nora encouraged them. 'Buck up, eh? I've told 'em they can come in for one minute to see yers, then they're all coming back indoors with me for their dinner.'

Katie sniffed loudly, rolled on to her back and struggled to prop herself up on her elbows. 'Give us yer handkerchief, Pat.' She wiped her eyes and blew her nose. 'Tell 'em to come in, Mum.'

Katie and Pat's five children filed in. Molly, then Danny followed by Michael, Timmy and last of all, hanging back, came Sean.

They stood there staring at their mum, the woman who always coped with everything and everyone; even when their dad had gone away like that. And now she looked terrible, and it frightened them. They tried not to let their fear show. Nora had warned them all, especially Timmy, that they weren't to cry or go upsetting her in any way, but Molly couldn't help herself. She rushed forward and threw her arms round Katie's neck.

'Mum!' she wailed. 'Aw, Mum!'

That was it, the floodgate had broken; within seconds all the other kids were weeping and sitting on the bed, getting as close to their mother as they could. Even Sean, the tough nut, was gripping one of her hands and sniffing noisily.

'You ain't gonna die, are yer?' wailed Michael, his little tear-stained cheeks puckering with the effort of controlling his sobs.

Nora was furious. 'What did I tell you lot about upsetting yer mammy?'

'They're all right, Mum,' Katie said, her voice faint with strain. 'It's making me feel better just having 'em here with me.' She did her best to smile for Michael. 'And course I ain't gonna die, yer daft 'apporth. Who'd chase yer off to school in the morning if I wasn't here?'

'Now come on, we all know what the doctor said, yer mam's gotta rest.' Nora held out her hand to Timmy, always the easiest of them to handle. 'All of yer. Back next door now. We'll leave yer mam and dad to a bit of peace.'

Each of her children kissed Katie in turn, while Molly still clung on to her as though she was scared she would run off and leave them all. But Nora didn't have to tell them again; without any argument they followed her out of the room.

'I know there's been times when I could've wrung their necks for 'em, but they're good kids, Kate,' said Pat, smoothing her hair away from her forehead. 'Yer've done a right good job with 'em all.'

'Have I?' Katie looked up into her husband's face, the face she had fallen in love with when she was just a girl, when she had known nothing of the pain and hurt that could come with being a wife and mother. 'And have I been a good wife?' she asked, in a barely audible whisper.

'Aw, Katie. Katie, I love you so much. You don't know how much. Nothing's ever gonna hurt you again. Nothing. I'd rather cut me hands off than ever hurt you again.'

He buried his head in her shoulder and they cried together.

Next door, Nora called Stephen in from the front room, where he had been looking through the Sunday paper, to carve the meat for her, while the kids sorted out the plates and cutlery, and she dished up the vegetables and roast potatoes.

Stephen did his best with the bit of silverside, which wasn't saying much; it wasn't something he had much experience of, carving meat. In fact, he was surprised Nora had asked him to even attempt it, and he said as much.

'I wanted yer by me so I could have a quiet word,' whispered Nora, as she dug viciously with a fish slice at the little crispy bits of potato in the bottom of the tin. 'I wanted to ask yer, Stephen Brady, what yer thought yer was up to, not coming in to see yer own daughter?'

Stephen put the carving knife down on the draining board. 'I was there when I was needed yesterday, wasn't I? I ran and fetched the doctor.'

He looked over his shoulder to make sure the kids were too occupied with their own thoughts and concerns to bother listening to anything he had to say, then he leant close to Nora. With his head angled sharply downwards, he murmured, 'And if yer want to know the truth, Nora, I reckoned I'd be intruding.' He held up his hand to still Nora's denial that he knew would come next, and glanced anxiously over his shoulder again. 'Sure, I'm no fool. I know exactly how she feels about me. And I can't say I blame her.'

'She'll come around, Stephen. Perhaps if yer popped in to see her later, for just a couple of minutes . . .'

'She's got enough on her plate, without me going in there and upsetting her even more.' He lifted his head and looked at Nora. 'I know me turning up here has only added to that girl's aggravation. And I can't help feeling partly to blame for what's happened to her.'

Nora touched him tenderly on the arm. 'You mustn't talk like that.'

Stephen shrugged dejectedly.

'Scuse me!' Trying to hide the tears that were streaming down her face, Molly dashed past her grandparents and out into the back yard.

Stephen picked up the knife again. Much as he hated to see Molly upset, he was relieved by the diversion; he had come very close to saying things that he would have regretted. 'Go on, go out to Molly. I'll sort this out,' he looked at the ragged chunks of meat he'd cut, 'somehow or other.'

Nora wiped her hands on the tea towel and went outside.

'It's all right, love,' she said. 'I'm here.'

She held Molly close to her, stroking her hair, just as she had done when she was a little girl and had grazed her knees falling in the street or clambering over the wall. 'It's been a shock, but she'll be just fine now. I promise yer.'

'I know, Nanna, but it's something she said to me. I can't stop thinking about it.'

'What's that then, darling?'

'She said she'd been upset 'cos of how me and Danny have been. You know, how we've not been close like we always used to be.'

Nora tipped back her head so she could look into Molly's eyes. 'Surely she knows he's busy with young Liz taking up all his time?'

'That's what I said, Nanna, but Mum said she didn't mean that, and it was making her really sad to see us. Then I said she'd got it all wrong.' She looked away from her nanna as more tears spilt from her eyes. ' "Honest, Mum, there's nothing wrong between us." That's what I said to her. And d'yer know what she said to me, Nan?'

'What, darling?'

'She said, "Yer not lying to me, are yer, Molly?" And I said, "Would I ever lie to you, Mum? Yer know us Mehans never lie." '

'Sssh, don't take on so. Yer just seeing a lad, that's all. Yer've not done anything wrong.'

'But I have, Nanna,' she sobbed. 'I've kept it all from Mum, 'cos I know what she'd say. I know she'd make me give him up 'cos he ain't Catholic. Yet I love him so much, Nanna. But I know what it makes me and all. A rotten liar.' She buried her face in her hands. 'You just don't understand.'

But Nora did understand. She thought of the night back in Ireland when she had left a note stuck on the pile of turf by the hearth, saying that she couldn't face living without Stephen and was running away with him to England. She had been just about Molly's age then – a child of seventeen, who thought she would die if she couldn't be with the man she loved, but whose heart was breaking at the thought of leaving her home and hurting her mother. And even when he'd gone and left her, and she'd had all those years of struggling to bring up their child alone, still she loved him. Yes, she understood all right.

'Right,' Nora said, 'here's what yer gonna do. Yer gonna come back in that kitchen with me, eat yer dinner, then get yer face washed and go off and meet this Sunday feller o' your'n.'

'But, Nanna—'

'No. I won't hear another word out of yer, Molly. Yer know that you lot being happy's the best medicine for yer mam. That's all she's ever wanted in life. So just do as I say and it'll all work out for the best. You just see.'

In just a few weeks, Katie was strong again – at least her body was – and, if there had been any chance of their taking her on again at the laundry she would have been back there like a shot. But being ill had cost her her job, and someone else had filled her place.

For Pat, too, the situation at work was becoming even more difficult. Dockers had never expected to be in a position where they could mess their bosses around by being ill or taking time off – whatever the reason – but, by the middle of November, even the most loyal and compliant of Pat's fellow employees were beginning to wonder what was going on.

Pat had been expecting something like it for weeks, but, when he read it right there in the newspaper in black and white, it still came as a shock. This was going to cause real trouble, he just knew it.

He slammed the paper down on the table and shoved his chair back across the lino.

'Pat?'

'It's nothing, Kate.' He folded the paper up and shoved it under his arm. 'Look, I ain't gonna bother with no breakfast, or nothing. I'm gonna get straight into work.'

'All right, love. Tell yer what, I could make yer a fried egg sandwich to eat going along if yer like.'

'No thanks, Kate, I couldn't eat a thing.'

'There's something wrong, ain't there?'

'Yeah, there's something wrong.' He pulled the paper from under his arm and waved it angrily. 'The union bosses,' he spat the words out contemptuously, 'have accepted a deal of *fivepence*, yeah, that's right, *fivepence* more a day. What's the point in being part of a sodding union when they ignore what the workers want?'

'That's terrible.'

'You ain't wrong there, girl.' Pat strode out of the kitchen and grabbed his jacket from the glory hole under the stairs. He stood in the doorway, jamming his cap down tight on his head. 'The bastards have let us down – every last one of us – and with no other jobs about, they know there ain't a poxy thing we can do about it.'

Michael didn't even giggle.

'Geezers in the big docks like our'n have been stuffed with a sodding eleven and sevenpence minimum.' He smacked the flat of his hand hard against the door jamb. 'Bastards! Marvellous innit, eh? And them poor buggers in the smaller docks, they're on a bloody shilling less. Their kids must have smaller bellies, I suppose. Don't need so much grub in 'em.'

Katie stood up and went over to him. 'Pat, you won't go doing nothing daft, will yer?'

'No, I won't do nothing daft.' He bent forward and kissed her distractedly on the top of her head, then he turned on his heel and muttered angrily to himself as he stomped towards the street door, 'But if I never had a family to think of, I'd have them bastards. I'd show 'em what it means to suffer.'

The situation at the daily shapeup on the stones outside the dock gates grew tenser every day as ever-increasing numbers of men gathered there earlier and earlier each morning hoping for the chance of some casual work. There weren't only the regulars who came from the surrounding neighbourhoods looking for casual, but there were desperate newcomers who had come flooding into London from all over the country, and even some of the stevedores – the skilled dock workers like Pat – were queueing up for bits of dockers' unloading work. With families to feed and landlords to satisfy, no one could afford to be particular.

It was a freezing February morning, one of those days when it would get dark almost before it had ever really got properly light, but Pat was on a promise of a decent job for a change, and, cold as it was, he was feeling quite chirpy, whistling tunelessly to himself as he walked up to the gates. But as he passed the anxious, care-worn faces of the crowds of men whose hope was draining away the longer they had to wait, he stopped his whistling. If he hadn't, he'd have felt like he was rubbing their noses in it.

He was about ten yards from the dock coppers' booth, the place from where suspicion of thievery and smuggling emanated like a physical force, when one of the gangers appeared at the gate, and the crowd behind him suddenly surged forward.

'Oi, watch it.' Pat, though considerably taller and broader than a lot of the others, was still carried forward on the tide of desperate men. It was literally every man for himself in the struggle to catch the man's eye who could make the difference between earning the rent that week or being forced to do yet another moonlight flit because you couldn't pay the landlord for the second week in a row.

Pat battled his way to the side of the mob. Rather than try to get to the gates, he reckoned he'd be better off hanging back for a while until they'd all calmed down a bit. He knew he could look after himself if it came to it, but he had no argument with these men, and if tempers were going to be lost then he'd prefer not to be part of it.

He watched, doing his best to remain dispassionate, as the majority of them jostled with one another, trying anything and everything they could think of to get the attention of the foreman. They stuck their heads forward, stood up straight, puffed out their chests – anything to make themselves look strong, willing and worth taking a chance with a day's work.

But then there were the others, the really pathetic ones who had turned up from who knew where to try and earn a few bob. They probably didn't really believe that anyone would ever pick them out of the crowd. They were the ones who had become used to being rejected wherever they went, the ones with that terrible sense of despair about them, the ones with the same look that Pat recognised in that poor bugger Milton as he dragged himself along Plumley Street, his head bent down into his hunched shoulders as though he were scared that someone might see him in his shame.

It disgusted Pat to see how some of the registered men were having a go at the more sickly-looking outsiders.

'We've been standing here day in day out, for hours on end in this sodding freezing cold and these bastards have got the cheek to turn up here like they're entitled,' one of the regulars yelled. He was jabbing his finger close to the face of a man who was quaking from what looked to Pat like a combination of fear and the icy wind that was ripping through the man's threadbare coat. 'Now look what yer've done, yer bastard. He's picked his crew and I've missed out. And it's your fault, yer no-good slag!'

Pat took out his tobacco pouch from his jacket pocket. He had been saving his last bit of Gold Flake to have after his dinner, but there were times when a man needed a smoke, and this was one of them. He'd have his cigarette, then he'd go through the gates.

He was just raising the paper to his lips to lick it, when an elbow jammed into Pat's side, sending his last precious bits of tobacco fluttering down on to the damp cobblestones.

'For Christ's sake!' Pat kicked at the stones, punishing them for taking his smoke. Then he took a deep breath and turned to face the idiot who'd made him drop it. He was about to say, 'All right, mate, just give us a fag and we'll forget it.' But as he looked round, he saw the wild look in the man's eyes. Instead of just apologising good-naturedly, the man drew back his fist and slammed it

388

forward with all his force, directing it at Pat's chin.

Pat, blinking with surprise, dodged back out of his way, but now he too had his fists up and at the ready.

'Look, moosh,' Pat said, weaving around in front of the man, who was a good head and shoulders shorter than he, 'I don't want no trouble. Let's just—'

But Pat's words were wasted. A torrent of frustration had been loosed in the man's head and he had to take it out on someone, and, small and weak though he was in comparison, he launched himself on Pat again.

The man was lucky that he had chosen Pat to start on.

Pat flung his cap to one of the bystanders who, glad of the distraction, had all gathered round, and went through the motions of fighting him. Everyone who knew him could see that Pat was just blocking and avoiding, dancing almost, around the skinny little runt who was barmy enough to take on Pat Mehan, a bloke who could take on fellers twice his size and beat them with one hand tied behind his back.

'My good Gawd, Pat,' one of the bystanders shouted. 'That the best yer can do with a little twerp like him? I ain't betting on you no more. Go on, bash him one!'

'Just keeping meself warm, Con,' Pat shouted back. As he bobbed around, avoiding the little man's flailing fists, Pat looked over his shoulder and treated Con to a wide, genial grin. 'If you fancy yer chances, I'll take you on next.'

'Watch it!' a voice hollered from the crowd.

Pat wasn't sure what happened next, he just knew that he was sprawling on his side on the hard, wet ground.

'What the hell?' Pat rolled over on to his back and propped himself up on his elbows.

'It's all right, Pat.' A hand reached down to him to help him up. 'It's me, Frank Barber. I shoved yer down out of the way.'

'Yer silly bastard,' roared Pat, smacking Frank's offer of a hand out of the way and springing to his feet. 'What d'yer have to go and stick yer nose in for?'

'Lucky he did, Pat,' said Con, handing Pat his cap.

'Eh?'

'Look.' Con lifted his chin towards the little man who had attacked Pat; he was being held by three men.

One of them lifted a docker's hook high in the air for Pat to see. 'You was lucky, Mehan,' the man said. 'He was just gonna use this to part yer hair for yer while yer was sodding about grinning at Con boy over there. I reckon you owe Barber for saving yer life.'

Pat stood there, dumbfounded, as two of the dock coppers came out of their booth and took custody of the man. 'Who else was involved in this?' one of them asked.

The crowd was silent.

'Fighting with himself, was he?'

'That's right,' someone shouted. 'He's barmy, see. It's having no money and no job and no grub in his belly. Makes yer go round the bend, don't it?'

'All right, all right, clever. That's enough of that. Now, we'll see to him while you, 'cos you seem to know everything, go and fetch the law.'

After that grudging, if veiled, acknowledgement that their jurisdiction was confined to the docks, the other dock copper added, 'Now the rest of yer, there's nothing more to see and there's no more tickets being issued. Fun's over and so's yer chance of any work. Now on yer way or there'll be more trouble, and we'll be the ones causing it.'

With that they marched the now ashen-faced man

back to their booth and locked the gates firmly behind them.

'Shit!' Pat dashed his cap to the ground. 'Another sodding day's work down the shoot.'

Frank Barber retrieved the hat and handed it back to him. 'Hard, innit?'

'Eh? Aw, yeah.' Pat brushed the dirt from his cap and jammed it back on his head. 'Thanks, like, for, yer know,' he began grudgingly. 'For what yer did just now.'

'Pleasure, mate. I mean, it's me what owes you really, innit? What with everything your family's done for me these last few years. Ever since my Sarah . . . yer know.'

Pat, a gorge of shame threatening to rise up and choke him, managed to say, 'Yeah. Yeah. I know.'

Frank pulled out a packet of Woodbines and offered one to Pat, who took it with a nod.

'Might as well be getting off home, I suppose, eh, Pat?'

Pat struck a match and held it out to Frank. 'I reckon I could afford to stand yer a cuppa tea first. For saving me life, like. What d'yer think?'

'Ta, I'd like that.' He shrugged. 'Yer know what it's like, I ain't got nothing to rush home for.' He laughed, an easy, self-deprecating chuckle. 'Except about half a hundredweight o' washing, me windows to clean and the tea to get on. It's a hard life for a feller being mum and dad to his kid.'

'Yeah. It must be.' Pat hesitated, then gave him a friendly slap on the back. 'Come on then, I'm getting bloody freezing standing here.' He looked over his shoulder towards the booth by the dock gates. 'And I don't fancy waiting round here for the law to turn up.'

As they hurried along towards Chinatown to find a coffee stall, Frank chatted away as though it was the most natural thing in the world for him and Pat Mehan to be going to have a cup of tea together.

'Makes yer wonder, dunnit, Pat, what's gonna become of us all when yer see men acting like wild animals, fighting one another over a day's pay?'

'There's a lot of unhappy people about, all right.'

'Yer can say that again. One of the blokes back there just now, he was telling us about some poor sod down the Victoria Dock. He got trampled the other day. When they got him to Poplar Hospital, he was dead.'

'I never heard nothing about that.' Pat ushered Frank towards a stall where a group of men were huddled around the big silver urn on the counter, doing their best to keep warm. 'Two teas, please, mate,' said Pat with a lift of his chin.

'S'pose they kept it out of the papers to stop the likes of us from hearing about it,' said Frank. 'Always the way, ain't it?' He nodded his thanks as the stall holder handed him his tea in a thick, chipped china cup. 'I mean, they don't want us poor bleeders whose sweat earns the profits for them rich bastards, knowing what's really going on in the world, do they? We risk life and limb, and wind up fighting amongst ourselves and getting bugger all out of it.'

As Pat listened to Frank, he stirred three heaped spoons of sugar into his tea; it was a luxury he didn't get much of lately, and a tight-fisted stall holder's angry glare wasn't going to put him off.

'I was talking to Harold the other day.' Frank sipped at his cup, the hot tea making him sniff and his breath form into white, misty clouds.

Pat glanced sideways; this bloke was really surprising him. 'Yer know, I don't think I've ever seen yer in the Queen's, Frank.' There, he'd called him by his name.

'No, I don't get the chance to do much drinking, do I,

with me nipper. No, I was in there doing a bit o' bottling up for Harold. I go in most mornings, right early, before Theresa wakes up, see. It brings in a few bob and I can do it before I get down the dock to see if anything's going down there. I mean, I can hardly tell me little 'un to stop growing just 'cos I ain't got no money for new shoes for her, now can I?'

Pat swallowed hard. Katie always worried about things like that. He just earned the money – when he could – and handed it over to her. He didn't know what he'd do if he was expected to think about sorting out shoes and washing and windows and stuff as well.

'Anyway,' Frank went on, 'Mags was telling me about her daughter, yer know Margaret, her what's living in Dagenham.'

'Yeah, I know Margaret.'

'Well, she told Mags how the Prince of Wales went down there to see the motor factory. And d'yer know what?'

'What?'

'All the silly sods was out waving and cheering him. They ain't got a pot to piss in, most of 'em, and they turn out to cheer the likes of him.' Frank shook his head at the mystery of it all. 'Don't understand it meself.'

'Yer a man after me own heart, Frank. Yer talk a lot of sense. Tell yer what, if yer can find someone to keep an eye on the little 'un, maybe I could stand yer a pint some time.'

Frank smiled, pleased by the idea. 'Maybe Katie'd let Theresa sit in with your boys for half an hour? A Friday'd be best, 'cos of her having to get up for school. You know.'

Pat's jaw stiffened and he felt a rush of heat creep up his throat. He gulped at his tea, emptying his cup in two swallows.

Frank put down his own cup, folded his arms, and looked Pat straight in the eye. 'Yer jealous, ain't yer, Pat?' he said matter-of-factly.

Pat blinked; he felt like he'd been pole-axed.

'I was a bit that way with my Sarah,' Frank went on, 'so I know all the signs, mate. I even asked your Katie about it once. When yer was away that time. I reckoned that was the cause of it.' He winked matily at Pat. 'And I was spot on about yer, wasn't I? Still who can blame you, eh Pat? Yer a lucky man, having a good-looking woman like her by yer side.'

Pat was silent for a long, uneasy moment, as images of Katie swam around in his mind. He could see her, smiling happily and chattering away to Frank Barber, while he was stuck in the poxy lodging house down by the docks.

He took in a slow, deep breath, telling himself to stop being so stupid. *He* had been the animal who had actually raised his hand to his wife, and it had been he who walked out on *her*, not the other way round. And this man had just saved his life . . .

'Yer right,' Pat said stiffly. 'She is a good-looking woman.' He beckoned to the stall holder. 'Two more teas over here, please, pal.'

'Ta, Pat,' grinned Frank, as the man topped up his cup from the urn. 'We'll drink a little toast to your Katie, eh?'

Pat frowned. Was this bloke taking the piss or what?

16

Pat never did stand Frank the pint he'd promised him, the main reason being that during the weeks since Frank had saved him from the man with the docker's hook, Pat had done his best to avoid Frank Barber at all costs, not trusting himself to be within punching distance of a man who had saved his life but who had also openly admitted he found Katie so attractive. Whenever he spotted him in the street or at work he would duck out of sight, and if ever Frank came to the house, Pat would make sudden, loudly announced dashes for the lavatory.

But Pat was now faced with a situation where he wouldn't be able to avoid meeting him; he had no choice. Katie and Mags were organising a street party to celebrate the Silver Jubilee, and no matter how ingenious his excuses, Pat was soon resigned to the fact that, unless he was hospitalised, he wouldn't be able to get out of it.

Not that he hadn't tried. He'd agreed with Katie that the King was, in his words, a harmless old geezer, all right even in his own way; but how could he, *Red Pat*, a man whose every belief was against all that the monarchy stood for, celebrate his reign? And anyway, didn't he have more important things to do with his time, like trying to earn his living?

Katie listened patiently but she still wasn't having any of it. It had caused enough rows when he hadn't gone to the Procession, she said – not spitefully, she didn't even raise her voice – but what with everything they had been through, a knees-up was just what they all needed. And it would prove to everyone, show them all, that the East End spirit couldn't be defeated by hard times and a run of bad luck.

So, he was coming to the party and that was that.

Katie had judged the mood exactly. Except for her husband, everyone else agreed that celebrating 6 May 1935, King George V's Silver Jubilee, was the perfect opportunity for people to forget the cost for just one day and to have a good time regardless.

Mags had actually come up with the idea, and had mentioned it one bright April morning when she and Katie had bumped into each other as they were going into the corner shop.

They had started to ask Edie what she thought of it, but were interrupted by two little kids who dashed breathlessly into the shop and pushed their way forward to the counter. Katie and Mags were now waiting patiently while the two children, whom neither of them recognised, tried to persuade Edie to give them back the money on the roll of lavatory paper they were returning.

The guests their mum had been expecting hadn't turned up after all, they explained, so she wouldn't need to waste her money on rolls of Izal, but could use squares of newspaper as they usually did. Edie, however, was questioning the pair closely; she wasn't convinced that they hadn't pinched the stuff off a stall and were trying to use Edie as an unwitting fence for stolen property.

'So what d'yer reckon, Kate?' Mags asked, as they waited for Edie to finish her inquisition of the two youngsters.

'I reckon it sounds a blimmin' good idea, Mags. As yer say, this street could do with something to liven it up, like the beanos we used to have every year when we could all afford 'em. They always did everyone a power of good, didn't they?'

Mags chuckled. 'Apart from that poor old cow from round Ricardo Street, what Phoebe used to wind up upping every year.'

Edie was listening to Mags and Katie with one ear, while she finished her negotiations with the two children. Her final offer was that she would pay them half now and the other half if they got a note from their mum. When they readily agreed to the deal, that was when she knew they were lying, and came from behind the counter and shooed them out of the door. No kid telling the truth would have dared to go home without all the money they'd been sent out for.

Satisfied with her detective work, Edie resumed her position behind the counter. 'Yer know Phoebe always reckoned that old girl from Ricardo Street had her eye on her Albert, don't yer?'

The three women sniggered at the thought of it.

'Even Albert's old mum would never have had him down as no oil painting.' Edie paused, locked for the moment into some private memory. 'We've had some good times in this street over the years, ain't we?'

'Yeah, yer right there, Ede,' agreed Katie. 'And yer know what they say, there's good times just around the corner and all. There'll be good times again.'

Edie crossed herself and cast her eyes up to the ceiling. 'Please God.'

'I thought we'd ask some of the other turnings round here if they wanna join in,' said Mags. 'Just like we used to do with the beanos. But I reckon Plumley Street'd be

397

the obvious place to have it, what with the wall and everything.'

'More the merrier,' said Katie, warming to the idea. 'Tell yer what, Mags, yer wanna see if your Margaret'll come. Get her to bring her old man with her.'

'I dunno if she'd want to, to tell yer the truth, Kate.' Mags pulled out her hankie from her sleeve and started fiddling with the lace edging. 'Not now she's got her place down there. Done up like a little palace it is.' Her bottom lip started trembling. 'I miss her, yer know. She said I'm always welcome, but I don't like to go, not unless I'm asked special like.'

Mags dropped down on to the bentwood chair that was usually occupied by customers a lot less well-preserved than the smartly turned out landlady of the Queen's. 'I worry, see, that my Margaret thinks she's too good for the East End now she's living down there.' She looked up, her gaze passing from Katie to Edie and back again. Her eyes were brimming. 'She's got a privet hedge and everything, yer know?'

Katie nearly burst out laughing at Mags's peculiar notion that a privet hedge might make a person superior in some way, but Katie would never intentionally hurt anyone, especially not someone as kind and generous as Mags Donovan.

'I reckon we should start collecting straight away,' Katie said brightly, trying to cheer Mags up a bit. 'We've got a couple of weeks, and I tell yer what, if you drop your Margaret a line I bet she'll be up here like a shot. She always loved a do.'

'Yeah, she did.' Mags seemed slightly comforted by the thought. She blew her nose genteelly and stuffed her hankie back up the sleeve of her brightly coloured print dress. 'I'll ask all me customers what come in today. See who's interested.'

'Good idea, Mags,' nodded Edie. 'I'll do the same.'

'And I can start going round giving all the neighbours a knock.'

'They'll all wanna join in,' said Mags, with a flap of her hand. 'Well, maybe not the Lanes.'

Edie looked thoughtful. 'I reckon she would, that Irene. Give her a chance to show off her latest frocks. She's got some lovely things, that girl.'

'Have to watch she don't go chasing Phoebe's Albert, though,' Katie said with great solemnity. Even though part of her was furious about the night she had caught Sean in the Lanes' house – especially as he still refused to say what he'd been up to in there – she was shaking with suppressed laughter at the thought of the glamorous Irene and smelly old Albert Tucker. 'I mean, we don't want no fights breaking out, do we?'

'She was good to me, yer know, Irene, after my Bert . . .' Edie said quietly. 'Never made no fuss. Just brought me flowers to try and cheer me up. Told me to make sure I was eating properly, and having enough sleep and that.'

Katie frowned. 'Did she? I never realised.' She turned to Mags. 'Did you?'

Mags started giggling. 'No,' she spluttered. 'Sorry, I was just picturing her sitting on old Albert's knee with her arms round his scraggy old neck!'

The three of them were still laughing when the door opened and Phoebe Tucker came bowling into the shop. She had a battered, black straw hat perched over her miserable, broad, fat face, with an incongruous bunch of cheerful, bright red cherries dangling over one eye.

'What's all this about?' she demanded, giving Mags

the evil eye until she took the hint and gave up the chair to her.

'We're organising a street party. For the Jubilee,' explained Edie, not daring to look at the others in case they set her off again. 'We was just sorting out collecting the money.' She looked at Mags and Katie. 'I know what'd be a good idea,' she said. 'If we get every one to give a bit extra, we could ask the Miltons without them knowing anyone's gotta pay anything.'

Mags nodded, liking the sound of the idea. 'We could say the brewery was stumping up.'

'Good idea,' said Katie.

'That's all you lot know.' Phoebe nodded her head wisely, sending the cherries into a jiggling little dance over her nose.

'Eh?' said Mags, unable to say any more without laughing.

'You lot obviously ain't seen him, have yer?'

The women's laughter was now forgotten.

'Is something wrong in number three?' Katie asked.

'Wrong? Pwwhhhuh!'

Mags folded her arms and looked Phoebe levelly in the eye. 'I ain't playing games with yer, Phoeb. If yer've got something to say, for Gawd's sake just say it. Has something happened in there, or what?'

Too keen to want to pass on her gossip to be worried about the tone Mags was taking with her, Phoebe leant forward, her chins spilling over the faded velvet collar of her serge coat. 'He's had it off, ain't he? That Milton. These last few days he's been walking about with a suit on and everything. And just yesterday, I saw her coming back from the market with enough shopping to feed a flaming army.'

Mags frowned. 'What? Ellen Milton?'

'Funny enough,' Edie said, 'the kids was in here buying sweets and showing me their new football the other day. I thought nothing of it. Just reckoned someone had treated 'em.'

Phoebe shook her head. 'No, you mark my word, it's him, he's come into a few bob.' She shifted her weight, making the chair creak alarmingly beneath her. ''Cos he certainly ain't got himself no job. I mean, he's indoors all day, ain't he?'

'Maybe's he's got nightwork somewhere,' Edie suggested, never one to see bad in anybody if she could help it.

'What, nightwork what pays the sort o' dough he's flashing about? Never. He's had some rich old uncle die or something. Them sort have all the luck. Breed like rabbits and don't have to lift a finger.'

Katie looked from Mags to Edie and back again, raising her eyebrows and sighing. 'I can see yer busy, and I've gotta get on and all,' she said. 'I'll be over later and we can sort out doing the collecting then.'

'I'll pop back later and all,' Mags said, following Katie from the shop.

'See yer,' Edie called after them. 'Right, Phoebe, now what can I do for yer?'

'Nothing,' she said, hauling her bulky frame from the chair. 'Yer don't reckon I'm paying your prices when the market's open, do yer?'

The day of the Jubilee dawned grey and overcast, with a steady drizzle laying down a glossy slick of water on the cobbles – not what everyone had hoped for at all. But bad weather was no match for the residents of Plumley Street. They were holding a street party that was being attended by people from all of the surrounding turnings and they had no intention of letting anyone say that they couldn't put on a decent show. So, raining it might have been but the work to transform Plumley Street went on unabated.

Bunting and paper garlands were draped between lampposts, looped from one house to the next, hung in wreathed swags around windows, and stretched from one side of the street to the other. Big, colourful flags, representing some unknown and probably unheard-of country – borrowed by Bill Watts from someone over Hoxton way who had the hump with his neighbours and had gone to his daughter's street to celebrate – were used to cover the row of kitchen tables that had been lined up along the middle of the road.

It was not even nine o'clock, but Plumley Street was already transformed.

Katie, having told Michael and Timmy to help her lug their kitchen table into the street almost before they had had the chance to finish their breakfast, was now busily decorating the outside of number twelve. She stood on a chair, while Timmy and Michael handed her the paper and crayon Empire flags and Union Jacks they had made at school. Carefully, she fixed each one around the door frame, leaning back to see if she'd got them straight.

'This is better than doing the laundry, eh, Peg?' she shouted across to her neighbour, who was concentrating on folding sheets of newspaper into Nelson-style paper hats.

'You ain't kidding there, girl. I could fancy having a party every Monday morning instead of lighting that flaming copper.' Peg stood up and stuck one of the hats on her tightly permed hair, then, in a moment of recklessness that could have only come from the holiday atmosphere, she added, 'Sod the washing, eh, Kate?'

'Yeah, sod it!' Kate called back, causing Michael and Timmy to collapse in fits of giggles at the amazing sound of Mrs Watts and their mum using such a word out in the street.

'Sod it!' gurgled Michael, clutching his sides. 'They both said sod it!'

Just then, Pat stepped out of the passage. Edging past Katie's chair, he stared down at the boys. 'What's tickling this pair's fancy?' he asked.

'Tickling our fancy!' squealed Timmy, his face scarlet with laughter.

'They're excited,' Katie said, with a little wrinkle of her nose. She smiled down affectionately at her two now almost helpless sons. 'Bless 'em.'

'I'll give 'em bless 'em,' said Pat, looking up at the first rays of sunshine breaking through the clouds, 'if they don't pull 'emselves together and start helping yer.'

'They're all right, love. They've been good as gold. Been helping me all morning, ain't yer, boys?'

The boys gawped at one another; their mother had obviously been replaced by a ringer. Instead of the woman whose only aim in life was to get them told off by their dad, she had been substituted by this nice, understanding lady whose only aim in life was to be kind to small boys.

'So,' she asked, still smiling happily, 'where you off to then, Pat?'

Pat winked at her behind his hand and held out a brown paper parcel. 'I'm just taking this over the Queen's. It's that, yer know . . .' He nodded towards the boys, signalling to Katie that he was now speaking in parents' code, an indecipherable language that could only leave the boys guessing as to the actual significance of its words. 'That whatsit, what I got from work last Friday.'

'Aw yeah, yeah. Yer'd better get it over to her then, hadn't yer?'

'What's that then, Dad?' asked Michael, his recovery from hysterics now almost complete as he struggled with this new puzzle.

Pat winked again at Katie and held up the package. 'It's a great big plate of air pie and windy pudden. Now, you two, I want yer to get up off yer arses and help yer mother. Now.'

More language! Michael's mouth dropped open. Had all the grown-ups gone raving mad?

Pat said nothing more. He just strolled over towards the Queen's and disappeared behind the glass and mahogany doors.

'All right, Mags?' Pat put his parcel down on the polished counter. 'Katie said yer was organising all the food from over here, so I thought I'd bring yer this. A bit extra never hurts, does it?'

Mags peeled back the wrapping and found herself looking at a great haunch of boiled ham. 'Blimey, Pat. This must have cost yer a fortune.'

'Not really,' he said slowly. 'See, I got a cotchell of it from work. This crate just burst open on the dockside. Right in front of me, it did. Seemed a pity to leave it there, so me and another bloke had a bit of a share-out. And Katie cooked it last night. Took hours it did.'

'I bet it did. And it was a bit of luck, weren't it? I mean, that it weren't a crate of old rusty nuts and bolts or nothing.'

Pat shrugged innocently. 'Yeah, I reckon yer right, Mags. It was a bit o' luck, 'cos I reckon we're all gonna

404

need plenty o' grub to line our guts. Right jolly-up, this is gonna be.' He stepped back to let Harold Donovan and Joe Palmer stagger past him with a barrel of ale. 'All right, chaps?'

They grunted a panting reply.

Pat laughed as the two men pushed their way out of the bar and lurched out on to the street. 'There's enough booze stacked up out there already for a fleet of charras going on a beano.'

Mags raised her eyebrows. 'Harold's kept saying all morning, "I'd better put out one more crate. Don't want no one going short."' She lifted her chin with a little tutting sound. 'Yer right, we're gonna need plenty o' sandwiches, all right. I'll take this out the back and get on with it. Thanks again, Pat.'

'It's a pleasure, girl. I'll see yer later on. I'm gonna go and see if I can give Harold and Joe a hand with anything.'

'All right, Pat,' Mags answered him, using her foot to push open the door that led out to the back kitchen. 'And if yer see Aggie out there,' she called over her shoulder, 'tell her I'm ready to get started, will yer?'

'Can I help till she gets here, Mum?'

Mags nearly dropped the ham at the sound of the voice she had been longing to hear. 'Margaret!'

By two o'clock, the time the party was due to begin, the sun was shining, and the street was full of people, most of them wearing some combination of red, white and blue. Even Phoebe and Sooky, still sitting outside their houses on their kitchen chairs and still wearing their slippers and rolled down stockings, had made a bit of an effort. Both of them had spent the night with their hair wound tightly round metal crackers and Phoebe was

405

even sporting a smear of scarlet lipstick – her loyal flash of red especially for the occasion.

Mags had organised all the other women from Plumley Street to help her carry the food out to the tables. Edie had been right about Irene Lane: she seemed only too pleased for the opportunity to join in. Making an odd partnership with Nutty Lil – who was sticking to Irene like a limpet after setting her eyes on Irene's dazzling blue and silver lamé outfit – she tottered in and out of the Queen's back kitchen on her red spiky high heels, carrying plates and bowls of food with the rest of them.

And there was plenty to carry. Apart from the money that Katie, Mags and Edie had collected over the weeks from friends and neighbours, the few who could afford to had produced plenty of little extras that they had made or bought, and others like Pat, who had somehow just come into a bit of 'luck', had brought their spoils along too, so that by the time the convoy of women had finished going back and forward to the pub, the tables were groaning with food. There were not just sandwiches, but pies and pickles, cheeses and shellfish, jellies and trifles, cakes and biscuits – and another two crates of brown ale and one of lemonade that Harold had brought out as an afterthought – just in case, he had assured Mags. But now that their Margaret and her husband Paul were there to share it all with them, Mags certainly wasn't complaining. Harold could have emptied the whole cellar for all she cared.

After everyone had sat down at the long row of tables and eaten their fill – then just a bit more, rather than see such bounty go to waste – the tea urn that Nora had commandeered from the church was set up outside the shop. Then, while the grown-ups settled down to get over their blowout, the older kids lifted the tables to one

406

side and organised their younger brothers and sisters into teams to play a boisterous, unorthodox game of cricket with the stumps chalked in their traditional spot on the high wall at the end of the street.

But Molly – so well known for her powerful swing at the wicket that Pat had once claimed if she'd been a boy she would have been the perfect replacement for Jack Hobbs when he'd retired – just wasn't interested in the game today. No matter how hard her little brothers tried to cajole her into taking her turn at bat, or any amount of her dad's good-natured coaxing, she just couldn't be persuaded to play. Instead she sat on the kerb, sipping moodily at her cup of tea, staring into space, preferring to be left alone with her thoughts.

Molly's absence was soon forgotten as the game got underway, and both sides were enthusiastically running up and down the turning as though their lives depended on it. When the two sides reached a draw, it was decided by the grown-ups – well used to how these things could get out of control and develop into a full-scale battle when kids from more than one street were involved – that the match was over and it was time to start on the next part of the celebrations, the part that included opening some of Harold's assorted bottles and barrels.

The remains of the food and the tea things were cleared away into the saloon bar of the pub for later attention, the first barrel was tapped, and with a glass of ale in his hand and the promise of plenty more to follow, Jimmo Shay was soon persuaded to give them all a tune on his concertina.

Jimmo only played the silver and mother-of-pearl-studded instrument on high days and holidays, but he prided himself on the fact, as he was never tired of telling anyone who would listen, that he had never ever pawned it, not once, had not even been tempted to, no matter how bad things had got. His old dad had left it to him as his inheritance, and he would never have forgiven himself if he had taken it round uncle's.

Jimmo emptied his glass in two gulps, and with a shout of, 'Right then, let's be seeing a bit of dancing here,' he launched into 'The Isle of Capri' and they were off.

Liz dragged Danny away from the beer and was just steering him towards the part of the street that had become the dance floor when she spotted Molly still sitting alone on the kerb.

'Come on, Dan, let's see if we can cheer her up a bit.'

'Yer'll have a bloody hard job,' Danny muttered grudgingly, as he followed her. He liked a dance, and would happily have had a few turns round the floor with Liz, even though it meant missing swallowing a few glasses of free beer, but when it came to listening to his sister moaning, that definitely wasn't on his list of what he fancied doing at a party. He could do that any day of the week.

'All right, Moll?' Liz asked her gently.

Molly shrugged. 'Yeah. S'pose so.'

Liz silently signalled for Danny to leave her alone with Molly. He opened his mouth to complain that she'd just dragged him over there, but Liz hurriedly shook her head and flashed her eyes towards Molly, warning him to keep quiet. So Danny just shrugged and headed back to where the men were gathered by the booze and where he at least would have a clue as to what was going on and what was expected of him.

Satisfied that Danny was out of earshot, Liz smiled down at Molly. 'That's him off to get another glass of ale. Still, who needs fellers, eh? Tell yer what, fancy coming to have a dance?' She laughed encouragingly.

'We've practised in me bedroom enough times over the years to be champions, you and me.'

Molly exhaled slowly. 'It'll be two years in August, Liz.' She looked up at her friend. 'Did yer know that? Two years, and we're still hiding round corners.'

'You really are fed up, ain't yer, Moll? You ain't even mentioned him to me for ages.' Liz sank down on to the kerb beside her and touched her tenderly on the arm. 'I hate to see yer like this. You was always laughing and joking, and now look at yer. Yer look like yer've got the weight of the world on yer shoulders.'

'See, the more I think about him, the more I know I'm really stuck on him. I can't help it. I just can't get him out of me head.'

'But it's no good, is it, Moll, you getting yerself all upset?' She paused, not quite sure how to put her thoughts into words. 'Have you ever,' she began slowly, 'thought that yer might be better off finding yerself someone else? Someone yer could eventually settle down with?'

'Don't yer think I would have done if I could? It ain't as simple as that, Liz.'

'I know. I know.'

They sat there for a moment, Liz now as glum-faced as Molly. But Liz suddenly brightened up. 'Here, look, Moll. There's that feller from Sussex Street looking at yer again.'

'Do what?'

'That feller. You know, Maureen Murphy's big brother. He can't take his eyes off yer.' Liz was on her feet, heaving Molly up from the pavement. 'Come on, you and me're gonna go over and talk to him. And you, Molly Katherine Mehan, are gonna dance with him.'

'Yer wasting yer time, Liz.'

'Yer like dancing, don't yer?'

'Yer know I do.'

'So what's the harm? One little dance.'

Pat was helping Harold pour drinks at the bar they had set up outside the Queen's, when Katie came rushing up to him through the crowd, seemingly not caring about the safety of the tray of used glasses she was carrying.

'You seen our Molly?' she asked Pat excitedly. 'Look, she's dancing with Bridget Murphy's boy.' She looked round, checking that her eyes hadn't deceived her. 'I'm that glad, Pat. I've been so worried about her.'

Pat reached across the bar and chucked his wife under the chin. 'We'll have a dance in a minute, shall we, girl?'

'Don't mind if I do,' said Katie, emptying her tray on to the temporary bar. 'But yer'll have to hang on a minute, I've just gotta collect a few more glasses or there'll be none left for you and Harold to fill at the rate that mob are drinking.'

'Yer right there, Kate,' said Harold, wiping the sweat from his forehead with the back of his hand, before slapping a much smaller hand that was trying to filch a bottle of pale ale from behind his back. 'It's flipping murder. My Mags is too busy chatting to our Margaret to do anything here, but I told her, if she don't give us a hand soon, I'll wind up in Colney Hatch at this rate.'

'Don't worry, Harold, I'll get Joe to take over when I go and take me wife for a turn round the dance floor.' Pat smiled the smile that still had the effect of making Katie feel like a young girl again. 'But she'd better not take too long fetching them glasses, or I just might have to go and ask Phoebe for a dance instead.'

Katie set down the tray and stuck her fists into her waist. 'If that's how yer feel, Padraic, I'd better go over and warn her off yer, hadn't I? No woman's gonna get her hands on *my* old man.' She leant forward and whispered so that only Pat could hear her. 'Especially not a woman with a nose like a strawberry, 'cos I know how yer like a bit of soft fruit.' With a saucy wink and a flick of her apron, Katie picked up her tray again and flounced over towards Phoebe and Sooky.

Katie was too busy finding empty glasses and Pat was too busy filling them up again to notice that as soon as Molly finished her dance with Bridget Murphy's boy, she thanked him politely and then ran home to cry in the privacy of their back kitchen.

Katie was just straightening up from collecting the row of empties that Phoebe and Sooky had lined up beside their chairs, when she saw Nutty Lil dance past, proudly displaying to the two miserable old women the blue and silver stole that Irene Lane had given her.

Irene was insisting that Lil take the wrap she so obviously coveted, when Arthur Lane had come puffing along the street, shouting for Irene to shift herself, as he'd got them a cab and it was waiting for them at the end of the street with the meter running, and he didn't intend paying out good money for her to take her time.

'It was nice of that Irene, giving her that, wasn't it?' Katie said as she watched Lil go weaving through the other dancers, the stole spread out across her arms like blue and silver wings. 'I don't think she wanted to leave, yer know. She looked like she was enjoying herself being with everyone. Still, ne'mind, Lil looks happy anyway, don't she?'

'Happy?' Phoebe was scandalised by the very idea. 'Pissed more like. And just look at that hat of her'n, will yer? Stuck on her head like a sodding flowerpot. Looks just like she got it with a pound o' tea, it does.'

Katie went to speak, but Phoebe had paused just long enough to draw breath.

'And while we're at it,' she went on, arms folded and chins wobbling, 'will yer look at that Milton feller over there? Bold as brass he is. Wearing that fifty-bob suit of his again. Parading about in it like he's the pox doctor's bleed'n clerk. And I hear as how they've paid the tally man off.'

Sooky nodded wisely. 'That's what I hear and all.'

'And have yer seen all the tom she's taken to wearing, that Ellen Milton? Even more'n that bloody Laney's old woman had on. Rings, earrings *and* a chain round her scraggy neck, if yer don't mind. Bit different to how it used to be, having to dress off o' the barrows. And look at her boat and all: she's got enough powder slapped on them skinny chops of her'n to cover a dozen babies' arses I reckon.'

Katie could hold her tongue no longer. 'And I reckon it's smashing seeing people having a bit o' luck in these hard times.'

'Luck? Luck?' Phoebe was incredulous. 'You seen that kettle he's got on that bleed'n chain across his weskit? Gold hunter it is.' She turned to Sooky. 'Bit like that one Bert Johnson had to sell to Laney now I come to think of it.'

'I thought even you'd have a day off for the Jubilee, Phoeb.' Katie shook her head wearily. 'I reckon if someone had a new pair of drawers on, you'd turn out to have a nose in case the wind blew their skirt up.'

Phoebe as usual was immune to anyone criticising her, too dedicated to her mission of judging others to bother with nonsense like that. 'You just wait and see,' she went on. 'I'm telling yer now, it'll all come out. He's probably turned that dirty hole of their'n into a sodding knocking shop, with his old woman doing the business upstairs. They could bring all sorts of blokes along that back alley behind the shop and no one'd ever know.'

'You spiteful, wicked-minded old—' Katie began, but there was no stopping Phoebe when she was in full flow.

'I'm telling yer, you just watch. She'll wind up having all sorts of troubles . . .' she dipped her chin, and stared in her lap ' . . . *down there*, and saying she don't know what's wrong with her. Well, we'll know, won't we?'

'Why can't you keep your nose out of nothing?' Katie snapped. 'If you was a younger woman, Phoebe Tucker—'

Sooky tutted in alarm. 'That's it, go on, have a go at an old girl what can hardly move what with that rain this morning bringing on her screws.' She turned to her old neighbour. 'You just ignore her, Phoeb.'

Katie was saved from working herself up any further by someone behind her coughing loudly in an effort to attract her attention. She turned her head to see Pat standing there; he was bowing theatrically.

'I thought yer'd forgotten our dance,' he said, and held out two bottles of milk stout to Phoebe and Sooky. 'Get that down yer, girls,' he said to the two women. 'But yer wanna watch yerselves, there's a baby in every bottle o' that gear. That'd surprise yer old man, eh, Phoeb?'

'Bleed'n would and all,' she said, snatching the bottles from Pat's hands. She jerked her head in the direction of the pub where Albert was trying to stop Jimmo playing his music. 'Just look at him, the silly old bugger. Pissed as a pudden. I know exactly what he's gonna do.'

'What's that then, Phoeb?' Sooky asked, as she poured her stout into a glass she'd retrieved from Katie's tray.

'One of his bleed'n recitations. I knew he would. And if he does that really rude one . . .' Phoebe shook her

413

head and had an expression on her face that was the nearest thing to shame that Katie had ever seen in her. 'Last time he dared do that was Armistice night. And I bent a bottle right over his bonce for his trouble and all. If I wasn't settled just nice on this chair—'

Pat roared with laughter. 'I'd love to see yer do that again, Phoeb. It's about time we all had something to smile about.'

'Dunno what you're laughing about, Pat Mehan. The smile'll be on the other side of everyone's faces soon,' droned a sour-looking elderly man who was leaning against the wall behind Sooky. He had a pint in one hand and a short in the other. 'Them Germans – we're gonna be in trouble with 'em again. You mark my words.'

'Who's he?' asked Katie, trying not to giggle.

'From round, you know, Ida Street way,' sniffed Phoebe, looking him up and down with unconcealed contempt. 'Dirty old bleeder.'

'Oi! Who you calling a dirty old bleeder?' demanded a grimy, but flashily dressed man in his forties. 'That's my old dad, that is.'

'Well, yer should be ashamed of him,' snapped Sooky, surprising everyone with her vehemence. 'I've had my eye on him. He's tried to have his hand up nearly every girl's skirt since he started pouring that Scotch down his throat.'

'He's what?' demanded Pat.

'Yeah,' said Sooky, warming to her role of informer. 'He wants to piss off back home; we don't like that sort of thing round here.' She twisted round to point directly at the man she was accusing, but he had moved away further along the street. 'My good Gawd, will yer look at him now. I don't believe it.'

Pat, Katie, Phoebe and the man's son all turned to

look in the direction Sooky was pointing, just in time to see him trying to drag Nutty Lil into the passage of the house where she and the Barbers lived.

Pat shoved his glass at Katie and took off down the road after him. 'Ain't yer gonna stop him?' he shouted back over his shoulder to the man's middle-aged son.

'Leave off. Leave him alone,' he yelled, racing after Pat. 'She don't even know what's happening. I had a feel meself earlier on.'

Pat stopped in his tracks and spun round. 'You what?'

The man laughed. 'I thought every one had their turn with her.'

Pat said nothing more, he just swung his arm back and lifted the sneering man right off his feet with a sharp upper cut that connected neatly with his chin. As the dazed man struggled to his feet, Pat followed it with a left cross that sent him sprawling backwards into the gutter.

By now there was a crowd clamouring for a look: a fight was always a big draw at a street party.

'What's going on?' Stephen asked Danny.

He just shrugged; he had no idea what was going on, but he wasn't surprised it had come to this, not with all the free beer that had been sunk. He stood by his grandfather and watched as Pat with his back to number eleven, crouched over the man, waiting for him to get to his feet.

Behind his dad, Danny saw Frank Barber appear in the doorway. He had hold of the old man with one hand and Nutty Lil with the other.

'Does anyone know what's going on here?' Frank asked, indicating his two prisoners as though they were exhibits in a court case. 'I came out of me lav and found these two staggering about in me back kitchen.'

Pat turned to face Frank. 'You wanna ask him,' he scowled, jerking his head towards the old man. 'And his no-good dirty bastard of a son.'

At that, the man's son hauled himself to his feet and launched himself at Pat again.

Pat ducked to one side, easily avoiding the man's punch.

Frank let go of his two uninvited guests and hurled himself at the man who was trying, and failing yet again, to land a punch on Pat's chin.

Frank pinned the man's arms to his sides. 'Oi, oi, oi, come on now chaps. Yer don't wanna fight. It was my flaming kitchen.' He looked at the old man. 'Now, are yer gonna tell me what all this is about?'

'They're a *pair* of dirty bastards,' Phoebe chipped in from the position she had established for herself at the front of the crowd. 'D'yer know what they done?'

'What?'

Pat dropped his chin, barely able to say the words. 'His son's been feeling up Nutty Lil, ain't he? And the old boy was going in your kitchen to have his turn.'

'You what?' Frank shook his head in disgust; he let go of the man's arms, and without any warning spun him round, grabbed his collar and stuck a straight right directly on to his nose, making blood spurt all over the pair of them.

'All right, Pat,' Frank said, keeping his eyes fixed on the man, watching as he dabbed at his bloody nose with the stained sleeve of his jacket. 'It's over. No more now, eh? We'll just get rid of 'em. We don't wanna spoil the party. They'll get theirs later on.'

Pat stepped round Frank, grabbed the man by his lapels, twisted him round and placed a boot up his backside. 'If yer know what's good for yer, just piss off out of it.'

As the two men slunk away, Frank called after them, 'And yer'd better watch yerself if yer go down any dark alleys.'

The crowd were torn between cheering Frank and Pat and jeering at the two men.

'All right, everyone,' Pat said. 'Show's over. Let's all have a drink, eh?'

'He's torn me pretty shawl,' Lil wailed.

Katie put her arm round Lil's shoulders. 'Come on,' she said. 'Don't cry. Let's get you inside and wash yer face for yer. And we'll make sure yer all right, eh?'

Peggy Watts stepped through the mob, holding young Theresa Barber's hand, having kept her back from witnessing the fight. 'You stand with Lizzie,' she said to Theresa, as she flashed a look at Katie that said they both knew what they were afraid of. 'Now give us yer shawl, love. And I'll mend it for yer.'

'No.' Lil shook her head, frantically clutching the torn stole to her chest. 'It's mine. Honest. She give it to me. Said I could keep it.'

'It's all right, I was just gonna darn that hole.'

But Lil was having none of it.

'Look,' Katie suggested gently, 'how about if we go in yours and mend it? You can keep hold of it while Peggy stitches it up. You ain't gotta let go of it or nothing.'

Peggy went over and stood by Lil. 'I could make it look good as new.'

Lil looked down at the ripped material, considered for a moment and then nodded warily.

'Good. Come on then, Peg.' Katie turned to Pat and said quietly, 'I just wanna make sure he ain't, you know, hurt her or nothing.'

Pat nodded, his teeth set rigid with anger.

'You and Frank'd better have a wash. You look a right

state, the pair of yer. Go over home, go on.'

With the drama at an end, the crowd wandered back
to the other end of the street, all voicing their own version
of how the events had unfolded and what the exact fate
of the two men should be. A bit of rough justice was
always a favourite conclusion to such matters in that
neighbourhood.

While Katie and Peggy escorted Lil up to her rooms
in number eleven, speaking softly and encouragingly,
doing their best to keep her calm, Frank was chatting
away nineteen to the dozen as he strode along, following
Pat into the passageway of number twelve.

'Like being down the docks a few months back, eh,
Pat? Maybe we should do this for a living instead of
wasting our time queueing up on the stones every
morning.'

'Who d'yer think you are? Joe Louis?' Pat snapped
without even bothering to look round.

'Good fighter, him,' Frank went on, obviously not put
off by Pat's terseness. 'Reckon he's got a chance against
Max Baer if they do have that fight. What d'you reckon,
Pat? D'you think he's got a chance?'

Pat stepped into the kitchen and just managed to stop
himself from making a very crude suggestion as to what
Frank could go and do to himself, when he saw Molly
sitting at the table.

'Hello, Dad. Hello, Mr Barber.' She stood up, frowning
at the blood. 'Here, you two all right?'

'Yeah, we're all right, darling. We just stopped a bit o'
trouble, that's all. But how about you? What you doing
in here all by yerself?'

'I just come in for a drink of water.' As she made for
the door, she just managed a smile. 'I'd better get back
and find out what you two have been up to. See yer later.'

'Yeah, see yer.' Pat rolled up his sleeves and turned on the tap.

'Reckon she's the only one drinking water in this turning tonight, eh, Pat?' Frank chuckled. 'That's a pretty girl yer've got there, and nice too. Yer've got every right to be proud of your family. I hope my Theresa grows up as nice mannered.'

Pat stepped back from the sink and signalled with a nod that it was Frank's turn to wash.

'Ta, Pat.' Frank stuck his head under the stream of cold water and rubbed his hands all over his face, making loud spluttering noises as he washed the blood and sweat away. Then he turned off the tap and straightened up. 'You being, yer know, a family man like, Pat,' he said, combing his hair back from his face with his fingers, 'you can help me – if yer wouldn't mind that is – 'cos I reckon yer've got more idea about how women's minds work. How they think, like. See, I've been on me own with me little 'un a bit too long and I've kind of forgotten.'

'What you getting at?' Pat sounded suspicious.

Frank grinned, his expression surprisingly boyish. 'What would yer think about me and Edie?'

'You and Edie?' Pat sat down at the table. He hadn't been expecting this.

'Yeah. See, I've been chatting to her a bit lately. When I go along to do the bottling up, she's usually opening the shop.' He scratched his head shyly, sending a shower of water across the table. 'But it's been a long time since I really, you know, even thought of speaking to a woman in that way. I asked her if I could maybe help her out with any heavy stuff she's gotta do in the shop, but what I really meant to say was I know how hard it is being alone. And it is hard, believe me. And I wanted to tell her that I thought she was a fine-looking woman. Kind

419

and all. But none of it never come out like that. But now she's practically out of mourning . . .' He sat down opposite Pat, and leant forward, resting his forearms on the table. 'D'you know it's nearly the year round now?'

'Must be,' said Pat quietly, doing up the cuffs of his shirt

'So, it won't seem like a liberty, will it, Pat, if I say something a bit more, you know, straightforward like? Like, ask her to, I dunno, the Queen's for a drink one night maybe.' He leant even further forward; his forehead was almost touching Pat's. 'So, would that be a liberty, d'yer reckon?'

'No, Frank,' he said, standing up and clapping him on the shoulder. 'I don't reckon it'd seem like a liberty at all, mate. Come on, let's go and enjoy the rest of this party. And who knows, yer might have a chance to have a few words with Edie now. A bit of a dance even, eh?'

Back outside, Pat crossed the street and went over to Katie, who was just coming out of number eleven.

'All right?' he asked, kissing the top of her head.

She smiled up at him. 'What was that in aid of?'

'Just counting me blessings.'

Lil stepped out of number eleven, followed by Peggy.

Peggy ducked her head and looked into Lil's eyes. 'You're all right now, ain't yer love? Happy?'

Lil nodded contentedly, smoothing the mended shawl in her arms as though it were a living creature. 'I'm happy,' she cooed.

Katie nudged Peggy and pointed along the street to where Frank Barber was standing, his body angled protectively round Edie Johnson to stop any stray dancers from bumping into her. 'There's someone else who looks happy and all.'

'He's a decent bloke that Frank Barber,' Pat said bluntly.

Katie looked at him in astonishment. 'Eh?'

'You heard,' he said.

If Katie hadn't known him better she would have sworn he was pouting, pouting like a kid; him, big, tough Pat Mehan. 'I think you need a drink,' she said, linking her arm through his.

As they made their way back along the street, Katie flashed sideways glances at her husband, trying to figure out what had come over him.

They weren't even close to the pub yet, but they both heard Mags clearly, screaming at the top of her voice.

Katie let go of Pat's arm. 'Whatever's happening now?' she wailed, shoving her way past everyone.

'Mags?' she puffed, bursting through the door of the pub. 'Whatever's wrong?'

'It's our Margaret! But there's nothing wrong!'

Katie could see that now; Mags was rosy and elated, clinging on to Harold on one side of her and Margaret on the other.

'Her and her husband's only coming back to the East End, Kate.'

Katie shook her head in wonder at this latest turn of events. 'Yer don't say?' Gratefully she took the glass of beer Harold was handing her. 'This party's having more turns than a blinking bed spring,' she said, raising her glass. 'Good luck to yer all.'

'So what's up then?' Pat asked, poking his head gingerly round the door. 'I waited outside for a minute in case it was women's business. You know.'

'Margaret and Paul are coming back home,' Katie explained.

Harold poured a whiskey and held it out to Pat. 'Didn't

get the work he'd hoped for, see.' Harold turned to his son-in-law who was making a not very good job of shifting an empty barrel. 'Did yer, son?'

Paul shook his head, unable to speak with the exertion.

'And Margaret felt lonely stuck down there, didn't yer, sweetheart?' Mags chucked her daughter under the chin. 'And now she's expecting!'

Katie threw her arms round Mags and kissed her smack on the lips. 'I'm that pleased for yer.'

'I always said this boy was a good 'un,' Harold added proudly.

Mags narrowed her eyes at her husband as much to say, 'Liar,' but what she actually said was, 'And he plays the banjo lovely. Go on, Paul, go and fetch it, and we can go outside and yer can join in with Jimmo on his squeeze box.'

Relieved that he didn't have to struggle with the barrel any longer, Paul left it where it was and disappeared into the back room to fetch his banjo.

When they all went outside again, they saw Stephen, with a piece of board laid out at his feet standing next to Jimmo. 'Right, young 'un,' he called out, pointing to indicate where Paul should stand, 'get yerself over here with that banjo. Jimmo'll tell yer what to play, and I'll do the rest.'

Nora threw up her hands enthusiastically. 'He's going to do his step dance, God love him.' She nudged Michael and Timmy in front of her to make sure they had a good view. 'Just watch this, boys, and learn. Your grandfather is the best step dancer this side of the Wicklow Mountains.'

Katie couldn't bear it, she rolled her eyes and went over to lean against the wall, determined to have her drink in peace.

Jimmo and Paul struck up a jig, the audience clapped and Stephen did his dance. His feet flashed and tapped as he moved with the speed and grace of a man half his age.

When he finished he pulled off his cap and bowed low, acknowledging the applause. Then he turned to his accompanists. 'Will yer be taking a drink with me? And give me the chance to tell yers all about me beloved Ireland and the dances we used to have there. And rare dances they were.'

'Yer love flipping Ireland so much, do yer?' scoffed a grinning, swaying man, his face patched red from the booze. 'Then why don't yer get back there? Go on, piss off out of it!'

Stephen stuck up his fists in the classic fighter's pose and glared about him. 'Who said that? Come on out and I'll fight yer. Sure, I'll fight all o' yers.'

'It was him,' Phoebe piped up, jerking her thumb at the now even redder man. 'Yer know, him from round Upper North Street what's married to that ugly old bag. He's round here just to get away from her, I reckon. Horrible she is. Nearly come to blows with your Kate once. Had a right go at her over the kids.'

'Is that so?' Stephen moved forward, his fists still stuck up in front of him.

His would-be opponent, less brave than his belligerent wife, began to back slowly away. Then, moving quicker and quicker, he mumbled to himself, 'Bugger this for a lark, the whole flaming family's barmy. All they ever wanna do is fight.'

The man's departure was met by a chorus of hoots and laughter. Even Katie, still leaning against the wall, caught herself smiling.

'I bet yer can fight really good, can't yer, Farvee?' Michael asked proudly.

'Sure, wasn't I the bare knuckle champion back home in Cork in the old days.'

Michael frowned. 'But I thought yer said yer was a champion singer?'

'Wasn't I just?' he asked, turning to Nora. 'A champion fighter *and* a singer o' songs?'

Nora nodded. 'A right song thrush, he was.'

'Go on then, Farvee,' Danny encouraged him. 'Give us "Red Sails in the Sunset",' he squeezed Liz close to him, 'so's we can all have a nice little dance.'

Stephen looked mortified. 'What, me sing modern rubbish like that? No fear, I only sing the classics. Here, I know, I'll teach me little grandsons one o' me old favourites. *Ohhhhhh . . . Auntie Mary had a canary, up the leg of her drawers . . .*'

This time, Katie did not smile. 'Teaching my boys that trash,' she fumed, marching over and dragging her protesting sons away from him. 'I'm getting fed up with yer, causing trouble and getting the boys at it all the time.'

Stephen looked at Katie for a long moment, seeing the anger in her eyes, then he swallowed down the rest of his stout, picked up the whiskey he had lined up as a chaser and knocked that back too. 'This suit yer better?' he asked stiffly. With that he began in a sweetly, lilting voice to sing the opening notes of 'Danny Boy'.

'He's got a good voice on him,' Pat whispered.

'The drink's making yer sentimental,' Katie snapped spitefully.

'Sssh,' Nora hissed at them. 'Let him finish.'

But Stephen never finished his song. Quite suddenly he stopped, staring over Nora's shoulder.

Everyone turned to see what had caught his eye.

Katie clapped her hands to the side of her face. 'I don't believe this.'

Sean was at the far end of the street by the house; Katie could see, even from where she was standing, that he had been fighting, but he was carrying something in his arms that she couldn't quite make out.

Katie and Pat ran to see what was wrong with their son, followed closely behind by Nora, then Molly and Danny and the two little ones.

Phoebe let out a long, noisy sigh. 'That bloke from Upper North Street was right: fighting mad the lot of them.'

Stephen shoved his face close to hers, the liquor on his breath almost choking her. 'Why don't you shut up, yer nosy old cow?'

'And why don't you bugger off back to Ireland like that bloke said?' Phoebe sneered. 'They don't want yer here poncing off 'em. Any idiot could see that.'

At the other end of the street, Katie had just reached Sean and had realised that the bundle of blood-stained fur that he was cradling in his arms was Rags. When she saw the state the terrier was in, she backed away, her hand covering her mouth to stop herself from vomiting, but as Sean's shoulders dropped and he crumpled into tears like a little boy, she took a deep breath, pulled herself together and motioned for him to get indoors.

Pat, Danny and Molly gathered round the draining board as Katie bathed Rags's wounds, watching and praying silently for him to be all right; while Nora, Timmy and Michael sat at the table, glaring silently at Sean as he stared wild-eyed at the floor.

'He's gonna be fine.' Katie gently lifted Rags from the side and set him down on the folded blanket that Molly had put by the Kitchener for him. 'The poor little thing wasn't as badly hurt as I thought, but he's whacked out.'

She turned to Sean. 'So, what's the story this time? And let me just guess what stupid, step-dancing, boozing, no-good idiot put the idea of dog fighting into that thick head o' your'n.'

Breakfast the next day was a solemn affair. Rags was sleeping contentedly on his new bed, but he was the only one who seemed to have anything to be happy about.

'Yer sure he's gone?' Pat asked Nora.

She nodded. 'He's taken everything.'

Timmy started crying. 'But he said he'd go down the Cut with me to find some old pram wheels and make me a cart. He can't be gone.'

'And he said he'd buy me a bike.' Michael's lip trembled.

'Sssssh, don't take on,' Nora said, pouring herself some more tea. 'Sure, yer can't tame a wild spirit; a dreamer like your granddad.'

'Tame him?' Katie crashed the side of her fist on to the table making the cups rattle in their saucers. 'I'd bash the living daylights out of him if I had my way. Dog fighting!'

Sean, who had been sitting staring silently at the floor, much as he had the night before, slowly lifted his head. 'He never said I should do it. He just said that some blokes he heard of did it sometimes, back in Ireland. It wasn't him. It wasn't.' He shoved his chair back and ran out of the room.

'Sean!' hollered Pat.

Katie stuck her elbows on the table and covered her face with her hands. 'Leave him, Pat.'

Nora too rose to her feet. 'Yer shouldn't be so quick to judge people, Katie. Yer father never meant no harm. He's a good man.'

'You trying to say it was my fault he's gone?'

'I just want him to come back. I don't care if he don't buy me a bike. I miss him, Nanna.' Michael started weeping noisily, and Molly joined him as she put her arm round his shoulder and tried to comfort him.

'So do I, love,' sniffed Nora, dropping back on to her chair. 'So do I.'

Stephen had been gone for nearly three months and Nora still hadn't resigned herself to the fact that he wasn't coming back. She hadn't really had one decent night's sleep since he'd left, but the oppressively hot August nights were making her even more restless. The weather had been in the eighties for over a week now, and, from how sticky it was, it felt as though there was going to be yet another thunderstorm.

It was half past three when Nora looked at the clock. It was no good lying there staring up at the ceiling, she told herself, she might as well make herself a cup of tea. So as not to wake the boys, Nora slipped into the kitchen in her bare feet and set the kettle on to boil.

She was draining her third cup and wondering whether to freshen up the pot again, when she heard a loud banging outside in the street.

Grabbing her coat from the banister and throwing it on over her nightdress, Nora cautiously opened the street door. It took her a moment to focus in the dim, pre-dawn light, but then she saw what all the row was about.

It was the police – two carloads of them – and they were bashing on the Miltons' front door. Nora wouldn't have been surprised if it had been the Lanes' house they were trying to get into, but whatever would they want with the Miltons?

In the time it took for Nora to run next door to fetch

427

Pat and Katie, all the doors in the street were open and everyone was on their street doorsteps to witness the sight of Mr Milton being dragged away by the police, while Ellen screamed at them not to take her Edwin away.

'Edwin!' they all heard Phoebe yell at the top of her voice. 'No wonder he never told no one his sodding name.'

Edwin Milton was thrown into the back of one of the cars and the police drove him off into the night.

Katie turned and looked up at Pat. 'I'll have to go over there and see if I can do anything.'

'Too late,' said Pat. 'She's gone back in and shut her door.'

'Perhaps it'd be better in the morning, eh?' Nora said with a sad shake of her head. 'The poor girl probably wants a bit of time to talk to her kids.'

But when Katie went over to number three the next morning there was nothing she, or anyone else, could do. The house was empty; Ellen Milton and her children had disappeared.

Phoebe, of course, had the solution to the mystery. 'That weren't no normal moonlight flit, you mark my words. She'd got a load more gear off the tally man, so's I heard,' she said, leaning against the wall as Katie squinted through the window into the empty front room. 'After she'd paid off all that other lot. But she only made one payment on all the new stuff, then pawned the lot and went and sold the pawn ticket.'

Katie rapped on the door again. 'D'you have to speak ill of everyone?' she asked over her shoulder.

'Why not? They ain't bleed'n dead, are they?' Phoebe snorted.

Sooky, breathless from the effort of dragging her flabby body along at more than a snail's pace, came

428

gasping to a halt beside them. 'Guess what I just heard down the market? I went down there special to see if anyone knew anything,' she added proudly. 'It's something to do with Laney.' She rolled her eyes in the direction of number six. 'He's only gone and grassed Milton to the law to save himself. They was involved in some big—'

'I ain't standing here listening to your poison,' Katie interrupted her. She looked the two women up and down, turned on her heel and left them to their gossip.

Katie winced as though she had been struck across the face when she heard Phoebe call after her: 'Dunno what she's so cocky about, Sook. Drove her own father away, she did. Hard-faced cow.'

17

It wasn't only the Miltons' misfortunes, and now Stephen Brady's disappearance, that hung over the little community of Plumley Street. There was also something less tangible, a feeling many people had that maybe those better times they'd been praying for weren't going to be just around the corner after all. If anything, things seemed to be getting worse, life getting harder. Even the weather seemed to have turned against them.

September brought floods, followed by gales in November and, by December 1935, a bitter freeze had set in. It might have looked picturesque, and was even fun for those who could afford to enjoy it, as all the pictures in the papers testified; taken at night, they showed literally thousands of happy people skating on a frozen reservoir by the light of bonfires dotted round the shore. But for the Mehans and their neighbours there were more pressing concerns than smiling for the camera. Concerns such as how they could afford to keep even one room in the house warm enough to be able to bear taking off their outdoor clothes when they got in from work, if they were lucky enough to have work. And knowing that just going to bed and getting up in the morning, in rooms with windows covered in frost as thick as that on the pavements outside, was a misery to be dreaded.

It was during the very worst of the weather that a new family, the Gibsons, moved into the Miltons' old house. Although mystery still surrounded what had happened to the Miltons and whether they would ever return, it hadn't stopped the landlord renting out the place as soon as the police had satisfied themselves that number three held no potential evidence in the case they were apparently trying to bring against Edwin Milton.

The Gibsons were not unlike the Miltons. They were a youngish couple, with a brood of wary-looking kids whose clothes looked more suited to the rag-and-bone man's barrow than a child's back. The man, Ted, did have a job; he was a skilled cabinet-maker according to Bill Watts, working for a firm Bill used to do business with. But from the look of him, old and worn out long before his time, Ted was working long hours for not very much pay.

The Gibsons had been living in Plumley Street for almost three weeks when Aggie Palmer went along the road to see Katie on a cold Thursday afternoon. The old year was almost at an end and it certainly felt as though they could all do with a taste of something new.

'I don't wanna stick me nose in, Kate, yer know me,' Aggie said, fiddling with her headscarf.

'Is something wrong, Agg?'

'Yeah, there is.'

'Well, come in a minute. Have a sit-down, and I'll make yer a cuppa. Then yer can tell me all about it.'

'I won't stop, if yer don't mind, Kate.' Aggie sounded, and looked, distracted, as she kept glancing over her shoulder across the street. 'Look, Kate, yer know how I'm up all hours, seeing to me animals and taking Duchess out for a run with the trap and that?'

'Yeah.' Katie wondered what on earth all this was

432

about, and wished Aggie would get on with it. She could just imagine all the heat from the Kitchener flooding along the passage and escaping out of the open street door. But then a horrible thought occurred to her and her worries about the heat disappeared like smoke up the chimney. 'Here, it's not my Danny, is it? He ain't been hurt? There ain't been no accident with the truck?'

'No, honest, it's nothing like that. It's the Gibsons. I ain't seen a sign of life over there for two whole days now. I'm worried about 'em.'

Katie was back down the passage, had grabbed her coat and was halfway across the street before Aggie had the chance to say another word.

'I don't know why, I just thought it'd be better if two of us went over. Less nosy like,' Aggie said, trotting after her, her breath forming clouds in the icy air.

They both knew that Aggie's concern wasn't really to do with the niceties of calling on their new neighbours, it was the thought of what she might find in there that was really worrying her. She was a very tender-hearted woman, always sensitive to others' sufferings, and had told Katie once that she had never really got over seeing Edie sobbing as she cradled Bert's body in her arms.

Katie leant back and gave the front of the house a quick once-over. 'Least the curtains look like they're open.'

'They have been since yesterday. That was one of the things what worried me.'

Katie went to the street door and started banging on it with the flat of her hand.

'It's no good, I tried that earlier. That's when I got really . . . you know . . .'

Katie moved to the front window. She leant forward, cupping her hands round her face and pressed hard against the icy glass.

433

She stepped back. 'Look in there, Agg,' she said grimly.

Aggie squinted through the window. Her hand flew to her mouth. Inside was a huddle of frightened-looking children, three of them not much more than toddlers, squatting in front of an empty grate, hugging big shapeless coats round their skinny little frames. There was no sign of either Ted or Eileen, their parents. 'Poor little loves!' Aggie gasped.

'Mind, Agg.' Katie eased her shocked neighbour to one side. She somehow pinned a smile to her lips before tapping gently on the glass. 'Hello,' she said brightly.

None of the children moved.

She tried again, louder this time. One of the older ones, a girl, looked round.

Katie drew in her breath at the child's eyes: they were dull, indifferent. She had a look about her, not of a little girl, but of someone much older who had seen too much and who had just given up on life.

Katie composed herself; with her smile pasted back in place, she spoke as loudly as she dared without alarming the child. 'I'm Mrs Mehan,' she cooed encouragingly. 'A friend of yer mummy and daddy. I live over the road. You know, on the corner over there. Where the two boys, Michael and Timmy, live.'

Still no response, other than the heartbreakingly blank stare.

Katie thought for a moment. 'Tell yer what, if yer let me and Mrs Palmer in, we can make yer all something to eat. Get the fire going for yer. How'd that be?' She crinkled her eyes. 'All nice and warm.'

One of the little ones began to cry. The older child, the girl who had been silently watching Katie, turned to the younger one and said something. Then she

434

dragged herself listlessly to her feet and trudged out of the room.

'I think she's gonna do it,' Katie said, as much to herself as to Aggie. 'Come on, girl, open the door. Please. Come on.'

Katie's wish was granted.

The child peered through the tiny crack she had made between the door and the jamb. 'You really Timmy's mum?' she rasped. By the look of her puffy eyes, Katie guessed that her throat was raw from sobbing. 'He said I could come over and play with him one day.'

'Course yer can, love. Yer welcome over home any time.' Katie could scarcely hold back her own tears. 'What's yer name, then?'

'Mary Ann Joan Gibson.' The child gulped, having to close her eyes at the effort of swallowing with such a sore throat. 'I'm ever so hungry, Mrs Mehan. And our David's got a dirty bum, but there ain't no clean napkins left.'

Katie and Aggie exchanged brief, anxious glances.

'Right,' Katie said, adjusting her expression back to a smile. 'Now, where's yer mummy and daddy?'

'They're upstairs,' Mary mumbled into her chest. 'They ain't very well.'

Katie nodded. 'Now, I want you all to wait here with Mrs Palmer. I'm just going up to have a little word with 'em.'

Katie was upstairs for only a few minutes.

'Right,' she said, all jolly smiles as she stepped back into the freezing room. 'I've spoken to yer mummy and she said it's all right for me to take yer all over to *my* mummy's house. Yer know, to Timmy and Michael's nanna's house next door to mine? And she can sort out David's napkin for him. Use a nice clean towel. How about that?'

435

Mary nodded and her dirty, tear-stained face relaxed; someone was going to take care of them.

'Then me and Mrs Palmer are gonna make sure yer mummy and daddy feel better. All right?'

'You all get them coats on yer nice and tight,' Aggie said, coaxing one of the littlest one's arms into the sleeves of the oversized jacket he had wrapped around him. 'Now, you all got shoes?'

There were nods all round.

'Make sure yer've all got 'em on then.'

While the children did their best to organise themselves, Katie put her arm round Aggie's shoulder and whispered to her, 'They've got a fever, the pair of 'em. Weak as kittens they are. And the place is in a bit of a state. I reckon she, you know, Eileen, ain't been well for a while. Hungry probably.' She sighed. 'Same old story, eh, Agg? Giving whatever there is to her old man and kids, and going without herself.'

As Katie and Aggie were just about to go back inside number three, after ferrying the children across to Nora, Irene Lane called to them from her street doorstep. Although it was now late afternoon, she was standing there wrapped in a fluffy candlewick dressing gown, but her yellow, bleached hair looked as though it had just been styled and she was wearing full make-up.

'Everything all right?' she asked in her girly, high-pitched voice.

Katie looked her up and down. Well, things were obviously all right for some people in the street. She silently reprimanded herself; she shouldn't be like that, it was none of her business if people had nothing better to do than sit about titivating all day. And, much as she felt like snapping Irene Lane's head off for that business

436

with Sean, Edie had said how she'd been good to her after Bert had died, so Katie did her best to control her voice as she answered her. 'Eileen and Ted – Mr and Mrs Gibson – they ain't too well.'

'Can I do anything? To help, I mean.'

Katie turned to Aggie, who just shrugged.

Katie considered for a moment. 'What yer like at cleaning?'

'Try me,' Irene said eagerly.

'Right,' said Katie, 'I'll leave the door on the jar.' She stepped into the passage of number three, paused and turned round. 'Aw yeah, and yer can bring a couple of buckets of coal over and all while yer at it.'

Aggie couldn't resist a little chuckle. 'That'll bugger up them lily-white hands of her'n.'

But Irene surprised them both when, less than five minutes later, she appeared in the Gibsons' kitchen with the coal.

'Right,' she squeaked, putting the two brimming buckets down by the hearth. 'I'm ready for action. You just tell me what to do and I'll get stuck in.'

Both Aggie and Katie instinctively raised their eyebrows as they appraised Irene Lane's cleaning outfit. She had her hair tucked away under a bright, spotted scarf that she had fastened at one side like a pirate's bandanna, and was wearing a pair of matching trousers, glamorously draped, silky evening ones, just like the film stars wore on the newsreels. But, Katie grudgingly admitted to herself, at least she was showing willing.

Within two hours, the three women had the house almost back in shape, a fire going in the bedroom grate, some pea and hambone soup taken up on a tray to Ted and Eileen, and two bags of shopping, most of it paid for by Irene Lane, the rest donated by Edie, put away in the cupboard. They were just finishing off before they left, doing a few final jobs to make the place ready for when Ted and Eileen felt well enough to get up again, which probably wouldn't be long now they had some decent food inside them.

Aggie was bundling the dirty washing into a bed sheet, ready to take home to do in the morning; Katie was balancing on a chair giving the kitchen window a quick rub over – she knew how she'd feel if she had to come down to grimy windows – and Irene was putting away the dishes she had just finished washing and drying.

'When I took the soup up,' Katie said, rubbing at a stubborn mark in the corner of one of the panes, 'Ted was asking if someone could get a note round to his work. He don't want 'em to think he's cleared off or nothing.'

Aggie straightened up from knotting together the corners of the bulging bed sheet. 'Shoreditch way, ain't it?'

'Hang on. I wrote the address down.' Katie dug into her apron pocket and pulled out a bit of cardboard that looked like it had been torn from a cigarette packet. 'Bethnal Green. If my Sean was about I'd send him, but he's helping someone round the market today. Thank Gawd.' Katie rolled her eyes towards the ceiling and crossed herself. 'That lark with the dog-fighting mob shook him up good and proper. Did him good in a funny way.'

Aggie shuddered at the thought of such cruelty. 'How about if I shot off home, got my Duchess tacked up and went round there now in the trap?'

Katie looked over her shoulder. 'It'd be a weight off Ted's mind, I reckon, Agg.'

'That's what I'll do then. Give us the address here, Kate, and if I move meself, I'll catch 'em before they

438

close.' Aggie hoisted her bundle on to her shoulder and hurried out.

With Aggie gone from the kitchen, the atmosphere between Katie and Irene became less easy.

'Nearly done here now,' Katie said stiffly. 'You might as well get yerself off home.'

Irene nodded, looking round the room to make sure that there was no other little job she might do. Not being able to find one, she walked towards the kitchen door. 'Yer a good woman, Katie,' she said abruptly.

Katie hesitated a moment before answering. 'Only doing what anyone else would.'

'It wasn't me what encouraged Sean to come indoors, yer know.' Irene was standing in the doorway with her back to Katie, staring down at her feet. 'It was him, Arthur, what started it. He likes having young people round him, see. Doing things for him. Makes him feel tough having someone to order about. But don't worry, he always paid him and it was only ever errands. Never nothing, you know, nasty.' She bowed her head even lower. 'He's got me for that.'

Katie bit her lip and sighed to herself as she climbed down off the kitchen chair and walked over to Irene. 'Don't upset yerself.' She reached out to put her arm round the young woman, but, just before she touched her, she withdrew her hand. She couldn't bring herself to do it.

'I know what yer must have thought when Sean got involved with them dog-fighting geezers,' Irene whispered to the floor, her voice sounding more childlike than ever. 'Well, I want yer to know that I hated the bastard for doing that. I would have killed him if I wasn't so scared of him.'

'You saying that it was your old man's fault? That

439

he . . . ?' Katie was confused; she'd been so sure it was Stephen.

'I'm gonna leave him, yer know.' Irene lifted her chin and turned to face Katie. 'Soon as I get meself a job.'

Katie reached out again; this time she folded her arms round Irene and pulled her close. 'Yer might have a long wait if that's yer plan, love.'

Irene gave a little shuddering sob and then stepped away from Katie. 'I'd better go.' She sniffed daintily. 'He'll be back soon and he don't like it if he don't know where I am.' She raised her hand and waggled her fingers in a babyish gesture of goodbye. 'See yer.' Her words sounded more like a question than a farewell.

'Yeah,' Katie smiled at her. 'See yer.'

With the coming of 1936, Plumley Street witnessed a flurry of activity and comings and goings that were all directed at making sure that the Gibson family – or any other family in the neighbourhood for that matter – would never have to go without again. Aggie had gone to everyone to ask what they could do to help. It had always been taken for granted, of course, that people in their community would always help one another, but during such difficult times, Aggie knew that it wasn't so easy to give to others when you had so little for yourself. That was why she decided it would be easier if the helping was shared around a bit.

Whoever could manage it gave clothes and food to tide the Gibsons over until they were back on their feet, and those who couldn't give things contributed in other ways, maybe putting the broom round Eileen's kitchen for her, or doing some of the Gibsons' laundry in with their own weekly wash; any good turn that would make life more comfortable for Plumley Street's newest residents.

It hadn't actually taken much effort on Aggie's part to get nearly everyone to rally around. People had been only too keen to do what they could, although their motives for doing so did vary somewhat.

Phoebe and Sooky, for instance, had insisted on doing their share for two reasons: first, they couldn't bear to think of being left out of a project that involved practically everyone else, including Irene Lane – the flighty bit from number six as Phoebe referred to her when she mused out loud how, for the life of her, she couldn't figure out how *that one* had got involved. And secondly, it gave them a chance, under the guise of polishing the Gibsons' front room, to have a good old nose round the newcomers' home.

But, whatever their motives, the residents of Plumley Street had pulled out all the stops and they had every right to feel proud of themselves, even if, as Sooky insisted on reminding everyone, Mags Donovan's elevation of her recently returned daughter Margaret to the status of sainthood was a bit exaggerated, seeing as all she did was look after the Gibson toddlers alongside her own new baby for a few hours every day.

In just a couple of weeks, the Gibsons were almost flourishing: Ted was back at work, the older children were back at school and Eileen, Aggie swore, had actually put on a little bit of weight. The family still had their share of worries and concerns, of course, but nothing exceptional.

But, as Jimmo Shay said to Albert Tucker, as they sat in the Queen's one miserable evening in late January, it wasn't only the poor who were suffering for once. Not only had old King George died, the rest of the world was having its ration of troubles too. There was Italy; Africa; and as for Germany, well, Jimmo could barely find words to express his feelings about what was going on over there. And now there was even talk, though most people dismissed it as scaremongering or barmy pessimism, that there was a very real threat of another war breaking out and gas masks were soon going to be distributed to every household in the land.

But, as always, with the coming of longer days and the summer sunshine filtering through the grimy London air to warm bones long chilled by winter, even the most hardened of pessimists couldn't help but feel that things were perhaps getting just a little bit better, and maybe those good times really were just around the corner after all.

It was the end of a balmy June day, and Katie was humming tunelessly to herself as she and Nora cleared the dirty plates from the kitchen table.

'Right,' said Katie, dumping her pile on to the draining board and sticking her hands on her hips. 'Anything more, Pat, before I get on with this lot?'

Pat leant back and patted his stomach. 'No thanks, girl, I couldn't eat another bite. That was flipping handsome.' He yawned loudly, making himself laugh. 'Blimey, I'm gonna have to watch meself. I reckon I'm going soft. I get the chance to do a full week's work for a change and I'm worn out.' He pushed back his chair and went over to the dresser to fetch the evening paper. 'Still, mustn't complain, eh? It's good knowing I'll be picking up a proper wage packet tomorrow.'

Pat sat back down at the table and began idly flicking through the pages of his paper.

'Can me and Timmy go out and play now, Mum?' Michael asked.

'Yeah, go on, but yer to come in the minute I call yer, right?'

The two youngest didn't need telling twice, they were out of the room before Katie had the chance to change her mind.

'You seen this?' Pat held up the paper to Katie. 'It's beyond me, the way kids behave these days. Yer can hardly believe it.'

'What's that then, love?' Katie asked him over her shoulder.

'They arrested some razor gang last night. And in Hyde Park of all places, if yer don't mind. And some of the kids was as young as our Sean.'

'I ain't no kid.' Sean glowered across the table at his father. He scraped his chair back across the lino, stood up and loped over to the back door.

'Sean . . .' Katie began, but he was gone: out of the back door and off over the yard wall. Still, she told herself, getting back to her washing up, she didn't have to worry about him too much any more. Irene Lane had promised to keep an eye on him, to stop him hanging around Arthur. And even though he hadn't got himself a proper job yet, he was still earning a bit of pocket money, doing odds and ends for the stall holders in Chrisp Street. He'd be all right.

'Razor gangs,' Pat repeated with a disgusted shake of his head. 'Whatever's the world coming to?'

'Can I see that when yer've finished, Dad?' Danny asked.

'Here, have it now, son. I'm going over the Queen's to whet me whistle.' He handed Danny the paper. 'Fancy coming over, Kate?'

'What? On a Thursday?'

'Why not? Come on. We're gonna be flush tomorrow, and it's been a while since we've treated ourselves.'

'But I've gotta do all this.'

'No you haven't. You go on,' Nora said, looking pointedly at Molly, who was sitting slumped listlessly at the table. 'We can finish this, can't we, Molly?'

Molly rose wearily to her feet. 'You go with 'em and all, Nanna. I'll do it. I ain't got nothing else to do.'

Nora untied her apron and handed it to Molly. 'Well, I wouldn't mind just a drop o' stout,' she said, squeezing Molly's cheek between her finger and thumb. 'For the iron in it, o' course. Good for me old blood.'

Molly put on her grandmother's apron and started the washing up. She didn't say a word as she scoured and rubbed and rinsed, but, the moment she heard her parents and nanna leave the house to go over to the Queen's, she rounded on Danny. 'Don't help, will yer?' she snapped, flicking the wet dishcloth at him.

'Oi! Watch it.' Danny ducked behind the paper. 'I'm trying to read.'

'Nice if yer've got the choice.'

Danny finished the rest of the article he was reading, and closed the newspaper. Then he got up and went over to the sink where Molly was still up to her elbows in greasy suds. He leant back against the draining board. 'I'm going over to see Liz in a minute,' he said casually. 'You doing anything tonight, are yer?'

'What would I be doing on a Thursday night with no money and no one to go out with?'

'So you ain't seeing no one then?'

'Me?' A hint of caution had entered her voice. 'No. I'm not seeing no one.'

'Don't lie to me, Molly. I know you are.'

Molly went to say something but Danny didn't give her the chance.

'Still that feller we saw yer with, the one over the fair, is it?'

'Has that Lizzie Watts been telling stories about me?'

'No, course not.'

'She better hadn't.'

'Look, Moll, I ain't interfering, it's just that stuff in the papers . . .' He rubbed his hand over his chin, just as his dad always did when he didn't know how to say something. 'I've heard talk. Talk that Bob Jarvis has had something to do with them razor gangs.'

'Bob Jarvis?'

'Yeah, and I just wanna make sure that if he starts hanging around again, that yer've got a bloke who'll look out for yer.'

Molly could have laughed out loud. She had really thought that Danny was going to try to warn her off of seeing Simon and here he was wanting him to act as her bodyguard! 'Bob Jarvis hanging around me?' she said. 'What, after I grassed him? He'd hardly be interested in me no more, now would he?'

'It ain't funny.'

'Am I laughing?'

'Look, Moll,' Danny grabbed his sister by the arms, not caring that she was dripping water all over him, 'he thought you was his girl. He told everyone, bragged about it. And he ain't the sort of bloke to forget it when he reckons someone's turned on him.' He let Molly go and rubbed his hands over his face again. 'I wish I'd never got yer involved with him.'

'Why are yer going over all this now? It's two years since he did that old boy in.'

'Yeah, and he still ain't been caught, has he? Blokes like him have places to hide. And they've got dangerous friends. There's even been talk lately that he's back round here, that someone's been hiding him.' Danny screwed up his face as though he was in pain. 'I've just

445

got this horrible feeling that he could cause a lot more trouble.'

Molly shook her head and made a sarcastic little tutting sound with her tongue. 'I dunno why yer getting yerself all upset about nothing, Dan. It's just a stupid rumour. Bob Jarvis wouldn't dare show his face round here.' Her words might have been brave, but deep down, Molly feared that Danny might just be right. 'And I don't know what yer mean about me seeing someone,' she added lightly, mentally promising Father Hopkins that she would go to confession for lying at the first opportunity. 'I don't need no bloke, thanks very much.'

But Molly did need a bloke, she needed Simon Blomstein; and, in the three years she had been seeing him, Simon had become the most important person in her life.

It was Sunday afternoon, and Molly, as usual, was going to meet him. But this was to be no ordinary Sunday meeting, it was 4 October 1936, the day that Mosley and his British Union of Fascists had marked for their long-threatened march that was to lead them through areas of the East End populated by Jewish families and their businesses.

For weeks now there had been whitewashed slogans, handwritten posters and printed leaflets appearing all over the East End declaring 'They Shall Not Pass'. The warning was clear: regardless of what it took, the Blackshirts were going to be stopped.

Also during those weeks leading up to the Sunday of the march, Molly had refused to listen to Simon's continual insistence that it would be far too dangerous for her to join him at the anti-Mosley protest. She was determined, no matter what, that she was going to stand by his side.

446

But it was a feeling of gut-churning terror, rather than her usual dread of being found out, that gripped Molly's stomach as she attended early Mass then rushed off straight after Sunday dinner – supposedly to meet a friend from work – without even helping her mum to clear the table.

As she neared the place where Simon would be waiting, Molly realised that it was going to take her quite a while to find him. Their agreed meeting place was Gardiner's Corner, the busy junction of Commercial Road, Commercial Street, Whitechapel Road, Whitechapel High Street and Leman Street; it was also the site of the anticipated clash between the demonstrators and marchers as the BUF approached the East End from the direction of Tower Hill.

Neither Molly nor Simon had imagined how many people were going to be there; there were so many, in fact, that some of the side streets were already impassable, and a number sixty-five tram on its way to Blackwall Tunnel had actually been trapped on its rails right in the middle of the junction, its path blocked by milling hordes of protesters.

At least Molly could move forward, if only at an agonisingly slow pace, as she was going in the same general direction as the crowds. But she had to hold her arms up around her body to protect herself, and keep twisting away from the unintentional pummelling she was getting from her fellow demonstrators. Molly was neither particularly short nor skinny, but, as far as she could see, she was the only female in the crowd and just about everyone else was taller and heavier than she. And, as was clear from their banners and posters and yells, the crowd was too set on its one intention of forming a solid line of defence to bother about who they were pushing or shoving out of their way. They had been gathering since first thing that morning and were now more than ready for action.

The ones who had come with their various political, religious and union associations, had first assembled at temporary campaign headquarters set up in houses, shops and cafés, and had received orders and gone over plans. The less organised supporters of the protest – mainly cockneys from neighbourhoods further east of the City – had just turned up with their friends and neighbours; regardless of their affiliations, they were united in their disgust at Mosley and his followers' violence, and were determined to do whatever was necessary to stop the march getting a single foothold in the East End. There were youngsters there too, gangly, long-legged adolescents of about Sean's age, who didn't seem to have much of a clue as to what was actually going on but knew the prospect of a good bundle when they saw one, and also knew that if the numbers so far were anything to go by, this definitely looked like the sensible side to support.

There were other groups of men whom Molly was doing her best to avoid as she pushed her way through the crowds searching for Simon. They were the heavies, the hardnuts, the ones who, so the whispers went, worked for an infamous local gangster. They were there in a show of honouring the tithes, the insurance money, that they collected each week from the Jewish businesses in the area in return for 'protecting' them from any trouble or accidents.

As well as the demonstrators there were observers and sightseers, some women amongst them, who dangled and strained from every high window available, in their efforts to ensure a comfortable seat, but more importantly a good view, for what was promising to be quite a show.

Molly had just reached the stage when she was making bargains with herself about how much longer she would give it, or how many more times she was prepared to be jostled almost off her feet again, before she would just give up looking for Simon and go home, when she caught a glimpse of him in the crowd a few yards in front of her. 'Simon!' she hollered. 'Simon! I'm back here.'

With many mumbled apologies, Simon heaved himself back towards her through a knot of complaining men who told him in no uncertain terms that they were *meant* to be moving forwards.

'Molly, I didn't think I'd ever find you.'

'Well, yer've bleed'n well found her now, mate,' one of the men shouted at him, 'so why don't yer get her off home. This ain't no place for no girls.'

Simon slipped his arm protectively round her waist. 'He's right, you know. You really shouldn't be here.'

If there had been room, Molly would have pulled away from him. 'Ain't yer glad to see me then?'

'Of course I am. But I'm worried about you. I couldn't bear you to get hurt.'

Satisfied, she smiled happily, even though they were now being dragged forward again and she was nearly being lifted off her feet. 'Have I missed much?'

'Funny way to put it, but yes, you have I suppose.' Simon staggered sideways as a group of oversized men carrying a banner proclaiming them to be 'Dockers united against the fascists' came barging past. 'Look, let's go down there or else we're going to get crushed by our own side. We can stand by that wall.'

'I think that's a good idea,' she said, thinking it

probably best not to add that one of the big men with the banner was her dad's work-mate from the dock and she didn't much fancy him seeing her there. Gladly, she let Simon grab her firmly by the arm and begin to guide her back along Commercial Road, although she found it much tougher struggling against the increasingly agitated and excited crowds as two o'clock, the time of the march, grew closer. So she could have kissed Simon, no matter how many people were watching, when he tugged her after him, away from the main crush, along Back Church Lane, and then jerked her to an undignified halt near the corner of Cable Street and Leman Street.

Puffing from exertion and relief, Simon wiped his forehead with his sleeve and leant back against the rough brick wall. When he had got his breath back, he told Molly about the skirmishes and violent clashes that had already taken place between the police and the protesters before she had arrived; and how the mounted police charges had only been halted when the senior officers realised that at least ten extra men were needed as escorts every time they had to get a single arrested demonstrator past the jeering crowds and to the nearby police stations.

Molly's eyes had grown wide. 'So the coppers ain't on our side?'

'It's not that, darling,' a gruff-voiced man, who had stopped to have a cigarette, informed her. 'It's just that they've had orders to get them bastards through so's they can have their poxy march.' He touched his cap in apology. ''Scuse me language, love.' He ground the cigarette butt out under the heel of his boot. 'I'd be getting off home if I was you, miss. They've got thousands of coppers, on horse and on foot, just waiting up between Tower Hill and Whitechapel for the signal to start

450

charging us again, and this time they'll really mean it.'

Molly gulped. 'Thanks. I'll be all right.'

The man raised his eyebrows, questioning Simon's wisdom at letting a girl hang around such a dangerous place. 'I suppose yer safer here than Gardiner's Corner.'

Simon nodded and the man was gone.

As the clocks ticked nearer to the appointed hour, and people looked at their watches every few minutes, the mood of fear and excitement that had weighed so heavily in the air was quickly being replaced by a lot of slightly bored offering around of cigarettes, and increasingly frequent suggestions that they might as well forget hanging around Cable Street and make their way along Leman Street over to Gardiner's Corner. After all, why be there at all if they were going to miss all the action?

There was some light relief, for a few of the men at least, when someone pointed out that there was a girl amongst them and made some crude suggestions as to what he thought she might do to scare off the Blackshirts, but Molly stubbornly ignored him and flashed a challenging stare at Simon to do the same. She had come this far and wasn't going to let a few stupid remarks upset her.

Completely unexpectedly, the mood suddenly changed as the word was passed urgently around that the march was not going to take the advertised route after all. The police were going to force a path from Royal Mint Street into Cable Street and let the marchers and Mosley's motorcade through that way instead.

The response was immediate. First the cry went up, 'They shall not pass!' Then the barricades of old mattresses and crates that had been thrown across the narrow road were hastily reinforced with whatever the now fully alert protesters could lay their hands on.

Despite Simon's renewed attempts to get her to go further back behind the lines, Molly insisted on standing by his side and helping him and the others. In their need to build up the roadblock, the men who had only moments ago been jeering at her, seemed to have forgotten that she was a girl. She stood in place, working alongside them as they passed lengths of timber that had been seized from a nearby furniture factory, and then dragged heaps of old furniture, slung from upstairs windows, into the middle of the road to help bolster the now shoulder-height barrier.

Molly only once stepped back, when a group of men broke into a nearby haulier's yard, stole a truck and shoved it across the road a few yards back from the main barricade. They began rocking it back and forth, trying to turn it on to its side. As the vehicle finally toppled over and smashed down on to the cobbles, the men cheered at the tops of their voices, but Molly could only think what the owner – a man like Joe Palmer with a little business and a wife to support maybe – would have to say about sacrificing his truck. But she didn't suppose that the hundreds of demonstrators, working to reinforce the barricades, were in any mood to listen to the reservations of a nineteen-year-old girl.

Their numbers were rapidly swelling into thousands now, as the men who had been defending Gardiner's Corner streamed along the side streets in a single-minded, massed effort to seal the narrow bottleneck at the top of Cable Street. They were ready, no matter what the cost, to stand their ground.

With no apparent signal that Molly could make out, policemen poured forward and began clambering over the barrier with their truncheons flailing. Then the missiles began to fly. Stones, bricks, milk bottles, roof slates and foul-mouthed abuse were hurled with complete abandon, the violence of the confrontation between police and protesters making the earlier encounters seem like children's playground scuffles, as men on both sides fell to the ground with bloody heads and screams of agony.

'Please, Molly,' Simon gasped, raising his arms to shield her from a half-brick that had been launched from their own side. 'Get back.'

But before Molly had the chance to object, the next onslaught was on its way from the police side of the barricade.

She watched, wide-eyed and dry-mouthed as four mounted officers, truncheons raised high above their heads, cantered their horses directly into the wooden roadblock, sending it splintering into the air like so much kindling. As one, the frontline protesters turned their backs on Royal Mint Street and surged back along Cable Street, sucking Molly and Simon into their tide as they staggered and stumbled away from the animals' hooves and the officers' truncheons.

Molly's ears rang with a cacophony of screams and yells, the blowing of police whistles, hooves clattering across the cobbles, and the ever-closer buzzing of approaching motorbikes and the rumble of car engines.

As she was buffeted from one dark-jacketed mass of men to another, Molly knew, even without looking, that Simon was no longer with her.

A voice shouted from somewhere high above her head, 'Gawd almighty, there's only a girl down there in that lot.'

Molly's arms were pinned to her side, but she could still, just about, move her head to look upwards.

She saw two men sitting on an upstairs window ledge of the Sailors' Home, their legs dangling down in front of them and their hands grasping the window frame as they strained forward for a better view of the madness below them.

'Yer right!' the other one shouted. 'For Christ's sake get yerself over here in the doorway, love. Yer gonna get trampled in that lot.'

His friend beckoned urgently. 'Yeah, come on, girl, yer've gotta try. Over here.'

Molly did try, with every bit of effort she could muster, to do as the men were urging her.

'Come on, darling,' the first man hollered again. 'Yer've gotta move. There's sodding thousands o' rozzers running towards yer. And they're leading that bastard's motors right down here. Come on,' he pleaded with her. 'Get over here. Quick!'

But before she had moved a single step towards them, another great dark expanse of rough serge jacket scraped across her face and blocked her view of her would-be saviours. As she felt herself being swept along again, she knew it was useless to try to reach the doorway. She had no choice. She was a piece of broken twig in a whirlpool; the crowd spinning her round and round until she hadn't even a clue in which direction she was facing.

Quite suddenly the shoving stopped and she went stumbling forward through a gap in the heaving mass of bodies. At last she felt she could breathe again. But her relief was momentary.

She blinked, hardly able to believe her eyes. Not only had she been catapulted right to the edge of the police lines, but there, right in front of her, was Bob Jarvis. But it couldn't be. Even he wouldn't be so arrogant as to think he could be here with all these coppers around.

Yet Molly was sure it was him. Even the pose was the same – his head held high, and his chin thrust defiantly forward, as he stood on the running board of one of the shiny black open-top cars that were poised behind the lines of police, waiting to make their way along Cable Street once the way had been cleared.

In her bewilderment, Molly made no attempt to conceal herself; she just stood there, staring. She soon realised that that was a mistake.

The man turned his head and, for a brief disturbing moment, he held her gaze with his. It might have been two years since she had last seen him, but she would never forget that face. It was Bob Jarvis all right.

She had to do something quick, and she knew exactly what it was. Hurriedly she skirted around the piles of shredded timbers that had once been the barricade and called to one of the mounted policemen.

The officer gently encouraged his sweating, trembling horse to move forward to where Molly was now standing in the shadow of a wall on the corner of Dock Street: a temporary no-man's-land between police and protesters.

'Please,' she said, 'help me. That man over there,' she pointed towards the car where Bob Jarvis was standing, watching her, 'yer've gotta arrest him. He killed an old man. Two years ago, it was. Just over in Back Church Lane.'

The policeman looked down from his saddle at Molly as though she was something nasty he had stepped in, and that had spoilt the shine on his freshly polished boot. 'A murder, eh? Two years ago, yer reckon?' He bent forward from his waist, his face almost touching hers. 'You wouldn't be trying to cause trouble 'cos he's one of the marchers, now would yer?'

He straightened up again. 'I saw where yer come from.

455

From down there.' He lifted his chin in the direction of Cable Street. 'I dunno what things are coming to. Young girls getting mixed up with scum like that. I tell yer what, yer lucky you ain't no daughter of mine, 'cos if you was, I'd tan yer arse for yer. Now go on, get off home.'

Molly felt herself being yanked sideways and slung back against the wall. 'Mind back!' her attacker yelled. 'I'll show him what we think of coppers.'

Molly watched, dazed and confused as the man simultaneously screamed and slapped the horse's flanks, making the already skittish creature rear up in terror, then threw a handful of marbles on to the ground just as its hooves made contact with the cobbles again. The horse's eyes showed white with terror as it plunged to the ground, crushing the policeman beneath it.

'You bastard!' Molly yelled at the man, who was running back along towards Cable Street. 'You're no better than the sodding Blackshirts!'

Molly fell to her knees, trying desperately to reach the policeman and pull him away from the horse; but the animal was panicking in its efforts to stand up, and its hooves were flailing dangerously close to her face.

Urgently she looked around for help, but the fighting had started again and no one seemed to care about what was happening there in Dock Street. She took a deep breath and made a grab for the horse's reins – anything to stop it kicking the policeman.

'Leave it,' she heard a man hiss into her ear.

She turned round and screamed. It was Bob Jarvis.

He clapped his hand over her mouth.

Molly flashed her eyes at the policeman who was now almost on his feet, almost upright. But he was staggering, barely sensible and blood was pouring from one of his ears.

As she felt herself being dragged backwards along Dock Street, Molly sank her teeth into Jarvis's hand and shrieked at the top of her voice.

'You'll pay for that,' Jarvis spat. He clasped her even tighter to him and whispered slowly into her ear, ''Cos I'm gonna show you exactly what I know you always wanted me to do to yer. But I don't think yer gonna like it very much. Not when I've finished with yer.'

A young foot policeman who would rather have been having a Sunday afternoon kip in his mum's front parlour than having bricks lobbed at him, turned to see where the unexpected sound of a female screaming had come from.

Bob acknowledged him with a confident nod and then jerked his head in the direction of the injured officer who had sunk to his knees again by his terrified horse. 'She saw him take a nasty fall,' Bob explained. 'Sent her hysterical. Yer'd better go and help him.'

The young man looked warily at the wild-eyed animal. Glad of no further complication with the girl, but with definitely no intention of messing around with half a ton of crazed horse meat, the young officer tipped the rim of his helmet with his gloved hand. 'I'll send someone over.'

With that he disappeared, leaving Molly petrified – and at the mercy of Bob Jarvis.

But she hadn't been forsaken entirely. The two men from their perch high up in the Sailors' Home had seen Simon frantically tearing his way through the crowd calling Molly's name.

'You looking for the girl?' one of them shouted down to him.

'The one with red hair?' the other one added.

'Where is she?' a man's voice yelled at them. But it

457

wasn't Simon, it was Danny. He had been frantically looking for his sister for what felt like hours, ever since he had spotted her in the crowd.

'She's over there. Some Blackshirt bastard got hold of her and dragged her off down Dock Street.'

The two men began to explain how they couldn't get down to help her, but Danny and Simon weren't listening, they were too busy fighting their way towards Molly, back through the maelstrom of heaving, struggling bodies.

Simon cursed himself over and over again. 'I told her not to come. I told her.'

'No one,' gasped Danny, barging forward, 'has ever been able to stop my sister doing exactly what she wanted.'

With a supreme effort of will and a disregard for injuries – their own and other people's – they reached the front of the crowd, only to be met with another obstacle between them and Molly: a would-be cordon of two very disgruntled police officers, hands clasped behind their backs, were guarding the entrance to Dock Street. They had been told to stand there and await further orders while their colleagues got on with what they considered was the real business of the day.

Simon motioned for Danny to keep quiet. 'Excuse me, officer,' he said in his nicest, speaking-to-his-Uncle-David tones. 'One of those Communists back there – I saw him grab a young girl and drag her down into Dock Street.'

'Aw yeah? And what would a girl be doing round here then?' He turned to the constable at his side and grinned. 'Looking for a bit of business down the dock gates, maybe?' He flashed his eyebrows. 'I wouldn't interfere if I was you, mate.'

Simon said no more, just turned to Danny and nodded.

Danny understood the signal perfectly. As one, they drew back their fists and landed punches squarely on the unsuspecting officers' noses, sending the now open-mouthed and bloody-nosed colleagues stumbling into one another.

Danny and Simon wasted no time; they raced along Dock Street towards East Smithfield before the policemen were even back on their feet.

'Over there!' hollered Danny, pointing towards the corner of Nightingale Lane, where Jarvis was struggling to keep hold of his frenziedly squirming, kicking, biting prisoner as he dragged her along the street that led between the docks and down towards the river. 'The bastard's still got her.'

They launched themselves across the road and into the lane, taking Jarvis unawares. Simon grabbed at Molly, wrenching her out of the way as Danny hurled himself at the unsuspecting Jarvis, knocking him clean off his feet.

While Simon wrapped Molly, shivering with fear and shock, tightly in his arms, Danny got on with finishing off Jarvis.

As Danny stood over him, punching at him, landing blow after hate-filled blow on the body of the man he had once thought so impressive and whom he now totally despised, Jarvis curled himself into a ball, pleading and whimpering for mercy.

Danny lifted his foot and was about to kick him in the kidneys, when Jarvis lifted his head and started crying like a baby, a trickle of snot dangling from his nose.

The sight of him grovelling and snivelling sickened Danny – he couldn't even bear to touch him, not even with his boot. Instead, he ripped the black shirt from Jarvis's back and threw it, disgusted, into the gutter.

'Some hero you turned out to be,' he sneered. 'Not so brave when it ain't a girl or an old man yer fighting, are yer, you bastard?'

'Danny!' Simon was next to him, pulling him away from Jarvis. 'The law!'

Danny looked over his shoulder. The two furious-looking bloody-nosed policemen were hammering up and down East Smithfield, obviously looking for him and Simon.

'Over here,' Molly called.

The three of them stood, flattened against the high dock wall, invisible in the shadows, hardly daring to breathe. As they watched Jarvis slowly haul himself to his feet and then lurch forward towards the main road where the two officers were looking for them, the shrill piercing note of a single police whistle suddenly sounded, followed by a whole chorus of others.

Danny really thought they'd had it, that reinforcements were coming to help beat them to a pulp, but, as if by magic, and with a stream of loud, crude expletives, the two young officers stopped in their tracks, turned round and started trotting back in the direction they'd come from – just as Bob Jarvis floundered his way to the corner of Nightingale Lane.

'What d'yer make of that?' Danny asked.

The answer wasn't long in coming. They heard wild cheers followed by jubilant shouts of 'They did not pass' come echoing through the streets.

'We've won,' Molly breathed, collapsing back against the wall. 'We've stopped the fascists.'

'We've won today, but it's going to take more than—' Simon stopped. He frowned and looked around him. 'Jarvis, he's disappeared. Come on, we can't let him get away.'

Molly grabbed Simon's arm. 'Please, no more. I just wanna go home.'

Simon nodded. 'If that's what you want.'

Danny inspected his grazed and bloody knuckles. 'I'm gonna have to get meself cleaned up before I can go home.'

Simon took out his handkerchief and gave it to Danny to wrap round his hand. 'We'll go to a café. They'll be proud to let you use their tap after what you've done today.'

As they made their way wearily towards Aldgate, there were very few police still on the streets, but there were still crowds of protesters everywhere. Most were vocally triumphant, but some, like Simon, were feeling more circumspect about just how successful they had been, and were getting on with the job of helping the injured, clearing away the debris and turning the battleground back into an ordinary East End neighbourhood.

It took Molly, Danny and Simon a while to find a steam-filled coffee shop that had room for them, as every café they passed seemed to be packed and buzzing with men, noisily swapping stories of their courageous deeds, and laughing at the Police Commissioner who had decided to stop the march because they, the heroes of the hour, had won the Battle of Cable Street.

As they sipped at their mugs of scalding tea, Danny leant across the table and said, so that only Simon and Molly could hear, 'You said they'd be proud to let me use their tap.'

Simon nodded. 'They were, weren't they?'

'Yeah, but I ain't so sure they would've been if they knew I'd been mixed up with Bob Jarvis.' He dropped his chin and stared down into his cup. 'I come here today

461

'cos I reckoned it wasn't good enough just regretting ever being fool enough to listen to him. I wanted to show whose side I was on.'

'You're a brave man, admitting that, Danny,' said Simon, holding out his hand across the rickety, oilcloth-covered table.

Danny shook Simon's hand, glancing sideways at Molly. 'I think it's about time he met the rest of the Mehan clan, don't you?' he said solemnly.

Molly almost choked on her tea. 'What!'

'Mine and Lizzie's wedding'll be the perfect opportunity. This Christmas, we thought. We've been saving for so long now we reckon it's now or never.' He gave a joyless little laugh. 'Times have been hard.'

Simon blinked with astonishment. 'Er, thanks. Thanks. I'll have to see if I can make it.' He looked at his watch then turned to Molly. 'Will you be all right now?'

Molly nodded dumbly. She was so amazed by her brother's invitation that she could hardly think straight, let alone speak.

'If you're really sure, then I'll get off home. I promised my uncle I wouldn't come within a mile of this place and if I don't get back soon he's going to start getting suspicious.'

Still Molly didn't answer him.

'Look, it doesn't matter. I don't have to go yet.'

'No, please,' Molly stood up, her legs wobbling unsteadily. 'I'll be fine, I've got Danny with me.'

As the three of them stepped outside into the cold October air, Simon looked up at the sky. 'It'll be dark soon.' He shook Danny's hand again. 'Take care of her for me.' Then he leant forward and kissed Molly tenderly on the cheek. 'See you Sunday, Molly. I'll come round to

Terson's in the week to tell you where.'

With that he dodged off into the crowd.

'Coming?' Danny asked.

Molly didn't move, she looked too dazed. 'I can't believe all this is happening. Yer don't know nothing about him, Dan. And yer've gone and asked him to yer wedding.'

'I know enough. Lizzie told me about him.'

'Eh!'

'I made her, when I was worried about Jarvis coming after yer. And now I've seen him for meself, I know he'll look after yer. He'd never let no one hurt yer, Moll.'

'D'yer reckon he could stop Mum killing me when she meets him?'

Danny shrugged. 'Sorry, I never thought . . .'

Molly's hand flew to her mouth.

'Look, Moll, we'll think of something.'

'No.' Molly pointed urgently. 'Over there.'

Danny twisted round and looked over his shoulder.

'I know he's got a bandage round his head, Dan, but I'll swear that's Dad. Come on, we've gotta make a run for it.'

'You sure yer up to running?'

'If Dad's gonna be after us, you bet I am.'

18

It was a cold dark Monday night, the last day of November, and Molly was again running as fast as her legs would carry her. Although this time she wasn't running away in case her dad saw her, she was charging along towards Plumley Street on her way home from work. But instead of stopping when she reached number twelve, she ran straight past, and didn't slow down until she came to a breathless halt outside the Palmers' yard, where Danny was backing Joe's truck in through the gates.

'Dan! Dan!' She slapped the flat of her hand on the cab door. 'Have you heard?'

'Hold up, Moll, don't do that. Joe'll do his crust if yer scratch the flaming paintwork.' He wound down the window and checked that she hadn't damaged the door. 'What the hell's got into yer?'

'Dan, it's important. Please.'

Irritated, but knowing that Molly wasn't one to give in when she got an idea in her head, he turned off the engine and got out of the cab. He folded his arms and looked bored. 'This had better be good. I'm trying to get finished for the night.'

'Simon come down the warehouse at dinnertime.'

'I'm very pleased for yer,' he said sarcastically.

'He come to tell me about Bob Jarvis.' She now had

her brother's full attention. 'Him and some of them other nutcases was planning another one of them revenge attacks.'

'Bastards!' Danny's fists balled up as his temper rose. 'What, breaking more shop windows and scaring old ladies, I suppose?'

Molly lowered her voice and looked around nervously. 'No. It was gonna be some sort of explosion, in some tailoring workshop off of Brick Lane. Last night it was gonna be. Jarvis and some other bloke. But they got really tanked up, didn't they?' She snorted contemptuously. 'Some heroes, eh, needing Dutch courage?'

'Molly . . .'

'Yeah, well, they got so pissed they started mouthing off in the boozer. Bragging about what they was gonna do.'

'Stupid bastards.'

'I'm telling yer. Anyway, they go round to the workshop, and while they was stuffing all these paraffin rags round the doorway, these other blokes turned up. Caught 'em at it. No one's saying who these other blokes was, mind, but the word is they was, you know, *protecting* the place.' She paused, letting Danny take in her meaning.

Danny nodded slowly. 'Right.'

'Well, of course, it turned into a fight. But the bloke what was with Jarvis got the wind up and had it away. Left him to it.'

'Typical o' that mob. So what happened?'

Molly leant very close to him. 'They done him in,' she whispered.

'They what?' Danny frowned. 'Who?'

'They mullered Bob Jarvis.' She straightened up and

466

took a deep breath. 'They found him this morning. With his throat slit. And a razor by his side. His own razor, so they're saying.'

'Jesus Christ!'

'It's over, Dan. He's gone. Gone for good this time.'

'Yer sure this ain't just a load of old toffee?'

'Course I am. The blokes what done it are making sure everyone knows all about it. And how that's what'll happen to anyone else who reckons they can start messing around on their patch.'

'I dunno what to say.'

'I thought yer'd be pleased. No,' she added hurriedly, 'not pleased, relieved. Yeah, that's it. Relieved.'

'Course I'm relieved that bastard's outta the way, it's just . . . Aw, I dunno, it's something Simon said after all that business in Cable Street. I keep getting it stuck in me head, going round and round.'

'What yer talking about?'

'About us winning that day, but how it's gonna take more . . .' He ran his hands through his thick dark hair. 'Look, it's nothing. It's a bit of a shock, that's all.'

'Yer can say that again.'

'Moll, can yer do us a favour? Tell Mum I won't be in for me tea straight away. I wanna go over and see Liz about something first.'

As soon as Danny had backed the lorry into the yard and sheeted it up for the night, he went across to number nine and rapped on the door.

'Hello, Dan.' Liz smiled up at him, her face dimpling prettily. 'I didn't expect to see you so early.'

'I knows it's a Monday night, Liz, and I know we ain't meant to be spending no money 'cos the wedding's in a couple o' weeks, but I feel like I wanna get out for a few hours. Fancy coming for a drink later on? Joe said I could borrow his bike and sidecar. We could have a little ride out.'

'Well, if yer let me get a word in edgeways,' she grinned, 'I'd love to. I'll have me tea and brush me hair and then I'll be ready. About seven suit yer?'

It was just gone half past seven, when Danny parked the motorbike outside a little pub close to the foot tunnel on the Isle of Dogs.

Liz shivered as Danny lifted the roof of the sidecar and helped her out onto the pavement. 'I'm glad I had that rug round me legs,' she said softly. 'You must have been frozen on that bike.'

'I didn't really notice,' he said, pulling off his goggles and leather helmet.

'On a perishing night like this,' she said, stamping her feet to get her circulation going, 'yer wouldn't credit yer could walk under the river to Greenwich, would yer?'

'No,' Danny said, stuffing his gloves into his pocket.

Liz pulled up her collar round her ears. 'Can we go inside, Dan? I'm freezing.'

Danny silently held out his arm and led her into the warm fug of the saloon bar. Then he settled her at a table, while he went to fetch some drinks, leaving her increasingly anxious about his odd behaviour.

Liz took a sip from her port and lemonade, thought for a moment whether she should actually be saying what she was about to say and then thought that if she didn't she might well burst into tears or start screaming. 'Look, Dan, I'm doing me best to seem all happy, but I know something's up. I can tell.' She dropped her chin as her tears won and her big round eyes filled with water. 'If yer've changed yer mind about getting married, or yer've met someone else, then I think I've got a right to know.

468

I'd rather yer told me now than made a fool of me later on.'

'Lizzie.' Danny put his drink down on the little round table, put his arm around her shoulders and pulled her close to him. 'Whatever give yer that idea?'

'I ain't used to yer being all moody like this.' She sniffed delicately, and licked away a tear that had run down the side of her nose. 'If something's up yer usually just spit it out. That's what I've always liked about all you Mehans, yer straight. But this is different. Yer bottling something up, and it's scaring me. I mean it, if yer wanna finish, I want yer to tell me now.'

'Daft. How could I ever wanna finish with you?'

'So what is it then? Here, you ain't in no trouble, are yer, Dan?'

'No. Nothing like that.' He ran his finger round the top of his glass. 'Yer gonna think I'm stupid when I tell yer.'

'No, I won't.'

'Yer won't laugh at me?'

She shook her head.

'It's the world.'

'The world?'

'Yeah. All this stuff about Japan and Germany and Italy and . . . And all that lark. And then there's Spain. It's all just getting worse and worse.'

'But why should that worry us? I don't even know where them places are.'

'I don't either. Well, not all of them. It's just . . . I've been thinking about things. And there's a lot that's going wrong in this world, Liz.'

'Yeah, but we'll be all right here, won't we? We won't have no trouble, not in England?' She looked around the bar, a bright, happy place, buzzing with laughter and good-natured chat. 'Not in the East End?'

Danny looked down into her big, trusting eyes and shook his head. 'No. We won't have no trouble here. We'll be all right.' He squeezed her to him. 'And anyway, yer've got Danny Mehan to look after yer, ain't yer?'

He felt Liz's body relax. 'I love you, Dan,' she whispered contentedly, and picked up her drink to hide her blushes.

The bar room door was suddenly flung back on its hinges and a man came rushing into the pub.

'Close that bloody door!' hollered the landlady. 'Letting all my heat out.'

'Yer've gotta come and see this,' the man shouted, beckoning furiously. 'There's a fire out here and yer've never seen nothing like it in yer life.'

Drinks were gulped down and coats and hats grabbed, as the bar emptied out on to the pavement. They followed the man up the little slope that led to thé footpath running alongside the Thames.

'Where?' complained a whiskery, middle-aged man, whose moustaches, stained yellow from years of filtering tobacco smoke and straining beer, twitched up and down as he spoke. 'I can't see no—'

'There!' The man who had run into the pub pointed for him to look across the river.

'Gawd bloody blink me!' the whiskery man gasped, as he stared at the night sky that was lit up like a blood-red travesty of daylight. 'What the hell's going on?'

A woman called down to him from one of the pub's upstairs windows. 'Here, George, did yer know there's a fire?'

'Yes, Min,' he snapped.

'All right,' she snapped back. 'I was telling yer, 'cos it's only on the wireless, innit? They're saying the roads are all jam-packed with people trying to get over there to see it all go up, and they're stopping the rest of the fire engines getting through. They reckon ships right out in the Channel can see it and all. Hang on.' She ducked her head back inside the window, then out again. 'They just said that if people really want to see it close up, they should go on the special trains they're laying on at all the stations!'

'Yes, Min, very interesting.' George was losing his patience. 'But what the bleed'n hell is it that's a-sodding-light?'

'It's only the bloody Crystal Palace, innit!'

They all stood there watching, huddled against the cold, unable, as they shivered, to imagine the heat that must be coming from a fire that would be big enough to be seen from such a distance. But, even though they were so far away, they automatically shielded themselves with their arms as three massive explosions sent the fire flaming even higher into the night sky.

George took his pipe from between his lips and stabbed the stem towards the river. 'Just like the last war,' he said, and gave a loud, shuddering sigh. 'Just like when we was in them trenches. You wait and see, it's an omen, that's what it is. An omen.'

'Go on with yer,' heckled Minnie.

Danny pulled Liz closer to him and kissed the top of her head. She was his rock of sanity in a world that he was terrified might just tip over the edge into madness. He thought of Bob Jarvis lying in the street with his throat slit. Good riddance as far as he was concerned, but the trouble was, as Simon had tried to explain that day, and Danny was now beginning to realise, there were plenty more like Jarvis, all over the world, just waiting to take his place if nobody stopped them.

He nuzzled Liz's sweet-smelling hair. 'I love yer, Lizzie Watts,' he breathed. 'No matter what happens, I want yer always to remember that.'

It was nine o'clock in the morning on 19 December, the last Saturday before Christmas 1936, and all thoughts of what might or might not be happening in the world outside of Plumley Street, had, for the moment, been forgotten. Everyone was far too busy fussing and panicking over last-minute arrangements for what was promising to be the neighbourhood event of the year – the wedding between Danny Mehan and Liz Watts – to concern themselves with troubles in places they couldn't even pronounce.

Preparations had actually been going on for over two years now, ever since the day Danny and Liz had become engaged. Peggy Watts had started a bottom drawer for her daughter that very evening, taking the cross-stitched chair backs right off of the front room furniture from behind Bill's head while he was trying to have a snooze after he'd sunk a few celebratory pints in the Queen's.

Bill reckoned that Peggy's collecting had become a bit of a mania. She hadn't only filled the one bottom drawer, but a whole chest of drawers, packing it tight with countless odds and ends from the market as well as from her own store of household bits and pieces. Then, when she had run out of space in the original chest, she had set Bill to making another one, bigger this time, a tallboy, one that would go with the dressing table and wardrobe she had decided he was going to make for the kids. After all, she told him, a young couple starting off in a few rooms in Grundy Street would never be able to afford to buy their own furniture, not at first anyway.

It wasn't only Bill and his cabinet-making skills that

were put on to overtime; Peggy and her talents with a needle and cotton were also going at full stretch. There wasn't a bit of linen in either of the chests that hadn't had the benefit of at least a bit of embroidery in one corner or another, and as for Liz's wedding gown and the bridesmaids' dresses, Peggy had sewn every loving stitch by hand.

But now the big day itself had arrived at last, and the preparations were on their last, frantic lap.

In the Watts household, Molly and Peggy were charging around like a pair of headless chickens. One moment they were making sure that the hems of the dresses were straight and that all the tacking had been removed; the next they were fiddling about with the curlers they had wound into Liz's blonde hair, desperate that they shouldn't come unravelled, or get damp as she splashed around in front of the fire.

Liz was concentrating on just the one job for now: scrubbing herself spotless in the big tin bath that Peggy had instructed Bill to lug into the front room and set in front of the roaring hearth she had got up at five that morning to light. Having the bath in the front room was definitely a once-only treat on account of the special occasion. Peggy would never usually have allowed the thing past the kitchen door and into the passage, let alone tolerate having water slopped all over her treasured hearth rug.

Across the street, Katie was working herself up into an equal frenzy, as she did her best to take some sort of control over the proceedings in the kitchen of number twelve.

'You did go across and ask the Gibsons in for a drink, didn't yer, Dan?' Katie asked the soon-to-be bridegroom as he stood at the overmantel, trying to shave amongst all the bedlam without actually cutting his throat. He had tried standing at the sink, where he usually shaved, but it was brimming over with pots, so he was having to manage where he could, dipping his razor into a bowl of barely warm water balanced on the side.

'Yes, Mum,' said Danny wearily, having answered the self-same question at least three times before. He caught sight of his dad's reflection in the glass and treated him to a jaded roll of his eyes. 'Like I told yer, I've been over to the Gibsons and they said thank you very much they'd love to come over the Queen's this afternoon. And it was right nice of yer to ask. All right?'

'Right.' Katie licked her pencil and ticked that off her list – again. The list had, over the last few weeks, become the bane of the Mehans' mealtimes, there being no escape from it when they were all trapped around the table.

Pat winked at Danny and got on with finishing the full breakfast that Katie had insisted they should all eat, it being such an important day.

'Mum,' said Timmy thoughtfully, his mouth full of fried eggy-bread, 'd'yer know Mary Gibson?'

'Yeah,' said Katie absent-mindedly, still concentrating on her list.

'Well, she said that Liz is having a baby. Is she, Mum? Is she having a baby? 'Cos I'd be its uncle, wouldn't I?'

'*What?*'

'She said that Liz must be having a baby 'cos her and Danny're getting married. And she said Liz must've sat on the lavvy seat while it was still warm after our Danny'd been using it, 'cos that's what yer do, see, when yer wanna have a baby.'

Katie slammed her pencil down on the table, and glared at Timmy.

Danny and Pat were finding it hard not to burst out

474

laughing, but they weren't stupid, so they both did their best to keep their amusement to themselves.

'I can't believe I'm hearing this,' Katie fumed. 'Can yer just imagine what Father Hopkins'd have to say if he heard yer talking such filth? I've a good mind to get that bar o' soap and wash your mouth out for you, Timothy Mehan.'

Timmy, his top lip curled and his eyes wide in wonder at such injustice – he had after all only been repeating what Mary Gibson had told him – opened his mouth to make his appeal. But Pat, his composure almost restored, knew when the line had been crossed and a full-flight row was not what was needed on the morning of the wedding.

He waved his fork towards the kitchen door. 'Go on, Tim, off yer go. And you, Michael. Leave yer plates there, I'll see to 'em when I've finished. Just go next door to Nanna's and get yerselves washed and ready.'

Michael, in the role of sensible older brother for once, grabbed Timmy by the arm, deliberately pinching his flesh. 'Come on, yer great daft baby,' he mocked, 'before yer get us all in trouble.'

As his brother dragged him away from the table, Timmy was going to sneak on Michael to his mum for hurting him, but she was looking a bit fierce, so he contented himself with the thought that he'd be able to tell his nanna of him in a minute, and she'd soon sort Michael out. She was always saying how Michael should look after his baby brother. And thinking about babies, maybe Nanna would know if Liz was having one. She always told him any secrets if she knew any.

'Leave it on the latch,' Katie hollered. She screwed her eyes tight as the street door was slammed to with a loud crash. 'I don't know why I stand for all the old

475

nonsense I get from them two boys. They'll turn out wrong 'uns the way they're carrying on, you just see if they don't.'

'Course they won't, Kate.'

'But how can yer tell, Pat? Who can tell anything nowadays? Look at that Mr Milton. Who'd ever have thought he could have done an armed robbery?' Katie went to rake her fingers through her hair, then remembering she had her curlers in she rubbed her face instead. 'Perhaps if we'd all done a bit more to help 'em. The thought of that poor Ellen and them kids . . .'

'Look, love, today ain't the day to start going over all that again, now is it?'

There was a knock at the street door, making Katie jump in her seat.

'Now who can that be? Everyone knows how busy I am.'

'All right, Kate, leave off,' he said, holding up his hand to calm her. Then he called out, 'Come in. It's on the latch.'

Even Pat looked surprised when Irene Lane appeared in the kitchen doorway. As usual, she was all dressed up. She had on a scarlet coat in the latest monkey jacket style with black frogging and brass buttons, and a natty little matching hat pulled down over one eye.

But there was something different about her today. She looked less hard somehow. Then Katie realised what it was: Irene had hardly any make-up on, just a touch of lipstick and a bit of eye black. She looked smashing.

'Sorry to bother yer on a busy morning like this,' Irene began in her tiny little voice, smiling apologetically. 'Eleven o'clock'll be here before yer know it, eh?'

'Yer right there,' said Katie looking around at the chaos that had taken over her usually pristine kitchen.

As her glance passed over Sean, Katie stored away the fact that he had hurriedly bent his head down and was making an animated show of using his bread to mop up every last bit of his fried tomatoes – the tomatoes he had earlier said he wouldn't eat even if she forced them down his throat. And he was blushing to the roots of his hair.

'I just wanted to pop in to give this to Danny for him and Liz,' Irene explained, walking over to where Danny was still standing at the overmantel.

Danny wiped his hands on the towel he had draped round his neck, and took the brown-paper-covered box that Irene was holding out to him. He looked bewildered. Lots of people had been really generous to him and Liz, giving them all sorts of things for their new home, but they hardly knew the Lanes. 'That's really nice of yer. Ta, Mrs Lane.'

'It's *Irene*,' she said with a tinkling little laugh.

'Thanks, Irene.'

'My pleasure, Danny.' She put her head on one side. 'I hear yer setting up a little haulage business of yer own.'

Now Danny was really confused. 'How d'you know that?'

'Danny,' Katie said sternly.

'Sorry. Yeah, I am,' he said, remembering his manners. He held up the parcel, smiled, nodded his thanks and stuck it on the overmantel next to his shaving water. 'And ta, it was kind of yer to think of us. Me and Liz appreciate it.'

'So, this business of your'n,' she squeaked. 'Exciting, is it?'

'Well, I'm gonna try and start up on me own. Yer've gotta give it a try, ain't yer?'

'Good for you.' Irene smiled at him for a moment longer than Danny would have expected before she turned back to face Katie, surprising her again with how much younger and prettier she was looking without all her usual powder and paint.

'I'm leaving Plumley Street, Kate,' she said abruptly.

'You're what?'

'I'm off. Right now. Me bag's outside on the step.' She opened her eyes wide and pulled her lips tight across her teeth. 'What a lark, eh?'

'So yer got a job then?'

'No.' She was suddenly serious, speaking slowly, more cautiously. 'There's this friend o' mine. He owns a couple of pubs over South London way. I'm gonna be sort of living with him.' She couldn't remain serious for long, she was all smiles again. 'I'm gonna be living abroad, if yer don't mind. In Bermondsey!'

Katie had to ask. 'How about Arthur?'

'Him?' Irene giggled and crossed her eyes. 'In bed snoring still, with a bit o' luck.' She took her gloves from her coat pocket and carefully pulled them on over her long, manicured fingers. 'I mustn't keep yer, and I'd better be getting a move on anyway. But I just wanted to say thanks, Kate. A lot round here never bothered with me, especially once they found out that it was my cowson of an old man . . .' She looked around at Pat, Danny and Sean. 'Excuse a lady's French, won't yer?' Then she thought about it and shrugged. 'Well, he is a cowson, ain't he? Getting that Milton bloke involved in that robbery like that. Poor feller, he would never have done it, yer know, if he hadn't have been so desperate. I just thank Gawd that no one was hurt.'

Katie wasn't sure what to say. She and Pat had guessed that Laney was involved somehow, but here was his wife telling them outright. 'Do the coppers know, Irene?'

'They will do, believe me, 'cos I'm gonna tell 'em. And I've made sure that that poor Ellen and her kids have got a nice few bob out of it.' She sighed, her pretty face clouding over. 'That bastard thinks he can control anyone and everyone. And he certainly controlled me these past four years. But that's all over. Sod him. I'm off. Anyway, I ain't wasting me breath talking about him. I just wanna say thanks again Kate, you was kind to me, right kind.' She looked over her shoulder and winked at Danny. 'If yer anything like me, yer won't be able to wait to see what's in that box. Open it as soon as yer like.'

Then she turned to Sean. 'Sorry I won't be around no more, love.' She reached out and touched his face. Then, she kissed Katie and ran out of the kitchen.

'And don't worry, Dan, what's in that box ain't no ill-gotten gains,' they heard her call along the passage. 'I sold the engagement ring the old bugger give me! Wish me luck, all of yer!' She giggled again and they heard the street door click on to the latch.

Katie plonked herself down at the table. 'I was never nice to her. Not really,' she said, shamefaced.

'Well, she thought yer was.' Danny took down the package and unwrapped the brown paper. 'Blimey!'

He walked over to the table and dropped down beside Katie. 'Look here, Mum. There's seventy quid in here! I can't believe it.' He waved a wad of money under Katie's nose. 'Hang on, there's a note and all. *You and Liz,*' he read, '*are going to need something to help you start your new life together. And I'd like to think you can have a better start than I did. Don't ever forget to love each other. Your friend, Irene.*'

Sean shoved his plate away from him. 'It ain't fair.

479

Some people have all the luck. He's got his own business and he's getting married. But look at me: no job, nothing. And now she's gone and all, so I won't have no money neither.'

'Sean?' Katie was having trouble understanding. 'What?'

'Are you saying it was Irene who's been treating yer? When you told me yer was doing jobs down the market?'

'She didn't give it to me for nothing. I used to . . .' Sean blushed.

'What?' Katie's voice was rising in alarm. 'What did yer do?

He shrugged. 'Nothing much.'

'*What?*'

'I used to talk to her,' he said flatly.

'Talk to her?' Danny repeated.

'When Arthur was out. She used to get so lonely.' Sean lifted his head and looked at Katie. 'She said she didn't have no friends but me and you, Mum.'

Katie got up and held out her arms to him. 'Come here and let me give yer a cuddle.'

'No. And I ain't going to no wedding neither.' Sean got up and backed away from her towards the kitchen door. 'And just look at this boil on me neck and all. Everyone'll be staring at me. I ain't going. I've changed me mind.' He pointed at Danny. 'Yer'll have to get yerself another best man, 'cos I ain't doing it.'

'Sean,' Katie said wearily, flopping back down on to her chair, 'I know yer upset, but don't start. Not today, darling.'

Sean backed further towards the passage, but instead of escaping, he stepped straight back into his nanna's arms as she tried to get past him into the kitchen.

'Whatever's going on in here?' Nora asked, peering

round her grandson. 'Will yer look at the state of it. We're all booted and suited and ready to go next door and you lot in here are dozing around as if yer've just got outta bed.'

'I've got a boil and I ain't going,' Sean said, his jaw rigid.

'A boil? Is that all? Well, don't I know exactly what to do about that!'

Sean turned round and was now reversing slowly away from his nanna back into the kitchen. 'No, Nanna. I ain't having you nowhere near me with them red-hot bottles and bread poultices.'

'Nanna ain't gonna touch yer, Sean. All right?' Danny laid his hand on his brother's shoulder. 'Please, it means a lot to me you being me best man. And it won't even show over yer shirt collar.' He slapped Sean matily across the back. 'Anyway, who's gonna be looking at us two, eh? Yer know what it'll be like. They'll be all cooing and grizzling over the bride, won't they?' He leant close to Sean. 'And Liz's cousin Lalla's gonna be there. She's one o' the bridesmaids, remember?'

'Lalla?' asked Sean carelessly.

Danny winked conspiratorially. 'Yer know, Lalla. That one from Grove Road. The one with the legs. And what with you being best man . . .'

Sean shrugged, not wanting to show any interest in anything, but still not able to conceal from his brother the very obvious appeal of being close to Lalla, the little blonde girl he had been dreaming of for months now, ever since she had started coming round to Plumley Street for her dress fittings.

Danny looked past Sean and grinned at Katie. 'Well, ain't yer gonna get yerself ready then, Mum? Me and Sean're only gonna be a few more minutes, ain't we,

481

bruv?' He lifted his chin and started scraping at it with his razor. 'I'm just gonna finish having me shave.'

Pat laughed amiably. 'Dunno why yer bothering with a razor on a bit of bumfluff like that, son. Yer wanna smear butter on it and let the cat lick it off for yer.'

'He might just have to do that if he don't get a move on,' said Nora bossily. She took down the apron from the hook and wrapped it over her wedding outfit. 'Now will yer all move yerselves? It's a quarter to ten already and if we're gonna be ready in time, me and Katie are gonna be busier than a pair of one-armed paperhangers with itchy ars—'

Katie glowered at her mother, and Nora corrected herself. 'With itchy bums. Now will yer get them crackers out of yer hair?'

Nora went over to the sink to get a wet cloth, and Katie began unwinding her curlers, tossing them on to the table. Visions of all the various humiliations her younger sons were capable of inflicting upon her during the ceremony danced before her eyes. 'If you get them boys going in church and make 'em show me up in front of the company, Mum . . .' she warned Nora.

'I nipped over to Frank Barber just now,' said Nora briskly, ignoring her daughter. 'I said it'd be nice if him and Edie came together, as a couple, like. What with Theresa being one of the bridesmaids, it'll be someone for them both to sit with in the church.' She pushed Katie's curlers to one side while she cleared everything else from the table – including Katie's list.

Katie frantically snatched the list from her mother's hand. 'I was gonna clear that meself.' She flapped the paper at Nora. 'Look, it's on me list.'

'I'm back,' a man's voice hollered along the passage.

Katie took a deep breath, looked around the kitchen to make sure that everything was at last as it should be, and then picked up her handbag from the dresser.

'Yer ready, Kate?' Pat asked, holding out his arm to her.

She looped her arm through his and nodded, then she pulled away from him again so that they could walk along the narrow passageway to the street door.

When they got outside Pat tried to guide her into the back of the taxi, but Katie resisted. 'Yer really sure yer've got everyone else there already?' she quizzed the driver.

'Yes, lady,' the cabbie assured her. His patience was beginning to wear a bit thin. He had taken this job, ferrying the wedding party round the corner to the Catholic church and back again after, thinking it would be easy money, a bit of a doddle really, but this woman was driving him bonkers. She had gone over her flaming list with him so many times he knew it off by heart. All he wanted to do was get them all round there and have time to have a cup of tea before he had to start carting them all back again to the pub for the reception. 'Now, can yer get in, so I can get moving?'

Katie got in, nodding haughtily at his reflection in the rear-view mirror as he released the handbrake.

'Hang on!' Katie yelled.

'What now?' The driver was definitely not a happy man.

'I just wanna run over the road.'

'Katie.' Pat put his hand over hers, stopping her opening the cab door. 'If we don't get to the church soon, the bride's gonna get there before us.'

'But I just wanted to make sure that Liz—'

'Kate, please?'

'All right.'

'Go on, mate,' Pat said to the relieved cabbie.

'Thank Gawd that fog's cleared,' Katie said, leaning forward and dipping her chin so that she could peer out of the window up at the sky. 'And I don't think it looks like rain neither.'

Pat pulled her gently back against the seat and put his arm round her. 'And with a bit o' luck the sun'll be out for the photos, and everything'll be smashing. Now will yer just calm down?'

'It ain't every day me son gets married,' Katie sniffled, pulling away from Pat and straightening the collar of her coat.

'And thank Gawd for that,' muttered the cab driver.

The journey to the church took less than a couple of minutes, but it still wasn't fast enough for Katie, who had practically shredded her handkerchief by the time they arrived. In her hurry to get out and start organising, she clambered inelegantly over Pat's lap and out on to the pavement, leaving him to sort out the pick-up time with the driver.

It took her a moment to spot Nora and the boys as there were so many people milling around, all clapping their hands and stamping their feet to keep warm, as they waited for the bride to arrive. In many ways it was like a Sunday morning before Mass, with people standing around chatting and gossiping, but this morning there were many unfamiliar faces and everyone there was dressed up to the nines – especially a huddle of young women, all giggles and whispers and fancy hats, who Katie guessed were Liz's and Molly's friends from Terson's Teas.

'Mum!' Katie called, waving frantically to Nora. 'I'm here.'

She nodded and smiled at all the people who greeted her as she dodged through the waiting crowd to get to Nora. She pecked her on the cheek and then gave Michael and Timmy the once-over.

'Don't you look grown up,' she beamed at Michael, who was proudly parading the long trousers that Nora had bought him from the tally man.

'I don't think it's fair,' whined Timmy. 'I should've had longs and all.'

'I told yer, yer want to think yerself lucky, young man,' Nora reminded him. 'If Liz would have had her way, you'd be all dressed up in a blue satin suit to match the bridesmaids.'

'And I told you, Nanna, if she'd have made me be a pageboy I'd have topped meself, truth I would.'

Katie shook her head. 'Talking to yer nanna like that. Just as one of yer gets a bit grown up and starts behaving himself, the next one starts acting like a little hooligan.'

Timmy stuck out his bottom lip and contented himself with a crafty kick at Michael's shin before escaping to the safety of the cluster of stiff-collared men who were standing with his dad smoking and cracking jokes.

Katie craned her neck to see over the massed hats. 'I can't see our Molly nowhere, Mum.'

Nora jerked her head towards the church door. 'The bridesmaids are standing inside. Those little capes might look pretty but they're no good against this cold. Mind you, it's just as cold in there, if you ask me. I think Father Hopkins could have got some heaters or something.'

'D'yer think I should nip home and get Molly a coat?' Katie's mind raced through the warm outer wear she possessed that might be suitable for a bridesmaid. 'I'm sure I could sort out some jackets or something for Lalla and young Theresa as well.'

Nora looked at Katie as though she had gone daft. 'Can you just imagine? Their big moment, all dressed up in gorgeous blue satin and you want them to wear big old coats over the top. Sure they'd rather freeze.'

Katie hauled her handbag further up her arm and headed for the church door. 'I'll just go in and see,' she said over her shoulder.

'You can tell 'em to get out here while yer at it,' Nora called after her, "cos here comes the bride! Come on, let's have a quick look before we go in,' she said, herding Michael forward.

All eyes were turned towards the street where Aggie and Joe, dressed in their finest, sat perched on the driver's bench of a ribbon bedecked governess cart, pulled by Duchess, their little grey pony. Behind them, in a froth of white, sat Liz, shivering with nerves and the cold, next to Bill, resplendent in his bowler and a new suit from the fifty-bob tailors in Chrisp Street.

Bill took off his hat and helped his daughter down from the carriage. There were gasps of admiration as the guests and the sightseers, who had assembled at the church gate, had their first proper look at the bride. Her dress fell in soft folds of lace from a simple satin bodice; her head was covered in a matching long, full veil held in place by a circlet of flowers, and a cascade of dark green ivy and pure white lilies trembled in her hands.

'Yer've gotta hand it to her, Kate,' said Nora, sniffling into her hankie. 'That Peggy is a genius with the needle. Sure, I reckon that Mrs Simpson'll be after her to make her wedding frock when she marries Edward.'

By the time the service was over and the guests were outside again for the photographs, Nora wasn't the only one who was crying. In fact, there was hardly a dry female eye to be seen, and there were quite a few men who suddenly needed to blow their noses as well.

Katie shuddered back a sob as she kissed Peggy on the cheek. 'Yer such a clever woman, Peg. They all look so lovely.'

Peggy dabbed at her eyes. 'How could I go wrong with beauties like them to work with?' Her tears started flowing again. 'Aw, I'm so happy for 'em, Kate,' she wailed, falling into her neighbour's arms.

But when they got back to the Queen's and the reception got under way, it wasn't long before most of the weeping was forgotten.

Everything had been prepared beforehand so it was just a matter of getting stuck in. The food was all laid out on big trestles in the snug, and most of the tables and chairs had been lifted through into the public bar, leaving plenty of space in the main saloon bar for dancing. Soon the little floor was filled with smiling couples swaying in rhythm to the unlikely trio of Sooky, bashing the life out of the pub's piano, Jimmo, strutting about with his squeeze box, and Paul, Harold and Mags's son-in-law, plucking away on his banjo.

As Molly watched the dancers glide by, she found it hard to stop her tears from flowing again, but these were bitter tears of regret that she couldn't be like Danny and Liz as they twirled around the floor in one another's arms, showing the world how much they loved one another.

Nutty Lil, who had been spinning around by herself, came to a halt next to Molly. 'Hello,' she said. 'Have you seen me blue and silver shawl?'

Molly nodded.

'It's mine. Irene give it to me to keep.'

'It's lovely, Lil,' Molly said, doing her best to smile through her tears.

'Yer can borrow it if yer like. Just for a minute, I mean, 'cos yer look cold standing over here by the door.'

'Ta, Lil, but I'm all right. Why don't yer go back to yer dancing? Yer like dancing, don't yer?'

She considered for a moment, then nodded. 'Yeah, I do. All right.' All thoughts of Molly being cold were forgotten, as Lil swooped away again, her shawl flying out behind her like a victor's banner.

Molly couldn't bear to look at the dancers any longer. Her tears stinging her eyes, she moved back into the doorway, right away from them, and watched Joe Palmer instead, as he led Sean up to the bar. He seemed to be giving him a talking to. She hoped that her brother hadn't got himself in trouble again. But she could hardly be bothered to keep the thought in her head.

She shivered as she felt cold air rush past her as someone opened the door.

'Sorry I'm late,' a voice said behind her.

She spun round. 'Simon! What're you doing here?'

'Aren't I welcome?'

'Er . . . yeah. Yeah, course you are. But I never thought yer'd really come.'

'I don't suppose I did either. Not until about an hour ago.'

She looked nervously over her shoulder. Everyone was still dancing, eating or drinking: too busy to worry about what she was up to.

'Will you come outside for a moment? I want to talk to you.' Molly nodded; he sounded so serious.

Simon pushed the door open and let her step out in front of him into the wintry afternoon sunlight.

'Over here, out of the wind,' he said, leading her over

to where the high brick wall that blocked the end of the street formed a corner with the wall of the pub.

He took off his overcoat and draped it round her shoulders. 'You look so beautiful.' He gently took her hand in his. 'I've been speaking to my uncle about you.'

Molly's mouth felt so dry she thought she would choke. 'And what did he say?'

'What I expected. He doesn't approve.'

Molly dropped her chin, unable to face him.

He squeezed her hand. 'But I don't care what he thinks. You're everything to me, Molly, and I can't live without you. Not now I know what it is to be in love and to laugh and be happy.'

Molly stared down at the pavement. 'You don't look very happy now.'

'I really love you, Molly.'

'And I love you, but it ain't doing us much good, is it?' She pulled her hand away and smacked it against the rough brick of the wall. 'There's some things yer can just hitch up yer skirts and climb right over, like this here. But there's others, they're just too high.'

He leant close to her. As he spoke, she could feel his hot breath on the top of her head. 'My uncle had something else to say.'

'Aw yeah? Found yer a nice Jewish girlfriend, has he?'

'No. He told me the truth about who I am.'

'Who you are?' she repeated.

He laughed ironically. 'I come from bad stock, apparently. I'm useless, just like my mother.'

'That's wicked, him talking ill of the dead like that.'

'There's more.' Simon shook his head as though he could hardly believe what he was about to say. 'My mother and father didn't die in an accident. The story he'd always told me was just that, a story. None of it was true.'

'They're alive?'

He shook his head again, hesitated for a moment. 'Well, my father might be.'

'I don't follow yer.'

'My mother, my *real* mother, became pregnant by the boy she wanted to marry. But the family didn't approve of him, so they sent her away to have her baby with some cousin in Manchester.'

'Didn't the boy go after her?'

'They refused to tell him where she was. When the child – me – was born, she started pining for the boy. She became ill. So they took me away from her, and the family brought me up, passing me around over the years like an unwanted parcel.'

'So what happened to yer mum?'

'She . . .' he spoke so softly, Molly could just about hear him ' . . . died. A few years ago, in an institution. I could have gone to see her if only my uncle had told me about her. She died alone, and I never even knew she existed.'

As he took her hand again, Molly felt her eyes brim with tears.

'He even took me to see the graves where my so-called parents were supposed to be buried.' He swallowed hard. 'When I was a child I cried over the graves of strangers, strangers who just happened to have the same name as mine. My whole life has been a lie.'

Molly dropped her chin again. 'Just like you lied whenever you came to meet me.'

'Don't talk like that, Molly, please. You're the only one who makes any sense to me any more. Molly,' he took her face in his hands, and searched her eyes for the answer, 'you've got to marry me.'

490

Molly shrugged away from him. 'Look, yer've rowed with yer uncle. It don't mean nothing. Us lot row all the time. You see, it'll all have blown over by the time yer get home, and then yer'll be sorry yer said that.'

'No, you're wrong. I'll never regret it. I'm going to find us some rooms, and I'll stay there by myself until we get married. I've got a bit of money, I can get by until I find another job, and then I'm going to find my mother's grave. My real mother's grave.'

'Simon, yer know I can't marry yer. When all this is sorted out, and you and yer uncle are mates again, how yer gonna feel then? Yer've said it yerself: he'd never forgive yer if yer didn't marry a Jewish girl.'

Simon closed his eyes. 'It's nothing to do with religion, Molly. That's something else I found out.'

'So what is it about then?'

Slowly he opened his eyes. 'All he cares about, all he really cares about, is that I should marry "the right sort of girl".'

Molly bristled. 'So I ain't posh enough for him, is that it?'

Simon grabbed Molly by the shoulders. 'He's a fool. He's the sort of man who thinks that men without jobs are all worthless loafers, and even if someone tried to give them work, they'd only live like animals, and spend all their spare time thieving and drinking.'

Molly laughed mirthlessly. 'There's a few from round Upper North Street what wouldn't change his mind.'

'Don't mock me, Molly.'

'I'm sorry.'

'It was one of those "worthless" types who my mother was in love with. That was why my uncle wouldn't hear of their marrying. She had no choice but to let them take me. It wasn't her fault.'

'Course it wasn't.' Molly reached out and touched his cheek with her fingertips.

'I'm going to find her grave, Molly, and you're going to be with me, as my wife, when I do.'

'But it ain't as easy as that, is it?' Molly buried her face in her hands. 'It ain't gonna be easy whatever we do.'

Molly felt someone gently take her hands away from her face. 'What's not gonna be easy, my little love?' It was Stephen, he had appeared from nowhere and was standing next to Simon. 'Sure, I'd fight the buggers with one hand tied behind me back if they tried to make things hard for my angel of a granddaughter.'

'Farvee!' Molly flung her arms tightly around his neck. 'Aw, Farvee!'

'And who's this handsome young feller?' Stephen gasped, trying to twist his head so that he could see Simon.

Simon held out his hand. 'Simon. Simon Blomstein.'

Stephen peeled Molly's arms away and shook Simon's hand. 'A good Irish name, Blomstein,' he said with a wink. 'Now you, Molly, my girl, you go inside and find them young grandsons o' mine for me. I want to see 'em before I have to face yer mammy. And don't worry, I'll look after yer man here.'

Molly nodded, wiped her tears away with the back of her hand, and ran into the pub to look for them.

She found Michael straight away; he was supposedly collecting empty glasses and taking them back to the bar, but was actually relieving unsuspecting guests of their unfinished drinks, which he then knocked back in one go, before piling them on to an over-spilling tin tray of empties.

'Yer'll be sick as a dog if yer carry on like that, and serve yer right,' Molly hissed into his ear. 'So before yer

492

do start chucking up or passing out, I'm going into the lav, and while I'm in there, I want you to go and find Timmy and Sean for me.'

'Aw, Moll,' he whined.

'There's a surprise outside for yers. But only if yer fetch the others and only if yer keep quiet about it,' she warned him.

When Molly had washed her tear-stained face she went back outside. Simon and Stephen were talking animatedly to one another.

'Me and yer man here have had a little chat,' said Stephen, clapping his hand on Simon's shoulder. 'He seems like a good boy to me.'

'Yeah, he is,' said Molly. She kissed her grandfather on the cheek. 'We've missed yer, yer know, Farvee.'

'And I've missed all of yous.' Stephen smiled ruefully. 'Sure, I found I couldn't live without yers, didn't I?'

Molly's three younger brothers appeared in the pub doorway. When they saw who was waiting for them they launched themselves forward like a rugby team on the attack. 'Farvee!' They were so excited, and had seen so many strange faces at the reception, that they didn't give Simon a second glance.

Timmy was almost beside himself. 'I've gotta go and get Mum. She ain't gonna believe this.'

Stephen raised his eyebrows in mock alarm as Timmy dashed back into the pub. 'Now I'm for it.'

'Don't worry, Farvee,' Molly said. 'Mum won't start, not today.'

'Has she met yer friend Simon yet?' he asked.

'Er . . .'

'Well, it might be better if I go inside and see her in there, eh? Don't want her coming out here and finding two surprises waiting for her.'

He winked at Molly, put his arm round Sean and guided him back towards the pub door. 'Now young feller, tell me all yer news.'

As they stepped back inside the warm pub, Sean felt the blush rising from his throat and colouring his face, but it wasn't the heat that was making him red. 'Joe Palmer was talking to me just now. He asked me if I'd be interested in working for him now that our Danny's gonna be setting up on his own.'

Stephen nodded approvingly. 'Setting up on his own, eh?'

'Yeah.'

'And what did you say to Joe Palmer?' he asked as he shoved the door shut behind him.

'I said I might be.' Sean grinned. 'No, I didn't. I said, yeah, I said thanks very much Joe, I'd love to work for yer!'

Stephen ruffled Sean's red curls. 'Good for you, son, good for you. But now it can't be that what's making yer go the colour of a beetroot, now can it?'

'No, there's something else,' Sean whispered, so that Michael couldn't hear. 'I've got meself a girl, ain't I? That pretty blonde one over there with Peggy Watts. She's Liz's cousin. Her name's Lalla. It's short for Alice.'

All the while that Stephen was admiring Lalla and praising Sean for his good fortune, he was aware of Katie threading her way towards him through the dancers behind the still beaming Timmy.

'Hello,' said Katie stiffly, stopping in front of him.

'We'll let you and Mum have a talk, eh?' Sean said, dragging the protesting Michael and Timmy away behind him.

Katie frowned suspiciously at this new mature Sean; strange things happened when Stephen was around.

'He's growing into quite the young man.' Stephen said, watching his grandsons' progress across the bar. 'And no more dog fighting, I hope?'

'No.'

'Yer know that had nothing to do with me, don't yer?'

'I know. But ne'mind all that. What're you doing here?'

He shrugged. 'I found I missed them little monkeys as much as I'd miss the fingers off me own hand. And sure I couldn't not come to me own grandson's wedding, now could I?'

'How'd yer find out about it?'

Stephen winked and tapped the side of his nose with his finger. 'Happiness has a way of making things happen for the best.'

Katie paused for a moment, then said, 'Thanks for coming. I know it'll mean a lot to our Danny.'

Stephen nodded. 'And it means a lot to me too.'

'I'll go and fetch him in a minute. But I'll get Mum first.'

'Where is she?'

'Only over there, talking to Edie and Frank.'

'Edie and Frank, eh? Sounds interesting.'

Katie's voice softened. 'Yeah, it's nice. They've got right close lately.'

'Well, I'm more than pleased for the pair of 'em. Being alone's a terrible thing. It's a hard lesson, but I've learnt it well, the older I've got.'

Katie began to walk away but she stopped again, turned round and said to him, 'Edie's always been right grateful about how good you were to her Bert, yer know. It was important to her, she said, knowing he'd been happy them last few months.'

Stephen smiled, but his eyes looked sad.

'Thanks for coming, *Dad*.' She emphasised the word

with a smile, then bowed her head. 'I never thought I'd say this, but I've missed you, yer know?'

'I've missed you too, my love.'

Katie hurriedly turned away and pushed through the crowds to Nora. 'Mum, there's someone here to see yer.'

'So, who would that be, darling?'

'It's . . . it's Dad. He's by the door.'

Nora's eyes lit up. 'So he came after all. I knew he would.'

'What?'

But Nora was already making her way across the bar to him, so Katie went off to find Danny.

She found him standing by the bar in his outdoor clothes. He had a leather helmet and goggles in his hand.

'Yer not going already, are yer, Dan?'

'Yeah, I've just told Dad. We've gotta be off soon, Mum. It's nearly two o'clock already and we wanna get there before it gets too dark.'

Katie bit her lip. It was just dawning on her that her child was really married. All she had ever prayed for was for her children to be happy, and Danny was happy all right. But she didn't know how she would cope with his leaving home. She swallowed back her tears. 'Give us that bell,' she called across the bar to Harold.

Harold handed her the brass bell he used to call time.

Katie rang it as loudly as she could; the music stopped and everyone turned round.

'Right everyone,' she sniffed. 'Outside, all of yers, the lovebirds are about to fly the nest!'

All the guests spilled out on to the pavement and waited while Joe Palmer went along to his yard to fetch his motorbike and sidecar so that the newlyweds could leave for their honeymoon.

As he wheeled it into place outside the Queen's, Liz

hid her blushes behind her bouquet as the tin cans he'd tied on the back rattled and clattered over the cobbled street. 'Everyone'll know we've just got married,' she giggled.

'The confetti's gonna be a bit of a giveaway and all,' shouted her friends from work, and showered her navy going-away costume with bags full of coloured paper shapes.

'Where they off to, then?' Sooky asked Phoebe who was standing next to her, right up at the front.

'They're having a week down on the farm where we go hopping, if yer've ever heard of such a thing,' Phoebe replied, with a tight-lipped grimace. 'We never had no week away when we got married.'

'Thank Gawd for that,' whispered Albert to Jimmo, behind his wife's back, raising his glass of beer in gratitude.

'Hang on. How about a smacker for yer old nanna before yer go?' Nora called.

'I wouldn't have gone without saying goodbye to you, Nanna.' Danny gave Nora a noisy kiss on the cheek.

'And would yer go without saying goodbye to yer grandfather?' Katie asked, pushing Stephen forward.

'Farvee!' Danny threw his arms round his grandfather.

Stephen patted his back. 'Good luck to yer both, Dan. Good luck.'

'Yer will be here when we get back, won't yer?'

Stephen winked. 'I hope so, Dan. I hope so.'

Danny winked back. 'Me and all, Farvee.'

He took Liz's hand and helped her into the sidecar. 'In yer go, Mrs Mehan,' he said to a round of noisy cheers. 'And thanks for lending us the combination, Joe.'

'You just make sure yer careful.'

'I will.' Danny grinned. 'That's twice I've said that today,' he said, straddling the bike.

'And make sure yer bring us back a hop bine for luck!' Sooky shouted, waving her hankie at him.

'Silly mare,' scoffed Phoebe. 'There ain't no hops this time of year.'

'So what they gonna do, down there in Kent then?'

'*How* long you been married?' Phoebe asked her.

Realising what she'd said, Sooky started tittering into her hand. 'I reckon I've forgotten what yer do with it, after all these years being married to Jimmo!'

Danny revved the engine into life. He was ready to go, but Liz wasn't. She threw open the top of the sidecar and shouted for him to wait. Then she clambered out on to the pavement again and ran over to her mum and dad. 'Thanks Mum, Dad. For everything.'

Peggy flapped her hand and took the handkerchief that Bill handed her without being asked. 'Don't, yer'll set me off again.'

'Come on, Liz, we've gotta get going. Them narrow lanes are bad enough without it being dark and all.'

'Just one minute.' Liz stood by the sidecar, closed her eyes and deliberately turned her back on everyone, then she heaved her bouquet over her shoulder in a high tumbling arc.

She turned round and clapped her hands with delight. Her flowers had reached her intended target; Molly, her best friend, was cradling them in her arms.

'You next!' she called.

Molly felt her face turn scarlet and, just as Liz had done earlier, she buried her blushes in the bouquet.

Danny helped Liz back into the sidecar and revved up the bike again.

'She did that on purpose,' Phoebe jeered. 'Threw them

flowers right at her. My granddaughter should have had them by rights. She's the next one who should get married round here. Not that there's anyone good enough for her, mind. And who's that bloke standing over there with that Molly Mehan, anyway?' she added without pausing for breath. 'Is he that foreign bloke they was talking about that time?'

'I dunno,' said Sooky. 'Handsome though, ain't he?'

'He's all right, I suppose,' Phoebe admitted with a grudging sneer.

'There they go!' someone shouted, and they all watched as the motorbike disappeared round the corner to a chorus of whistles and yells.

Pat bent forward and kissed Katie tenderly on the forehead. 'Come on, let's go back in the warm.'

Inside the pub, Katie shooed Pat over to the bar while she waited by the door until the guests had filed back in. As she had expected, Molly and the dark-haired young man, who had been standing by her side, weren't amongst them.

Katie took a deep breath, reminded herself that all she ever wanted was for her kids to be happy, put a smile on her face, and then poked her head outside the door.

'Why don't yer bring yer friend inside and get him a drink, Moll? He must be freezing out there.'

Molly and Simon stepped warily inside and stood there in awkward silence.

Katie smiled at them, trying to look relaxed, but her hands were clenched in tight fists behind her back. What should she say to them? What *could* she say to them?

Just as Katie thought her jaw was going to break with the effort of keeping up her smile, Jimmo announced loudly that the dancing was about to start up again. She could have kissed him.

'Listen to that row,' she said, taking a step away from Molly and Simon, as the three musicians began to bash out a well-intentioned but slightly strangulated rendition of 'I Only Have Eyes for You'. 'They're ruining me favourite song.'

As she took another step back, she gestured vaguely. 'I'm gonna go straight over to yer dad, Moll, and get him to have a dance with me before they bugger it right up.' She put her hand to her mouth. ''Scuse me language.'

She turned and fled across the room, almost bashing into Stephen and Nora who were already whirling around to the music with effortless grace.

'Your grandfather dances really well,' Simon said, and began humming along to the twanging rhythms.

'This is bloody awful,' Molly said, staring at her mum and dad as they took to the floor.

Simon stopped humming. 'It's not that bad. Maybe they're a bit out of tune . . .'

'Simon, you know very well what I'm talking about.'

'I know it won't be easy, but your grandfather promised me he'd help us convince everyone that we should be together.'

'My *grandfather*?' Molly knew she couldn't even begin to explain, not now. She started laughing, she couldn't help it.

'What's so funny?'

'Nothing. I think I'm getting a bit hysterical.' Molly turned to face him. She stuck her fists into her waist and appraised him as though she was seeing him for the first time. 'D'yer know, I've dreamt about this moment so many times: you asking me to marry yer, and me introducing yer to all me family. And it was never like this.'

She closed her eyes tight as though she was making a wish, then opened them wide. 'Have you ever heard that old saying: there'll be good times just around the corner?'

Simon nodded.

'Well, I reckon there just might be.' She grabbed him by the hand and pulled him into the middle of the floor. 'And now I'm gonna teach yer to dance.' She put one of his hands round her waist and pulled him close to her. 'Hold me like that,' she instructed him.

'Like that?'

She nodded. 'Yeah, exactly like that.'

And there, in the middle of the bar in the Queen's Arms, an ordinary little East End pub at the end of Plumley Street, Molly Katherine Mehan and Simon Blomstein began to dance; not very well at first, but at least they had taken their first steps together, and were holding each other tight for everyone to see.